PRAISE

"*Where Labyrinths End* by Nick Padron will keep you turning the pages with the kind of breathless abandon you'd feel if you ran with the bulls in Pamplona. As if Charles Willeford and Elmore Leonard had collaborated on a novel."
VIRGIL SUAREZ, FIVE TIMES PUSHCART PRIZE-NOMINATED AUTHOR OF *LATIN JAZZ* AND *GOING DOWN*

"When a novel opens with young love and the running of the bulls in Pamplona, as does *Where Labyrinths End*, you know it will be a mad race to the end. Nick Padron uses his deep knowledge of the power and dark underbellies of both the Basque and Mafia worlds to paint a picture of lawlessness, greed, courage, and undying love so shocking and poignant the pages seem to turn themselves."
NANCY SARTOR, AWARD-WINING AUTHOR OF *BONES ALONG THE HILL*

"*Where Labyrinths End* is an intriguing mix of literary and popular fiction and an intriguing mix of political and human follies, which are among the hallmarks of Nick Padron's fiction. This story grants the reader access to the back rooms of the big stages, and instead of being left with the impression that the performances are the characters' deceitfulness, one sees that they are the product of their individual, basic human drives—and the deceptions themselves are probably in our own minds."
T. D. BADYNA, AUTHOR OF *FLICK*

"Nick Padron has taken his sharp literary skills and honed a razor's-edge thriller novel that will absolutely satisfy the appetite of readers from Spain to New York, Miami to South of France."
WILLIAM WILLIAMSON, AUTHOR OF *SOME CAME NAKED*

"Powerfully evocative of the Basque countryside, it also explores with true insight the worlds of ETA terrorists, the wealthy who are their kidnap victims, and the Mafia of the New York area. Suspenseful and intelligent, the driving action never lets up, while we find ourselves strangely sympathetic to both victims and their cruel captors."
LAURENCE DE B ANDERSON, AUTHOR OF *THE REDEEMED*

"Nick Padron's unique style imbues this story with an emotional edge not often found in crime novels. Padron brings the fast-paced prose of a classic page-turner."
JURIS JURJEVICS, AUTHOR OF *THE TRUDEAU VECTOR*

ABOUT THE AUTHOR

Author, composer, Nick Padron was born in Havana, Cuba. His stories have appeared in numerous literary magazines and anthologies in the US and internationally. His first fiction collection, *Souls in Exile*, includes his award-winning short story, "Dreaming in America." He is the author of two other novels, Gabriel Hemingway's *The Cuban Scar*, and *The Exhumation*. He is a former recording artist and the creator of the rock opera, *Diablero*, based on Carlos Castaneda's books. He currently resides in Madrid, Spain and in Miami, Florida.

www.nickpadron.com

WHERE LABYRINTHS END

NICK PADRON

NATIONAL LIBRARY OF AUSTRALIA

A catalogue record for this book is available from the National Library of Australia

For Lourdes, as always, and Donald Ciccone for his unwavering support

PART I

ONE

"The singular remarkable fact about the Basques is that they still exist ... Without a defined country other than Euskadi and no known related ethnic groups, the Basques are an anomaly in Europe."
Mark Kurlansky, author of *The Basque History of the World*

Pamplona, Spain

ON THE MORNING OF the abduction, Symphony Messina rushed to the wrought-iron balcony and watched her fiancé disappear into the red and white mass of runners on the hill. It was a quarter to eight and the pale light of daybreak had given way to a blinding July morning. She raised her binoculars and focused tighter into the crush of bodies by the stable gates. They were bouncing and waving rolled-up newspapers in the air under the statue of San Fermín, behind a chain of arm-linked policemen at the starting line. The spot where Miguel Angel had told her he would be, where the most daring start the run.

Below her in the canyon-like street, every flat surface, every oriel, every balcony, was crammed with people gesticulating, drinking and hollering for the run to commence. Virginia and her sisters, three tiny old women in the solemn black of widowhood, came out to the balcony. They were Miguel Angel's grandaunts and they spoke Castilian Spanish to her. It sounded nothing like the little Spanish Symphony had learned in New York. The old women talked to her at the same time and patted her arms with sympathetic taps as if they knew what she was feeling. Symphony grinned and nodded, venturing the occasional *sí sí* not to seem rude, assuming they were telling her the same things Miguel Angel had told her. Reassuring her of his bull-running skills, comforting her as they might other first-timers to this world of *hombres* and *toros*.

Symphony raised the glasses to her eyes and scanned the strange crowd.

It had been a journey of firsts from the start. Her "maiden voyage" across the Atlantic, her first meeting with her future in-laws in San Sebastián, her first time ever so far from her Brooklyn-born, Jersey-girl world. Miguel Angel hadn't changed her mind on the running of the bulls' nonsense. She still thought it stupid, a glorified game of tag with a one-ton beast. But since their arrival, Miguel Angel's relatives and friends had been wonderful to her, and she couldn't find it in her heart to speak against it.

Besides, she also knew something about Old World traditions from her own Italian-American upbringing, the unquestionable acceptance and the silence it demanded.

Symphony squinted into the binoculars and scanned the hilltop again. The sun was beating down on the balcony now. She could feel it on her shoulders and bare legs, in the heat rising from the street two floors below along with the men's stares. It was the first time she and Miguel Angel had been out of each other's sight since they arrived and it made her feel out of place, too far away from home.

"Damn it, Miguel," she muttered under her breath. All she wanted was a glimpse, one last look at him, but all that showed through the lenses was a seething blur of faces. "Where are you?"

~

Across the street, two thickset men with red neckerchiefs and matching beards jostled their way through the scrum behind the barricades. They glanced up surreptitiously at the young *americana* on the second story balcony. Their names were Aitor Urra and Patxi Mitxelena, and they had been on the couple's trail since Madrid.

Aitor, a balding, solid man dressed in the feast's colors to blend in with the multitude, scowled at his wristwatch. "Call Baldo," he told his partner, the taller and huskier of the two.

"We called only a minute ago," Patxi grumbled even as he pulled out his mobile telephone.

They spoke in a combination of Spanish and Euskara, the ancestral language of the Basques, with its ancient phonology without contractions or abbreviations.

"What if the girl convinced him not to run? You know how women are."

"Do not say that even in jest," Aitor replied. "Call them. Minot has probably returned by now."

Despite their tense sweaty brows, they were glad Miguel Angel's American girlfriend had decided to stay at the old women's apartment. It not only gave them a break from the complications of tailing her through the chaotic streets: it had also settled a delicate part of the operation that had gone unresolved until this moment. Now the problem was they were five minutes from the start of operations and were yet to receive eyes-on confirmation of the target's position.

Two blocks away, Baldo's mobile phone played an electronic version of the Basque anthem. Baldo and Minot, the rest of their team, were in the process of changing into their runner's outfits inside a bone-colored van parked behind the old houses facing Estafeta Street.

"Has Minot returned?" Patxi said from the other end of the line.

"Yes," longhaired Baldo smirked at the malformed head of the man beside him. "He says the target is in place, by the *corralillos*."

Out in the barricades, Patxi gave Aitor an affirmative nod. Then said into the mobile, "What took him so long?"

"Breakfasting," Baldo replied.

Upon hearing that, Minot, a unibrowed man with oval bovine eyes, sneered at Baldo from across the sweltering shadows inside the van.

Out on the street, Patxi glanced skyward. "The next rocket will go off at any moment."

"We are ready. Have the costumes on. But I have to tell you, it is like a furnace in here."

"Go over the moves with Minot again. Make sure he knows them by heart."

Patxi pocketed his mobile telephone.

"What was Minot doing that he took so long?" Aitor said.

"Breakfasting. Would you believe it? Whose idea was it to assign the *iparralde* to us?"

Aitor shrugged. "Iñaki said we need a man like him."

"What is so good about him? He makes me uncomfortable. I never can tell what he is thinking."

"He has been reliable so far," Aitor said.

"That does not make him necessary."

"True. But Iñaki swears he is something serious to behold when things get ugly."

Patxi let out a smoker's wet laugh. "I am completely in accord with that. All he is missing is a pair of horns to look just like a Miura. How could anything get uglier than that?"

Out on the balcony, Symphony readjusted the focus on her binoculars. Narrow Mercaderes Street looked like an anthill of black berets through magnifying lenses. Up on the hill, the oblivious bulls in the corral stirred as herdsmen picked up their long wooden poles. Outside the bullring, TV reporters shoved their microphones in peoples' faces and hyperbolized for the cameras the happy and tragic odds connected to the event about to unfold. Police units blocked off all adjacent streets.

Several ambulances pulled up unnoticed in the rapture of *fiesta*.

Three blocks away on the roof of city hall, a team of pyrotechnics waited for the Mayor's cue to fire up the skyrocket. The signal to let the bulls out of their pen.

The streets tremored in anticipation. Bagpipes squealed. Drummers beat on their snares, rolling to a climax. Symphony could feel all of it pounding in her breast.

Two flights below, Aitor and Patxi huddled inside a dilapidated doorway. They lit up cigarettes and glanced at the sky. All that was left was to wait for the rocket to fly and kick off the run.

Patxi gave a look around. "Your idea of seizing the *pieza* during the *encierro* is a good one, I give you that. But is it necessary that we take him today, on the first run of the season? Look at this place."

An amused grin formed behind Aitor's curly beard. He and Patxi had known each other all their lives and needed but few words to communicate their feelings to each other. "The decision has been made," he said. "It must be today, and it must be Minot, you know that."

"Yes, but Minot has never run in an *encierro*, yet I am the one with all the experience. To anyone else it would be clear who should be running with Baldo. But not to you. It could all end up a disaster with this guy."

"Patxi, if this operation, which has already taken so much of me, ends up being a disaster, it would not be because of that. We were not the ones who squandered the organization's funds in New York and came back with a report that is nothing but crap."

Patxi nodded his sweaty head in agreement. "How could we have known the boy was coming with his fiancée? But the *iparralde* running with the bulls? That is not intelligent. Maybe we should wait—"

"Wait? Two years of planning and waiting have not been long enough?" Aitor scowled over his shoulder at his man. "*Vamos*, stop turning this into a big tragedy only because you want to run with the bulls. They are only going to run as far as the curve into Estafeta Street. The whole stampede practically comes to a halt there."

"That is why I should be there. It all bottlenecks there, runners slip and fall, many of the bulls do too."

"Precisely. The curve is perfect for our purpose."

"Perfect? There will be hundreds of people and cameras."

Aitor turned to face his compeer. "Listen Patxi, if you know of another place where we can get our hands on the *pieza* without the girl being there too, tell me it. If you do not, keep your mouth shut. I need your solidarity, not your protests. The leadership left it very clear: the girl must not be touched. And I am in complete accord."

"Hold it," Patxi said, his mobile vibrating in his pocket. "It is Baldo … They are in position with eyes-on the *pieza*."

"Let us enter now," Aitor said, pushing the door behind them. "We must not attract attention."

They gave one last look at the *americana* in the cut-off jeans up on the iron balcony across the street and they disappeared into the darkness inside the building.

T W O

The Encierro

A SHUSHING WHISTLE rose over the great noise of the multitude, followed by the flash and snap of an explosion high above the red-tiled roofs. A tense, material silence descended over the packed streets. The vast silence of an entire city holding its breath.

The moment had come. A man howled and Symphony and everyone else on the street turned to face the corral gates. The metallic gates slammed open with a roaring gasp, and six massive fighting bulls and their oxen retinue burst out in a violent charge. Like a herd of mythical beasts, the galloping animals wedged straight into the packed crowd, hooves pounding on the cobbled street, black-horned heads bucking, chasing and being chased by hundreds of runners.

Symphony, binoculars over her face, let out an involuntary yelp. "I see him!"

Virginia and her sisters grinned at each other, pleased to see their grand-nephew's *novia* at last smiling. Seconds later, the stampede boomed like a tornado passing under their balcony. The old women huddled around her, making swift signs of the cross on themselves.

Symphony could barely keep Miguel Angel's lanky figure in focus. She leaned on the railing as far as she could, not to lose sight of him. Miguel Angel kept disappearing and reappearing from view inside the crush of runners, a snort's distance from the biggest bull she'd ever seen. She could not understand why he kept tapping it with a rolled-up newspaper on its hump. She wanted to yell at him to stop it, but they were moving so fast that by the time the idea entered her mind he was already zooming away down the street, one more head bobbing in a flood of bobbing heads.

The tumult reached the turn-off into Estafeta Street and Symphony squinted into her binoculars. There she saw or thought she saw two men prying Miguel Angel out of the bulls' path and into a doorway. She focused tighter on the spot, confused by what she'd seen.

"What's going on? Is he hurt?"

It was impossible to distinguish anything in the crashing orgy of bodies, runners and bulls, sliding into a heaping pile against the wall as they made the bend.

Symphony looked at the old women. But they were busy talking, oblivious of what she'd just seen. She tried to tell them, but it was of no use. Her Spanish was too limited, and she was unsure of what she herself had seen.

After a moment of indecision, she threw the binoculars and the camera she had forgotten to use back in her backpack and, without giving the old women time to protest, dashed off down the stairs.

By now, the rampage of runners and animals had migrated around the bend, leaving behind them the distinct smell of fresh manure in the morning breeze.

Symphony followed the last of the stragglers toward the doorway where she'd last seen the men pull Miguel Angel out of the mob.

She stood in front of the door. The building looked condemned. The ground floor windows were shuttered and its balconies the only ones on the street without potted geraniums.

With the side of her fist, she knocked on the dilapidated door. No one answered. She rapped harder on it. No sound came from within. For a second, she wondered if she had the wrong place. Took a step back. No chance, this was the right doorway.

She looked around her, waited until the man smiling at her went by, and slammed her right shoulder hard against the door. It opened with a scraping screech.

She sidled into the narrow hallway and waited until her eyes adjusted to the dimness inside. Dust specs floated like live insects in the shaft of light from the half-opened door behind her.

At the foot of the stairway inside, she noticed the ash-like dust covering the floor disturbed by recent-looking shoe marks, as if there had been a scuffle. Not a good sign.

She took two steps forward into the darkness and shouted Miguel Angel's name several times, louder each time.

"Are you in there? Can you hear me?"

Symphony waited for a reply. But all she could hear was the sound of her own agitated respiration over the rowdy background street noises. If the scuffle marks meant that someone had taken Miguel away, then she needed to run and call the cops and be quick about it. Luckily, there were dozens of policemen outside.

She turned for the door at the exact instant the sound of a man's heavy shout broke out from within the building. It stopped her cold.

"Miguel, is that you?"

Symphony backtracked toward the only opened door in the dark hallway.

With a hand outstretched before her and the other feeling the walls, she followed the footmarks on the dust-covered carpeting barely visible in the indirect gray light filtering through the uneven boarded windows. All sorts of cobwebbed, broken furniture and shadowy junk lay in her path.

Like a blind person in a strange place, she stumbled into what was once a kitchen. Its doors hung like broken wings beside the doorframe. A streak of golden daylight shone from under a side door. A way out?

Symphony worked her way over the discarded plumbing fixtures cluttering the floor and halted by the door, afraid of what she'd find on the other side. She turned the doorknob and the door creaked open. With an arm up to shield her eyes against the glaring sunlight, she stepped out. She only had time to take one breath before it was knocked out of her.

Three ski-masked men jumped her from all sides. A thick hairy forearm locked her in a chokehold from behind, his callous hand on her mouth. The longhaired one clutched her legs like a football player. A third man clamped her by the waist and tried to pull her down to the kitchen floor. Symphony kicked and tried to scream but all that came out was a stifled squeal.

"*Tranquila*," the huge man holding her from behind kept saying as if afraid to break her. "*Tranquila*."

A French-sounding voice warned the brawny man to show some restraint. The big man showed it, lessening on the pressure around her neck—a miscalculation they could not have anticipated.

Despite her panic, Symphony managed to call on the Taekwondo skills her Jersey instructor had literally knocked into her head, driven into her instinct, and with a swift contortionist's twist, she rolled herself into a solid ball and all four of them crashed to the kitchen floor in a pile.

Free from their hold she vaulted into the labyrinthine house, back to the front door, tearing through any opened doorway she found. She leaped over missing floorboards, knocked over everything, anything to slow them down. It gained her a little distance.

With the beams of their flashlights twitching ahead of her, Symphony made an abrupt turn and dashed into a room. She slammed the door shut, threw the latch, and leaned back against it, trying to catch her breath.

Then she heard their muted footsteps coming closer. She squeezed her lips tighter and held her breath not to make a sound. The light of their flashlights slipped through the crack under the door. The doorknob rattle sneakily but the latch held the door locked. They whispered to each other. "*Aquí no*," she heard one say, as in not here. A moment later, they moved away.

A long hissing breath came out of her. They were leaving.

Except they had only stepped away to pick up speed. Now she heard their stomping footfalls zooming in with an upsurge of hollering voices.

The door exploded against her back and Symphony and a large piece of wood panel catapulted together across the room and smashed against the opposite wall.

Next thing she knew she was flat on the floor, blood dripping from her nose. Half stunned, she pushed herself back on her feet while the men proceeded to kick down what remained of the door. She dashed to the only other exit in the room. Locked. The damn door was locked.

She picked up a stool and with hard desperate swings beat on the doorknob, hoping just as hard it didn't lead to a closet or a bathroom. She'd be trapped. With one last fierce swing, the knob broke off and she kicked the door open. She smashed into the wall-less dark outside just as the men tore into the room.

With their heavy footfalls and frenzied shouts behind her, Symphony came upon an inner stairway. She padded up the narrow steps into the heavier darkness at the top. She stood very still, leaning her forehead on the wall, taking lungs-full of the staled air. Her trick of hiding on the second floor, from where there was no visible escape, would have to work or else it was all over for her.

She wiped her nose with her arm and felt tears trailing down her sooty cheeks, but she wasn't crying. Hell no, she was thinking, trying to think. Working it out ... How would her father handle it? Wait, wait, yeah, what if she just came out and said "OK guys, let's talk about this. Huh? ..." Maybe it was all a big misunderstanding. What if the building belonged to them and they had taken her for an intruder? What if Miguel Angel had really gotten hurt and they'd taken him somewhere to be looked at? Yeah right, a misunderstanding with three beasts in black masks chasing after her ...

She heard them barging into the room downstairs.

Symphony glanced at both ends of the hallway. It made no difference which way she ran. Either way, it would be like running into solid blackness. A fusion of panic and fury such as she'd experienced only once before, long ago in the Brooklyn tenement of her childhood, erupted inside her. The inner fire that made it impossible to resign herself to submission. Symphony had no idea what those men wanted from her, nor cared to imagine it. Whatever it was, she decided, they would never have it while she was alive.

Downstairs, the three men started to work themselves up again. They hollered and argued with one another as if unable to agree on which direction to give chase.

Symphony leaned down slowly and picked up a broomstick on the floor beside her. She held it in front of her with both hands like a baseball bat, a hopeless, pathetic weapon, yet a weapon.

A crackling noise at the bottom of the stairs came next, followed by the beam of a flashlight tracing the prints she had left on the grimy steps.

She dragged herself into a nearby room and rolled herself up behind a huge armoire, her legs pressed against her chest. She listened to her pursuers going from room to room, coming ever closer. The realization that she had cornered herself where there was no way out hit her in full then. Every adrenaline-soaked fiber in her body yelling at her this was it.

The light of their flashlights entered the room first.

Symphony wiped her eyes and rose to her feet, the wooden stick in one hand and a small shower pipe she had found on the floor in the other.

They followed in slowly, one at a time, three out-of-breath shadows whispering instructions to one another, determined to put an end to their frustrations.

When their footsteps were almost upon her, Symphony let out a piercing cry and lunged at them like a fiend out of the blackness.

She hurled the foot-long pipe at the first dark shape she saw. The shadow let out a painful cry and dropped the light. Without missing a beat, she swung the broomstick hard at the head of the silhouette coming at her. The stick bounced out of her hand when it hit, and she burst out of the room at full speed into the dark hallway.

Her rubber soles flew over the creaking floors, a taste of deliverance dawning in her palate, until she collided with a wall. It wasn't exactly a wall, but something almost as solid and wide as a wall.

It was Patxi, who immediately locked her in his wooly lumberjack's arms. He lifted her kicking feet off the floor, his mitten-sized hand over her lips, careful to keep it clear of her teeth this time.

Longhaired Baldo came running, the side of his head bloodied from the blow with the broomstick. "Leave her to me," he said.

Patxi yelled "No!"

But Baldo swung his flashlight and smashed it on Symphony's head and she ceased moving. "Solved," he said, rubbing his hand on the side of his trouser legs. "Now she will behave like a lady."

"You could've killed her."

"She is all right," Baldo said.

"Shut up and take her legs. Help me get her out of here."

At that moment, Minot came out of the dark, rubbing the part of his chest where the led pipe had hit him. "Don't touch her," he growled, cutting in front of Baldo. "Take your hands off her." He gently took hold of Symphony's legs. "What is wrong with you? Do you like to beat up women? Is that it?"

"The hell with her. I am still bleeding from the blow she gave me, *la muy puta* ..."

Symphony woke up with her sore head inside a filthy pillowcase. Her hands, feet, and lips were bound together with duct tape. She felt someone grab hold of her arm and a needle stabbed into it. She tried to fight it but the burning liquid injecting into her vein was almost pleasurable.

The pillowcase came off her head and she saw a black-masked shadow looking down at her. She wanted to scream but it was so much easier not to make a sound, not to move a muscle, only to breathe as the strange voice coaxed her to do.

In the metallic heat inside the closed van, Symphony caught a glimpse of Miguel Angel lying beside her with his back to her and his hands taped behind him, as hers were. She made a dull attempt at wriggling herself free before she passed out, defeated by the chemicals in her veins.

Aitor, Patxi, Baldo, and Minot pulled their masks off their heads, soiled and drenched in sweat as if they had run with the bulls. Stooped over their catch, each man lit up a cigarette, except for Minot.

"We might end up paying dearly for this," Patxi declared with a puff of regret.

"The whore gave us no choice," Baldo snapped.

Minot fixed his bovine eyes on Baldo, glassy with disgust, but said nothing.

Aitor clapped his hands. "All right, men. *Vamonos*," he said. "The leadership is expecting us by lunchtime, and we have over an hour of highway ahead of us."

Patxi grunted in agreement. "Yes, let us go already. Before we have to shoot our way out of this *fiesta*."

THREE

San Sebastián, Spain

WHEN MIGUEL ANGEL'S father, gray-haired Orlando Estrada-Uribe, received his first call from Pamplona that afternoon, it caught him on the second course of a delicate business luncheon with three of his company's key stockholders from abroad. Tall and impeccably dressed in a tan suit, he excused himself to take the call. He walked to the glassed terrace overlooking the white sandy arc of La Concha Beach and the city below.

His chin sank as he listened to his Aunt Virginia's distressed inflections on the telephone.

"We are so worried, Orlando. We haven't seen Miguel or his *novia* since the *encierro*, many hours ago."

"Don't worry, Aunt Virginia. They'll be back by tonight. You'll see."

"But they left everything here and that is not normal."

"What do you mean everything?"

"All their things. Both of them. And I don't like the way Miguelito's *novia* just ran out of here like a *loca* this morning, without saying anything."

"They weren't together?"

"No. *Ay*, Orlando, we're so afraid something bad has happened ..."

Señor Estrada-Uribe tried to calm his emotional aunt. "I'm certain they're out having a good time as any young couple would during the *sanfermines*. Let's wait a little longer. We'll talk again this evening."

He returned to the table, concerned but unalarmed.

Later on, at home, he withheld from mentioning anything to his wife to avoid worrying her, in case it was just another of his free-spirited son's escapades.

Estrada-Uribe waited until nightfall. Then he went directly to his office at home and looked up the telephone listing of his corporate representative in the Pamplona area.

He found him at home.

Flattered by a call from none other than the company's elusive chairman, Señor Ruíz, his man in Pamplona listened attentively to his boss's brief description of the situation. He immediately agreed to look into the matter.

"And one other thing, Ruíz," Estrada-Uribe added, as he studied his young executive's round face in the photograph on the monitor screen. "Let's keep this strictly between us. The last thing we need is for the authorities or the press to get a whiff of it, particularly if there is nothing wrong."

"Consider it done, sir."

Ruíz covered all the places the Chairman had suggested. His first stop was the local hospital, to check if Miguel Angel was among the handful of runners hurt during the *encierro*. Then he braved the *fiesta* traffic to the Tres Reyes Hotel where the manager, a business acquaintance, escorted him to the couple's room for a visual inspection that turned up no clues. Lastly, he visited the old women's apartment on Mercaderes Street where he telephoned the Chairman.

Señor Ruiz's uneventful report seemed to confirm Estrada-Uribe's earliest suspicion that the emergency was only in his old aunt's overprotective mind. Except for one detail.

"Are you certain both of their mobiles are in their backpacks?"

Miguel Angel never went anywhere without it.

"Most definite, sir. As far as I can tell, all their personal documentation is there. Their mobiles, passports, wallets, credit cards, even his wristwatch, which I suppose your son removed for safety before the *encierro*."

"Do you have them with you?"

"No, sir. Your aunt would not give them to me. She was rather adamant about it."

"I understand. I will take care of it from here."

Estrada-Uribe thanked his officer and reminded him again of the importance of maintaining the utmost discretion on the matter. Then he rose from his desk chair and walked to the liquor cart. He was beginning to pick up the red flags that might be involved but did not want to acknowledge them yet, too soon.

He dropped a couple of ice cubes in a glass, poured himself a generous stream of scotch, and returned to his desk, a massive walnut escritoire in the center of the wood and leather elegance of his office.

He took small sips as he stared into the glow of his computer screen. Going back a few days, he found no emails from the boy. No lost calls on his iPhone either.

Miguel's mobile kept pestering him.

How much did he pay for it? It was the one Miguel had to have, a Zebra MC something or other, cost a fortune. No, he thought, his son wouldn't have gone out the door without it. Clearly, he had left it behind for the running with the bulls. But afterward? Not his Miguelín, he was certain of that.

In the same methodic manner with which he governed his enterprises, Señor Estrada-Uribe evaluated every detail and made his decision. His son and his *novia* had until morning to return to the hotel or show some sign of life. If not, he would personally fly to Pamplona and take command of the situation.

"And may God catch us confessed and in his good graces," he whispered to himself. For if some misfortune had in fact befallen his son and his fiancée, the repercussions would reach clear around the world.

~

At eight a.m. the next morning, Estrada-Uribe came back to his desk and looked through the fresh morning dailies while his wife was still asleep. No word about his son or his fiancée's fate in any of them. He stood by the French doors to the garden, his silk pajamas under his silk house robe. The Andalusian gardener was pulling weeds in the rose patch. Back at his desk, Estrada-Uribe drew his teacup aside, untouched, thinking. What happened to Miguel Angel and the girl had to have happened while the bulls were running, he decided. He picked his mobile phone ready to make the call he'd spent all night dreading to make, just as the call came to him.

The voice greeted him in Basque. "Estrada-Uribe *jauna*?"

"Speaking," he answered in Spanish.

"My name is Ignacio Gaztelu. You may recall I served as a councilman in your wife's hometown of Guernica for the Batasuna Party some years ago."

"Did you say Batasuna?" Estrada-Uribe could only imagine one reason why a member of the illegal Batasuna Party would call at this time, at his home telephone number, and on this morning of all mornings.

"Yes sir. The reason I am calling is because I've received an urgent message from ETA's political leadership, which I've been instructed to convey to you."

A glacial spasm rippled down Estrada-Uribe's back. "A message from ETA?" The telephone almost slipped out of his hand. "I thought they were a dead issue."

"No sir, ETA is very much alive. I was requested to inform you on their behalf that your son, Miguel Angel, is now and has been since nine a.m. yesterday morning a prisoner of ETA."

Estrada-Uribe bit his lower lip. "Have those sons of bitches kidnapped my son? Is that what you are saying?"

"Señor, please, I am afraid it is not that simple."

"Is my son all right? Is he hurt?"

"Miguel Angel is in perfect state of health," Gaztelu said switching to Spanish this once. "That I can assure you—"

"Have you seen him, personally?"

"No, I was instructed only to relay this information."

Estrada-Uribe pressed his hand over his heart and said with a quivering voice, "How much do they want? How much are those bastards looking to get from me?"

"Again, sir, there are other considerations that we must take into account." Gaztelu waited until he sensed Estrada-Uribe's breathing eased before he went on. "First of all," he said softly, "it is imperative that we establish whether my clients will receive your full cooperation."

"That is a rather stupid question, don't you think, Señor *letrado*? If it's true ETA has my son. Why not just tell me how much they want? And let's get on with it—"

"Señor, ETA's leadership will set a rescue fee in due time. But before they take the next step, there are details that we must establish without leaving any room for misunderstanding. Your son's life depends on it."

"By God, man, don't you think I know?" he growled, rubbing his temple, his brow tense. "Everybody knows what your ETA wants …"

"Then you agree to collaborate?"

"Yes. I said yes," he let out, shifting on his desk chair, unable to focus under a sudden onslaught of fury and frustration.

"You are aware that from this moment on any attempt on your part to try to derail the process of negotiation, or conspire with the authorities, or deceive my clients in any manner would be considered an act of treason, punishable by death?"

"I expect no less from your so-called clients."

"Sir, a yes or a no would be sufficient."

"Look Gaztelu, I am a Basque. The same as you and your clients. I have lived all my life in Euskadi. I know very well what ETA does. What else do you have to tell me?"

"I have other instructions to pass on to you, but we would have to meet in person."

"Why?"

"Your telephone is not a secured line. I was requested to furnish you with a copy of ETA's official communiqué, explaining the reasons for this action."

"A communiqué?" Estrada-Uribe repeated, repulsed.

"Do not miscomprehend me. I, as an attorney, am bound to my clients, but I am neither my clients' nor an ETA spokesman."

"I know what you are, Señor *letrado*—"

"That is correct. I am a *letrado*, a lawyer acting within the boundaries dictated by the Law of this autonomy. Now, if you allow me to continue."

"Please do, but I already know what comes next," Estrada-Uribe said reddening with contempt. "Your clients are going to wait two or three weeks before they admit publicly to the kidnapping. Isn't that the little trick they usually pull, for the publicity they are sure to reap from it? Then they're going to demand some exorbitant rescue fee meant to ruin me. Is this not how it functions, Gaztelu?" Estrada-Uribe kept getting louder, working himself up. "Is this not how it goes?"

Gaztelu replied calmly, "I doubt their aim is to ruin you, *señor*. Besides, everyone knows the weight of your purse is quite considerable."

Estrada-Uribe's nostrils flared. "You …"

"Sir, ETA has no intention of ruining any Basque citizen. On the contrary, as you well know, these operations are forced upon my clients. It is the only means left to them to persuade our more fortunate citizens to partake in our national struggle for independence. Nationhood will benefit you as well."

"Spare me that crap, Gaztelu. You are a lawyer and you know all too well that kidnapping is a crime in every civilized society. A criminal act, regardless of how you dress it up."

"Sir—"

Estrada-Uribe didn't let him finish. "You may go and tell those criminal friends of yours not to worry about me. Tell them that as long as Miguel Angel is alive and doing well, they can count on my cooperation. But you can also tell these clients of yours, if my son is hurt in any way—"

"Hold it there, sir. Be careful of what you tell me. I am obligated to inform my clients of everything you say. And in the spirit in which you say it. So, I strongly recommend that you do not say something now you will regret later."

After a long pause, Estrada-Uribe released a long sigh and continued, now sounding a decade older than at the start of the conversation. "Do you have any children, Señor Gaztelu?"

"I have two sons, but I do not see what that—"

Estrada-Uribe cut him off. "Then I do not need to explain to you how I feel at this moment, do I? Have your clients given you any idea as to how long it will take them to come up with a ransom fee? And will the ransom cover both my son and his fiancée?"

"Pardon me, sir, just so there is no misunderstanding. I was only instructed to contact you with this matter concerning your son."

"How can that be? They were abducted together."

"I know nothing about that. I am sorry—"

"Are those criminals of yours going to try to get another ransom for her, an American student visiting our country?"

"I have absolutely no knowledge of what you are referring to."

Estrada-Uribe shook his head, sickened by it all. "Listen Gaztelu, we Basques know what to expect when ETA kidnaps a family member. God knows you have done it plenty of times before. But kidnapping an innocent American girl? Gaztelu ... *Hola ... Hola ...*"

The line went dead.

F O U R

Brooklyn, New York

A FEW MINUTES PAST midnight, Terry Messina was watching TV at home in Cedar Grove, New Jersey, when she received Estrada-Uribe's transatlantic call informing her of his son's and her daughter's disappearance. She spent the next hour in tears, trying to track down her husband on the phone at all his usual haunts.

She finally reached him on a landline at the Greenpoint Social Club in Brooklyn, wrapping up a card game with his crew.

Joey Messina, tired and in a nasty mood after losing every big pot of the night, called her back on his cell. At first, he couldn't grasp what his wife was saying. "Calm down, Terry," he snapped. "What'd you mean they can't find them? Since when?"

All eyes inside the smoky cone of light over the card table peered up at the boss as he listened to the unbelievable things his wife was telling him.

The fair-skinned man seated across the table said, "What's the matter, Joey?"

Joey Messina put up his free hand, signaling his man to shut up. "Michelangelo's father said that. The Spanish Police and who else? Them too?"

As if choreographed, every glassy-eyed face at the table fixed on Joey's. They could see something was terribly wrong but could not figure out what.

"Listen to me, Terry. Take it easy, OK? Just give them Spillman's number when they call back ... Yes, Spillman ... cause he'll know how to deal with them ... My cell? Are you out of your mind? Look, it's probably nothing. Maybe they've just gone somewhere. Meantime, get a hold of yourself … Yes, I'm leaving now."

Somehow, those last words eased Joey Messina's men's immediate worries. Whatever the emergency was, it seemed to have nothing to do with their business. Still, they could see the boss had a family crisis on his hands, a serious one.

Joey's cell phone disappeared inside his fist. He sat back on his chair, motionless, scowling at the play cards on the green felt tabletop in front of him. His tense, suntanned features blanching to a pallid whiteness as the news sank in. No one, from the old man behind the counter to the two teenage boys by the front door of the sleepy social club, dared to break the silence.

"Can't fucking believe it," he finally said.

"For Pete's sake, Joey. What's going on?" Coppertone Tony, his right-hand man, said.

"It's Symphony. We got a call from Spain saying she and her boyfriend are missing."

"Missing?"

"Yeah. Her boyfriend's father had some interpreter call the house. Looks like Michelangelo's been abducted by somebody. They're not sure who. The Spanish police said they might've taken Sym too."

"Symphony? … Your kid? … Kidnapped? … That's crazy," his men let out almost in unison.

"Didn't say she's been kidnapped," Joey said, intentionally vague. "They just don't know where she is."

He was not about to admit to them that the FBI and a State Department agent in the US Embassy in Madrid had called his house and left messages asking him to call them.

"I got to go." He pushed himself off the creaking chair.

Joey's men bunched around him pouring out the obligatory curses, expressing their outrage at such an inexplicable event. "It's got to be some kind of mistake, boss … Them Spanish cops probably got it all wrong … Got to be some kind of goof up … Who'd freaking dare?"

"Got to get home," Joey said, and headed out the door, his quick-moving feet too small for his girth, making the cuffs of his silk trousers flap violently.

Joey Messina's crew watched their boss storm out of the club. They could only remember one other occasion when Joey's face had turned that pale gray. They had been sitting at the same table that time too, when two-dozen FBI plainclothes and NYPDs led by the DA himself busted in and personally handed out the court summons, the indictments that put an end to their profitable golden days in the carting industry.

With the boss gone, the crew drifted back to the table where they stayed all night, drinking and smoking in hard debate, wondering whether this unprecedented event was in reality the preamble to a war no one had seen coming. Or just more evidence of the messed-up shape the world was in.

FIVE

San Sebastián

FORTY-EIGHT HOURS after the abduction, the Spanish police found the kidnappers' getaway van abandoned and scorched in a wood near Pamplona, then lost their trail in the hazy green fields of the Basque countryside. The next morning, Estrada-Uribe held a press conference outside his corporate headquarters, where he announced his part of his secret settlement with ETA.

With his wife and daughter and his son-in-law with their children standing behind him, Estrada-Uribe addressed a group of reporters under an overcast sky.

Microphones, cameras, and small sound recorders were aimed at the magnate's distinguished figure.

"With all due respect and appreciation to our Ertzaintza and Guardia Civil agents and our excellent intelligence services," he began. "I have requested this press conference to announce our decision to comply with the demands set by the persons holding my son, Miguel Angel."

Instantly, the reporters broke into a shouting struggle, each trying to have their questions heard.

Estrada-Uribe held his hand up for silence. "Needless to say," he said. "This has been a very difficult decision for us to make. But after two long days of meditation and prayer, we believe this to be the only course of action left to us to ensure his safe return."

He folded the page with the notes he had brought and glanced at the funereal faces of his family behind him.

"As it is to be expected," he continued, "we are not free to discuss any of the details of our arrangement, so, please, I beg you not to ask. I would also like to add: we must withhold the name of my son's fiancée for the time being—"

There, he was again interrupted by another round of shouts. "Please," he repeated almost pleadingly. "Ladies and gentlemen, just allow me to say this one last thing. This is important."

He waited until the reporters quieted down.

"All I have to add is that neither I, nor any member of my family, have any information regarding the whereabouts of my son's fiancée. Nor do we feel that it would be prudent to venture any opinions on this delicate situation at this time—"

The shouting broke out again, but Estrada-Uribe ended it there. "Thank you very much to all for coming." He turned around and took his wife's arm, and together with the rest of his family, they marched back up the steps into his six-floor glass building, surrounded by his corporate retinue and private security agents, blocking off the microphone-wielding reporters chasing them.

New York City

Six hours later, Joey Messina drove his Porsche Cayenne into the Lincoln Tunnel and out into Manhattan's hot July sun. Terry's shrieking voice was still ringing in his ear.

"I can't do that, Terry. I can't," was all he could tell her.

"Don't you say that to me, Joey. Like you're some helpless—I don't know what. I don't want to hear about your passport troubles or your goddamn business either. Symphony is your daughter and you've got every right to go to the police to help her—"

"Can't do it, Terr."

"You could at least call the FBI guy who offered to help us with it—"

"What?" he shrieked. "Are you listening to yourself? Are you fucking insane?"

"Then talk to Tommy, to the goddamn Pope if you have to. But do something already ..."

Joey couldn't understand how something like this could be happening—that it could happen at all. To him, a capo in the Luciani Family? A man who never had a nickel stolen from him that was not returned with high interest or soaked with the blood of those who tried taking it. And now Terry wanted him to fly to Spain and talk to the Spanish cops, to talk to the damn FBI.

It felt like a knife twisting in his gut every time she opened her mouth.

"Jesus Christ, Terry. You've known me since forever. Do I have to explain it to you? Do you really expect Little Tommy to give me the go-ahead to have a sit-down with the Feds? Is that what you think?"

"But you're her father, for god's sake," she cried out. "Your own flesh and blood—"

"If I did that the next thing you know, you'll be a damn widow. Forget about it. This has got to be dealt through the Family. No two ways about it."

"But—"

"Goddamnit, Terry. I'll take care of it. OK? Just give me some time."

"Time?" She let out a sinister laugh. "Have you any idea what your daughter may be going through right now? She's our daughter, Joey. Yours and mine and nobody else's. Our little girl—"

Joey had to slam his cell phone on the passenger's seat so he wouldn't have an accident on Route 495.

Terry just couldn't understand the complexities of the situation. This wasn't something he could solve with a phone call. He had to handle it the right way or he stood to lose a lot more than his daughter.

Joey moved up another car's length into Manhattan's bumper-to-bumper traffic. On Lexington Avenue, he stopped for the light, sweat beads rolling down his sideburns despite the A.C. blowing on high. He pounced on the horn and cursed at the traffic. No, Terry had no idea how much worse it could all get. How messed up it was already.

Then there were those other thoughts he'd been getting, those other silent, soul-crushing visions of his little girl helpless in the hands of that scum. Thoughts that only the fathers of young girls torture themselves with.

"Man, why did I let her go? Why did I do that?"

Joey was amazed at himself, forgetting how charmed he'd been by the idea of his daughter meeting her filthy rich, future in-laws. Once the boy's family background checked out, he'd been delighted to approve of their engagement, charmed.

The same with Terry, who became fascinated by the idea of becoming part of a distinguished Old-World family, with all that sophistication and gentility.

Joey took his lighter and cigarettes out of his coat pocket and lit up, the smoke exhaled onto the windshield. He hadn't told Terry that the night before he had spoken to Little Tommy, the Family's current acting don. And that their two-minute phone conversation hadn't gone any better than theirs had.

All Little Tommy had told him was "Go see Spillman," his favorite Jew lawyer. "Talk to him. You're going to need specialized help with this problem of yours. You're going to need somebody like him to act as a buffer between you and whoever else is going to come asking questions about your daughter. Meantime, I can put a call to our people up in Boston. Those micks are tight with the IRA out there in Europe. It wouldn't surprise me if they got some connections with them Basques. You know, terrorists of a feather. But you talk to Spillman. Let me know how it goes."

Joey had done as the don had told him to do, made an appointment to see Spillman, which was a hell of a thing for a man as himself to have to do with a flesh-and-blood matter like this one, downright degrading. But it had to be done, for more reasons than he knew, and that was exactly where he was heading to right now. Little Tommy's final words still echoed in his head, even louder than Terry's. "I know this has got to be real tough on you and Terry. But I expect you to handle it the right way by us. Don't forget that. In this Family, we all got families to protect ..."

Joey drove down the ramp into the building's parking and took the elevator up to Spillman's office just like another working stiff in the building.

Glazed-eyed, lips compressed to a lipless line, he strutted in the fancy lobby, mentally telling the don off "... I don't need you to remind me this is a 'personal' problem. Don't need you to tell me I can't go anywhere near a lawman neither. I'm a made-man since '68, been one since you were a brownnose punk running numbers downtown, don't forget that. I know where I stand. Don't worry about me forgetting what I got to do ..." What he wouldn't dare tell the little don was what else he wouldn't be forgetting. The fact that every other wise guy in the city, from his boss on down to his closest colleagues, would be watching him like vultures when word got out. Watching his every move, waiting for him to fuck up and take over his business. He could forget some things, but he had better not forget that.

All right then, he made up his mind alone in the elevator. What is it all kidnappers ever want? Money. OK, he'd give them money. Whatever the sons of bitches ask for. That would be his punishment. A million bucks? He'd come up with it. It ain't so hard. But oh ... the minute Symphony's safe at home again. When that gets done, well ... then those pieces of shit would be his, bone by bone, limb by limb ...

SIX

THE INSTANT JOEY Messina walked in the door Arthur Spillman stood up and dismissed his junior associate from the room. "Joseph, Joseph," he moaned, rushing to meet him, his hand extended before him.

Joey stepped on the swirling marble floors and Persian carpets toward the glass desk. A bright tinted view of skyscrapers in the sun shone through the floor-to-ceiling window, coating the room with an amber sheen.

"My goodness, Joseph," Spillman said with uncharacteristic drama in his tenor. "What's wrong with this world? This is awful. Terrible. Please, have a seat."

Joey remained standing. "What do you got for me?"

"We have more news from Spain." Spillman wandered back to his desk as he spoke. "I got through to one of the councils at our embassy in Madrid, a nice lady. She said they're keeping watch on the case, doing what they can for now. The Spanish authorities have only just opened the investigation—"

"What about that other thing?" Joey wanted to know about the Feds.

"I spoke to Special Agent Fletcher. I have him on hold for now. However, you know they're not going to tell us anything worth hearing unless you consent to speak with them. And that is out. Correct?"

"You got that right." Joey let himself drop onto one of the leather armchairs.

"I also had a talk with Judge Garzón. He's the Madrid judge in charge of the case. He was very forthcoming, spoke surprisingly good English too.

He said they have witnesses who saw Symphony going in the building where Miguel Angel was abducted. He suspects that was where they captured her—he has an interesting theory on that."

"A theory? Is that what he's got?"

"Don't underestimate this man," Spillman said with a reverential nod. "Judge Garzón is a highly respected investigator, a world-renowned figure. He's handled many high-profile international cases in recent years. He's been after these Basque terrorists for years, decades. He knows how these people operate. We should consider ourselves lucky he's involved."

"Lucky? Jesus fucking Christ." Joey shook his head. "So, what's his theory?"

"He's not convinced that Symphony was their target. So far, all the evidence shows they were only after the boy. This might explain why they haven't admitted to be holding her or demanded a ransom. The positive side is that when this sort of screw up happened in the past, these ETA people usually set the hostage free. So there's hope. For all we know, they might already be planning to release her."

Joey let out a bitter laugh. "Or maybe these guys don't even have her. Or they're waiting to ask for a ransom. Has that genius judge thought of that?"

Spillman drew up his shoulders. "That's possible too. In either case, whatever they decide would have to be acceptable to ETA's leaders, and that might take a few days. You have to keep in mind Symphony's disappearance is still regarded as a missing person's case."

"The one that burns me is Michelangelo's father," Joey said. "The son of a bitch. He's got to know if them Basques have her. He's got to."

"I'm sure he's only doing what he was told to do, Joseph. His son's life is on the line."

"So is my daughter's, goddamn it." Joey gazed away at the sunlit cityscape, his eyes blinking non-stop. "Did he say how much of a ransom they want for Michelangelo?"

Spillman had been ready for that one. "They've asked for eight million euros. Around nine, ten million dollars."

"Ten mill?" The sound of it alone made Joey's hands clammy. "You think they'll ask that much for Sym?"

"It's too soon for that kind of conjecturing, Joseph. You shouldn't—"

"Is Michelangelo's family going to pay up?"

"It looks that way. Mr. Estrada announced it at a televised press conference."

"In the news?" Joey began to hyperventilate. The whole mess just kept getting worse, one damn thing piling on top of another. He couldn't think of a worse torture than needing to kill somebody and having nobody to kill. "What if the reason they haven't said anything about Symphony is that she's already, you know—"

"No, please, Joseph." Spillman leaned forward on his desk. "I know what you're going to say and that's not what you should be thinking about now."

He hurried toward a cabinet built into the wooden paneling and pulled out a bottle of twelve-year-old scotch. He poured some in a glass and handed it to Joey.

"Thanks." Joey sipped it until the glass emptied.

At another time, Spillman might have been delighted to watch a smug Mafia goombah like Joey the Bear get a taste of his own medicine. He had seen his share of them swagger through his office with their arrogant conceit. Not this time. Symphony and his son had gone to the same high school together and he remembered her as a good girl. Besides, no one deserved anything like this. Still, business was business and other priorities compelled him.

"Now listen to me," Spillman said. "There is absolutely no evidence to indicate anything like that has happened to your daughter. None."

Joey shut his eyes and opened them again, redder now, unable to focus on anything. "Easy for you to say." Then he checked himself and peered at his lawyer of six years. "Sorry. Didn't mean that."

"It's all right." Spillman returned to his desk and leaned back on his wingchair.

Joey looked up at Spillman, his biddy dark eyes in a squint. "Anyway, so who the hell are these eh-tah sons-of-bitches, exactly? I mean are they Spanish, Spanish?"

"Sort of. They're a Basque group from northern Spain. Similar to the IRA. Considered one of Europe's most dangerous terrorist organizations. They had supposedly disbanded—apparently, they're still in business. I have Tess doing research on them as we speak. I'll call her in, if you have the time."

"Yeah. I want to hear this."

Down at the far end of Lance Cohen & Spillman office's long corridor, Tess Bernard gathered the four unlabeled folders on her desk—the blue ones to differentiate them from her other files, her everyday work. Holding them to her breast, she marched out of her cluttered associates' cubicle and across the great divide toward the senior suites.

She was not yet over her surprise when Spillman called her to his office the previous morning and asked her, all full of mystery, to open a file on Messina's daughter and to look into whatever she could find about her abduction in Spain. What business a missing person's case had in a firm that specialized in tax law she had no idea, but she owed the firm and Spillman in particular much more than that. So she'd dropped everything and had the presentation ready for the client.

Upon reaching the smooth teak double doors of Spillman's suite, Tess brushed her natural blonde hair off her face, smoothed her pantsuit, and put on a grave smile. It takes forty-three muscles to frown and only seventeen to smile, her dad used to say. The less important you are, the more they expect you to smile.

She knocked and assessed the atmosphere as she entered. She went as far as the great Persian rug. Spillman waved her in. "Come on in, have a seat."

With her chin high, she settled on the armchair next to the client, the rustle of her stockings calling attention to her legs. "Afternoon, Mr. Messina."

Spillman said, "Please give us an idea of what has been published on the case so far, and tell us a little about these ETA people."

"As you know," she said, addressing the client. "Symphony's identity and nationality has been withheld from the media with the actual cooperation of ETA. Supposedly, so as not to embarrass the US government, quote, unquote."

"The last thing those kidnappers want is the FBI or the CIA on their backs," Spillman added.

"However," Tess went on. "The Spanish press is having a field day with what they do have on the case. As it appears, Mr. Estrada, your future son-in-law is a minor celebrity over there because of his family's wealth."

She showed the client the Spanish newspapers with the front-page articles on the kidnapping. "This one is one of Spain's most influential dailies. They're already referring to the case as the Kidnapping of the Century."

"Tess is fluent in Spanish," Spillman threw in.

Joey eyed the Spanish newspapers, focusing an instant on Miguel Angel's picture and handed them back. "It's all Greek to me."

Tess extricated several printed sheets from the folders. "This material I got from the Institute for National Strategic Studies. It's the Institute's report on the ETA—pronounced Eh-Tah in Spanish. They basically describe them as a major terrorist organization now—"

"Now?" Joey let out. "What were they before, a jai alai team?"

"Prior to 9/11, the international press usually referred to them as a Basque separatist organization. Now they're officially recognized as a terrorist group."

"How long have they been around?" Spillman said.

"According to the Institute, ETA's criminal activity begins in 1968. To date, however, their terrorist acts have caused over one thousand casualties in Spain. This was in part the reason why the Spanish government rushed to blame them for the Madrid train explosions in 2004. That is, until the al Qaeda connection was established."

Joey made a bored face and Spillman motioned his junior partner to cut to the chase.

"In regard to ETA's tactics," she said. "They do everything you would expect a terrorist outfit to do. From coercion and intimidation of the opposition, to extortion, sabotage, organized street violence, demonstrations and other low-intensity urban terrorism, up to the more serious terrorist acts such as assassination, bombings, and kidnapping."

A streak of optimism flashed in the dim mess in Joey's head when he realized how little difference there was between terrorists and wise guys. The notion that these Basque spics might just have some code of respect he could work with shone with a measure of hope.

"How successful have they been with their kidnappings?" Spillman said.

"Very, I'm afraid. Over the years, they've taken in tens of millions of dollars from their kidnapped victims' families."

"How long they've been getting away with this?" Joey said. "How many have they pulled?"

"Around eighty known kidnappings, dating back to the Seventies."

Tess paused and cleared her throat.

"Maybe I should mention two encouraging details worthy of noting," she said with an apologetic grin. "Despite their long criminal history, ETA has never abducted a female or an American citizen before. And out of these eighty or so kidnappings, only in seven cases have their victims been hurt, fatally or otherwise. So, if we were to look coldly at our chances here, at the odds if you will, I would have to say that, A: there is less than ten percent probability that Symphony's life may be in physical danger. And B, that there's a better than a good chance they might release her, as it hasn't been their practice to abduct non-Spanish citizens, much less an American."

Spillman nodded at his associate and thanked her for her eloquent analysis.

Tess gathered up her paperwork. "I'll be in my office if you need me."

Both men observed her in silence as she moved toward the door.

Spillman said when the door closed, "What do you think?"

Joey shook his head and stood up. "Got to go."

"Me too. I'll walk you to your car."

Spillman slipped on his suit jacket, picked up his attaché, and accompanied his client out to the lobby. "Oh," he said as if just remembering. "I spoke to my friend at the State Department this morning. He agreed to look into some people he knows in Langley, who might be able to help. His only advice is not to accept whatever ETA's initial demands may be—if and when it comes."

A smirk formed in Joey's face. "So, he thinks I should negotiate with my daughter's life?"

"He only wants us to know how these Basques work. They not only expect you to barter the ransom. They'll even accept payments in installments. But you're right. That's neither here nor there for now."

"So, make it your job, goddamn it," Joey said, working himself up again. "Find me somebody to negotiate with. Get me an address; get me a name, someone I can get my hands on."

"Joseph—"

"Don't look at me like that. What's it to you? Aren't we covered under the attorney-client privilege deal?"

"Not when the attorney is an accessory to a crime."

"What crime? Who's the victim here?"

Spillman waited until they exited the glass doors to answer. "Listen Joseph, we've been through this already. I'm your lawyer, your legal counselor. You can depend on me to do everything necessary to help you. My entire staff is at your disposal. But," he said with his courtroom baritone. "Please, don't forget I am in the business of law."

Joey waved him off, his lips pressed together as if exerting great force. They walked into the white-light confinement of the elevator car together. Joey gazed at his lawyer, watched him staring up at the numbered floors lighting up as they descended. Spillman with his tan face and Yale suavity had been good to him in the past. Saved him a fortune in money and grief back when the Family's Long Island business went to hell. He was a good man to have on his side. Little Tommy swore by him. So why did he all of a sudden look so useless?

"Just so it won't come as a surprise later," Joey said. "I'm going to have some of my people start looking into this too. Work my side of the fence."

Spillman's eyebrows rose in warning. "Look, Joseph, you know I can't stop you from doing anything. But just for the record, I want you to know I'm against it."

"Oh yeah," Joey sang, sneering. "Any reason in particular, counselor?"

The elevator doors rolled open to the dusty fumes of the basement garage.

"Most definitely. It might spoil things for the Spanish investigators, the ones who know how to deal with these terrorists. Besides, I'd bet they're just waiting for the right moment to set your daughter free, just like the Spanish judge said."

The parking attendant gave Spillman a nod and rushed off to get his car.

"Wait up," Spillman called out. "Get Mr. Messina's car first. He's in a hurry."

When the attendant shuffled off, Spillman went on. "I think those Basques are just looking to save face, not to show to their constituency they've botched the job. You know how important honor is over there in the old continent."

When Joey saw his wine-red Porsche Cayenne coming, he reached into his pocket for some cash to tip the parking attendant. "You know," he said with a melancholic, ominous voice. "I do want you to tell that Spanish judge something for me. Tell him I'm ready to cooperate and pay whatever cash those sons-of-bitches ask for. But—and this I swear on my mother's eyes—if my daughter is not returned to me alive and unhurt by next week, then tell'm—"

There Joey cut himself off and looked around as if someone might've been overhearing. "Forget it, counselor," he said and climbed into his SUV. "You just go ahead and do what you do. Me," he said with a tired but cocky grin, "I'm going to do what I got to do."

SEVEN

Mondragón, the Basque Country, Spain

AITOR PARKED HIS Citroen in the shade under the bat-winged gargoyles on the church wall. The wet, sparse strands of hair on his head, his burly figure garbed in a bright summer suit and a dressy T-shirt gave off a fresh, dapper air as he strolled the three blocks to Café Donosti.

Well-known for its nationalist clientele, the place was packed with people drinking and discussing Orlando Estrada-Uribe's declarations on the afternoon news.

Upon entering, the café's proprietor signaled Aitor to proceed to the private room at the rear where the others were waiting.

Aitor nodded and grinned at the regulars lunching at the marble tables as he traversed the length of the restaurant.

For the first time in his life, Aitor felt worthy of a celebration such as his team had insisted on holding. The operation, the kidnapping of the son of the third richest man in the Basque Country, had been his operation from the start. He had conceived it, made the initial proposal to the leadership, and campaigned for it for a year until it was approved. He had rented the plant, had the underground *zulos* built under it, set up the routines, and planned the abduction itself. So yes, for once in his life he felt deserving of the loud cheer he got when he entered the private dining room.

"Here he is!"

Everyone gathered around him, backslapping and bombarding him with questions as if he had been away for ages. "Well, come on, tell us, how did it go in Toulouse?" They all wanted to know.

"What do you expect?" Aitor said of his meeting with Iñaki, ETA's chief of operations. "We have become their favorites."

The group roared with laughter and raised their glasses in a toast. "*Gore Euskadi Askatuta!*" Long live the Basque Country!

Aitor took the chair they had saved him at the head of the table.

From their perspective, they had plenty of reasons to celebrate. The signed accord between Orlando Estrada-Uribe and ETA that the organization had obtained almost guaranteed a favorable conclusion to their operation. The Spanish government's policy of limiting their assistance to victims who negotiate with terrorists practically shot down the investigation before it began. It left the Madrid government without the support of the victim's family, perhaps the most essential element in any successful kidnapping investigation. The Estrada family's decision to pay the ransom in installments, in addition to their willingness to not interfere in Symphony's case, also presented ETA with a public relations victory of sorts, as it had eased the hostility the abduction had initially sparked nationwide.

As Iñaki had said to Aitor that morning in Toulouse, "Nothing like a settled accord to cut off the impetus of those in Madrid. How the hell are they going to justify now accessing those special funds they like so much?"

Aitor had agreed, of course. But as the one in charge of the day-to-day supervision and security of the prisoners, one question still begged to be answered.

When everyone settled down around the table, bearded Patxi wasted no time in asking it. "So, tell us, what do they want us to do with the *americana?*"

Aitor filled his wine glass and answered the question as he'd been instructed to do.

"High command remains undecided on the matter."

"Is that it?" Patxi said, frowning from his end of the white banquet table.

"As it appears," Aitor explained, "some of our senior comrades in prison—you know the ones—they feel we should get something in return for the girl's release."

A stir traveled around the table. "She was never part of the plan," Patxi reminded him. A series of grunts of approval followed.

"As you yourself told us the other day," Pedro, the one in the business suit, said, "Madrid could use her as an excuse to involve the Americans."

"Yes," Aitor said. "But you know our historic ones. For them, it is as if time does not pass. They still think things are the same as before they went to prison—as if September 11 or March 11 or the London bombings never happened."

"This is not logical," Pedro said. "The moment a ransom demand is made for that girl, she will cease being a missing person's case and become a statutory kidnapping, and the Americans will gain jurisdiction."

"They know that."

Patxi said to Aitor, "Then give me the order to set her free and it's done. Who needs more complications now that the money matter with the boy has been settled?"

Aitor shook his head. "Too late for that now. Now we're stuck with her until we can release both of them together. We cannot let her go at this point. There's no telling how much information she may have picked up since her capture."

Baldo swept his hair off his face and cocked his head. "We have spoken nothing but Euskara around her and she has seen nothing outside of the *zulo* walls and our masks. Nothing. What could she tell them?"

"Even so, it is possible that she may have obtained enough information for Madrid to find a trail back to us. Do you want to take that risk?"

"Then I must warn you, my compeer," Patxi cut in. "This girl will not survive until the last payment comes in next month, not in that *zulo*."

The dark cloud the *americana* had suddenly cast over the celebration vanished the moment two waiters came in with the main course, a seafood spread.

The eating and drinking marathon continued until six o'clock when Pedro and his wife Mertxe, the two non-action members of the command, took their leave carrying two plastic bags filled with leftover seafood from the banquet to feed the prisoners.

"The boy's going to eat well tonight," Patxi said, his mood improved by the Chacolí wine.

"Much better than the canned food we've been feeding them," Aitor said. "We wouldn't want his Tomato Sauce King father to think we feed his prince only from his canned food selections."

His statement made the men explode with laughter.

"Certainly not now when he is worth a fortune to the cause," Patxi said.

Minot sat up on his chair, to catch Aitor's attention.

"Pardon me, chief," he said with his French-Basque inflections and his misshapen head tucked inside a black beret he never removed. "One question, am I the only one who has noticed that our 'import'—another code name for Symphony—does not eat fish or seafood?"

The laughter across the table dissipated, thrown by his remark.

"So?"

"So," Minot said, "the leftovers are mostly *kokotxas* and salted cod. She will not eat them. Wait—" Minot focused his brown, oval pupils at the faces around him. "Could it be that I am the only here who knows she's been only eating bread and little more?"

"So what?" Patxi broke into a belly laugh. "At least the boy will appreciate it. He is one of us ..."

Minot snapped, "I am not talking about him."

Patxi narrowed his drunken eyes. "Monsieur Minot, you seem to know the import's habits very well after only a few days."

Minot turned to face the big man. "Why do you say that?" he said, his voice dripping with scorn. "Is it that you disapprove of my observations?"

"I just find it rather curious how rapidly you have learned such details about her, in the middle of getting all those bites and scratches she's given you."

Baldo let out a giggly laugh.

"Oh, I see," Minot sang out, his sarcasm unclear on his taurine features. "You find it curious that I use my intelligence. I suppose that does not surprise anyone, coming from you."

Patxi shot Minot a menacing look from across the table. "Are you implying that I do not use my intelligence?"

"Quite contrary, *mon compère*. I believe you do—the little you have."

Patxi sprung to his feet, the muscles around his eyes twitching, his rosacea nose flaring. "I defecate on the virgin! You take that back or I will rip your ugly head off your shoulders, you disgusting cow."

Minot slipped his hand inside his jacket, a forced grin on his lipless mouth. "I do not think you are stupid enough to try it."

Patxi's body swelled up with fury. "What did you say to me?"

Aitor slammed both hands on the table. "Enough! Both of you, stop it. Patxi, sit down. And you Minot." Aitor peered at him. "This is the damn limit. Did you really have the *cojones* to bring a *pipa* to our reunion? And threaten a comrade with it? A pistol? Here? Today?"

"Why not? Am I not permitted to defend myself from a gigantic monster like this one?"

"A gigan—" Patxi again made as if ready to leap over the table.

"Shut up, both of you. The first one who opens his mouth, I swear I will have him sanctioned. Patxi, give me your car keys."

"What?"

"Your car keys, come on. Do as I say."

Patxi handed Aitor the keys.

"Now go home. Go."

"On foot?"

"Yes, on foot. Baldo, accompany him. Make sure he does not do any more stupidities on the way. Go on."

In silence, Aitor and Minot watched their compeers walk out of the banquet room, then glanced at each other, the only ones left.

"Tell me one thing," Aitor said. "What in the world made you bring a pistol to this meeting? Why did you do such a stupid thing?"

"Aitor, I respect you, but do not call me stupid."

Aitor leaned his fists on the table, his eyes fixed on Minot's. "I call it as I see it. And you have acted very stupidly. Why did you bring a firearm here today? What do you think would happen if the Ertzaintza came in with a search warrant?"

"I always carry it. Always, since my last arrest. I thought Iñaki might have told you that about me. I went to prison once because I was unarmed. I will never give myself up again. I would rather die."

One by one, all the rumors Aitor had heard about the *Taureau du Aquitaine* came back to him. He gave a long harsh look at Minot's far-set eyes, at the wide shaft of his nose, at his out-turned nasal holes of an angry bull. "So, you would have killed one of your own, just like that?"

"Not just like that. But in self-defense, I would."

Aitor nodded his head as if saying, I know your kind. "This is what you are going to do," he said. "You are going to drive to the plant and make sure that Pedro and Mertxe give the girl enough to eat, then report back to me. But before you go, I want you to leave that *pipa* here." Aitor tapped on the table with his index finger. "Here, now."

Minot started to say something but Aitor cut him off. "You have but two alternatives. Either you give that pistol to me for safekeeping or you leave Mondragón and never return. One or the other. You decide."

Minot, the line of his lips compressed together as if holding back a scream, slipped his hand inside his jacket, pulled out a 9mm automatic and dropped it on the table. Then he gave Aitor one last look.

"Don't forget to report back to me after the prisoners are fed," he was told.

Minot tucked his beret and stormed out of the dining room without a word.

Alone in the banquet room, Aitor let himself down on his chair. He knocked back the last of the *orujo* in his glass. Patxi in his boorish way had hit upon something that he himself had noticed: Minot's special interest in the *americana*. There was something unnatural about it.

So far, Minot had proved to be a disciplined and reliable compeer, he thought. But the poor guy had the pitiful looks that only a mother could love, worse than that. No doubt he had to be suffering from some serious deficiency in the women's department. He would have to keep a close eye on him from now on. Make sure to keep him away from the girl.

Aitor searched through the empties on the table until he found a bottle of Chacolí wine from Guetaria. He poured what was left in his glass. The wine made his lips pucker like bitter lemon.

I can deal with the gun-crazy *iparralde*, he told himself, and I can deal with the money-hungry historics. But the *americana* ... anything we do with her is wrong. We cannot free her because it would jeopardize our arrangement with the boy's family. We cannot admit we have her because of the Americans and the risk her mafioso father might represent—another detail high command had failed to determine prior to the operation. And we cannot keep her long because she might get ill and die in that hole in the ground. And now, on top of everything, the deformed *iparralde* has a thing for her.

Aitor let out a sad, ironic laugh and sipped the wine.

Still ... it felt good to complain about it in the privacy of his beer-wine-scotch-*orujo*-soaked thoughts. He had earned the right. He had served Euskadi well. The world can call us terrorists if they want to, he thought. But is there a single nation in this world that has gained its independence without some bloodshed? No. But when we Basques do it, they call us terrorists ... like we're no different from those damn turbaned Taliban and al Qaeda Moors.

He stood up and downed the last of the wine, wincing as he swallowed. Why is it that nothing ever comes easily to us Basques? Why?

"*No es justo*," he said aloud. It is not fair.

P A R T II

E I G H T

In the Zulos

KEPT UNDER HEAVY sedation, Symphony and Miguel Angel would retain no memory of their first days in the two subterranean rooms Aitor's crew had dug under a tool-and-die plant outside Mondragón. Although separated by only a meter of earth and rock, neither Symphony nor Miguel Angel had any idea of their proximity, nor where in Spain they were.

Twice a day, when their daily dosages of sedative began to wear off, two masked men would enter their cells. Then, while one of their captors handed them their meals and watched them eat with a club in his hand, the other one inspected their grimy cells. An hour or two later, another masked duo appeared to administer another intravenous injection of sedative and emptied out the toilet buckets and whatever else they did while their prisoners lay unconscious.

Miguel Angel's *zulo*, although it resembled a Middle Ages dungeon cell, had the better accommodations. At two meters wide by six meters long, it gave him enough space to exercise and stretch his legs. It was equipped with a field cot with a flat pillow and two blankets, a portable toilet with a roll of paper, a bucket with fresh water and a plastic cup, a towel and a taboret. The basic amenities Aitor thought their prisoner would need for the next two or three weeks—the time the leadership believed it would take for the ransom to come through.

Symphony would not be so lucky. Since her capture had not been part of the plan, they had had to keep her in the only space available, an unfinished storage space next to Miguel Angel's *zulo*. Really a closet-size hollow without a ventilation system or insulation. The single mattress where she lay took up most of the shabby wood-planked floor. On the ceiling, a single light bulb enclosed in a meshed box kept the space permanently lit. The bare earth walls, soaked with humidity, crumbled alive with crawling things that appeared and disappeared in and out of the cracks. Even by her captors' standard, her cell space was the closest thing to being buried alive.

By their fourth day in captivity, Aitor's planned routine, which had looked so well on paper, began to break down when put into practice. It soon became apparent they could not continue to sedate their captives indefinitely, or keep the girl in those conditions for long. So Aitor and Patxi came up with an alternative strategy, a system of punishment and reward they hoped would keep them docile as well as in good physical shape. In exchange for their peaceful obedience, the prisoners would be given candy and cold refreshments, reading material, play cards as rewards for their good behavior; as well as improve the girl's *zulo* with proper ventilation. As punishment, they would be fed only survival rations of food and water and be forced to empty their own toilet buckets.

The system worked well with Miguel Angel, whose single act of defiance on his arrival in the *zulo* became his last. In Symphony's case though, it had the opposite result.

From her first day of captivity, Symphony never missed an opportunity to try to make trouble for them. Anytime they allowed her sedatives to wear off and her limbs responded to her will, she'd turn on them like a wild animal charging for the door. Had Symphony known that to escape from the *zulo* would've been no different than escaping from a maximum-security prison, or that she was only three feet away from Miguel Angel, it might have helped her control her rage. But it was not to be. Regardless of how roughly they treated her and how drug-tamed they kept her, the instant her door opened, she tore into her masked captors like a woman on fire.

For Aitor and his men, who were forbidden by high command to use excessive force to subdue the *americana*, their dilemma became a serious one as the days passed.

For Baldo in particular. "I can't take my eyes off the sneaky bitch for a second," he said. "Every day we have to wrestle her to the mattress. I am not Minot," he warned Patxi. "I am not going to let her claw and bite me like she does to him … If that whore touches me again, I swear she's going to get a whipping just like her boyfriend got."

The problem worsened after Pedro and Mertxe refused to enter Symphony's cell altogether. "We will leave her food just inside the door, but that is it. We can't take any more chances with that *loca*," Pedro said. "She almost broke Mertxe's head open the other night, kicked me in the groin …"

Only Minot and Patxi volunteered to enter her cell at feeding times. Minot used a reverse approach. He took her punishment like a martyr, ducked, blocked her blows, dodged her clawing, and held her back from biting him until she tired. It took a bloody toll on his arms and legs but not on his face, which for some reason she refrained from touching.

On Aitor's and Patxi's turns, Patxi's tree-trunk limbs and wrestling experience gave him a powerful advantage. He could easily put her down and hold her whenever she tried to jump him until she finished making her point and ran out of steam.

But then, after a week in captivity, when Symphony no longer had any energy left to get up from the mattress and launch her attacks, she came up with another form of retaliation: she refused to eat.

That day Aitor and Patxi arrived at the plant unannounced and found Baldo sitting on the factory's kitchen counter, his longhaired head shaking.

"Guess what," he said with a sardonic laugh. "Now the bitch is on a hunger strike."

Aitor and Patxi looked at him, waiting for more.

"She was sleeping when we went inside her cell. Did not even stir. That part went well. Then I saw she had not touched her dinner. It was stuck on the wall and the plate upside down on the boards. Bugs all over it."

"And?"

"And I picked up the plates and left the food there for her to clean up if she wants to. Couldn't find the plastic spoon, though. I think she hid it somewhere."

"Did you look for it?"

"Minot looked, but he didn't find it." Baldo grinned. "She went easy on him today. I think she thinks the *iparralde* likes it when she hurts him and does not want to give him too much pleasure."

"Did you look for the spoon?" Patxi asked him this time.

"Had no time. She woke up and threatened to throw her shit bucket at me."

Aitor gave him a narrow-eyed look.

"So, she hasn't eaten anything?"

"Minot brought her some Burger King, but I haven't looked to see if she's eaten any. Ask Minot, he is in the *zulo* cleaning up."

"How about the boy?" Aitor said.

"He is as always. A perfect gentleman, as he has been since we straightened him out."

Aitor said to Patxi, "This situation with the *americana* keeps getting worse." It had been part of their plan to keep the prisoners a bit underfed, to avoid excess energy, but not this. He shook his head. "This cannot continue."

"What can we do?" Baldo said. "That bitch is crazier than a goat."

"Is she sedated now?"

Baldo shrugged. "I left it up to Minot."

The clanking noises of the hand-cranked, one-man elevator coming up from under the factory floor broke the stillness among the shadowed machinery. Designed without steps or a ladder to access the underground area, the miner's cage-like elevator was the only means of entry and exiting the subterranean chambers.

Minot, his deformed skull disguised inside the folded shape of his beret, climbed off and walked to the kitchen area, carrying a trash bag. "*Hola.*"

"How is it down there?" Aitor said.

Minot picked up the garbage pail cover. "Normal. The boy had his dinner. She threw the hamburger at me when I unstrapped her."

Patxi addressed Aitor as if only for him to hear. "The boy could handle a month down there. But she will not make it if she does not eat."

Minot filled the plastic bottle with water. "She will eat the French fries."

"How do you know?"

"She hid them and kept the ketchup bags."

"How about the plastic spoon. Did you find it?"

"I will look again when she is fully asleep."

It made Aitor wonder how often Minot entered her cell while the girl was asleep.

"Even if we force-feed her," Patxi said. "She could fall seriously ill very quickly. And then what?"

"We have our orders," Aitor said, still thinking of Minot alone with the girl. "We will watch her carefully. That we will do, trust me. The rest is not up to us."

Patxi let out a grim chuckle. "It will be if she dies on us."

NINE

A LONG WHITE LINCOLN limousine, all shine and lights, pulled alongside Joey Messina's bulky figure in the shadows under the Brooklyn Bridge. He was leaning on his wine-colored Porsche Cayenne, stifling a sneer as he watched the limo come to a stop, thinking the word inconspicuous meant nothing to Little Tommy anymore.

The back door flew open and Joey ducked inside. He first shook hands with the small-framed man seated at the far end of the spacious cab. "Thanks for seeing me on such short notice, Tommy. Appreciate it."

"No problem." Tommy Pacelli spoke through a cloud of cigar smoke. "We just finished eating at Peter Luger's." Meaning he hadn't gone too far out of his way to meet him.

Joey shook hands with the man seated between them. "Hey, Dom."

He also knew the man at the wheel, but the soundproof glass partition was up. The three men had known one another since their early years "in the life," and in honor of those years of collaboration, Thomas Pacelli, the acting head of the Luciani Family, tolerated some of his older captains' the intimacy of addressing him as Tommy. "You said it's urgent."

"You ain't kidding. Urgent's not the word no more."

Tommy knew what was coming. "This about your daughter?"

Joey lowered his curly head.

"I figured." Tommy muttered a few sympathetic curses, sympathy that came from the consoling notion it had nothing to do with business, at least not directly. "Bad news from Spain?"

"That's just it. Not a thing. It's like the earth's swallowed her." It wasn't the god-honest truth but what difference did it make? He was desperate. "I'm not even sure if she's alive anymore."

Domenic Costorino, the man Pacelli referred to as his consigliere, cut in. "We heard about those Irish guys you hired."

"Well then you heard more than I have, 'cause I haven't heard a thing from them. They told me they'll get in touch with me in three days and it's been a week. They don't take my calls. That's why I had to call you, Tommy. Maybe you can do something."

"Those micks up in Boston have no shame," Domenic grumbled. "Why you even bother with them?"

"Why?" Joey's voice shot up an octave, his contorted expression half lost in the dimness. "You got to ask why?"

Little Tommy turned to face him. "Listen, Joey. I know what you're thinking. But talking to those micks in Boston was just an idea I had. You can't expect me to vouch for them too."

"You paid them?" the consigliere said.

"Hell yeah, I paid. You know anybody who works for nothing?"

Domenic shook his head. "That's tough."

"Tough?" Joey snapped. "I'm talking about my flesh and blood here."

"You tried talking to Hogan, George Hogan?" The consigliere went on as if the deal with the micks was news to him.

"I talked to the son of a bitch myself," Little Tommy told him. "Did what I could. But you can't fucking trust a single one of them up there." He pointed at Joey with his cigar in his fingers. "But I also warned you about them. Told you to be careful. I did, didn't I?"

Joey looked at his boss from across the smoky shadows, thinking, the son of a bitch. "You did, yeah. A little too late, though."

"That's wrong," the consigliere said, his head still shaking. "I mean the way they took your money. Unforgivable."

Little Tommy said to Joey, "There's only one thing we can do about that now, but it can't be done. You know why."

"That's a fact." The consigliere confirmed it. "This problem of yours is outside our capabilities. Your daughter, out there in Spain. She could be anywhere, with anybody."

Joey took a deep breath, as if oxygen and patience were the same thing. He leaned forward to face the don. "Tommy," he said, pleading sneaking into his voice. "I don't know what to do anymore. Don't know what to tell Terry. She's on my case all the time now. Get on a plane to Spain, she says. As if I could get a damn passport of my own." Joey rubbed his brow. "But she's one hundred percent right. I can't sit around like this anymore. Just can't."

"How about Spillman?"

Joey snorted like a bull. "With all due respect, Tommy. But what the hell can a New York tax lawyer do for me in Spain?"

"He hasn't helped you any?"

"Sure. But what can he do except keep calling the Spanish police and keep chasing the news people away? This is way out of his league."

"Give him a little more time. He'll get on top of this."

"Tommy, I'm talking about my kid, Symphony. Who you've seen grow up. Who's played with your kids at birthday parties."

Domenic cut in, "Look, Joey, there's only so much Tommy can do about this—"

"Fuck that, Dom. Has any of your kids ever gone missing? Got any idea what that's like?"

"Take it easy there," said the don, softly. "You're right. This may not be business, but it is family. So, tell me what else you've been doing?"

"I'm in the process of checking out some people who said they can get me into Spain from Morocco. That way I'll be off the radar, you know. Truth is I don't know what good that would do—"

"None," Little Tommy hurried to say.

The idea of one of his top earners leaving his business unattended for any amount of time was unacceptable enough, but he had other reasons.

"Not only that," the consigliere added. "You talking to the police over there is only going to make a lot of people here nervous. And who needs that?"

"Forget that, Joey," Little Tommy insisted. "What's happening to your kid over there, and your family here, it's fucking terrible. But you going to Spain?"

"Besides," Domenic said, driving in the boss's point. "What could you do over there that you can't do from here, anyway?"

"Yeah, but I'm going out of my mind over here. It's been a fucking week since I've heard from my daughter—"

"Look, everybody feels for you," Little Tommy said.

"That's right," his consigliere pushed on. "From every mouth I've heard nothing but the highest respect for the way you're handling yourself."

Little Tommy waved his lit cigar in front of him. "Takes a big man to do the right thing when our interests get so ... how can I put it? Get so conflicted. Like they are. Nobody's in the dark about this, believe me."

The acting don paused and rubbed his chin as if in deep reflection, his pinky ring catching the light from the street. Then as if against his will, he looked at Joey and dipped his head twice with a papal nod and asked the question his captain had been waiting to hear.

"So, Joey, you tell me what else I can do for you?"

Joey huddled closer to his boss, the heavy twenty-four-carat chain around his neck dangling forward and gave him the answer they already knew.

"I need your help to get my daughter back before it's too late. No more, no less."

Little Tommy Pacelli, his small-barreled frame enshrouded in the phantasmagoric light of the luxurious cab, took a deep puff of his cigar.

Many issues prevented him from involving himself with his capo's problem. Some had to do with his Neapolitan prejudices, his natural dislike of Sicilians and their descendants. Some had to do with Joey the Bear himself. He never liked the man. He could've washed his hands on the whole affair and would've, had he not still been involved in the process of consolidating his power within the Family. As acting boss, he was in no position to ignore Joey's appeal, not while the eyes of all his captains were upon him. Not to mention the business opportunities the situation presented, which he had only just begun to work out.

The acting boss glanced through the cigar smoke at the Brooklyn Bridge, its arching lights shining like a giant diamond necklace across the river.

"OK," he finally said, reaching across and tapping Joey's jittery leg. "I'll take care of this for you. My way. I'll do it because you have so far handled this very difficult situation like a true made-man. Showed us your loyalty. Kept your head. Done the right thing by us."

Joey nodded in solemn gratitude. "I appreciate it, Tommy. Really do."

The two heavyset men turned and gave each other an uncomfortable, back-patting hug.

"Hey," Little Tommy said as he stuck his cigar back in his tiny mouth. "If we don't take care of our interests, who will?"

Joey nodded meekly. "It's all I ask."

T E N

Essex County, New Jersey

OUT OF THE LINCOLN Tunnel, Joey lit up a cigarette with the car lighter. He was breathing easier now. Having Little Tommy's word didn't necessarily mean it was a done deal, or that his support would come cheap. He knew better than that. Little Tommy's blood-sucking greed was legendary. In fact, he knew he could never trust him all that much. Still, the idea that an authority he recognized and understood was at last committed to bringing his daughter home restored his confidence in himself. Something definite had been accomplished, he felt. Something he could bring home to Terry.

Driving under the highway lights, he settled back into the soft, warm leather of the driver's seat, again feeling like the made-man that he was. He could almost see his daughter's return within sight. Perhaps in a matter of hours.

Time he could use to plan his payback, such was his optimism.

He pulled in a filling station off the New Jersey Turnpike, a couple of miles from his house. He bought three pints of Ben and Jerry's ice cream—the kind Terry was crazy about. Back in his SUV, he checked his cell phone for lost calls. Spillman's private number was listed several times.

Joey speed-dialed it. "It's me."

"Glad you called, Joseph," Spillman said with unusual verve. "I have news for you. A good one for a change. Guess what? We've found someone who can help us get in touch with those Basques."

"What do you mean? You talked to Tommy already?"

"No, why? Should I?"

"Never mind that. Just me wondering. So, talk to me, who is it you found?"

"Remember my contact at Langley—the CIA guy I told you about?"

"I think so, yeah."

"Well, he's located a man in Miami who used to work with certain members of the ETA network. The guy's got a straight connection to those people. Isn't that something? I've already scheduled Tess Bernard to fly down to meet with him and confirm whether the information is reliable. If it's good, I'm going to need your OK to make him an offer."

"What kind of offer?"

"To talk to his ETA friends in your name."

Joey meditated a moment. "Sure, go ahead. What have I got to lose?"

Spillman made an extended pause of his own. "I thought you'd be pleased. Everything OK?"

"I've been better. But, yeah. Follow it up."

"I'll call you as soon as Tess gets to Miami."

"Do that."

Joey was about to close his cell phone when he said, "Wait up. How come you're sending your secretary down there? Why can't you go?"

"Joseph, Ms. Bernard is not my secretary. She's an associate in our firm. Besides, I can't do it until next week, and I don't think we should wait that long. I'll send you her schedule if you like."

"That would be nice."

Joey narrowed his eyes at the trail of red taillights in front of him, thinking that maybe he should talk to the guy himself. Then decided Spillman was right. It would be better if they feel him out before he gets involved. "OK. Just keep me posted."

~

By midnight, everyone in the Messina residence had gone to bed. Joey walked in the kitchen. Terry, Aria, and Junior always seemed to be going up to bed when he got home. Yet not one light was off in the house. He stuck the ice cream in the freezer, then ripped open a family-size bag of Doritos, cracked open a can of Heineken, and knocked back half the beer with one swig.

Joey dropped himself on the white-leather sectional in the family room, dragged the ashtray and the remote closer. He stayed up most of the night staring at his 85 inches of flat-screen on the wall of his family room. Sometimes he'd zap through the sports channels, looking for the Giants, watching nothing, going over the night's events, flipping them in his head.

Entirely new scenarios opened up to him the more he thought about this new development in Miami. Alternatives he didn't have before. Spillman's timing couldn't have anything to do with Little Tommy and whatever he had in mind to do for him. No question about that, too soon, he told himself. He might even be able to bring Sym home and take care of the Basques himself without Little Tommy's help, which would save him a fortune. On the other hand, if worse came to worse, and Spillman's Miami guy crashed, he still had his boss's word.

Working both sides of the tracks might pay off, after all, he thought, as he lay down in bed next to Terry and went out like a light.

Long Island Expressway, New York City

A Frank Sinatra tune came on Tommy Pacelli's cell phone as he rode on his palace on wheels. He squeezed it and said, "Talk to me, counselor."

Arthur Spillman's compressed voice came from the other end of the connection. "I just had a chat with Joseph about the Miami connection, as you asked."

"And?"

"He sounded a little aloof at first, but I made sure he understood it was his best alternative. He gave me the go-ahead."

"Good for you." Pacelli grinned at his consigliere sitting by his side. "Can't have him going off to Spain on a wild goose chase like that. Got a lot on our plate here. This guy you got—"

"The Miami connection?"

"Yeah. He's not going to be a problem, is he?" Pacelli blew a mouthful of smoke that the limo's ventilation system instantly sucked away.

"As I said, he's an old CIA something or other, a Cuban who knows those Basques personally. There's a good chance that he'd be able to work out a deal with them without having the authorities interfere. I believe he just might be the safe alternative you're looking for to keep Joseph on this side of the Atlantic and keep his conscience clear."

"And his wife off his back," Pacelli added with a smoky laugh. "Just make sure Joey and that Cuban don't meet face to face. It might change things."

"I'll try."

"Don't try. Just do it. You know how to handle it. Come on."

Spillman remained quiet.

"You just keep doing what you're doing, counselor. You going to thank me when this is over."

"I'm doing the best I can, Thomas. But it's not easy. You know."

"Hey, I feel bad for his kid too. But he's got responsibilities to all of our kids. We all got to eat. Am I right?"

"That, you are."

"You just work with me on this and everything's gonna work out fine. Guaranteed."

Pacelli tossed his cell phone aside and puffed his cigar.

"You were right about both these guys," he said, addressing his consigliere. "The Jew lawyer and the Bear. Men under duress will believe anything."

Domenic wasn't so sure. "This could turn out to be an overkill," he said with a tone of warning. "You've got the German going to Spain to work on this too. Doubling up could mean problems later."

"Listen, Dom, I've got to be sure Joey stays put until it's time. Besides, who's this Cuban anyway? Probably an old fart Miami retiree."

"He's not the one that worries me. It's the German running things over there, where he could do whatever he wants without us knowing. While we're picking up the tab."

"So what? He's on Joey's tab. And if I recall correctly, the German was your idea."

"He was when we weren't looking for a negotiator. Now I'm not sure. What if the Cuban cuts a deal with the kidnappers?"

"Fine if he does. I'm not against deals. But if there isn't one, we got the German on the job. Truth be told, I rather see the German find those cocksuckers first. This is bigger than you're thinking, Dom. Can't have a bunch of half-assed Spanish terrorists moving into our business. And I don't got to tell you how much better we could do with Joey's business."

"But what's to stop us from putting the German on hold for now? Until the Cuban plays out. It'll keep us out of the picture. If there's a settlement, whatever Joey's got in mind of doing over there won't touch us."

"You're missing the point, Dom. I want to see the German put the fear of God in those sons of bitches. I want to see them on their knees begging us to take the girl back at no cost. And when that happens, then everything will move on as planned. Joey will go to Spain to get his daughter back, a big man, and get his payback. And that's when we'll make our moves in Brooklyn and get ours."

E L E V E N

Mondragón, Spain

HOT DUST CAME blowing out of the city's industrial park when Aitor made the turn out of the highway. It was Saturday, one of his scheduled days to feed the prisoners. He waved at the two helmeted workers standing around a noisy cement mixer. They waved back.

The *polígono industrial* had been slow in attracting business for two years, the reason why he had chosen it. Now there were new construction sites springing up all around their small tool-and-die plant. These new buildings so near were no cause for concern, he thought. It made theirs seem less conspicuous. Besides, the two-room *zulo* they had built under the factory was their best one yet. Anything less than a bomb explosion would be inaudible outside of it.

He steered onto the parking area in front of the unpainted cinderblock structure. Before exiting the car, he made a quick visual inspection of the surroundings and picked up the plastic bags with the groceries.

The instant he unlocked the three locks on the metal door, a half-asleep German shepherd appeared tail wagging out of the greasy gloom within.

"Hello, you." He patted the dog's head. "Done much defecating overnight?"

He walked across the length of the building, the dog hopping beside him.

They went past the tool-making machines that had been so useful the previous winter, turning out explosives, rebuilding and remodeling weapons, but now sat silently in the shadows since the prisoners arrived.

In the kitchen area, Aitor opened a window that looked out on a high cinderblock wall. He opened a can of dog food, emptied it in the bowl, and watched the dog go for it. Then he got busy with the cooking—his and Patxi's job on weekends.

Aitor felt his watch with his fingers. "That *cabrón* of Patxi is late again."

He did not mind cooking for the prisoners but hated Patxi's continual tardiness. After only a week, he'd noticed a slack sense of routine settling in with both prisoners and his men. He welcomed it gladly in the prisoners' case. But he would have to keep a watchful eye on his compeers. Becoming too over-confident was the greatest danger in their business.

While the pasta boiled on the electric burner, Aitor heated up the content of two cans of precooked Orlando-brand meatballs in the microwave. When it was ready, he mixed them up in two plastic soup dishes. He had just set the plates on the aluminum tray when he heard the squeaky front door opening.

"*Cojones*," he hollered without looking at the person approaching. He could tell it was Patxi by the noise of his keys. "Could you not come any later?"

"I told you Mari wanted to go to Alcampo this afternoon. Here." He handed him a loaf of bread. "I brought him the *Marca*—did not have to clip off any part of it."

"Did you read the entire newspaper? You know the boy will."

"There is nothing to censor out."

Aitor gave him an askance look.

"Why do you look at me like that? *Marca* is a sports daily."

"You know why I say it."

"So we found one small mention of the kidnapping before. So what. That is not the norm."

"To hell with the norm."

"I will check through it again if you want to."

"Too late now."

Aitor cut the loaf of bread in halves. The smaller half for Miguel Angel, the bigger one for the girl. "She has only been eating bread for the last three days."

Patxi filled two plastic bottles with tap water and set them on the tray with the food dishes and the bread. Aitor opened one of the shopping bags on the counter and brought out a wedge of cheese and two chocolate bars. He put those on the tray as well. Patxi picked up the tray and followed him out.

"Any word from Iñaki?"

Aitor shook his head. "The *americana* stays until the operation is over. That is final."

Patxi made a lip noise of disapproval but said nothing.

Four days into the abduction, Iñaki, ETA's head of military operations, had summoned Aitor to a clandestine meeting in Toulouse and informed him of the leadership's final decision on the *americana*.

"It is not what any of us want," Iñaki had told him. "But to set her free at this time, even with an official declaration of regret, would be a total disaster. First, because it will jeopardize our negotiations with Estrada-Uribe. And second, because I do not believe an apology would prevent a retaliatory response from the girl's father and his Mafia associates. I know that everyone suspects that we abducted her, yes. But do they have any proof? No, they do not. This is why now our strategy should be to keep them guessing until we can complete our transaction with the boy's father. A quiet, peaceful period of a few days is all we need. So let us keep calm and move on as planned, and pretend the girl does not exist."

Iñaki had also spoken candidly about those in the leadership who were pushing to set a ransom on Symphony's head.

"Why not? They're asking. Don't we already have her?"

Aitor, who felt he had tactically the last word on the issue, flatly disagreed. "That, I cannot do."

"Neither will I," Iñaki assured him. "Those spiritual leaders of ours sitting in the comfort of their prison cells, they've lost touch with reality. They're not scared of gangsters, they say. Demand a hefty ransom. But, Aitor, what we need now is peace and tranquility until our transaction with Estrada-Uribe is completed. Because, as you well know, without those funds, all the work we have done to keep our ETA alive will go to hell. And that is the one thing I will never allow to happen, not as long as there is a breath of life in me."

Aitor nodded but remained in cautious silence.

"And that's not the worst that's been said," Iñaki added with a laugh of disgust. "Some of our least constructive members have proposed that we could have the girl disappear. Solve the problem in the same manner the Mafia does it, they say."

"If that is what they want the new ETA to be ..." Aitor started to say.

But Iñaki stopped him. "Do not even think of it, brother. We may be combatants, but we are not murderers. Ours is a struggle for independence, not that. And as long as I am military commander, I will never allow our Basqueland to be dishonored that way, not again. Not while I am alive to prevent it."

In the semidarkness of the Mondragón plant, Aitor, Patxi, and the dog walked toward a heavy milling machine sitting by the grease-stained wall.

Aitor took hold of a chain hanging from an overhead pulley. He hooked it to a heavy machine sitting on a rusty bedplate. Then, together with Patxi, they hoisted up the ancient contraption by pulling on the rattling chain, drew the machine to one side, and set it down on an empty space next to the wall.

Patxi dragged the heavy iron bedplate aside with a hand hook, exposing a manhole-sized opening on the concrete floor: the entrance to the subterranean rooms where the prisoners were held, the infamous Basque *zulos*.

A metallic dome inside the manhole was visible just below the floor. Aitor hooked the pulley chain to a loop on its top, pulled the chain, and up came a cylindrical-shaped cage reminiscing of a miners' one-man elevator, the exact size of the round opening.

They lowered the trays first, as one man and a tray did not fit in the elevator. When it hit the ground, Aitor tugged carefully on a cord attached to its side and the trays slid off onto the *zulo* floor without its content spilling. They pulled the elevator up again and Aitor stepped inside it and watched the dark outline of the machines on the factory floor rising as Patxi lowered him into the pitch-black underground.

Aitor flicked on the lone light bulb and the operation reversed, Aitor cranking the chains from below as Patxi descended.

They slid on their ski masks. In the key ring, Aitor found the one to Miguel Angel's cell door.

Patxi pressed play on the dusty boom box on a shelf. It started blasting heavy metal music—Baldo's idea to prevent the *piezas* from hearing each other's voices when the doors opened. At first, both Patxi and Aitor had opposed the idea, but the loud music had proved so reliable in masking their voices and noises that after ten days in captivity, the prisoners still had no idea their cell doors were only three feet apart.

T W E L V E

In the Zulo

THE CD MUSIC HAD already made Miguel Angel get up from his cot. The trapdoor built in the gray armored door dropped with its usual bang. He still had to resist the urge not to attack the hands that slid his meals through the opening twice a day. He had paid too high a price for it on his first night there. The beating Baldo and Minot gave him with their rubber hoses only lasted one minute, but the excruciating pain continued for two miserable sleepless nights. Then they kept him at half-rations for the next three days. Now he did not know what was worse, the swollen black-and-blues or the hunger pains.

"Stand up and face the wall," the man he knew as José yelled over the deafening electric guitar music.

"I'm in position," Miguel Angel shouted, his back visible in the brown light of the caged bulb.

Aitor placed the tray on the flat of the trapdoor and peered through the opening. He flinched back when the stench from inside hit him.

"*Hola, chaval,*" he said. "How are you today?"

The smell of factory-cooked tomato sauce and meatballs wafted into the cell. It made Miguel Angel salivate, although he hated it. "As you can see," he said, with the same faked good humor. It was all an act, which his kidnappers played as well, part of the spirit of camaraderie his captives thought they deserved. It drew better results all around. Particularly from José and his partner, the ones who brought him the sports newspaper and told him the exact time of day so he would not go mad. The other two, the silent French-Basque and the cocky young one, were another story. "What time is it?"

"Three forty-five p.m."

"You're a little behind schedule."

"You must be hungry."

Aitor tried to make it easier for Miguel Angel whenever he could. Not only because he liked the boy and was thankful that he was nothing like his problematic fiancée next door, but because of what he represented to the organization. And how their treatment of him now would reflect on them later when the ransom was paid in full and he was set free.

Miguel Angel picked up the food bowl, the newspaper and the plastic water bottle. Then he slid the empty plate from the night before and the empty bottle onto the trapdoor.

"Enjoy the cheese and the chocolate," Aitor said over the loud music.

"Any news from my family?"

"Not yet. I've told you these things take time."

"Any word on the electric fan and the dehumidifier?"

"No, but we have not forgotten. We are waiting for our petition to be approved. Anything else?"

"How about the keys?" Miguel Angel muttered under his breath.

"What?" Aitor shouted from the door.

"*Nada.* Thanks for the chocolate."

Patxi shut the trapdoor and slid the black ski mask off his head. Aitor rolled his up to his forehead. "It stinks very badly in there," he said, lighting up a cigarette. "Tell Pedro and Mertxe to come tonight and empty the crap bucket."

"It is not the bucket. The stench comes from that filthy creek near the highway. The underground water filters in. The engineer said it could happen."

"Then make sure the buckets are emptied every day. We owe the boy a little consideration, now that his father has paid the first installment. And what is delaying Baldo with the dehumidifier and the wall fan?"

"He says there is only a single A/C line for the lights. He would have to rewire both cells to install them. I think he is procrastinating. He is afraid the boy might make a weapon out of the fan or the machine."

"Why would he? He knows he will be freed soon."

Patxi blew a long puff of smoke and stubbed the cigarette in a tin can. "I suppose. Are you ready to feed the tigress?"

Aitor shrugged, resigned.

"Who goes in first?" the big man asked with a teasing grin, knowing well whose job it was.

"Baldo says she has been housebroken," Aitor said with a grin of his own.

"And you believe him?"

"Not for a second."

They rolled their black masks over their faces.

Patxi picked up Symphony's food bowl from the tray and handed it to Aitor.

"Let us see what new surprises she has for us today."

Built as a weapons' storage room, Symphony's cell door was not furnished with a trapdoor opening as Miguel Angel's. It required of her captors to physically enter and hand her the food, a task the entire team had come to dread. Patxi unlocked the door and flinched back when the foul smell hit him.

Symphony, a shadow in the dull overhead light, wrapped herself to her neck with the blanket, her knees under her chin.

"I bring food to you," Aitor yelled in his English over the noisy CD.

She glared at him in stalking silence.

He surveyed the tomblike hole. Sections of the raw plywood planks on the ground had buckled with the humidity that filtered in from the nearby blackwater creek. The fetid smell made breathing a form of perpetual torture.

He showed her the tray before moving any closer. "Is OK?"

Although she no longer was the dangerous biting and clawing, kicking tigress of the first few days, he thought it a good idea to proceed with caution.

"Spaghetti *y albóndigas*."

Aitor set the tray on top of the wooden banquette beside her. The lentil soup dinner from the previous night was sitting untouched and crawling with insects on the floor planks where Baldo or Minot had left it. The bread and the water were gone, he was relieved to note. He picked up the bowl with the dried-up lentils and handed it to Patxi.

Symphony followed him with her gaze, eyeing his every move from behind matted spikes of hair.

Aitor leaned over to have a closer look at her face. "I bring cheese and one Kit Kat chocolate to you. Good, yes?"

Symphony held him off with a vicious look. She detested their phony generosity, their stupid English, the smell of cigarettes they brought in on their bodies, further polluting the already foul air.

"This girl does not look well," Aitor said in Spanish.

He picked up the Spanish/English phrasebook Minot had brought her. Aitor looked quickly through it. "Ah," he said when he found the phrase. "Miss, do you feel ill?"

"Go to hell." Symphony turned abruptly to face the wall.

Aitor tried to show her the phrase in the book. She would not look at it. He tried to feel her forehead for fever and she recoiled tighter against the wall, her burning eyes on his.

"Don't you touch me," she warned him.

Aitor backed off. "You, you," he said, his head shaking with frustration. "You are a big, big problem for nothing. I bring good food. Why no eat?"

Symphony, glaring straight into the mask's eyeholes, brought her hand out from under the blanket, grabbed a lump of humid earth from the wall, put it in her mouth, and chewed it with defiance.

Aitor let out a string of angry curses. "You eat this, this dirt and not the food? Why?" He jabbed his forefinger on his temple. "You crazy? *Loca*? Why no eat the food? Why?"

Symphony spat out a mouthful of dirt and showed him her dirt-smeared tongue. "Fuck you."

Aitor threw his arms up and switched to Spanish, facing Patxi. "Bah, to hell with her. She can eat all the dirt she wants. The entire wall if she wants to. I have taken all I can take."

He turned to her again, his face flushed, fuming. "Don't eat. What do I care? Better you stay silent with a mouth full of shit than screaming like a witch on fire. I have had it with you …"

He started for the door but then wheeled unable to let it go. "Why no eat? I make good food to you. Why you no eat?"

Symphony turned her face to the wall.

Patxi gave Aitor a fatal shake of his head. "I do not like this. Look at her. She looks worse than ever."

Aitor cursed and rubbed his wool mask, dying to rip it off his face. "We're going to have to force-feed her if she keeps this up one more day."

He took a deep breath and slowly neared the bowl closer to her. "Look, only taste a little bit. OK? Just a little," he said as if talking to his own daughter. "Because if you no eat then you ill ..." He unwrapped the chocolate bar and waved it like a cigar at her. "Delicious, yes?" He held it closer to her, encouraging her to take it.

Symphony squinted at the holes in his black mask. She could see him grinning, or trying to, his teeth almost sticking out of the mouth hole.

He placed the plastic water bottle beside her. Symphony lifted it and washed her mouth with the water, spat out the mud on the planks, and wiped her soiled lips.

"Yes. Good," Aitor said, urging her with a baby talk-like tone, thinking that at last he was getting through. "Now eat the chocolate, yes?"

"How much longer you're going to keep me here?" she said, at first with a labored whisper, then raising her volume by degrees with each syllable. "How long? Huh, you bastards."

Aitor and Patxi watched her mud-browned rubber slippers hit the planked floor one at a time.

"So where's Miguel? What did you do to him? Did you kill him? Is that it? You sons of bitches—" Symphony raised herself off the mattress, her face twisting with fury. "Or are you waiting to get your ransom? Is that it? Is that why you're keeping me in this shit hole? To get your blood money?"

She started to move toward Aitor as he backed toward the door. "Well dream on, pal. 'Cause I got news for you. Even if you bastards get your ransom, you're never going to spend that money. Never."

She was screaming now. "You don't know who my father is. You don't know me either. And I'm never going to eat your crap. Never. And there's not a thing you can do about it. So if you're going to kill me, go ahead. I'm not scared of you, you shits. Go on kill me and get it over with—" She screamed louder than the singer did on the CD. "Go ahead. Kill me already if you got the balls."

Patxi cut in front of her brandishing the rubber hose, but Symphony kept staggering forward until she stood nose to chin with him, yelling the filthiest obscenities, curses he understood only by the venom in her cries.

He shoved her back and slammed the door in her face. Symphony wrapped herself inside the filthy blanket, cocooned in the corner. She could hardly breathe without holding the towel to her nose. She was beyond starving but the smell of spaghetti sauce together with the offal stink that lived there with her made her empty insides turn. She had nothing left to throw up but water.

"*Jodía americana*," Patxi growled as he pulled his mask off his sweaty face and hurled it to the floor. "It is not food this girl needs. She needs a damn exorcist. God, listen to her wail. Between that damn music, the heat, the stench, and this girl, I am warning you, Aitor, this is not going to end well. She is either going to die of malnutrition or one of us is going to kill her."

Aitor yanked the plug on the blaring boom box.

"I've had enough of that lunatic," he said, his face red with pent up rage. "It's over. If she does not eat her food today, tomorrow we will feed her intravenously. She is not going to die in my *zulo*. Not while I am in command."

Symphony threw herself on the mattress, buried her face in the smelly towel and screamed into it until her rage began to subside. She tried to stay awake, alert, but the black-faced ghosts always succeeded in mainlining her for hours, blending days into one another in an endless hallucinatory night.

After a while, she heard the metallic clanking of the one-man elevator as the men climbed out. Then everything grew quiet and dreary again.

Symphony lay on the bare mattress with her face to the raw dirt wall. Only sleeping made her agony bearable. Except sleeping was hopeless since they stopped drugging her. With the 100-watt light permanently on her face, she just couldn't. Sometimes she'd close her eyes, slip into a dormant state, and collapse from exhaustion into a dreamless pretend sleep. But real sleep was impossible. Had she not been taught that suicide would only lead her to an even worse hell, she would have ended it all right there and then.

So she prayed, dozens of Hail Marys, one after another like a mantra, until she fainted or fell into a sort of trance, seeing visions superimposed over the mud walls ... a dear face, a hovering glow in a long-flowing dress of pure white ... the image of her grandmother, Mama, holding a bouquet of white flowers, a fresh-smelling grin on her lips. The ancient wedding picture in her Brooklyn living room coming to life through her tears ...

Symphony felt a shifting inside her, a murmuring behind her navel, a mysterious hunger stronger than her self-pity.

She picked up the Kit Kat bar off the floor planks with a vague sense of hope, swatted the ants off it, and took a tentative bite. The taste brought her home, to her family, to life.

She sobbed with every bite until she finished it.

Next, she dragged the bowl toward her, dug the trembling spoon into the food, and filled her mouth with it. She squeezed her stomach and fought back her nausea as she chewed and swallowed it until all of it was gone.

It would be some time before Symphony would identify the source of this newfound strength, but she would, without anyone's help, alone inside her womb of rock and dirt, because even there, so far from the warmth and light of the living, the forces of procreation would not go unheeded.

PART III

THIRTEEN

Miami, Florida

Tess Bernard of Lance Cohen & Spillman pulled into the only unpaved driveway on the block. She lowered her dark sunglasses and peered through the cluster of palm trees at a flat-roofed bungalow in the sun-blistering hush of suburban Miami-Dade County. She took the modest home as a positive sign after the rows of ostentatious sheet-rock Mac-mansions she'd passed on the way. The mysterious Zeus Aguirre would not be averse to making a little money. She figured she'd be back in New York by dinnertime.

A breath of burning vapor hit her face the instant she climbed out of the air-conditioned rental. She hurried on her high heels into the screened porch as if running out of the rain. She stood still by the door, listening for a moment to something she thought she had imagined. The melancholy strains of Chopin's Prelude No. 4. It wasn't a recording. Someone was playing it. She had never heard her favorite piano melody performed at such a delicate tempo or in such an improbable setting. The doorbell silenced the music in mid-phrase.

The wooden door swung open and the figure of a barefoot man in faded jeans and a white T-shirt appeared through the cloudy screen door. "Tess Bernard, right? You got here quick."

"No time to waste, Mr. Aguirre."

Her host gestured toward a small couch next to an old flat-black grand piano that took half the living room space. In his baggy T-shirt, lean and mild-faced Aguirre didn't look like much to her, definitely not the war hero she had read about in the CIA dossier Spillman had given her. She noticed no sheet music on the piano, as if the ghost pianist had been playing Chopin from memory. That impressed her.

"Have a seat, Miss Bernard. It is Miss Bernard?" Mr. Aguirre said with an air of concern.

Tess nodded in silence. Zeus Aguirre's cottage bore a worn but cozy atmosphere, a fading woman's touch. Colorful Caribbean paintings and mahogany carvings shared the living space with a handful of modern home electronics, exuberant houseplants, worn-out rugs, and squeaky floorboards.

Aguirre sat on one of two matching rocking chairs in front of her. Noticing her interest in the piano, he said, "Miss Bernard, do you play?"

"Goodness no. Do you?"

"A little. Would you like something to eat? A drink maybe?" Aguirre said with a trace of an unidentifiable accent.

"Bottled water, if you have it."

Zeus called out, "Maria."

Tess expected the real pianist to materialize, his mate perhaps, when a small brown woman with Indian features and an apron around her barrel-shaped waist came out and spoke in a whistling, choppy Spanish to Aguirre. Her fingers were stubby and short, not those of a pianist.

While Aguirre inquired about her drive from the airport, the traffic jams and the awful heat, the Guatemalan woman left and came back with a tray she placed on the center table. Aguirre's "divorced and retired" status seemed to check.

Still, Tess was having trouble seeing the special ops-type she'd read about in his dossier. If not for the mysterious, elusive quality which she for some reason associated with secret agents, he seemed quite average in height and build. Definitely nothing like "the only person in the entire country with a direct line to ETA's leadership in Spain, and who is not wanted by the Law," as Spillman's Washington connections had described him.

And definitely not the type that would impress a man like Messina.

Aguirre took the Presidente beer. Tess sipped her iced water and smiled politely. She had learned from previous dealings with Hispanic clients that they never went straight into business, but rather meandered into it. She prepared herself to wait until her host took the initiative. To her pleasant surprise, she didn't have to wait long.

"Tell me, Miss Bernard—"

"Call me Tess, please."

"OK Tess. Why do you think ETA is responsible for the girl's disappearance?"

"The evidence pointing at ETA is immense. In fact, the most persuasive clue came from the man who represented them in the ransom negotiations with the Estrada family."

"The Batasuna councilman?"

"Precisely," Tess said, delighted the Cuban had read the report she had sent in advance. "We've also obtained information from another source supporting this allegation. Are you familiar with Judge Garzón?"

"Yes. Did he say ETA is holding the girl?"

"Not in so many words. But he's of the opinion that ETA's reluctance to admit to Miss Messina's abduction might be the result of an internal dispute between those who want to profit from her capture and those who oppose it."

"It's possible. How about the FBI, what do they have to say?"

"Well, I'm afraid they haven't been much help," she said, recalling Spillman's instruction to keep off the subject of the FBI and Messina's line of work.

"Strange," Aguirre said with mild surprise. "The Bureau has jurisdiction over missing US citizens' cases abroad. I know they have several special agents in the Madrid embassy trained to handle this kind of situation."

"It goes back to the problem the Spanish authorities have with this case," Tess said. "Since no one has claimed responsibility for Ms. Messina's abduction or asked for a ransom, she's technically regarded as a missing person's case. Except for her connection to Miguel Angel's case—"

"When did the abduction take place?"

"Eleven, twelve days ago."

"I've heard nothing about it on the news."

"I'm not surprised. It didn't get much coverage here. Then it died out completely. I suppose the lack of new developments may have cut the media's interest."

Aguirre placed the half-full bottle of beer on the coffee table. He was thinking.

"It's natural that ETA and the Estradas would want to keep their ransom arrangement out of the scrutiny of the media. Both of them have plenty of influence in the region to implement it. But I can't see how that would benefit the girl's investigation."

Tess could see Aguirre was sensing something wrong with the picture. The silent Indian woman brought two coffee cups and a sugar bowl on a tiny silver tray. She offered Tess a cup, but she declined.

Zeus drank his in a single gulp. "I can't understand why the FBI hasn't given the Messina family the kind of assistance they would anyone else in the same situation. It's their obligation, by federal law."

Tess didn't have an answer.

"Why haven't the Messinas gone to the press? Relatives of kidnapped victims do it all the time."

"They're afraid it might endanger Symphony's situation."

"Ah," he said, folding his arms as he studied her.

"Mr. Aguirre," Tess declared with a gesture of impatience.

"Zeus."

"Right, Zeus. What do you think, sir? Can you help us bring this girl home to her family?"

"The truth? I haven't the remotest idea—"

"Zeus," she said, talking over his words. "I came to Miami to engage your services because our friend in the CIA assured us the ETA leadership trusts you and will speak candidly with you. They might even owe you a favor or two. My client is willing to pay you one hundred thousand dollars just to speak to them on his behalf. But," she added as if to let him in a secret, "if you can arrange Symphony's safe return, I have it from the best of sources that you could pretty much write your own ticket."

"What if they don't have the girl?"

"The one-hundred thousand dollars fee is secured even if the girl is deceased. The same as the expenses. The cash would be deposited in an account of your choice, anywhere in the world. The advance fee will be negotiated on acceptance."

Aguirre released a soft chuckle of disbelief, the melancholy laugh of a man who had just been offered what he had always wanted but no longer needed. "I'd have to study the situation before I can make a decision."

Tess leaned forward. "What is it, Zeus? Is this money not enough?"

"The money's fine. But this is much more complicated than you think."

"Oh? Enlighten me, please."

"There's no telling what ETA's reaction will be if I were to approach them with this. It could scare them into a more defensive posture. Tell you what, give me a day or two and I'll give you my answer. You have my word."

Tess opened her purse, fished out her phone and speed-dialed her boss, as instructed to do should the negotiations hit a snag. It had.

She averted her glance not to look Aguirre in the eye, wondering what kind of paranoia he could be suffering from to turn down that kind of money. "Hi." She exchanged a few words with her boss and gave the handset to Aguirre.

"Mr. Spillman would like a word with you, if you don't mind."

Aguirre's conversation with Spillman ended just as theirs had. "No, Mr. Spillman, I am sympathetic. But I need to assess the situation more carefully before I can give you an answer either way." He listened on and added, "Yes. A couple of days," then handed her the cell phone.

Tess listened to her boss's new instructions and threw the phone back in her purse.

"OK Mr. Aguirre," she said as she stood and headed for the door. "I'll call you later when I know the hotel I'll be staying in. As Mr. Spillman informed you, I'll be in town until you give us your final answer." She was about to add, "If Symphony Messina is still alive," but checked herself. "Keep in mind, time is of the essence. This girl's life just might be in your hands now."

FOURTEEN

Mondragón

THAT SAME DAY AT 2:45 p.m., Spanish time, Aitor and Patxi were halfway through their midday meal at the Café Donosti when Xavier, the proprietor, white apron over his round belly, wandered over to their table. He looked over his shoulders as if to make sure no one was listening and said with a tragic undertone, "Have you heard what happened in San Sebastián?"

"Heard what?"

The proprietor eyed the uneaten food on their plates. "Come to the counter when you are finished," he said to avoid ruining their meal. "You can see it for yourselves on the three o'clock news."

Aitor and Patxi moved to the bar counter to have their coffee as the punctual three o'clock TV newscast from Madrid began.

"*Una genuina carnicería en Donosti,*" the newscaster began. "A massacre that has horrified the city and has Ertzaintza investigators puzzled as to its motives ... The shocking discovery of the mutilated bodies of former Batasuna councilman Emilio Gaztelu and those of his wife and two sons were found last night in the basement of their home ... alongside the body of José Navarro, president of Banco Vasco, who had been reported missing by his family only a day ago ... According to local sources, Gaztelu and Navarro were the key negotiators responsible for the ransom agreement made by the family of kidnapped victim Miguel Angel Estrada and ETA ..."

Aitor and Patxi glanced at each other in tense silence. For the murdered bodies of bank president Navarro, the man in charge of paying out the ransom for the Estrada family, and that of former Councilman Gaztelu, the ETA spokesman who negotiated the ransom, to have been found tortured and killed in the same location could only mean one thing. Some monstrous force was coming after Miguel Angel Estrada's kidnappers, and it was on the right trail.

They rushed out of the café and drove directly to the industrial park. They hadn't been to the plant in the last two days and they needed to see with their own eyes that their prisoners were safe in their cells and everything was where it ought to be.

Aitor opened the glove compartment and took one of the three mobile telephones he kept there. He typed the numbers with his thumb as he steered the Citroen with his other hand.

"Are you calling Iñaki?" Patxi said.

Aitor nodded yes. He waited for the call to go through but there was no answer. He slammed his hand on the steering wheel and left Iñaki a voice mail. "Primo, it is me," he enunciated slowly. "Do not forget today is my wife's birthday. Call her as soon as you can. Repeat: My wife's birthday."

Their Code Red signal.

Pau, Pyrénées-Atlantiques, France

Iñaki felt his mobile telephone vibrating in his pocket, ignored it and kept walking. He was on a life-or-death mission. Txatxi, his friend and most trusted man in France, had been hospitalized the night before, victim of an unknown assailant. And it was Iñaki's obligation as head of ETA's Military Operations to find out what happened and report it to the leadership.

On Boulevard des Pyrenees, he found the main entrance of the clinic sealed off by the police. His first reaction was to perform an abrupt about-face. But then he mingled with a crowd of onlookers across the street of the hospital. Pau's Our Lady of Lourdes Hospital was perhaps one of the most secure places in the world for an *etarra* to get treatment, thanks to its director, a French Basque and staunch ETA supporter. Also, the number of uniformed gendarmes standing outside the building set him somewhat at ease. Had the French come after an ETA member, he reasoned, there would have been dozens of plainclothes DCPJ types, Reisegnemant Généraux agents, even black-hooded men from the Special Forces, and not so many local police officers. The crime unit vehicle would not have been there either. They used those only on murder scenes.

Cautious but unworried, Iñaki meandered toward a group of people that had gathered around a heavyset gendarme. The bystanders were bombarding him with questions and the reluctant gendarme kept repeating, "A man patient was murdered in his bed by some out-of-towners. That's all I know."

An old woman gasped. "*Tué sur lit? Quelle horreur!*"

"Was the victim from Pau?" someone said. "Anyone we know?"

"No. The patient was also an out-of-towner. *Espagnol.*"

Iñaki's back stiffened up. But he held himself from jumping to conclusions, there could be other *espagnoles* in the clinic. He hurried back to the car. As he made the corner, he spotted a male nurse in green scrubs coming out of a side door of the clinic. "*S'vous plaît, infirmier,*" he said in his best French. "Do you know the name of the Spaniard who was killed?"

The nurse regarded him for an instant as he continued walking. "I don't know. Valdez, I think."

Iñaki halted abruptly. Valdez was Txatxi's cover-name.

It took him a while to find where he had parked his beat-up BMW. When he did, he dropped down on the driver's seat, dug his mobile out of his pocket and dialed the clinic's administration. His face wet with perspiration.

"*Allô.* May I speak with patient Roberto Valdez, if you please? I believe he is in room 209. Yes, I will hold."

Seconds later a man's voice came on the line. "Are you the person calling to speak with Monsieur Valdez?"

"Yes."

"May I ask you to identify yourself?"

"By all means, I am his cousin Daniel. And you are?"

"I am Police Inspector ..."

Iñaki squeezed the phone until his knuckles turned white. His closest friend and brother-in-arms shot to death in bed? Who would dare do such a thing in a hospital, in the middle of the day?

He pressed his fist on his chest as if to keep his arrhythmic heart from bursting out. He took a plastic vial out of his pocket, placed a nitroglycerine pill beneath his tongue and closed his eyes.

His mobile began to vibrate again. He recognized Aitor's voice.

"Listen, Primo," Aitor said in Spanish, then in Euskara. "We have a very serious problem. Did you see the afternoon news from Madrid?"

"No, but they cannot be worse than the one here," Iñaki said short of breath.

"What happened?"

"Are you on a sterile mobile?"

"Yes, yes."

"Txatxi is dead." Iñaki eyes reddened just to hear himself saying it.

"But I thought he was out of danger."

"Someone shot him in the clinic, as he lay in bed. Can you believe that? There are uniformed *txakurras* all over the place here."

A heavy smoker's sigh hissed through the line. "Any idea who did it?" Aitor said.

"No, but I will find out. Of that you can be sure."

"I think I have an idea who had it done," Aitor said.

"You?" Iñaki said, incredulous.

"Yes. And if you had seen Madrid's three o'clock news, I believe the same idea would have occurred to you."

Aitor gave him a quick report on the San Sebastián killings.

Iñaki uttered a string of curses in Euskara. "Only the *americana*'s father could've had this done. Only he has the motivation and the resources to try something like this."

Aitor agreed. "Primo, we knew keeping this girl was a disaster waiting to happen."

Iñaki exhaled a long, labored breath.

"What do we do now?"

"We hunt them down," Iñaki said. "Whoever they are. They have gone as far as they are going to get. They only got this far because of the filthy traitor of Gaztelu. Who else could have told them where to find Txatxi?"

"Do not judge him too harshly," Aitor felt obliged to say.

"I'd shoot him myself if he wasn't dead already."

"I don't think you know what those people did to him and his family. It was even more horrendous than the press reported. They tortured his wife and slid the throats of his children in front of him, then chopped off his extremities with an ax. They strapped three explosive charges in sequence on Navarro the banker. The police have yet to recover all his body parts. I am not surprised he talked."

"He is still a traitor. Had that soft-belly lawyer been a true patriot, Txatxi would not have been killed today."

"I'm not sure—"

"You're not? What if Gaztelu had known where the girl is? You might not be around to be so considerate."

Aitor withheld from comments and let Iñaki vent.

"The most important thing we have to do now is to reassure the boy's family that all is well. That should take priority."

"I am in accord," Aitor said. "The news of these killings is not going to go down well at the cannery."

"Have the boy write a letter to the family," Iñaki said. "Make sure he tells them he is in good health and being treated well. The second installment is due in two weeks and I do not have to remind you how much we need those funds."

"Consider it done."

"Make certain it gets delivered without delay."

"What about the girl? Maybe the time has come to let her go. Those assassins would have no alternative but to go back to where they came from if she is freed."

"I believe so too, but not yet."

"Then when?"

"The political branch has to approve it. But do not worry. I doubt the old-timers will demur anymore. The last thing they want is to jeopardize our arrangement with the boy's family. In the meantime, get her some new clothes, maybe some makeup for her face, feed her well. I want her to look good when the press gets their hands on her."

Aitor glanced at his mobile telephone. "Maybe we should terminate this connection. We are past the limit."

"*Agur.*"

"One last thing," Aitor said. "You should get out of Pau as soon as you can. These people might be waiting for you."

"Do not worry about me, my compeer. I am not a soft-belly politician like the councilman or a helpless man lying in bed in a clinic."

The instant Iñaki started the car, a smiling woman rode up and asked him if he was leaving the parking space. Iñaki lowered the window. "Yes," he said, waving at her to get out of the way. "I'm in a hurry."

He had not finished saying it when the passenger's door of his car snapped open and he came face to face with the barrel of a Glock.

"*Déplacez un muscle et vous serez un mort,*" a Moorish-faced gunman told him. "Move a muscle and you're dead."

While Iñaki was looking over his right shoulder at the gun, the door on the driver's side opened and a blond heavyset man with a childlike smirk slapped a T-shirt sopping with ether on his face while the Moor held him down.

Iñaki tried to fight them off, arms flapping, legs kicking like a drowning man until all strength drained out of his body in one swift gush and he blacked out.

The sneering heavyset man hurled the T-shirt to the back seat and grinned at the Moorish-looking man.

"We got ourselves a live one."

FIFTEEN

Miami, Florida

FLANKED BY FIELDS of yucca, beans, and other vegetables in demand in Miami, narrow Krome Avenue reminded Tess of a highway in some third world country. She followed the GPS's directions to an unmarked graveled road off the highway until she reached a discolored sign. Garrigo Ranch.

The weed-choked, rusted gate was open, permanently. A leathery-skinned man in rubber boots and baseball cap came by pushing a wheelbarrow. "*Perdón,*" she said from inside the car. "*Con el Señor Aguirre, por favor.*"

The man waved her onward past a stand of palm trees to a sky blue and baby pink cottage up ahead.

At the other end of the finca, Zeus was in the stable stalls, brushing down his brown and white Appaloosa mare when he heard a shout reminiscent of a cattle hoot.

"Your visitor has arrived," old man Garrigo shouted from the distance.

In a bathtub outside the stable, he washed his arms and face with tap water, put on his shirt, and walked to the visitors' palm-thatched roof kiosk.

Tess, her blonde hair in a ponytail, watched him walking from the stables, his surefooted gait and easy frame, his tanned face in the sun, seeing for the first time the man of action of the CIA report. The dispensing machine behind her made a loud fumbling racket. Old man Garrigo, the ranch owner, handed her a Coke can.

"It's the diet kind."

"In that case," she said, taking the sweaty can.

Zeus climbed the three wooden steps up to the kiosk.

"How about you, Aguirre?" the old man said. "They're nice and cold."

"Sure," he said, surveying Tess in the sunlight. She looked different sans her high-power attorney's suit and makeup, younger and curvier in jeans. "Had any trouble finding the place?"

"Your directions were OK."

Old Garrigo gave Zeus a furtive wink and walked away and sat down with his Cuban friends waiting to start a domino *partida* under the ceiling fans.

Zeus escorted Tess to a corner table. A muggy July breeze rustled through the tropical vegetation fencing the kiosk. "I hope you've had sufficient time to consider our offer," she said.

He regarded her with kind eyes. "I hope you're not sore at me."

"Why should I be?"

"The way we left it yesterday."

"Not at all. I think the Messina family and our firm are very fortunate to have you come aboard." Then she added with a probing smile, "That is why you had me drive all the way out here. Right?"

Zeus frowned at the wet coke can in his hands.

"Zeus, every hour that Symphony remains a prisoner of those terrorists is—Well, I don't think I have to tell you what it means. So please, I'd like to hear your terms. New York's waiting."

"Last night," he said. "I found out something about your client that I am surprised you didn't mention." Zeus scrutinized her for a moment. "Joe the Bear Messina."

A single wrinkle formed between her eyebrows. "I thought Mr. Spillman gave you that information."

"Apparently, he forgot."

"I'd be more than glad to tell you, Zeus," she replied with an evasive shrug. "Only I really don't know what there is to say, aside from the fact that he's the grieving father of a kidnapped nineteen-year-old girl who needs our help."

"So you don't think there's anything about him that I should know, before I go to work for him?"

She let out a tiny sigh. "You disappoint me, Zeus. I know what you're driving at. But even if those rumors about Mr. Messina are true, what do his sins have to do with his daughter? Are you going to turn your back on her because of her father?

Zeus lowered his eyes and remained silent.

"Zeus," she said. "Symphony Messina needs your help. She really does."

"It's not only that this guy is a known Mafia type," he said. "Why didn't you tell me about the hit squad hunting down ETA members connected with the kidnapping?"

"What in heaven's name are you talking about?"

Zeus's eyes narrowed as if he could not see her well. "You expect me to believe you don't know about that either?"

Tess had seen something about it on the Internet that morning, but there was always news relating to ETA in the Spanish press. "You're not implying Mr. Messina has anything to do with it. A hit squad, that's ridiculous."

"I called you here today because I believe we should help this girl. But—" He gave her a terminal headshake.

"Tell me something, Zeus. Can you really afford to pass up on the quarter of a million dollars you stand to make? How long has it been since you've seen your daughter?"

"Hold it there, Tess." Zeus's face hardened. "Look, I appreciate the pressure you might be under. But don't try so hard as to make matters worse. This has nothing to do with my private life. It has to do with your client's stupidity. Does he actually think he can send a hit squad to knock off the kidnappers, and have me negotiate with them too?"

"My client may be everything you think he is, but he's not foolish enough to compromise his daughter's life that way."

"Then how do you explain the ETA members killed in the last seventy-two hours? Every one of them connected to the kidnappers. We know it wasn't the boy's father. He's made a deal with ETA. Who else is there?"

"For god's sake, Zeus. There are legions of people who'd like to see those Basques dead."

Zeus wasn't buying. Tess looked away at a group of children horseback riding on the grassy paddock beyond the kiosk, fighting a sudden urge to call it quits. But she gave it another go.

"You know, I thought my boss was sending me on a fool's errand when he told me to come. I honestly didn't think you would agree to represent our client. But later, when I read about your daughter Anna in your dossier, the way her mother legally robbed her from you. I thought there was a chance. I thought for sure you'd be willing to help this innocent girl who's being ignored by every law enforcement agency in the world."

"Sorry to disappoint you."

Tess closed her briefcase and slid her chair back with her matter-of-fact, graceful blondness. "Don't be," she said, strapping her purse over her shoulder. "Symphony Messina, she's the one you should feel sorry for."

"Can't do it, Tess."

They walked together to the kiosk's steps. The rattling of the domino bones and the stealthy glances of the old men at the game table followed their every step. "Let me ask you something," Zeus said. "Do you think a man like Messina is not going to want his pound of flesh when this is over?"

Tess observed his expression from behind her sunglasses. Was the negotiation ball rolling again? "I don't know. You tell me. You're the expert."

"Revenge would be the normal reaction from any father. Practically unavoidable from a captain in the Luciani Family. Wouldn't you agree?"

She leaned against the car door, the hot sun on her uptown skin. He was now atop the kiosk's steps, his shirt unbuttoned and flapping in the hot breeze, suddenly like a man with a sense of cause. She understood the implications of what he was saying. Why should his colleagues negotiate with a gangster who would retaliate against them once he got what he wanted? But she said what was her job to say: "Who are you trying to protect, Zeus, the victim or the terrorists?"

"Both, actually. Do you honestly think my friends would listen to me without having Messina's complete guarantee that there'll be no retaliation?"

"OK." Tess stepped into the shade of the kiosk. "Let's re-cap a moment. Would I be correct to assume that if my client provides you with complete assurance that he has nothing to do with the so-called hit squad and there'd be no retaliation, would you then be willing to accept his offer?"

Zeus switched on his mysterious grin. "It would at least bring us back to the table."

SIXTEEN

Southwest, France

THEY REMOVED ONE of Iñaki's BMW bucket seats and duct-taped him to it. Then they dragged it to a flat at the mouth of a remote grotto in a forest in the hills. The spot had been chosen not only for its isolation, but for its natural beauty and the storied caves and grottoes, some still bearing markings of prehistoric people dating back to the beginning of time.

Gunther Crimmil, breathing heavily, rubbed his thinning hair and grinned at Iñaki taped to the car seat. He opened a leather satchel and pulled out a tripod and a digital video camera. He set them up a few steps in front of Iñaki, whose half-closed swollen eyes were the only part of his face not covered with blood.

The dark-skinned Moorish man stood to one side watching the operation, holding a Glock with a sound suppressor. At his feet sat a ten-liter container with gasoline.

Stooped over the camera, Gunther Crimmil put his right eye to the lens. "There you go." His Bavarian features curled into that sinister boyish grin of his. "The light's good."

Back in New York, when Tommy Pacelli asked his consigliere to suggest an independent enforcer to take care of Messina's problem, only one name came up: Gunther Crimmil from Staten Island. In only two years, Crimmil had established himself as New York's top hitman, the one who the city's crime families turned to whenever their own triggerman would not do. Three days later, Crimmil was on a flight to Marseille to meet the European crew hired to assist him in the rescue of Symphony Messina. And to exact revenge.

Crimmil scowled at the slanting afternoon sunlight now coming broken by the pine trees on the hillside. He pulled a hacksaw out of his leather satchel and sawed off the branches that cast the shadows on Iñaki's face.

Crimmil was aware of the personal qualities that those who sought his services looked for. His ice-cold professionalism and Germanic strictness no doubt were among them. His three-month stint in Afghanistan as a private contractor working as an interrogator in American-run prison facilities was perhaps his most impressive calling card. But Crimmil knew the real secret of his success. He was holding it in his hands now, aiming it at the terrorist: His HD movie camera. The camera and his willingness to risk personal ruin so his clients could watch in the comfort of their privacy the horrors their enemies suffered before dying.

"Nice," he said as he fidgeted with the camera.

Iñaki watched his every move from under his bloodied brows. Wrapped inside layers of duct tape around his chest, his legs and the backrest of the car seat, every breath he took was a struggle. Crimmil raised the palms of his hands in front of his face like a film director, thumbs to indexes, framing the view Iñaki would cut on a screen. "Not bad. What'd you think, Rashid?" he said to the young Moroccan man. "You think they're going to like our reality show?"

Rashid, who knew no more than a dozen words in English, shifted his weight from one foot to another and nodded at the American, confused.

"Dumb ass," Crimmil muttered as he readjusted the tripod. He gave another look at the sun. "Better get on with it. I'm losing my light."

The idea of filming executions was nothing new in the trade. The Iceman, Crimmil's mentor in Trenton State Prison, had done it for selected clients in his day. "The easiest money you'll ever make, if you got the balls to do it." Crimmil never forgot Iceman's words. "You just get yourself a hundred-dollar movie light, a three-hundred-dollar video camera and a tripod, and let it run. Then bill the client an extra five thousand. And you know what? They love it."

Even in the best of circumstances, it was an insanely risky undertaking, and only a handful of professional hitmen would offer the service. But Crimmil, a frustrated filmmaker with the soul of a serial killer, had made it his specialty. And these movies, in turn, had made him a rich man in two years' time.

Recording graphic evidence of torture and murder complicated the work in many unpredictable ways. "It sounds a lot easier than it looks," he always warned his clients. He had to be supremely careful that no incriminating image or sound got on the recording. He always ran every frame through a post-pro program on his portable Mac to be sure it was clean before he parted with the DVD. This was the kind of cleanness he was looking for as he began to test-record the terrorist.

Crimmil zoomed into a close-up and opened the shot again, then played it back and watched it through the tiny screen on the camera. "Nice."

The subject on the bucket seat and a bit of dirt and stones in the shadows behind him, it was all he needed. A little low on light, but it'll do. The more grainy the better, more realistic that way.

He gave Iñaki a final look. "Yes siree bob. You're going to be a big hit in New York. Like the song says, if you make it there, you'll make it anywhere."

Crimmil turned to the Arab. "Rashid, go down and get Guy and the girl." He pointed at the trail back to the car. "Go on, get."

Rashid the Arab marched down the wooded hill to get Guy Charnier and Mademoiselle Albi, the French-Basque interpreter, who'd been keeping guard by the road.

Crimmil took a step toward Iñaki, the gasoline container in one hand and his Ronson lighter in the other. He kept opening and closing the lighter with his thumb—click-clack, click-clack. He peeled off the tape on Iñaki's lips.

"Hurt, ha? What's the name of that town again?" he said without expecting a reply. He knew the prisoner did not speak a word of English. "What's it called, Mon-drag-on? Is that it?" He laughed. "Yeah, that's it. Your pal in the hospital, he told me so."

Click-clack, click-clack, click-clack.

"You know, when I look at you, pal, I ask myself, 'How far will I have to go before this spic gives me the names and the address I got to have?'" He chuckled. "You, I must say, you look like one hardheaded mother, with that shaved head of yours and that pimp's mustache. The thing is, my terrorist friend, with you it'll be different than with your pal in the hospital. I'm in no hurry. We'll be here till tomorrow if you want to. Got plenty of light and fresh batteries. I'll cook marshmallow off your burning limbs if I have to. You understand me, you freak?"

Crimmil looked hard into Iñaki's unfocused eyes. Click-clack, click-clack. "You ever seen that movie, *Reservoir Dogs*? Huh? You know, 'Stuck in the middle with you—'" He did a little dance. "Well, that was nothing. Baby puke in compare with what I'm going to do with you, pal." Crimmil shook his head. "Ah the hell with you. I'm wasting my breath. I'll wait for the interpreter and get this show on the road."

Iñaki closed his eyes. The duct tape that had almost cut off all blood flow in his legs had loosened with his constant squirming. It was better with the tape off his face too. He could breathe a little better. Something else was happening inside him. Something he had not expected. The trembling in his hands and legs had eased. He could see everything around him as if magnified through a telescope, the summer grass, the patches of earth, the moving insects in the shafts of sunlight, even the red roofs and stone towers of Pau hinting through the forest of gray-bark pines. His nose hurt where it broke and so did his crushed ribs, though not as much. The pain in his swollen upper lip and inflamed left eye had eased too. He could see through his right eye. All the hurting came now through a layer of numbness. He wondered if it was because part of him had died already. As a child, he had heard people say that death entered through one's feet. He could not feel his feet, his toes. Had he begun to die? Was that it? He swallowed the dryness in his mouth. "*Agua*," he uttered without meaning to … Stop. Do not waste your last moments begging for what you will never get. Do not beg. Do not give this monster the satisfaction of seeing you break. Think of the people that you have taken to the other side. Think of them if you think you are so good and worthy. Did their begging change anything? Did it stop you? No. It is not going to stop him either. It will be much better to think of the people you are dying for, yes. Do that. You are an ETA *gudari*, a Basque soldier, and you must die without regret. And you will not beg for water nor will you make your death worth watching on TV. It will not be entertaining. All they will see is a human being dying, not a coward. Your life is not yours to beg for. You gave your life to Euskadi long ago. And leave God out of this, too. He has nothing to do with it …

Still, there was the step by step of dying yet to come. And it was coming. He could see it now. The camera was on, the Basque woman was here, they were all there. Oh God, do not let me panic. Make it a quick death.

Mademoiselle Albi, a faux redheaded woman in high heels and too small a dress, stepped to Iñaki's side and murmured to him in clumsy Euskara.

"Listen to me. Do you want to undergo the most excruciating pain imaginable before you die? Because that is what is going to happen if you do not tell this crazy American what he wants to know. Do not be a fool. Tell me where the kidnapped girl is, and I promise you he will let you live. Go on. Tell me."

Iñaki squeezed his eyelids closed.

"I warn you, do not be an idiot. All you have to do is tell me where to find Symphony Messina and we can all go. Tell me. Look, he is getting ready to hurt you, hurt you badly. Talk, please—"

Iñaki moaned and looked away. Crimmil stepped up beside him and kicked him on the side of the head with his boot heel, then yelled at Mademoiselle Albi. "Ask him again. Where's the American girl."

"Look at me," she yelled at Iñaki in his language. "I cannot believe you are so insane as to want to provoke this American. He will burn off your hands and your feet, cook you piece by piece and make you eat your own cooked self, without letting you die. That is what he said he would do to you. Spare us all this horror. Tell me where in Mondragón the girl is ..."

Iñaki glanced up at Crimmil and turned his head.

"So you want to test me? Is that it? Want a little action before you talk? Well you got it, asshole. We're going to make a blockbuster, you and me. The first live recording of a self-eating cannibal—well done." He laughed. "I promise you, you're not going to be such a hard-ass when you taste your own cooked flesh, my terrorist pal."

Crimmil turned to the woman as he picked up the fuel container, "Keep asking him for the girl. Don't stop. Just keep drilling him."

She did as she was told.

Iñaki's horrified eyes kept moving between her and Crimmil, his heart beating so hard he felt it about to explode. The American pulled his right shoe off and poured a stream of gasoline on his foot, soaking his gray cotton sock with it. A mouthful of vomit shot out of Iñaki's mouth.

"Don't you faint on me now," Crimmil shouted between curses. "Don't you dare."

Iñaki could not breathe anymore. He felt an icy coldness swelling up from his legs, a glacial numbness spreading throughout his body.

"Let's see if you have any star quality. Quiet," Crimmil yelled at the others. "Aaand action!"

He switched on the movie camera. Then, from outside the frame, he flicked the Ronson and set Iñaki's foot on fire like a torch. Charnier, Rashid, and Mademoiselle Albi stepped back, cringing with disgust.

Iñaki looked at his foot in flames as if it did not belong to him. Then muttered a string of words in Basque skyward.

Crimmil pulled Mademoiselle Albi by her arm. "Is he praying?"

She had her hands over her mouth in a mixture of repulsion and amazement. "Singing, I think."

Crimmil kicked Iñaki's face to shut him up. "Ask him where they're hiding the girl. Ask him now!"

She tried but Iñaki, his foot ablaze and his face a bloody mask, went on chanting until he began to choke and turn blue with the fumes from his own flesh.

"You ain't supposed to die yet, you prick," Crimmil yelled.

Iñaki's taped-up body went into a contorting fit. Then a long choking noise like that of a large slaughterhouse mammal came up from his throat and he collapsed onto himself on the bucket seat. His left foot and ankle a blackened and flaming flambeau while Crimmil's digital camera recorded every stage of it.

SEVENTEEN

Mondragón

THE DAY AFTER THE massacre, Aitor summoned his commandos for an emergency meeting at the plant. It was probably the worst location at the most terrible time. But the confusion caused by the killings and the urgency of Iñaki's disappearance more than justified it in Aitor's mind.

They gathered in the kitchen area at the rear of the plant. Carcelero, his tail wagging at everyone, was the only one upbeat.

Aitor stood with his back to the shadowy machinery, his hands clasped behind him in a martial stance. "This morning I received this encoded communiqué from high command." He held up the printout and read it. "It is with great regret that I must inform you that as of the above date, compeer Iñaki Arguelles has been officially declared missing in action. And a new military chief is to be named within hours."

A silent cloud of blue cigarette smoke rose over their heads. The loss of Iñaki, a living legend in the Basque underground, the *etarra* no lawman could catch after ten years on their most-wanted list, was unimaginable.

Baldo spoke up first. "Am I the only one who thinks this declaration is too premature?"

Pedro's wife, Mertxe, thought so too. "I agree. I heard the DNAT was conducting secret operations in the Pau area that day. For all we know he might be in a Paris dungeon at this moment."

Aitor shook his head but said nothing.

"What if he made himself incommunicado for some good reason?" Baldo said. "He has done it before."

"Iñaki is required to maintain daily contact with headquarters," Aitor said. "He knows that is the rule. Even more so during a Code Red alert he himself called. Besides, to declare him *desaparecido* does not mean he's gone. But we must maintain our chain of command operational. That is of the utmost importance. He might yet turn up. Who's to know?"

"I believe he will," Pedro said. "Iñaki isn't easy."

"*Claro que sí,*" Mertxe said, drawn in by her husband's optimism. "Let us not forget who we are talking about: Iñaki the Untouchable."

Minot glanced around him as if surrounded by fools. "Has it not occurred to anyone that maybe, just maybe, Iñaki might have met the same fate as that of Gaztelu and Txatxi?"

Baldo, his pale features half-hidden behind his straight sable bangs, raised his hand. "Aitor, do you truly think Iñaki could have been disappeared by these people? Because I cannot—"

"No," Aitor answered, determined to prevent morale from sinking any lower. "The theory of hired assassins from America remains a theory."

Minot grinned without showings his teeth. "A theory that has butchered five people connected to our prisoners. Is that the theory you're referring to?"

Aitor gave the *iparralde* a hard look. "Iñaki's disappearance could have been the work of the Guardia Civil or the DNAT. Hell, the one thing we do not suffer for is people trying to make us disappear."

"If that is what happened, it would have appeared on the TV news by now," Mertxe said.

Pedro agreed. "That is for certain. On every network."

Big Patxi released a bull's snort. "I knew something like this was going to happen. This is what we get for holding onto the daughter of a mafioso." He gave an accusing look at Minot and Baldo, the ones opposed to freeing the girl. "If there is a squad of assassins from America coming after us, it is because of those like you who are against setting her free. I say, enough. Let her go. She has been a curse from the start—"

"That is not a decision we can make on our own," Aitor said.

Baldo slid off the countertop and took the floor. "To surrender the girl now, after what they have done to Txatxi and Gaztelu and his family, would be shameful. But if they have also hurt Iñaki, it would be unforgivable. What we have to do is hunt them down like the animals they are."

"I do not expect any less from you, compeer Baldo," Aitor told him. "But that is not up to us either."

Pedro kept gnawing at his lower lip. "What if Iñaki was captured? What if they torture him and get him to talk? These people are beasts."

"*¡Jamas!*" Patxi boomed. "Never. Iñaki is a true patriot."

"He is a good man," Aitor said. "But even if he talks, it changes nothing for us."

"Truly?" Minot said, stifling a laugh. "Must I remind everyone that compeer Iñaki knows the names of every one of us?"

Patxi pounced on the counter, frightening Carcelero under the table. "Iñaki is a true Basque from Bilbao. They could boil him alive and still he would never tell them a word."

"You must forgive me then," Minot said, sneering at Patxi—the *boule de suif.* "I was unaware of Iñaki's superhuman powers that make him invulnerable to torture. He seems like such a regular fellow to me."

Aitor held Patxi's arm and turned to face Minot. "Whether Iñaki gives those phantom assassins any information or not, it does not change our obligation to protect our prisoners with our lives. And let me remind you of something else, Minot: Iñaki may know our *zulo* is here in Mondragón. But he does not know the exact location. This town may be small, *mon frère*, but not so small that complete strangers can come here and find it. We are not in France."

"Then how did they manage to find Txatxi so easily when we ourselves did not know where he was?"

"They did it by doing what the police and Madrid cannot do, by torturing and killing our people," Aitor replied. "It is not difficult to deduce that, after they found the banker, the most accessible link in the chain, they had no problem finding Councilman Gaztelu, who surely told them everything he knew, hoping to save his children and his wife."

Pedro, tense in his salesman designer suit, stopped rubbing his manicured mustache. "But why did these assassins go to Pau and not to Toulouse where our people walk around freer than they do here?"

Aitor had already asked himself the same question. "Gaztelu probably did tell them about Toulouse and someone there steered them in Txatxi's direction, someone whose body parts are yet to turn up."

"So who is the next weakest link in the chain?" Minot said with an insolent grin on his furry cheeks.

"You know something, Minot," Aitor said as if sniffing a foul smell. "I strongly recommend that you do not preoccupy yourself so much with

Iñaki. It is not for you to do so, nor do we need your sarcastic comments at this time."

"I beg your pardon, chief," Minot said, tipping his malformed head. "But if I may." He turned to address the group. "I only wish to say this. Each of us is free to think what he or she wants, but the truth is that those assassins are leaving a very real trail of blood directly to us. My question is: are we going to surrender to those butchers by setting the girl free?"

A momentary silence materialized.

Minot broke it, aiming his impassive bovine eyes at Aitor. "You can have my answer now. I will never surrender anything that is ours, not to those pigs, not to anyone."

"You will not have to," Aitor told him with a severity no one expected. "Because there is nothing here that belongs to you, except the obligation to follow my orders as your commander, as I am duty-bound to follow mine. In the meantime, I remind everyone not to forget that we are undergoing a Code Red. And that any act of insubordination during this time can and will be regarded as an act of treason. And I believe we all know the consequences of that."

Later, when everyone was gone and Aitor and Patxi were the only ones left in the tobacco cloud in the kitchen area, Patxi said, "I did not want to add to your problem by siding with Baldo and the *iparralde*. But they are right. We must not allow these assassins to get away with what they have done."

Aitor took the shopping bags out to the floor of the plant. "Right now we have a very delicate situation with the boy's father. For all we know, he could be reconsidering our arrangement."

"After paying out two million euros? I doubt it."

"Two million doesn't mean the same thing to them as it means to us."

Patxi grabbed the pulley chains and began the rattling operation to enter the underground *zulo*. "You know, I have been all for releasing the girl from the beginning. But I hope you are not expecting us to lay down for those assassins."

"So you want to take on the Mafia?"

Patxi wiped his sweaty face with a rag. "By God, Aitor, for sixty years we have fought Madrid and the French government. Governments, the biggest Mafia there is in the world, and we have survived. Even I know the American Mafia is not what it used to be."

"Neither are we, my friend." Aitor bent down and hooked up the chain to the one-man elevator.

"I am not afraid of gangsters. They are nothing but a bunch of common criminals."

Aitor let out a laugh. "That is what the world thinks we are."

"But we are soldiers, struggling for the independence of our country," Patxi said. "We live and die by our ideals. Can they make the same claim?"

Aitor picked the shopping bags and stepped inside the one-man elevator. "Going down."

A blast of distorted CD music tore through the sweltering stillness inside the *zulo*.

Without getting up from the cot, Miguel Angel grimaced at the armored door. He could not tell whether his biological clock was running slow or his keepers were early with his dinner. The key turned and the bolt on the trapdoor dropped. He was about to assume his position facing the wall when the man he knew as José said in Euskara. "*Kaixo mutil.*" Then switched to Spanish, "*Por favor*, be kind enough to come to the door."

"*¿Que pasa?*" Miguel Angel did not move. "Is it mealtime?"

"Stand where I can see you."

Miguel Angel took two tentative steps toward the armored door.

Aitor crouched on one knee and peered through the slot. "We have brought you some things." He placed a pad of blank paper, a pencil, a box of crayons, and a cardboard box with a puzzle on the trapdoor. "Was this what you asked for?"

"About a year ago."

"*Vamos hombre*, do not exaggerate. It is never too late if it is for the best. They tell me this is a very complex puzzle."

"God knows I have the time."

"Perhaps not as much as you think. We have also brought you these comfort items, a new toothbrush, another bar of soap, aspirins."

As he picked them up, Miguel Angel stole a peek at the hooded head outside. "Tell me, José, why all this sudden generosity? Has my father agreed to pay the rescue money?"

Aitor let out a loud patronizing laugh. "You are too intelligent for us, Miguel Angel. Now you will not allow us the pleasure of surprising you with the news. *Pues, sí.* Your father has at last assumed his patriotic responsibilities and reached an accord with the leadership."

"When?"

"That is of no importance. What is important is that your release has been approved. We are yet to receive an exact date, but we are convinced it will be very soon."

Miguel Angel stepped back and sat on the cot. He remained silent for a moment, trying to control his emotions. "What do you mean by soon?"

"What?" Aitor said, unable to hear the boy over the annoying loud CD music.

"How much longer do you estimate I will be here?"

"That is up to our commanders. Remember, we are only foot soldiers. We are not even permitted to guess," he said in a wasted effort at empathy. "Tomorrow one of our compeers will install a dehumidifier. It will make it a little more comfortable for you."

"Not that I am ungrateful, but it seems like a lot of bother for only a few days?"

"Would you rather we—" Patxi started to say but Aitor cut him off.

"You got us again," Aitor said. "You are correct. These comfort items do not come without interest on our part. We need you to write a letter to your family. You know, to tell them you are being treated well and you are healthy."

"So this is a bribe?"

"More or less." He laughed. "Except it is non-negotiable. We need the letter by tonight."

Miguel Angel remained silent.

Aitor slipped a paper with the information the letter had to include. "Guide yourself by these notes." When the boy failed to take it, he added with menace in his voice, "You write this letter now and make it a good one. Do we understand each other?"

Miguel Angel read the instructions. In essence, it was to be a letter extolling the treatment he was receiving as well as to reassure his family that he and their accord with ETA were in good condition, despite the San Sebastián events.

"I will do the best I can," Miguel Angel said and added in an offhand sort of way, "May I ask you something? Who is in the cell next to mine?"

Aitor and Patxi looked at each other's masked faces. "What cell?" Aitor responded. "What the devil are you talking about?"

"*Vamos*, José. My neighbor next door. Who is it?"

Patxi was going to speak up and Aitor again stopped him. "Listen to me," Aitor said. "There is no one in this *zulo* except you. No one."

"*Vale*. Whatever you say."

"Look, Miguel, we know what you are going through is not easy. We know what long periods of isolation can do. It plays tricks on your mind. You start seeing hallucinations, hearing things that are not there. There is no one here but you."

"Yes, yes," Miguel Angel replied, pouring on his contempt. "You are right. I must be hearing things."

Unsure of whether the boy was putting him on, Aitor glanced inside the cell. "Have the letter ready by dinnertime. And make the best of the few days you have left doing your puzzle, painting your pictures, and do not waste your time thinking about things that do not concern you. It will save you and us much unwanted complications."

Aitor pulled the trapdoor shut. Patxi bolted it. They pulled their masks off and looked at each other.

"He knows," Patxi said, wiping the sweat off his brow.

"No," Aitor said. "He is not certain. If he were, he would not have told us."

They glanced at Symphony's cell door.

"This has to be Minot's fault."

"I swear," Patxi said. "If that's so, I will strangle the freak with my own hands."

"Stop that talk."

"We must get rid of this girl, Aitor. Now, before this explodes in our faces. It may already have."

~

In the perennial dank night of her cell, Symphony lay facing the dirt wall, oblivious to the noises outside. She had found out that she could dream awake, let her hunger hallucinations carry her out of her muddy grave, sleepwalk through memories unrestricted of the stipulations of time or place. For some reason, her family's old two-story frame house in Brooklyn was often the setting. Those sun-stained Sundays that felt as if they had happened to someone else, in another life. Visions of Mama asleep on a deck chair, Junior worshipping the ballgame on TV, and Aria locked inside her air-conditioned room, assailed by adolescent pangs. Mom and Dad gone to the stores and the hunger in her belly, some part of her was always hungry then ... and the heat, god, the summertime fever that cooked her body ... The blue above-ground pool was no refuge from those kinds of heat waves ... Bobby's dripping face surfacing out of the soupy water. That smile of his, shiny with wetness and sunshine, the stew of first love, his body pressing against hers, pinning her to the plastic wall of the pool ...

Child's play until that early snow in Washington Square when Miguel Angel materialized before her like a new dawn, hotter than the sun. With him, she heard new music, new poetry, felt the smoky breaths of redis-covery everywhere, all in a pure milk-warm light. She floated over solid ground.

"Why are you always giggling?" chubby Aria would ask her. "Are you high on something?"

On weekends, she posed for Miguel Angel Estrada de Orueta while he sketched her and made portraits of her with long brushes. With him, she felt at ease in her skin. She read his books, watched him work, his intense blue eyes, the cute bump on his nose. They watched movies together and made love on his bed. She learned to pronounce his name.

"It's not Mee-goo-el Angel, Daddy. It's Mee-gehl Aan-hel."

"Can we just call him Michelangelo?" her mother suggested.

Daddy liked Michelangelo much better too. Once she presented him with the evidence of his bloodline, his racist objections vanished like hot pizza on Super Bowl Sunday. "So, the kid's worth millions?"

"He's heir apparent."

Bright eyes, Old World charm, natural elegance, everyone was happy. No one thought the engagement too premature. Except for some of her friends, her NYU friends. Jealous voices. "Marrying the matador ... You're only nineteen!"

She did not doubt it for a moment. Neither did Miguel.

She saw it with clairvoyant eyes. Miguel, more handsome than an arch-angel, waiting for her in the golden glow at the foot of the main altar.

She, arm in arm with her father, taking slow ceremonial steps along the flower petal-strewn center aisle.

"Where's Miguel, Daddy?"

The long flowing white train of her dress shushing behind her like a cotton cloud in front of two giggling, tiny pages in matching satin.

"Where's Miguel?"

"We're almost there, sweetie."

She searched the veiled world around her. Everyone was there. Her mother's side of the family on the right row of pews, Daddy's on the left. Kathy and Trish, her best friends in the universe, stood behind them, smiling and holding back tears. Then she saw the grotesque, five o'clock shadowy faces of her father's other family. Their overweight, scarred faces next to the loud painted faces of their wives.

"Where's Miguel, Daddy? I can't see him."

She could hear Miguel calling her, faint as though the sound was coming from another world. His cries growing louder, rising from ghost cries to metallic screams. She tried to answer him, but her voice died in her throat, her eyes to the wall of stony dirt.

EIGHTEEN

On the Arrasate-Mondragón Highway, Spain

GUNTHER CRIMMIL RODE in the front seat of the stolen Audi, a roadmap spread out over his lap, his cell phone in one hand. "What is it with these people?" he snarled. "They've got to have two names for every goddamn town?"

Everyone in the car ignored him. Guy Charnier kept steering, his Mediterranean-green eyes on the road. Mademoiselle Albi, her round face bright with a fresh coat of makeup, smoked in silence in the back seat next to Rashid, both in their own world. After three days under Crimmil's orders, they had learned to ignore his irritating ranting.

"What kind of messed-up names are these?" Every road sign annoyed him. "Nako Harria, Zarautz, Ordizia, Urretxu. They sound right out of fucking Star Wars or some crap like it."

He poked Guy with his elbow. "So what's the name of the town? Is it Arrasate or is it Mondragón?"

"It's both," the Frenchman said.

Most towns in the Basque Country had both Spanish and Basque names, often very dissimilar as in the case of San Sebastián or Donosti. But Guy did not explain this to him, rather enjoying his frustration.

It had been this way since Iñaki the terrorist had gone and died of a heart attack before Crimmil could make his DVD. It drove him into a mouth-foaming fit of rage. He stumped and bashed Iñaki's dead body with the biggest stones he could find. Then when he tired of that, he chopped off the hands, stuffed them in a plastic bag, and poured the entire can of gasoline and pitched a lit lighter on the bloody mess that was left. The mutilated corpse burst into a foul-smelling bonfire while he hollered and cursed at it as if the flames were consuming him too. "The son-of-a-bitch terrorist ruined my movie."

For Crimmil, the Basque Country was more than bizarre names and his growing dependence on his companions because of the language, the very landscape seemed to conspire against him. Nothing looked as he'd expected, not the green valleys or slate-roofed country homes, nor the orderly streets and towns. It defied his Hollywood preconceptions of Spain in a most irritating, disappointing way.

He let out a noisy sneeze, then scowled over his shoulder at chain-smoking Mademoiselle Albi and back at Guy. He had already warned them about smoking in the car, but they thought he'd been joshing, laughed at the presumed unreasonableness of his request. "We cannot stop every time we need to smoke," Guy had said. "We'd never get there."

"Listen Guy," Crimmil said now. "That's it. I'm sick and tired of sucking up your smoke. Put out your cigarette and tell her to get rid of hers or else."

Guy gave him a silent side-glance. He was sick of the American, enough to have driven back to Marseille long ago, but he was determined not to let his emotions interfere. There was too much money in the balance and only two days left on the job to spoil it now by letting his feelings get the better of him. He flipped the cigarette out the window and gave Mademoiselle Albi a nod to do the same.

She took one last deep puff before throwing it out. "Happy?"

Guy gave Crimmil a twisted glance. "Do you truly think we're going to find the girl in Mondragón, after the carnage you've left behind?"

Crimmil kept scowling at the road ahead. He could not tell whether the Frog was being a smart-ass or asking him a legitimate question.

"It will be a good trick if you can do it. Except I don't see how," Guy insisted.

"Don't worry about it. That's exactly why I'm here."

"I thought you said you're a man who believes in planning ahead. Are you not going to need some kind of plan?"

"That's none of your business. You just drive and don't get us lost."

Guy went on with his Southern French intonation. "No one here is going to help a foreigner hunt down an *etarra*. Not even those who hate them."

"Look, Guy, if something's eating you, spit it out. If not, shut the hell up. You're going to get your money no matter what."

"Oh, I'm not worried about that. What has me a little concerned is how some of us are going to get out of this country once the *etarras* find out what we came here to do."

"I'll let you in a little American secret, pal. Money talks, nobody walks."

Guy forced a laugh, his yellow toothy mouthed opened. "You think you will buy the information?"

"What we can't kill, we can buy."

"Very American of you."

"Everybody loves money. Just like you do."

"Not everybody."

Crimmil laughed at the idiocy. "Money's like sex or the movies. Everybody goes for some form of it. Hell, you ought to know. You're French," he said with a mocking French accent. "Aren't you the nephew of the famous Monsieur French Connection? Talk about a money-hungry bastard, your uncle. Filling up New York City with dope."

Guy rolled his eyes. "Then how do you explain Bin Ladin?"

"What about that prick?"

"Your country put fifty million dollars on his head for years. Dead or alive, as Sheriff Bush said. Did anybody turn him in? No. Maybe money doesn't talk to some people." Guy chuckled without feeling like it. "Not everything can be reduced to money. Maybe in the United States, surely there, yes. But not everywhere."

"You don't know what the hell you're talking about."

Crimmil was about to tell him of the six weeks he served as a private contractor in an Afghani prison interrogating Taliban and al Qaeda suspects, softening them up for the Agency boys. Talk about what Arabs were capable of doing to their own for money, for peanuts. Nothing that a man could do with a sharp butcher knife to another man was off-limits. When it came to money, even Allah took a back seat.

"All we need to do is find ourselves one of them ETAs and we'll be OK."

"You mean another one?" Guy said with a mocking grin.

"Shut the hell up and drive. That's what you're paid to do."

Five-hundred Gs Little Tommy Pacelli had guaranteed for Symphony Messina's rescue. A paycheck that would not only be Crimmil's single biggest take yet, but half of the million dollars he would need to attract backers to his secret dream "film project"—the movie of his life story. He could either go back to New York with Messina's daughter in one hand or in a casket, but he wasn't going back without her. "How long to Mondragón?"

"Another twenty minutes, maybe less."

"Tell your girlfriend to book us a couple of hotel rooms outside of town. I need the rest."

Guy glanced over his shoulder at Mademoiselle Albi. "You heard him."

"I don't know hotels in these parts," she said with her halting English.

"Call the directory," Guy said. "Try tourist information. Do something."

Mademoiselle Albi tried her mobile telephone. "The battery is dead."

Crimmil flipped his cell to the back seat. "Use mine. It's set up to work in Europe."

"Is it secured?" Guy said.

"It's American."

Guy gazed back at the road. Patience, he said to himself. Thirty-six more hours and the job would be done one way or another.

~

Mademoiselle Albi made the calls she was told to make. First, she dialed the information operator. Then she called the Basque tourist office and a hotel directory. Lastly, she phoned the three-star hotel outside Arrasate and made reservations for two doubles and one single room under the name of Ira Blacker—the name on Crimmil's U. S. passport and Amex card.

Crimmil's cellular telephone radio electromagnetic signal traveled in the usual manner, up to the satellite then relaying from one antenna tower to another as the Audi drove on, until it reached the Mobile Telephone Switching Office in Madrid. There, in a windowless room in the emblematic Telefónica building on Gran Vía, two agents in civilian clothing sat at their stations, facing a wall of high-tech surveillance equipment.

Without taking his eyes off the monitor screen, the younger man pecked a short volley of letters and numbers on the keyboard before him. "Alfonso, come here. Look. I have one from the DNAT program."

Grinning, they both watched the accelerating countdown on the LCD window on the Echelon satellite system unit monitoring Crimmil's SIM mobile telephone. The PCM system tracing the pings not only pinpointed the phone's location during Mademoiselle Albi's four-call sequence, it also latched onto her conversation with the hotel desk.

The agent wearing hip-hopper knee-length pants slipped on a set of headphones and switched on the digital recorder. Automatically, it triggered the voice-to-text translator. When the call terminated, he handed his partner the printout of the exchange.

"The mobile is still on," he said, both delighted and amazed. "I will stay with it."

The older man with the pallor of a lifer bureaucrat smiled at the document. "I will run it to Lope." Then he hurried out the door.

Several blocks away at the Tribunal Courts building, Judge Garzón's secretary received the call from the Division Nacional Antiterrorista headquarters, DNAT.

Jetlagged from a long transatlantic flight but full of energy, the judge interrupted his conversation with his staff and picked up the telephone on his desk. "*Dígame.*"

"Welcome back, your honor," the DNAT officer said and congratulated the judge for the award he had received in Buenos Aires three days before.

"Thank you, Lope," Judge Garzón replied. "What do you have for me today?"

"Good news. We have just received a confirmed location on the American suspect in connection with the Miguel Angel Estrada case."

The prolonged pause that followed urged the DNAT officer to refresh the judge's memory. "He is the US national the DSS and the FBI at the embassy requested us to look into."

Auburn hair neatly combed back from his face, Judge Garzón's handsome features grinned with satisfaction. "Ah, yes. *Vaya*, hombre, that is phenomenal news, and about time. Where is he?"

"It appears that he entered the national territory through Irun, just as you predicted."

Judge Garzón covered the telephone with his hand and looked up at the members of his staff standing around his desk. "The New York *matón* is in Spain."

Their eyes widened with excitement.

"Where is he heading?" the judge said.

"By the manner in which the relay signals registered, the technicians placed him in the vicinity of Éibar, moving south on the Vergara-Arrasate highway."

"Are you sure? Don't want to send my people out there for nothing."

"We went over the report with our unit. There's a short text from the piece of conversation, if you want to hear it."

"You have a recording of his voice?"

"No, sir. A female was using the mobile to make hotel reservations."

"Who is she?"

"We do not have that information yet."

Judge Garzón let out a breath of disappointment. "Have you checked if the mobile has been reported stolen?"

"Yes, sir. It has not. Not only that, the very location indicates that it has to be our man. If you recall, we narrowed out the kidnappers' location to the Guipuzcua region, precisely where we have traced the mobile."

"So it is confirmed?"

"Yes sir."

"Very well." Judge Garzón nodded at one of his assistants. "I will send you an authorization to intercept and record conversations on that mobile number. You will have it within the hour. Give my commendations to the technicians at Telefónica. Tell them that I said they are doing a fine job. Better than the British." He laughed.

"Thank you, your honor."

"If anyone has any questions you tell them my office has given you all clearances. I want this investigation to have top-priority. I have a presentiment that this Mr. Blacker is going to lead us directly to both the American hostage and Miguel Angel Estrada. Make sure our men do not move against him until we give the order. It is crucial that we know who he is going to meet before we do anything. Is that clear?"

"No one will make a move against him until you say so."

"We will also have to inform the Ertzaintza," the judge added.

"Do you not think it might be a bit too premature to include the Basque authorities?" the DNAT captain said with a tone of reluctance. "They have too many leaks."

"I am aware of the problem, Lope. We'll keep the operation at top-secret level for as long as it is practical. But we are obligated by law to inform them. They are the Basque Police."

"As you wish."

"Cheer up," the judge said. "This *matón* not only might solve this kidnapping case for us; he might even set off the downfall of this so-called New ETA."

"*Sí señor*. Good to have you back."

NINETEEN

Miami, Florida

SPILLMAN FINALLY returned Tess's call after her meeting with Zeus. She was in her hotel room doing caged-tiger circles around the bed, the white terrycloth fluttering behind her.

"My god, Arthur," she said, holding her cell phone to her ear. "What are you saying? You knew Aguirre was bound to bail the moment he found out who our client is. It's not my fault it took him less than a day to do it."

"Tess—"

"Not only that," she went on. "You told me this assignment was more like a PR maneuver, just to show the client we're on top of things, so he won't take his business elsewhere. Now you're making it sound like my life depends on it."

"Not just yours, my dear."

"What's that supposed to mean?"

She was shocked and amazed at Spillman's sudden change of attitude about an assignment that until then he'd made seem more like a personal favor to him.

"I sent you down there to gain this man's trust."

"But our client's put a death squad together, Arthur. And I had to hear it from Aguirre—"

"We don't know that."

"What? We intentionally omitted crucial information about our client, and he caught us, Arthur. How do you expect him to trust us now?"

"Can you make this work, Tess?"

"I don't know. Aguirre's afraid he's just being used to get at his friends over there. If we could assure him it won't happen—"

"Then do so."

"Please Arthur, the man's no fool. He wants proof our client won't seek revenge afterward—"

"Out of the question."

"Why?"

"We can't involve the client, that's why. How would that reflect on us? Listen to me, Tess. You have to close the deal tonight."

Tess couldn't stop pacing. "I don't know how you expect me to do it now. I don't know if anyone can at this point ..."

"Listen, just give him the facts," Spillman said louder now. "We have no knowledge of our client being involved with any paid assassins. Or whether he has any plans for reprisals, legal or otherwise. Those are facts. You can tell him that. You have tonight and part of tomorrow before you have to get back. Just make sure Mr. Aguirre sees the light without involving our client. I know you can do it," he added softer, now. "The firm and I will owe you one, a big one if you succeed. If you don't, well ..."

Spillman left the ellipsis there to hang and for her to interpret anyway she wanted to, knowing all too well what her reaction would be. Tess dropped on the edge of the bed, her head spinning, her eyes welling, a choking feeling in throat. Her iPhone fell on the carpet.

T W E N T Y

Greenpoint, Brooklyn

DOMENICK COSTORINO, the consigliere, dipped his head and peered at the sooty facades on Manhattan Avenue. A caravan of honking vehicles crawled behind his Cadillac Escalade Platinum Edition. A dead water smell wafted up from the hot flow of the East River below. It had been a long time since he last been to Joey's place and was unsure whether he'd recognize it. He was almost down by the river when at last the familiar black plate-glass window of the Greenpoint Social Club storefront came into view.

A group of four of Joey's wise guys stood loitering outside the door. One of them waved him over a few cars down to the only free parking space on the busy avenue. "This way, Dom."

He took the spot, grumbling to himself for not having come in his Mazda. Packed with Polacks, Ruskies, Ricans, and a new wave of hippie-types up from Williamsburg, Greenpoint was no place for a hundred-grand vehicle like his.

"Keep an eye on my wheels, will you?"

"Don't worry about nothing, Dom. On this block, your vehicle's safe as in your own garage, believe you me."

In truth, Costorino would have rather not come to Joey the Bear's place even if it were on Park Avenue. As with his boss, he barely tolerated the man and resented having to be there playing Little Tommy's personal bagman, a job he deemed beneath him. But the boss's instructions had been clear. "Go to Brooklyn. Show the Bear what we're doing for him. Give him the stuff the German sent us. Then make him understand he's got to do right by me. Just don't get him excited, for pete's sake. We don't need him giving us any grief."

So there he was, huffing and sweating in a short-sleeve Armani shirt draped over his rotund torso like a barber's smock, wide enough to project a movie on his back. Dominik Costorino, the Family's consigliere, dragged his lumbering girth under the rumbling 50,000 BTU air conditioner in the transom and the faded "for members only" sign, back in the grimy gloom of Joey the Bear's lair.

A card game was on inside under a cloud of smoke. Costorino halted for a polite hello to Lucio Ratti, Joey's prune-faced, sack of bones uncle. They slapped each other's back and called each other *paisano*. Coppertone Tony came out of the private office with a gold tooth smile on his face. "How you doing there, Dom?"

Costorino grabbed the napkins dispenser on the bar counter. "OK, if it wasn't for this damn heat," he groaned, wiping his face with a handful of napkins and throwing them in an ashtray.

Coppertone swept his hand out like a headwaiter and showed the guest into the Bear's inner sanctum. Joey was already coming from behind his desk, arms opened for the obligatory backslapping. "Dom, good to see you."

"Glad to be here," Costorino replied with a labored smile. They seemed to take a certain amount of genuine pleasure in their salutations. It wasn't all faked. Something about being worthy of a demonstration of affection, the illusion of esteem filtered through.

The two men rushed through the customary small talk, as neither wished to make the meeting any longer than it had to be. One of the boys came in and handed the guest a diet ginger ale. Coppertone sat in front of Joey's desk beside the consigliere.

Costorino opened his hard-shell, alligator attaché case. "The boss asked me to give you this." He placed an unwrapped shoebox and a DVD jewel case on Joey's beat-up brown desk.

"What's this?" Joey scowled at it.

"Open it," Costorino said with a reassuring nod. "Go ahead. It's a surprise."

Joey looked at Coppertone and back at his guest. "What'd you mean surprise?"

"No big deal, Joey. It's from the German." Costorino was grinning friendly-like. "Think of it as a token of our concern for your situation."

With a shrug of indifference, Joey picked up the unmarked DVD case and narrowed his eyes at his guest again.

"Like I said," Costorino insisted. "A gift from our guy."

Joey pushed the DVD aside and drew the box to him. He shook it and lifted off the top. "What the fuck is this, Dom?" he let out when he saw what was inside the box.

Costorino had a playful grin in his tiny mouth now. "A souvenir from our man in Europe. It belonged to one of those Basque terrorists who took your daughter."

"Somebody's chopped off hand? Whose idea was this?"

"It wasn't Tommy's idea. Or mine, I have you know. But since the German took the trouble to send it, we figured you might want it."

Messina looked at the brownish decomposed hand with a different disposition, now. He passed it to Coppertone who was eager to see it. "So what am I supposed to do with this?"

"Tommy figured you'd get a kick out of it. We sure as hell don't want it back. He did promise to give you a hand with this."

Costorino's remark made Coppertone Tony burst out laughing. Joey didn't think it was funny. "And this?" he said, waving the DVD. "Another gift from the German?"

"It came with the hand."

"Is it what I think it is?"

Costorino nodded yes. "Disgusting. I couldn't watch it."

"What's on it?" Coppertone said.

"A video of what happened to the man before and after he lost the hand."

"You gotta be joking." Coppertone was impressed. "The German videoed it?"

Costorino made a head gesture of reluctant indifference. "Nobody asked him to."

Joey leaned over his desk, his face tight as if he had just bitten into a green lemon. "Is that what that son of a bitch is doing over there? Chopping them Basques up like that before finding out whether my daughter's alive? Tell me it isn't so, Dom. Just tell me that ain't it."

"Hey, the guy's getting things done. How do you expect him to get anything out of those people? They're terrorists. Don't understand no other way."

"Don't you see what that's going to do?" Joey pushed himself up off the desk chair, head shaking at all that was coming into it now. "That animal's going to get my daughter killed. Tommy knows about this?"

"Take it easy, Joey. What are you getting so hot about? Things are going well."

"How you figure that?"

"Look, the German goes overboard sometimes. I give you that. But he's already on these people's trail. Which is more than you can say about the cops over there."

Joey could not stop shaking his head. "Got to tell you, Dom." He pointed at the DVD and the gift box. "If you think this crap's going to bring me any consolation, you're wrong."

"I know that. We're not where we want to be yet, not by a long shot. But, hey, you got to admit he's made more headway in the time he's been there than the entire world police's done in two weeks."

"You keep saying that like it's a big freaking deal. Hell, anybody can do better than the cops. They're not doing a goddamn thing. The FBI, the Interpol, none of them are lifting a finger to find her. Just because she's my daughter. They're not doing crap for Michelangelo either, 'cause his father is putting out. What do the Feds call it, 'No ransom or no help?' Geez, anybody can do better than them."

"Joey, you just can't expect the guy to fly over there and crack them just like that. I don't think I have to remind you what happened with those mick friends of yours. This Basque group is a major outfit. A terrorist army like in Iraq and such. This is like the War on Terror. New territory for everybody. Got to give it a little time."

"What do you call a little time?"

"A few days, no more. We all want to see this terrible situation come to a happy conclusion. Tommy's made your daughter a top priority. But these things take time and money."

Joey let out a long suspiration and glanced away at the peeling paint on the stamped patterned tin ceiling of his office. "OK." He nodded his head once. "Tell Tommy that I, you know, I appreciate what he's doing, sure."

"That's all he wants to hear."

"Tell him I'll wait a couple of more days. But he's got to know I can't go on waiting much longer. Spillman warned me he can't keep holding off the news people. Says this thing could turn into some 'Teen Missing in Spain, Day Fifty' kind of crap coming out every minute on CNN. I don't need that."

"Nobody does."

"But it's my daughter we're talking about," he thundered. "And I'm only going to wait so much. Get my meaning?"

Costorino fixed him with a heavy-lidded gaze. "Joey, I'm just here to pass on Tommy's wishes. 'Cause this problem of yours concerns us all. We're all hurting by it."

A lethal smirk formed at the ends of Joey's lips. "Nobody, but nobody's hurting any way like my wife is and like Symphony's grandmother is. Nobody. I know I've been a little distracted lately. Sure. But the work is getting done and everyone's getting their cut. The same as always. So I'm not going to let nobody throw that crap at my face."

"Nobody's saying anything, Joey. Tommy knows you're a professional and won't allow anything to interfere with business."

"That's exactly why the Family has to come through for me on this." He halted in front of his desk. "Got to tell you something else, Dom. Don't take this the wrong way or anything. But if Symphony's not back home in the next few days, I'm going to be forced to look for other ways to deal with this. I hope it don't come to that. Going outside the Family is not how I want it. Specially with certain individuals belonging to other families. You know who I'm talking about. Those by-the-numbers old-timers and their ideas of how a Family should be run. God forbid it comes to that. But nobody can expect me to give up on my daughter. Would you give up on any of your sons?"

Costorino wet his lips and swallowed something bitter. "No."

"Then that's all I got to say. Tell Tommy that my family and I, you know, appreciate the assistance he's giving us."

"I'm glad you put it that way 'cause there's another thing Tommy wants you to have." He placed a thick envelope on Joey's desk and grinned. "No body parts in there."

"What's this now?"

"Expenses Tommy's had to cover so far. He wants it taken care of."

Joey opened the envelope and looked through the list of plane tickets receipts, hotel bills, car rental contracts, gun shop receipts, cash advances, adding up to forty-seven thousand dollars. "What the hell's this? I sent Tommy sixty Gs to cover this stuff."

"As far as I know, Tommy took that first installment as a gesture of goodwill on your part."

"What the hell's that supposed to mean?"

"Look Joey, what you've asked Tommy to do for you is taking a lot of his time. Sixty Gs is peanuts. So yeah, a little goodwill and gratitude is in order. But if you think he made a mistake by assuming as much—"

Joey glanced at Coppertone who was looking back at him as if saying, "Can you believe this bastard?"

The consigliere, in an effort to make his boss's extortion more palatable, added, "Look at it this way. The only reason there's somebody working on your problem there in Europe is because of Tommy. You asked for his help and you got it. No questions asked. You don't expect him to cover your expenses too?"

"Helping a Family member in need is one thing," Joey said, waving the gift box. "But a sixty thousand-dollar rotting hand and a DVD?"

The grin on Costorino's face died. "What are you saying, Joey? You telling me Tommy made a mistake by having me bring these things to you? Because if that's what you're saying, then maybe I should just go back to Howard Beach now."

Joey slumped on his squeaky desk chair and tried to control himself. He knew he had no choice but to swallow whatever condition the "acting" boss of the Family set for him. There was nothing he could do about it, not now, probably not ever. Had this thing happened twenty, maybe even ten years ago—No way, none of this could have happened back then. No head of the Luciani Family would have stooped so shamelessly low as to squeeze a captain this way.

Joey took a deep breath, stood up, and walked a few steps to the corner of the office where an ancient safe sat concealed behind a secret door in the wainscoting. He crouched in front of it and gestured at Coppertone. "Get me an envelope."

The instant the consigliere was out of his office, Joey handed the gift box to Coppertone. "Get rid of that piece of shit. Dump it in the river, throw it in the incinerator. I don't care. Just get rid of it. And here, take the DVD too." Next, Joey grabbed his cellphone and called his lawyer. "Spillman, it's me," he said. "Yeah, good. Listen, talk to me about the Cuban ..."

T W E N T Y-O N E

Miami, Florida

FROM HER SPOT AT the dimly lit end of the lounge bar, Tess watched Zeus Aguirre entering the Doral Marriot's restaurant. He stood next to the one-man-band's keyboard and surveyed the room. It was dinnertime and most of the tables were taken. She restrained the urge to wave him over to give herself time to inspect him further. She was already working on her third vodka-martini, her father's favorite tranquilizer. Her conversation with Spillman had left her with an irreconcilable urge for it. She moved the plastic toothpick with olives aside and took a drink while following Zeus out of the corner of her eye.

A silly grin lifted one end of her lips … Is that a motorcycle helmet in his hand? How about that? Tess had yet to get over the idea of Zeus Aguirre the classical pianist and Zeus Aguirre the equestrian, now it was Zeus Aguirre the biker. The man was so full of surprises.

Funny, she thought, because that was precisely what she needed from him tonight, another surprise. A big one.

With a hand half-covering her face, Tess continued to watch him searching for her in the dining area. There was a distinct brightness about him as he walked around the tables, his shoulders back, loose-limbed like a dancer. Perhaps it was the silky cream-colored shirt or the sheen in his hair, combed back tight over his scalp as in olden days, which reminded her of his dossier photograph, taken during his youthful days in the military.

"Hope I'm not late," he said as he approached her.

Tess pointed at the barstool next to hers.

"Are you hungry?" he said.

"A little. It is dinnertime."

"Do you like seafood?"

"I do."

"Then allow me to invite you to dinner. I know this excellent place by the Miami River. We can talk there."

Tess regarded him from behind the arch of her eyebrows. "Very kind of you, Zeus. But I was hoping we'd get right to business, if you don't mind. My associates in New York are expecting my call and it's getting late."

He looked heartbroken. "Whatever you prefer. But I guarantee you'd be missing a fine seafood meal."

Tess lowered her chin and smoothed her skirt.

"It's only dinner. Come on," he said almost sweetly.

She looked searchingly into his smiling eyes. "OK," she declared. "Why not? I got to eat, right?"

Zeus looked at her two-piece suit. "I have a motorcycle out there. You might want to change your outfit."

"Sorry, I'm not getting on a motorcycle. And I already gave back my rental."

"No problem. I'll have the desk call us a taxi."

On their way out to the cab, the concierge called Zeus to the desk. "If you won't be needing your motorcycle helmet, I could have the attendant run it up to the room."

Zeus glanced at Tess for approval.

"Go ahead," she said.

~

El Emboque was a lively restaurant on the Miami River, loaded with gaudy maritime décor and a singing trio going from table to table. The maître d' showed them to one of the outdoor tables on the deck over the water.

A jolly-faced waiter set two tasseled menus on the table before them. "*Bienvenidos ...*" he spoke in Spanish to them.

Zeus asked for a bottle of Galician white. The waiter then asked him what the lady wished to drink, assuming her blondeness made her a non-Spanish speaker. Tess addressed him in flawless Castilian Spanish: "*Por favor, nada de vino para mi por ahora. Traeme un vodka-martini.*"

"*¡Pero, muchacha!*" exclaimed the waiter in Spanglish, laughing. "You speak Spanish *mejor que yo*! Chica, why didn't you tell me? Be right back with your drinks."

Zeus said, "I'd been meaning to tell you, your Spanish is very good. Where did you learn to speak it so well?"

"In high school. Then I took it up again at the university and in Salamanca, Spain, for a semester. Got a lot of practice there and the year I lived in Miami Beach."

"Well, I am impressed."

A waiter set a plate of fried plantain chips and a small bowl of garlic sauce on the table. Tess watched Zeus pick up a couple of the coin-sized chips, dip them in the sauce and pop them in his mouth. He smiled at her as he chewed.

"So tell me, Zeus. Am I going to go back to New York tomorrow with more bad news for Symphony's parents or are you going to become their hero?"

"The way we left it, the ball was in your court."

"Not anymore. Our client will go along with all your conditions."

"That was quick."

"Not really. Time is the one thing we don't have."

"Did you talk to Messina yourself?"

"Mr. Spillman did."

"Ah." He folded his napkin and set it on his lap.

The expression on his face prompted her to add, "Zeus, whatever you might think of our client is one thing, but we're a reputable law firm."

"What did Messina say about the hit squad?"

"He denies it categorically."

The waiter came with their drinks. Zeus took a sip of wine. "How did he respond to the question of reprisals?"

"As I said, he's ready to meet all your conditions."

"How could I be sure?"

"Mr. Spillman recommended a work-for-hire contract, wherein each party's responsibility is established, and indemnification described if either party fails to fulfill its obligation."

Zeus grinned. "A contract?" He wiped his fingers on the napkin. "Do you really think that's going to prevent Messina from seeking revenge once this is over?"

"What would you propose then, to have him swear on a stack of bibles?"

"I don't think there are enough bibles in the world for that."

"Come on, Zeus. You are the father of an adorable teenage girl. I've seen her picture. Do you honestly believe it's impossible for Messina to agree to it if it'll get his daughter back?"

"That's just it. I believe he'll say anything to get his daughter back." He paused, then, "What if I go to New York and meet with him—judge his sincerity for myself?"

A mysterious shade suddenly darkened Tess's face. "That would not be a good idea. Messina is convinced that you two should not meet yet, to prevent giving the kidnappers the wrong idea."

"Which is?"

"That you are working for him rather than for the girl's release. He's concerned that his reputation might stain your credibility when dealing with your colleagues in Spain."

Tess watched the mysterious grin reappeared on Zeus' lips. Actually, he preferred it that way. It was the same thing Judge Arsenio, an old compeer from his time in the military and ETA's man in South Florida, had told him the previous night. "If you take the job, keep away from the gangster. It would put you in a better position with ETA."

Zeus and Tess sipped from their glasses and glanced in silence over the wooden railing at the river. A long white yacht decked with strings of party lights and packed with salsa dancers came floating by, motors rumbling on its way to *fiesta* out in international waters far from the Law.

Tess placed a bank check made to cash on the table in front of him and said with a delicate voice, "I need you to say yes to me on this."

Zeus glanced at the check. "Twenty-five thousand dollars?"

"Your retainer."

He raised his wineglass at it, but made a pessimistic gesture with his shoulder. "I don't know."

"You're a hero, Zeus. All that men like you need is a maiden in distress to set you in motion. I know you want to do this."

He laughed. "So you got my number, huh?"

"Don't I?"

"This is tricky, Tess. Vengeance is a way of life for some people."

She took another sip of her drink. "Vengeance has no foresight."

Zeus's face lit up. "Napoleon, right?"

His eager reply surprised her. "I think it is Napoleon's quote. Boy, nothing gets by you. How about this one: 'Is it to be thought unreasonable that people, in atonement for wrongs of a century, demand the vengeance of a single day?'"

Zeus gave it some thought. "No idea. Simon Wiesenthal?"

"My, my, Zeus. I figured you'd know that one for sure. Try Robespierre the French revolutionary leader—not unlike yourself."

"I've never thought of myself as French, and I was never a revolutionary."

"Well, had your parents moved to Cuba a few days later, you would've been born in Paris. Isn't that right? And you were an officer in Cuba's Revolutionary Armed Forces."

"I get it now," he said, grinning. "Which dossier did you read: the CIA's or the one from Homeland Security? I warn you they are both loaded with blatant inaccuracies."

"I think I got the Agency's version."

"Good. I like their inaccuracies better."

Pancho the waiter arrived with his kitchen helpers. They set the dishes and refilled the glasses. It was then when Tess noticed with a breath of relief that Zeus had taken the retainer check. "Everything looks delicious," she said with a big smile.

For the next few minutes, they stayed off the Messina case and enjoyed their dinner. Now and then, a salty breeze worked its way upriver and ruffled Tess's hair. Zeus smiled every time she doffed it off her face.

His expression reminded Tess of her father on the day of her high school graduation. For reasons she ignored, the old boy had been on and off her mind all that day. The waiters cleared the table. Pancho lit up the candle that had gone out in the breeze. "Dessert?"

Zeus asked for an espresso. Tess said she was all set.

"For conversation's sake," Zeus said. "What do you think would happen if I turn down Messina's proposal?"

"For conversation's sake, I'd say the firm stands to lose one of its most important accounts, and who knows how it would reflect on me."

It was not the answer he had expected, but he did not pursue it. He could see by the dreamy look in her eyes that she was no longer at work. Their candlelit glances wandered out into the Miami night.

The singing trio surrounded their table, guitars strumming, voices soaring in three-part harmony. Tess recognized the song from her other time in Miami, a lifetime ago, a romantic bolero. She closed her eyes, carried away by the sweetness of the moment. She heard Zeus speaking to her through the trio's dreamy harmonies and felt the warmth of his hand on hers. She was unable to resist the sudden good feeling stroking her body.

"Take me home," she whispered.

Twenty minutes later, they arrived at the hotel. Zeus accompanied her to the room. Tess unlocked the door with the card and leaned against the doorjamb as he walked inside for his motorcycle helmet. On his way out, she cut in front of him. He was about to say something, but she shushed him with a kiss. The door closed. His helmet fell on the carpet, and then one by one the rest of their garments followed.

Neither spoke a word after their skin-to-skin embrace.

The last sound Tess heard before a deep delicious sleep overtook her was the distant tremor of Zeus's motorcycle roaring off into a new Miami dawn.

TWENTY-TWO

Five kilometers outside Mondragón

THE STOP-AND-GO TRaffic roused Crimmil out of his snooze. "What's this, rush hour?"

Guy removed his sunglasses and stuck his head out of the driver's window. "Can't tell."

A moment later, they started to move again, picking up speed and slowing down every few yards. A couple of cars in the opposite lane switched their headlights on and off as they went by.

"Uh-oh," Guy said, familiar with the Basque's way of alerting fellow motorists of a police check control. "I think there's a roadblock ahead."

"Pull over," Crimmil said.

"I don't think that's a good idea."

"Don't think, Guy. Just pull over."

"What if the cops see us?"

"Do I have to pull the key out of the ignition?"

"I will not stop the car here and call attention to us."

"Goddamn it, Guy." Crimmil looked about to sock him. "We're in a fucking stolen car with an arsenal in the trunk. Stop the car. Don't make me tell you again."

"Please, Guy," Mademoiselle Albi said from the back seat. "Don't drive to a police control."

"You shut up." Guy then said to Crimmil, "What are you going to do?"

"Going to get out and have a look. Then you're going to drive us out of here. Do you approve? Good. Now pull over."

Furious, Guy slammed on the brakes and stopped by the side of the road. Crimmil gave him a squint-eyed look and jumped out of the car.

From their seats, Guy, Mademoiselle Albi, and Rashid watched him climb on the hood, cup his hand over his eyes like a field marshal to shield himself from the sun, then jump down and duck back in the car.

"We're about fifty yards from the roadblock," Crimmil said between curses. "They'll probably see us backing out, but we've got to."

"This is stupid," Guy said, his French accent getting thicker by the second. "We should hide the guns someplace and come back later."

"That's your big idea? Open the trunk."

Guy pulled the lever and the trunk snapped open. "You're going to get rid of the guns?"

"Everyone stays in the car." Crimmil went around and pulled out the RPG launcher out of the trunk and leaned it on the side of the car. Then he came to the window and tossed the Uzi and a box of ammunition on the passenger's seat. "That's for you."

Guy muttered something in French.

"Say what you want, pal," Crimmil told him. "But we've got a job to do and I'm not leaving 'til it's done."

He handed Rashid the AK-47. "We can't let those cops come anywhere near us. OK?"

"OK," Rashid replied.

Crimmil could see by the dull look on the Arab's face he was only parroting him. "Guy, translate. I got no time for this crap now."

Back by the opened trunk, Crimmil picked up the DVD camera, looked at it for a moment and put it back. He lifted up a heavy canvas case and pulled out a rocket grenade for the RPG. He crouched next to the rear tire, out of sight of the passing cars, loaded the launcher, then stood it on the car floor by his seat.

"Guy, keep the engine running. Rashid, remember, if you see any cops coming near you let it rip, bang bang bang. OK?"

"OK."

"Yeah, right. And you," he signaled at Mademoiselle Albi. "You come with me."

"Me? Why me?"

"Get out of the car. You're going to stop the traffic for me."

"What?"

"At my signal, you're going to stop the traffic coming on the other side of the highway. You got to be quick so Guy can make a U-turn without stopping and get us out of here. You *comprehend moi?*"

"How I do this?" Mademoiselle Albi was getting nauseous. "I can't ..."

"Just go out there when I tell you to, stand in the middle of the damn road, flash those big plastic tits of yours, lift your skirt, whatever, but make sure the cars stop. Got it?"

"But the cars will run over me."

Crimmil grabbed a fistful of Mademoiselle Albi's copious bottled red hair. "I'll run over you myself if you don't. So shut the hell up and do what I say." He pushed her and Mademoiselle Albi tripped on her stilettos and plopped backward on the flat of her buttocks.

Crimmil glared around him. "Get up. You stop the traffic when I tell you to. Not a second before, not a second after, get it? Then we'll pick you up on the other side of the road."

Too frightened to sob, Mademoiselle Albi moaned in agreement.

Crimmil stuck his head inside the car. "Is everything clear?" The men nodded yes. "I'll be right back."

The *Américain Monstre* slid down into the drainage ditch parallel to the highway and vanished into the tall weeds.

Cursing him in every language she knew, Mademoiselle Albi lit up a cigarette while holding the lighter with both hands to keep it from shaking, and filled her lungs with the smoke.

In the car, Guy was already puffing on a Gitane, his chest swelling and depressing with every puff, watching Crimmil do his Rambo act down the ditch. The Uzi was on his lap. He had not killed in a decade and never in cold blood, but now he could not stop thinking how easy it would be to put one right between the American Monster's eyes and do the world a favor. "The damn lunatic."

Crimmil hoped the cops were just checking for DUIs, but had to see what he was up against. Crouched inside the tall growth behind a culvert under the highway, he got a view of the police roadblock. Three squad cars and eight men from two different police corps, judging by the different getups. They had laid a nasty-looking spike strip across the width of the pavement, designed to shred the tires of any vehicle that dared to ram the roadblock. Two policemen in riding boots were in charge of removing the spike strip and pulling it back every time a car drove up for inspection.

They weren't looking for drunks.

He counted nine cars in the queue between the Audi and the road-block. "We better get the hell out of here pronto, boys," he said to his imaginary platoon.

On his way back a group of children in a van saw him hunched over, sneaking along the ditch. They started yelling and pointing at him, more in fun than in alarm. It attracted the attention of other motorists. Two agents wearing the red and black uniforms of the Ertzaintza came to see what the racket was about and spotted him clambering out of the ditch.

Crimmil broke into a sprint toward the Audi. He yelled at Mademoi-selle Albi to stop the traffic. He reached the car, picked up the RPG, and aimed it at the two Ertzainas running after him. When the policemen saw the rocket-propelled-grenade launcher leveled in their direction, they jumped out of the way and disappeared between the cars.

Crimmil threw the RPG on the floor of the car and dove inside. "Let's go! Step on it."

Guy kicked down on the gas pedal, making the Audi perform a U-turn on the spot. The skid tracks left a black rainbow across the roadbed.

It came to a smoky halt in front of Mademoiselle Albi who stood waiting across the road. "Get in," they told her.

She froze, speechless.

"You stupid bitch, get in!" Crimmil was about to order Guy to leave her behind when Rashid jumped out and dragged her into the car. The Audi took off burning rubber away from Mondragón.

As they sped away, the four of them kept looking behind them expecting the police to come in pursuit, but it did not happen.

"They're not chasing us." Guy squinted into the rearview, astonished.

"See that? Woohoo," Crimmil howled like a rodeo star. "I told them wops in New York. This RPG's worth every penny. Shit, I should've had the camera rolling …"

TWENTY-THREE

Mondragón

AITOR MARCHED ACROSS the sunlit plaza like a man whose time was running out. He made the corner and glanced up the stone walls of San Juan Bautista Church at the bulging-eyed gargoyles shaped like hell-cats with batwings over the brown-wood portal, the same ones that had frightened him so as a child. He pushed the worn-smooth wooden door and scanned the shadowy temple.

A man with a short ponytail was standing by the holy water font in the echoey silence. Aitor stood beside him, facing the elaborate main altar.

"Are you here for the wedding?" the man said.

"No," Aitor answered. "I am here for the baptism."

"Then I must be in the wrong church."

"You are probably looking for the San Francisco Church. I can take you there, if you like."

With catchphrases exchanged, Aitor looked at the man. "I am Zurgin," he said in Euskara as they shook hands. "Let us talk. We are running late."

"It is best if we sit in the chapel." Aitor pointed at the other end of the church.

Zurgin motioned him to lead and gave an almost imperceptible nod to a young woman kneeling on one of the pews by the door. "She is with us," Zurgin said. "There are more outside."

They walked across the colonnaded central nave, past the imposing medieval main altar and the five-centuries-old choir stalls. Two elderly women were knelt in prayer on the steps by the altar.

In the chapel, Aitor and Zurgin sat down on the last row of pews. No one else was there except for the statue of bearded John the Baptist, who in the uncertain light from the multi-colored stain glass bore a curious resemblance to Aitor.

"Am I looking at the new military leader?"

Zurgin exhaled a breath of modesty. "You are."

"Permanently?"

"As permanent as these pronouncements can be."

Thick-boned with dark, bushy eyebrows joined together over his nose and a perennial five o'clock shadow, the new military chief reminded him of the classic Basque specimen from the funnies. "Should I congratulate you?"

Zurgin shrugged. "This was not the way I would have liked to be given this command, but here we are." He looked into Aitor's eyes. "It looks like the future of our organization depends much on how you and I resolve the situation here in Mondragón. Are you in accord?"

"Yes. But I believe the solution is simple."

"Simple, you say."

"As simple as setting the *americana* free. Once she is gone, the assassins will follow."

"Too late for that."

"It was Iñaki's last direct order to me."

"The assassins are already here."

"That is precisely why we should act now."

"You do not seem to understand. They are here, in Guicuzpua, as we speak."

Aitor frowned, confused. "How do you know?"

Zurgin looked away as if reluctant to share the intelligence. "Our compeers in the Ertzaintza gave us the information. They identified a team of three or four, including an American. They arrived in the area last night. It is confirmed."

"Then we have to let the girl go this very moment."

"Negative," said Zurgin. "The girl stays."

"Whose decision is that?"

"Mine."

Aitor let out a deflating breath. "This is madness. We'd have serious security problems if we have to confront the assassins anywhere near this town. Madrid will come down on us with everything. How will we protect the boy then? Our only alternative is to let her go."

"That alternative became invalid the moment they killed our brethren."

"Do you have the leadership's approval on this?"

"*Así es*," he said, switching to Spanish.

Zurgin came from the hard side of the organization, Aitor could tell. Still, "I cannot believe the leadership would risk the financial future of this organization when all we have to do is let the girl go."

"Do you think that we're going to give the assassins what they want after they killed Iñaki and Txatxi, and God knows what other compeers yet to be found? Is that what you think?"

Aitor straightened up his shoulders. "What I'd like to know is what makes you think they can just come to my town and take her? Do you think we have been twiddling our thumbs for two years? No foreign hit-men will find this girl if we don't want to." Then, Aitor said to avoid an argument, "Why not simply set it up for the Ertzaintza to take care of them? It's been done before. It's a more intelligent solution than battling it out and ruining this operation completely."

"Well rejoice, my compeer," Zurgin answered with a sardonic grin. "Because that is exactly what is going to happen. Understand this, neither the Guardia Civil nor the DNAT have any intention of stopping that death squad. Judge Garzón's orders."

"That is absurd—"

"Maybe so, but that is precisely the Judge's plan. He wants the assassins to find you and save his men the effort. Now you understand? He wants to catch you and your team and the assassins and the prisoners, everybody with one single swoop."

Aitor slumped back on the wooden pew.

"Fortunately," Zurgin said, "a group of our compeers in the Ertzaintza have owned up to their patriotic obligations and offered to stop the assassins with our help."

"Can they do that?"

"*Claro*. That is why we have to get moving."

"Now?"

"We've been on it for two days. Do you think we have been twiddling our thumbs? It's all set."

"How do you plan to do this?"

Zurgin glanced across the dusky nave. "Come and I will show you."

On a side alley by the church, they hopped into a panel van and drove out of town to the Arrasate-Bergara highway. All through the drive, Zurgin kept his mobile to his ear, following instructions from whomever was on the other end of the line. Passing under a tall railway viaduct between two round-topped green hills, he said to the driver. "This is it."

The van pulled into the rear lot of a roadside restaurant. Aitor, Patxi, Zurgin, and his two commandos entered the building through a service backdoor and went up a stairwell to the rooftop. Out under the gray Basque sky were several empty outdoor tables with benches under folded canvas awnings. Zurgin told the group to sit there quietly and wait until he came back.

Patxi looked into Aitor's eyes, his bearded face squint-eyed and puzzled. "What's with all the mystery?"

Aitor answered with a shrug and sat down.

The female member of their little posse, who had heard him, turned around and said with a knowing half-grin, "Look and learn, my Mondragón compeers. You'll be talking about this day to your grand-kids."

What she knew and Aitor and Patxi were about to find out was an entire Basque police brigade and a half-dozen squad cars were gathering on the quiet by the banks of the Deva River.

~

Highway GI 627 was clear of traffic as far as Crimmil could see. "How fast are we going?"

Guy glanced at the speedometer. "One hundred and fifty five."

"How much is it in miles?"

"About one hundred."

"Yeah," Crimmil let out.

The Frenchman gave him a look. If the monster was in a good mood, he might as well take advantage of it. "Mind if I smoke?"

Crimmil considered it for a moment. "Go ahead," he said. "You too, Albi baby. Hey, I used to smoke. I know what that's like." He was all heart.

Even Rashid lit up.

Crimmil rolled down his window a slit. "Did you guys see them cops running from the RPG?" He laughed over the roaring hundred-mile an hour wind. "They ran like rats."

He peered over his shoulder at Mademoiselle Albi, at her eye makeup streaming like black tears on her flushed cheeks, at her lipstick-smeared Marlboro squeezed between her lips, then at the fat silicone twins bulging out of her blouse. She reminded him of a battered whore he once met at the 17th precinct in New York, a transvestite who became one of his earliest clients. It stimulated his libido. "Sorry I had to get rough. You did good back there."

Mademoiselle Albi regarded him a moment then blew a mouthful of smoke. She recognized that kind of men's laugh. "Happy you think so."

"I'm going to buy you a dress when we get back to Marseille. Any dress you want. Would you like that?"

"A dress? How wonderful." The promise of a new dress did not do a thing for her, but Crimmil's approval eased her overpowering fear of him, so she played along. "It will be an expensive one, I promise you."

Stooped over the steering wheel, Guy shot them a smoky sneer. When the New York people asked him for someone fluent in Basque, he had gone out and found her. Mademoiselle Albi, a former dancer he'd met one night at a discotheque in Perpignan. Not an easy find, either. Only twenty percent of the Basques spoke their own language. She just happened to be one. It had been his job to take care of her since, indulge her obsession with cocaine and her phobia of boredom whenever she was in the mood, which wasn't always a pleasurable experience for him. Mademoiselle Albi was his find and it was the principle of the thing. He thought it deserved some exclusivity.

He glanced at Crimmil. The bastard had given up on Mademoiselle Albi. He was again caressing the RPG launcher between his legs as if it were a lapdog. Crimmil caught him looking.

"What?"

"We have to change cars."

"You got that right. Only I haven't seen a car on this road."

"Maybe they have another roadblock."

Crimmil wasn't listening. "Didn't we see a gas station on the way up, a trucker's place just outside that other town?"

"We are going to come up to it very soon. Beyond those hills."

"We'll change cars there."

They drove under a viaduct. Guy looked up from the road, expecting to see the restaurant's sign between the trees ahead. The twilight sky reminded him of the religious oil paintings in Catholic school, with their multi-color clouds and sunray-filled heavens of Resurrection Day. It filled him with a strange melancholia, like after a long night of blow and bourbon.

Out of the curve, a roadblock appeared. A wall of squad cars with swirling roof lights flashing. Out of nowhere a silver spike snake flashed across the pavement. The four tires exploded. Guy sunk his foot on the brake and snatched the emergency brake. The Audi fishtailed out of control, its rear end going from one side to the other. Mademoiselle Albi let out one long jarring scream.

Guy jerked hard on the wheel to keep from barreling into the eucalyptus trees lining the highway. Dusk became a blur of shifting horizons, a smudge on the windshield. The stripped wheel rims screeched over the pavement leaving a trail of orange sparks.

Guy parried one, two trees, sideswiped another, until a huge gray trunk materialized in front of his eyes.

The Audi rammed it in a headlong blast of flying glass, plastic, and twisted metal.

Crimmil could not open his eyes for the blood pouring from a deep gash on his brow. He tried to wriggle himself free, stuck between the dashboard and the twisted bucket seat. He pulled the RPG launcher behind him. Rashid had flown off the backseat and landed on Guy's right shoulder. He was trying to squeeze himself out of the driver's window, dragging his dislocated arm beside him like a dead animal. Mademoiselle Albi's cries of pain would not let anyone hear what the agent with the bullhorn was saying.

Fearing a gasoline tank explosion, two Ertzaintza agents came running with fire extinguishers to put out the engine flames. The rest watched with weapons drawn from their cover positions behind their patrol cars.

Concealed inside the fire extinguishers' white mist, Crimmil crawled out of the half-opened passenger door. He fired three desperate pistol shots in the air. The Ertzaintza agents dropped the extinguishers and ran for cover. The bullhorn went silent.

Crimmil wiped the blood off his eyes, untangling the RPG and the canvas knapsack out of the smoking wreckage. He laid flat over the pavement and debris behind the car. He loaded the weapon with quick reckless motions and fired at dead reckoning into the cluster of headlights and ducked for the blast.

The rocket shot in an arc over the smoking Audi and landed on the roof of a patrol car with a loud metallic bang. The grenade bounced off it without exploding.

"A dud," Crimmil growled. "A goddamn Chinese dud."

The police responded with a deafening barrage of small arms fire aimed to kill whatever was moving inside and outside the wreckage.

Crimmil curled into fetal position on the roadbed, hugging the RPG launcher. Bullets pierced and ricocheted inside the Audi. Jagged pieces of metal and plastic flew off like shrapnel. In the midst of it, Mademoiselle Albi tore out of the shattered rear windshield, shrieking down the road.

Her escape halted the police fusillade. They yelled at her to stop. Crimmil and Rashid watched her stagger for a few meters, her hands and face dripping with blood, then drop behind a tree.

"The crazy bitch."

Rashid, the only one who had checked the police fire with his AK-47, slumped himself next to Crimmil.

"Where's Guy?"

Rashid pointed to the car. Crimmil lifted himself and saw the Frenchman's silhouette still strapped to the driver's seat, his chin on his chest, the deflated airbag drooping on his knees, blood all over it.

The man with the bullhorn started again. Neither Crimmil nor Rashid could understand what the policeman was saying, no matter how loud or how many times he said it. Rashid looked into Crimmil's bloody face and mumbled in broken English, "Allah is merciful."

Crimmil didn't laugh. "We got to go. You understand what I'm saying to you?"

Rashid looked at him with vacant eyes. Crimmil tried the few phrases he knew in the Uzbek language, but it was the same as speaking English to the Arab.

Blood kept dripping from his frown. He sneaked a peek across the highway. Through the cordite fumes of gunfire, he saw what was aiming at him from the other side of the road. "Got to get the hell out of here."

From the roof of the roadside café-restaurant, ETA's men watched the gunfight.

"The trees are blocking my view," complained the man holding a high-power rifle with a telescopic sight. "I do not have a clear shot."

The same eucalyptus that had wrecked the Audi now obstructed their view of the crash site. "It is getting too dark to distinguish anything," Zurgin said. "How many are there left?"

"At least two more," the rifleman said, his gaze switching between the Audi and the squad of red-beret Ertzaintzas barricaded behind the squad cars. "The woman is down by those trees, dead."

Zurgin crouched behind the masonry railing. He raised his chin and scanned the darkening sky for the Guardia Civil helicopter. "Keep watching," he told his man. "We can only fire at what we can see."

Aitor peeked over the railing. "I only see the one in the car."

"That is all I can see too," Patxi said.

"The one in the car is dead, too," the rifleman said. "But chief, I can make sure if you want."

Zurgin answered with a silent sneer.

All they could see from the police's position now was the swirling blue lights that filled the trees with an unreal glow, and hear the tiny voices coming from the patrol car radios. The Ertzainas seemed to have no plans of getting out of their cover positions.

Patxi slid his back down the masonry railing and sat on the roof's tiled floor. "What are they waiting for?"

"They are probably shitting in their pants, waiting for the Guardia Civil to get here," the rifleman said.

Aitor said, "Maybe we could attack from the rearguard and get it over with."

"I was thinking that too," Zurgin answered. "But we are only to provide them with cover, nothing else. And only if they ask for it. We cannot be seen taking part in any of this." Then he addressed the group, "Remember, the moment we hear the Guardia Civil helicopter approaching, we get off the roof. Our Ertzaintza compeers will have hell to pay if they see us up here. And so would we."

The sky grew darker over the highway. There was a stir behind the police roadblock and the bullhorn sounded again, giving final warning to the ones left hidden behind the wrecked Audi.

Crimmil knew without understanding the words this was their last call. He gave his last rocket grenade a sinister look and loaded it on the launcher. "You better work, you piece of Chinese shit."

He crawled behind the most solid remains of the Audi, out of the headlights, and took a good look at the patrol car barricade. The beaming and swirling colored lights blinded him to every detail except for the target itself.

With the safety catch off, he wiped his brow with a headscarf Mademoiselle Albi had left behind, then positioned the RPG at an angle with the road.

An inspired grin formed in Rashid's dusky features when their eyes met.

"You happy I'm going to shoot this thing, huh? Yes you are, you stupid freak."

Rashid genuflected beside him and raised the AK-47 with his uninjured arm, ready to die fighting. Crimmil fired the RPG in the general direction of the bullhorn.

It worked this time, too well.

On hearing the shot, the police fell back into self-protecting spasms. The grenade detonated on a patrol car. It tore up the hood, spraying everyone and everything around it with metal and glass debris. In a chain reaction, the squad car beside it burst into fire when flames reached its leaking fuel tank and exploded.

Shocked by the double explosion, the police did not return fire. Instead, they spread out to tend their dead and the wounded.

Crimmil and Rashid crawled into the roadside ditch and lay together in the shadows looking back dazzled by the fiery destruction across the road and listening to the snapping of the burning cars and the screaming voices.

"I see heavy damage, Rash. They didn't like this one."

Crimmil pointed his chin at the dark river waters roaring softly beneath their feet. "Our way out of here."

Rashid shook his head. The river was not an option for a boy from a desert village where the local well had been the biggest body of water he'd known until age twenty-one. No death could be more horrible than drowning. "I fight here," he said as sure as he could be.

"Can't swim?" Crimmil said as he started to move out. "Tough luck, my Muslim buddy."

The big noise of a helicopter's flapping rotors came then, louder and louder in its approach. The ETA men on the restaurant's roof cleared out the moment they heard it reaching the highway.

In a dusky flat field off the road, a squad of heavily armed black-hooded agents poured out of the hovering chopper. For a few minutes, the assassins seemed forgotten in the clamor of squealing ambulances and police cars rushing from nearby towns.

Crimmil watched it all from the dark of the ditch. "The cavalry's here," he muttered, looking at the Arab. "The entire spic cavalry coming to get us. How you like that?"

Rashid was not sure because of the curdling blood over Crimmil's expression, but he could've sworn the American was smiling at him. The notion filled him with a warm brotherly feeling. Did this mean that Allah had chosen them to die together as martyrs? The American devil and he? Was Allah giving him the opportunity to redeem himself by killing the infidels in this humble jihad as his last action in life?

Rashid took his shirt off and used it to wipe himself clean. This was his time. He could hear it as clear as a call to evening prayer. He could feel it in his opened wounds, in the blood purifying him for the ultimate sacrifice securing him a privileged place by Allah's side. An eternity replete with everything denied to him in life. "Allah is great."

Crimmil wiped the blood off his face. Even on the verge of his own demise—or because of it—he could not resist doing what he always did whenever reality became unbearable. He fantasized about his movie, the final sequence. His original idea, the one with him rescuing the girl from the terrorists and coming home a hero to become an acclaimed film director, no longer suited the current setting. It called for a different climax, a new grand finale.

Crimmil grinned, remembering *Butch Cassidy and the Sundance Kid*, one of his all-time favorite endings. Two men going out in a blaze of glory as they faced a battalion of riflemen, a climax the audience never saw. Not in his ending. In his, he'd leave no horror left to the imagination. The audience would see every nuance of what happens when a hailstorm of bullets rip through human flesh, in slo-mo, like in *Bonnie and Clyde*, but bigger, with a blood-splashed lens.

The idea brought an inspired smile to his face, the bloody smile that had mesmerized Rashid.

They reloaded their weapons and looked into each other's eyes. Neither spoiled the moment with words. Crimmil grabbed Rashid's hand and held it tightly in his. "You and me, together. Yes?"

Rashid nodded from the shadows. They helped each other to their feet. "See you on the other side, friend," Crimmil cocked the Uzi, ready for the final act. "Let's go."

"Praise be to Allah," Rashid yelled in his language and charged out of the ditch to meet his fate, the AK-47 in his good hand. In an instant, the night lit up with a vicious roar of fireworks as he emptied his last clip into the dozens of headlights on the other side of the road.

Crimmil did not move from behind the Audi. He emptied his Uzi at the roadblock, then threw it into the river below, grabbed his backpack and slid down the weed-covered riverbank into the cold dark waters of the polluted Deba River.

He let the current carry him downstream as he listened to the receding gunfire and tried to keep afloat.

"Hey Rashid," he muttered between mouthfuls of water as he drifted away. "Save some of that virgin pussy for me, you dumb fucking Haji ..."

P A R T IV

T W E N T Y-F O U R

Madrid, Spain

THAT MORNING, ZEUS Aguirre rode out of Barajas Airport's futuristic Terminal 4 in an air-conditioned taxi with a GPS unit and a digital meter, and he had to admit he was impressed. Madrid had gone through a serious makeover since he was posted there, back in the '80s. Modern office buildings, hotels, and other stylish structures now lined the super-highway all the way into the city.

Tall glass and metal towers loomed over the old seigniorial stone *palacetes* along traffic-choked Paseo de la Castellana. International chain stores and fast-food eateries stood where shadowy bodegas and noisy *chir-inguítos* once gave the city a town-like flavor.

On busy Gran Vía, shaved-head boys, men in short pants, tattooed girls, and bottle-blonde "third-age" women in jeans rushed along the sidewalks talking on their mobiles as if the world was part of their conversation. A city beset by modernity.

The taxi dropped him off on Fuencarral Street, in front of an aparta-hotel Zeus had used on occasions during his service at the Cuban Embassy. The hotel had been an old favorite because of the concierge, a charming old Catalonian anarchist who for a reasonable fee would let rooms without registering the guests.

Neither the hotel nor the concierge had survived Madrid's progress frenzy. The once tranquil lobby was now illuminated with stadium-bright lighting and noisy with tourists coming and going in and out of buses.

Zeus waited his turn at the desk. He requested apartment 413, on the fourth floor, facing Fuencarral Street.

"*Lo siento.* That one is unavailable," the clerk told him. "We have one facing Tribunal."

Zeus nodded no. "How about 313, on the floor below?"

That one was available.

He dropped his suitcase on the bed and drew the thick window drapes. The sunny view that unfurled brought a squint-eyed grin to his face. He nodded at the figure of Saint Fernando in his suit of armor atop the baroque gateway of Museo Municipal building across the street. The statue was a former silent partner of his, from the hundreds of surveillance hours he spent by that window, or a nearby one, keeping tabs on the local Soviet and British secret-service agents who used the museum as a mail drop. Neither side knew of the other, only he and old San Fernando were in on it—him and perhaps one or two of the females that used to keep him company.

He opened the mini bar and closed it again. What he needed was an espresso from his home coffeemaker. He stripped to his underwear and rubbed the phantom pain stinging his scarred lower back.

During the flight, he had gone over his planned agenda and reached the same conclusion with which he had left Miami: the assignment was too open-ended for the kind of game plan he was accustomed to following. It was going to be the same as in his early counterintelligence service days, when they handed him a handful of dollars and a Beretta and cast him off to fend for himself by his own wits. The same thing, but without the Beretta.

Perhaps Tess was right, he thought as he unpacked his khaki pants. Maybe the job was as straightforward as it looked, and the reason why he was unable to discern the possible complications was that they didn't exist. Sure, it would be so much more comforting to think of Messina as no more than a grieving father and not a Mafioso from Jersey. Or to imagine that Txomin, the man he'd come to see, was only a dear friend from the war and not a notorious ETA terrorist serving twenty-seven life sentences. He could even think of himself as a man on a humanitarian mission, as Spillman had described the job, protected by a legal contract and a legitimate American passport. He could look at it that way. But he knew it would be a gross miscalculation.

Thinking of Tess was good, though. So good in fact that he had to mind when and how he thought of her, whether it was for business or pleasure. The problem was that she fitted in both categories.

He dug into his coat pocket for his Stealth phone, one of the items the firm had delivered to him by UPS before his flight. It came in a satchel with a false lead and osmium bottom to avoid detection, containing ten thousand euros in cash and a platinum credit card from a bank in Gibraltar. He would have liked to give Tess a call, just to hear her voice, but there was nothing yet to report. He gave the fancy untraceable phone his first try. He dialed one of the numbers he had memorized.

It belonged to his ETA handlers. He left a message on the voicemail, a single phrase: "*La áve llegó a su nido.*" The bird arrived at his nest.

On his next call, he had a brief but cordial conversation with a man named Pablo. They agreed to meet an hour later at an outdoor café at nearby Dos de Mayo Plaza.

Before he left, Zeus glanced at the mirror by the door and caught the early symptoms of jetlag in his droopy eyelids. He told himself not to worry. By next weekend, he'd be back to his Italian coffeemaker and his dull, carefree life again, only richer. Meantime, he'd see what he could do for the girl.

The plaza was a short walk from the hotel. In August, many of the youth bars along narrow San Vicente de Ferrer were shut, yet the street was busy with wandering bands of students who found their way into the area every summer. Zeus spotted Pablo sitting at an outdoor café in the shade of the sand-colored buildings facing the plaza.

Fifteen years his senior, Pablo looked like a suit-and-tie Buddha bulging out of the plastic armchair.

"*Vaya, vaya,* it is you, *compañero* Aguirre," he said. "How long has it been?"

"Too long, my friend," Zeus said.

Back before the Wall came down, Pablo and Zeus had worked under the command of the Cuban Directorate of Intelligence in Havana, where their paths crossed on occasions. Pablo was in charge of the document reproduction section, a one-man counterfeiting operation that earned him a life of privileges until computer technology and Castro's whims rendered his skills useless. In Madrid, Pablo had resumed practicing his craft.

"To make ends meet, you understand," he said with fake modesty. "Small scale stuff, passports, official documents, university diplomas."

"Not worthy of an artist of your caliber," Zeus said with playful sympathy.

"Can't compete with those new computer programs. They can do a month's work in an hour." Pablo gave a languid look around at the sunken arch in the middle of the plaza, Madrid's monument to the uprising against Napoleon. "Are you comfortable out here?"

"Didn't Judge Arsenio tell you? I'm not on that kind of job."

"Then why do you need a new identity?"

"For extra personal insurance," Zeus said, grinning. "It is a criminal case. And I figured you could use the business."

"Business, yes; trouble, no."

Zeus chuckled. "You're as safe now as you were before we met."

"Don't know if that's any more comforting."

A young woman stepped out of the café to take Zeus's order. "Double espresso, please." When the girl walked away, he said, "The judge told me that you hear a lot of cross-reference from your clients. What do you know about the Estrada kidnapping?"

"The son of Estrada? Is that why you're here?"

"Not exactly."

"I didn't think so. That business is closed. The *etarras* made a deal with the family."

"How about the boy's fiancée, the American girl?"

Pablo opened his beady eyes wide and grinned as if to say, 'So that's it.' He actually said, "I heard she's also a dead issue. No one knows who has her."

"What do you think happened?"

Pablo waved his pudgy hand. "Don't know and don't care. Those new *etarras*, they are *loco*. And they are in the poorhouse."

"That's not what I heard."

"I suppose that depends on who you talk to."

"I read the papers."

"The government may be helpless from stopping those renegades from going into business for themselves. However, no Basque is going to lift a finger to help them when the crap hits the fan, believe me. I'm surprised Judge Arsenio's still does. But he lives in sunny Florida, like you. The Atlantic Ocean is a mighty wall."

None of that concerned Zeus. It was all regional politics to him. "What have your sources told you about the assassinations?"

"Well, it's not hard to figure out who's pulling the trigger, is it?"

"Estrada-Uribe?" Zeus proposed, as a hook.

The Buddha chortled. "Come on, Aguirre. So far, the man's paid four million euros to get his son back. Do you think he wants to take out the very same people he's paying?"

Zeus sipped the last of his coffee. The same logic could apply to Messina, he thought. Why would he send out a team of hired killers and then hire him to negotiate his daughter's release? Even as an incentive to force his hand on the kidnappers, he saw no logic in it. Too dangerous a stratagem. Then again, "Anything's possible."

Pablo peered into his empty glass with a doleful look on his beefy face. "This much I will tell you, *compañero*. I'd stay away from those *etarras* like the plague if I were you. They're dropping like flies all over the place. Someone might confuse you with the exterminators or worse yet, with the pests themselves."

Zeus raised his espresso cup. "I'll keep it in mind."

Pablo paused for a meditative drag of his cigarette. "Interesting," he said after a prolonged silence. "You always seem to end up dealing with those Basques."

"It looks that way, doesn't it?"

With a circular motion of his index finger, Pablo signaled the waitress for another round of drinks. He leaned his rotund frame forward over the tiny table. "Tell me the truth," he said with a mischievous little grin hinting on his diminutive mouth. "You came for the girl. *¿Verdad?* Come on, you can tell me."

Zeus's expression dissolved into a grimace of forbearance. "All I can tell you, old *amigo*, is that I'm working for the good guys."

"Ah, the good guys, yes," the Buddha replied with mocking sorrow. "As we were back then? Guardians of the Revolution?"

"It wasn't the Revolution we guarded."

Pablo snapped his lips with disgust. "We were the Comandante's whores. That's what we were."

"We were many things."

Pablo downed his cognac. "So you're going to need a complete set? Passport, DNI, the whole thing?"

"*Eso es.*"

"How about credit cards?"

Zeus nodded yes.

"Ho, ho—"

"Problem?"

"No. But I'm going to need cash to open the accounts. How much do you have to spend?"

"I'm good for 1986's prices."

Pablo let out a belly laugh and put his hand over his mouth, coughing until his eyes watered. He lit another cigarette. "When do you need it by? Yesterday?"

"Sure."

"What nationality?"

"One Spanish and one US, if you got them."

"I got them."

Zeus pulled a folded manila envelope from his jacket. "There are three thousand euros in there and some passport-size pictures." On a napkin he wrote down the name and personal information he wanted on the documents and dragged it across the table.

Pablo read it. "Aha, first name Ernesto, born in Madrid. Only fifty-one years old? OK. This will do." He pocketed the napkin and raised his glass. "Another one?"

"Like to, but I got to run."

Zeus paid for the drinks and gave the old master forger a hug. "I'll call you tomorrow."

He strode toward Callao Plaza, glad that the meeting with Pablo had gone well. And glad to know he'd be able to count on additional covers in case of complications. In covert operations as in war, every forward move demanded a corresponding layer of security, such as the flexibility a double identity could provide.

Zeus narrowed his eyes at the sun-drenched traffic on Plaza de Callao and joined the flock of pedestrians swarming to the other side of Gran Vía, ready for his first face-to-face contact with ETA.

He walked to a *telefonía* shop off Puerta del Sol plaza and purchased a disposable mobile telephone, according to the specifications he received from Judge Arsenio in Miami. He installed himself in a booth in a nearby cafeteria and programmed the telephone as he sipped an iced lemonade. That done he sent the coded message. A text came back with instructions.

He had a few minutes to kill and sat back looking out at the busy plaza outside, marveling at the intricate series of events that had brought him back. He could trace it all to that equally sweltering day in Angola, a million years ago, it seemed. When a local UNITA chieftain in the Quimbele Province captured three Basque exiles who'd been making their way to the Cuban lines. HQ picked him to lead the search-and-rescue operation and bring the Basques to Luanda. The ambush, a by-the-book night raid on a village of straw huts, was a success. It earned him a field decoration and the profound gratitude of the men he rescued, among them Txomin, who would later return to Spain and become one of ETA's most admired and feared leaders. That his mission in Africa would lead two decades later to a girl named Symphony … he let out a single chuckle, it was nothing short of amazing.

~

Zeus strode across Puerta del Sol Plaza and stood beside the statue of the bear climbing the madrone tree, Madrid's rendezvous spot. A fierce Iberian sun was beating down on the organized chaos of people, cars, and buses streaming through the square.

A young, pale-skinned woman in black jeans and tank top approached Zeus from out of the cluster of people at the base of the statue. She had a *Segundamano* newspaper rolled under her arm, for identification purposes.

"Cristina?"

She greeted him with a formal kiss on each cheek. "Let's walk this way." She pointed toward Arenal Street, now a pedestrian street. "How was your flight?"

"Too long. I hope you have good news for me."

"You are in luck. You will see Txomin Sunday."

"Sunday. That's five days away."

Cristina regarded him for an instant as they walked. "We can only obtain a visitor's permit like this one once a month. Normally he is not permitted to receive visitors who are not family. Prison rules."

"I can't wait that long."

She chuckled to herself. "Then rearrange your schedule."

Zeus shook his head. Sunday would set him back three, maybe four days, too long of a delay, particularly for Symphony Messina. "It has to be sooner. What options do we have?"

"Options? None."

"There are always options."

She glanced up at him, a smirk on one side of her face. "You should be satisfied with what we've done for you. We only did this because Txomin asked as a favor to him. There are risks for us—in case you don't know."

"The organization will be better off if it's done sooner," he said.

"There's no other way, if you want it done quietly. I was told that you want to keep a low profile."

"Yes, but Sunday's too late. It could—scratch that—it will ruin our plans."

They crossed the street into one of Plaza Mayor's centuries-old archways. She reflected on it for a few more steps. "There is another kind of special request we can try. But it would be impossible without the press finding out. Someone in the prison system always alerts them when it's done this way."

"How soon can I see him with this other special pass?"

"We might be able to set it up for the day after tomorrow, if we work fast. But you will face a gauntlet of reporters if it is done in this manner."

"That can be solved."

Cristina gave him her full smirk and a one-shoulder shrug. "It's your call."

"How long will they let me speak with him?"

"Ten minutes, more or less." Then she added with a tone of warning, "They videotape the entire visit. So you will have to maintain your conversation strictly within the glossary code or else he will walk away."

Zeus knew what Cristina meant by a "glossary." It was a list of word substitutions prepared beforehand to codify the conversation he would have with Txomin, to prevent the prison officials listening in from understanding what they said. The problem was that a glossary would require Symphony Messina's identity to be revealed to whoever was charged with preparing the glossary, and that Zeus couldn't have, as it would be the same as informing the entire ETA organization.

Txomin was the only ETA leader left with the kind of authority to order the girl's release and get it done without the different factions interfering. But if the purpose of his mission were to get out before Txomin secured Symphony's protection, it would be a disaster, maybe even her death.

"Cristina," he said. "Our friend approved this visit of mine knowing very well that we have to keep my business strictly between him and me. A glossary would reveal classified details that would ruin everything."

"Then I don't see how it can be done." She shrugged again. "It is standard procedure, necessary to avoid slips."

"A glossary is an effective system, no question, but the wrong one this time. It will endanger the lives of friends, colleagues of yours as well."

"I don't know how it could be approved without a glossary."

"Let Txomin decide. I know he will agree. He and I will do fine without one."

Cristina halted in front of a souvenir shop window along the plaza's grand courtyard. She folded her arms over her breasts. "All I can do is pass on your request."

"Fair enough. But, please, time is the one thing we don't have. OK?"

They looked at each other for an instant. Zeus realized Cristina's expressionless face was as close as a smile he was going to get from her.

"I will see about a press pass for you. But remember: there are no guarantees."

TWENTY-FIVE

Mondragón

BALDO MANEUVERED his van into a parking space down the street from Café Donosti. "You can't come with me," he said to his brother, Gorka, sitting beside him. "They are waiting for me to talk about serious matters and you can't be there—you shouldn't even be here."

"I can help you with the cooking for the prisoners but I cannot go sit with them?"

"You listen to me well." Baldo grabbed him by the shirt. "You better not utter a word that you have seen the prisoners. If you do, you will get me and yourself killed. You tell your shadow about it, you tell Mother or Father, and I will kill you myself."

Baldo and Gorka, their matching long hair sweeping angrily, jumped out of the van and marched off in opposite directions.

The café's outside lights were off. Baldo knocked on the glass. The proprietor, apron over his round paunch, unlocked the door. "*Pasa. They're in back.*"

Aitor and Patxi stopped talking and watched Baldo's approach. They each had a tall *cubata* in hand and a relaxed, celebratory look in their eyes.

Baldo knew why. That morning the leadership had received Estrada-Uribe's second ransom installment. Baldo didn't think it befitting a celebration. Not after the loss of so many of their compeers and definitely not with the American *matón* still on the loose.

He pulled a chair. "Your pets have been fed. I washed everything so you do not have to do it tomorrow. But I have to confess I am getting very tired of doing everything myself. When is the *iparralde* coming back?"

Patxi grinned at Aitor.

Aitor offered Baldo a cigarette. He had always liked the boy, reminded him of himself at another time. Although at times, he could not remember why. "You took care of them well?"

"Yes. But Minot, where is he?"

"He is doing his duties, the same as all of us. What is the problem, are you dissatisfied with your chores?"

"These chores, as you call them, have always been carried out by two persons. But Minot is never here to help."

"Ha!" Patxi let out. "As if you two get along so well."

"Look who's talking. Besides, we get along professionally."

Patxi forced another laugh. "That *iparralde* does not get along with anyone."

"Never mind that," Aitor broke in. "He will be back when he is done with his assignment. For the time being, you have to continue doing the shopping and going to the plant twice a day."

Baldo swung his arms up. "How about you two? I have done kitchen duties for three days in a row. Tomorrow is the baptism of my nephew. Am I expected to miss it?"

"Patxi and I have to go out of town tomorrow to see Pedro and Mertxe. The new *zulo* is not yet finished. There is no one else to relieve you."

Baldo puffed hard on his cigarette. He wanted very much to protest but he knew the limits. "I cannot miss my nephew's baptism."

"So work it out around your schedule," Aitor said. "How are the humidifiers and fans working?"

"I did the electrical work well so they are functioning well. I just don't like to leave the fan exposed where *la loca* can get at it. She could use it to attack us."

"So be careful."

"It looks like she's up to something. She has been eating all her food, cleaning up the plate. It's not normal for her."

"Perhaps she is eating for two," Patxi said. "She has not used the compresses, at least not for the use they were made for."

"I am certain she is hatching a plan of some kind," Baldo insisted. "I can feel it. She's been acting very docile and behaved. What if she and the *pieza* have been communicating?"

Aitor and Patxi glimpsed at each other. "Not possible," Aitor said, despite his own suspicions, but to avoid feeding Baldo's. "She is making an effort to take care of herself and that is good for us."

Baldo drew the ashtray to him and snuffed out his cigarette. "I do not trust her, never have."

Aitor glanced at the wall clock and gestured for the others to put their heads together. "As for the American hitman," he said with a smoky sigh. "We still do not know whether he's dead or alive. They have searched the riverbanks in every community within a fifty kilometers radius. The Ertzaintza is waiting for orders to start dredging the river. But—" He shook his head and added, "It would be perfect if he is dead. But if he is alive, we know he'd be coming our way."

The proprietor came out from behind the counter and signaled it was time to go. "Everything is still open in the plaza," he said, "if you want to keep drinking."

Outside the café, Baldo drove off in his van and Patxi rode home in Aitor's Citroen.

The night was hot but pleasant. The bars and cafés in the town's main plaza were packed. "It looks like Sunday evening out there," Aitor said as they drove by.

Patxi studied his friend for a moment. "You look like you are enjoying this thing."

"What thing?"

"The assassin on the run and all the commotion it has caused since the newspaper reported it. You know what I'm saying."

Aitor turned his head in a weak attempt to deny it. "That is nonsense."

"I know you, *amigo*. I can see you are delighted with the rumors."

"You make it sound as if I wrote those newspaper articles. They are also rumoring Miguel Angel and the girl are in San Sebastián, in Bilbao, even in Pamplona. People always talk. This is why we are building a new *zulo* far from here."

"Yes, but they're not in any of those places. They're here."

The car lurched to a stop at a traffic light. Aitor glanced at Patxi. "What do you propose we do then?"

Patxi's graying brows shot up in fake astonishment. "You are asking me? You, the one with all the ideas? Besides, you and I know what the solution is."

Aitor was not listening. "When was the last time you saw anything like this?" He pointed his chin out the window at a crowded outdoor café. "Look at the town. They are ready for war."

Patxi winced. "War? I think you're seeing things that are not there, my friend. They are angry now, yes, because a few of our compatriots have been killed. But they will get over it just as fast. What I see is a great catastrophe if we don't set the girl free, now.

Aitor agreed. "But," he said with a dreamy tone that Patxi had never heard his old friend use, "Can you not see what that assassin has done? He has created a collective menace for us. In their minds, we did not fail to catch the assassin. It exposed the incapacity of Madrid to protect the Basque Country. Foreign aggression always strengthens the cause of independence."

Patxi shook his graying head. "Bah, now you sound like our newspapers."

"Do not misunderstand me. We will keep our noses to the ground and accomplish what we have set out to do. But, damn it Patxi, are you not glad to have Euskadi on our side again? For me, there is no price you can put on that."

~

The couple inside the parked Peugeot across the street from Patxi's building sank under the dashboard when Aitor's Citroen came up the unlit street.

"That is the car," said the big-hair silhouette in the Peugeot. "It's them."

"You're sure it is them?"

"Uh-huh. Every people here know they are ETA," big hair said with a heavy Andalusian intonation.

"You better be sure."

"I know them. How much more sure you want me to be?"

Aitor's Citroen stopped in front of a two-story building further up the block. The narrow street was empty and dark except for a single corner lamppost. Patxi stepped out of the car and walked around to the driver's window. He spoke to Aitor for a minute, waved good night, and entered the building. Aitor's Citroen disappeared up the hill.

Big hair watched the American at the wheel, captivated and a little frightened by the lacerations and bruises on his arms and hands.

"You did well," Crimmil said. "What's your name again?"

"Brandy is my name and love is my game," said the husky-voiced Andalusian.

It made Crimmil laugh. "Who taught you to say that?"

"I have many British and North American friends."

"No shit."

"So, I go now?" Brandy said with coquette hesitancy.

"You haven't finished your job yet."

"My job?" Brandy said, feinting confusion and broke into a bawdy laugh. "Oh, that job. It will cost you extra for that."

Five minutes later, Brandy sat up, straightened up his mammoth red wig, shored up his sequined dress, reapplied his lipstick by the glow of the courtesy light, and lit up a cigarette.

"Put it out."

Brandy switched off the light.

"Put out the cigarette."

"No. I want to smoke. You Americans—"

"Get rid of it."

"If you don't like, then pay and I go," Brandy said with a conceited swing of his chin.

A hand came out of nowhere and backslapped the cigarette out of his painted mouth.

"Hey!" Brandy opened the car door to go, but a brute grip pulled his bony frame back inside.

"Don't get your panties in a bunch. We made a deal, you and me."

"You pay me or I scream. *Tu no me coneces, gilipollas.*"

"Oh, shut the fuck up."

The car door flew open again. Brandy stretched one of his stockinged legs and began to shout *Auxilios* and *Socorros* in a combination of falsetto and full-voiced cries. No pretense in his booming masculine voice anymore.

Crimmil pulled out a wad of cash. "Look. I'll give you all of it if you stay with me." He handed him a few bills to draw him back in. "Take this for now and close the door. Come on. *Por favor.* You are so beautiful," he sang.

The lure worked. "OK." Brandy took the money and sat down, pouting and adjusting his red wig. "But I don't believe you are a Hollywood director. Um, um. You have no art, no elegance. What do you want me to do now? I told you I don't like pain."

"Just keep me company, that's all. But you break our deal and you get nada. *Comprende?*" Crimmil locked the roll of cash in the glove compartment. "You see what I just did? That money there is for you. All of it. I'll give it to you when I come back. But you have to wait here. OK? Here," he handed over a small folded paper. "You finish it if you want to."

"Where you go?"

"Right over there. To see a friend."

"A friend? The *etarra*? Ha!"

"I'll be right back. Promise. Wait for me."

Brandy gave his wig a reluctant shake.

Crimmil pointed at the glove compartment. "Don't you force it open while I'm away. Can I trust you?"

"Yes, of course. What do you think I am?"

"Beautiful. That's what I think you are."

Brandy's makeup cracked with a smile. "I wait a little. Only a little."

Crimmil took the car keys and went around to the back of the car, pulled out a knapsack from the trunk and walked up the cobbled street toward Patxi's building. Brandy brought out a small brass tube from his purse, unfolded the little paper pack, and sniffed the cocaine right out of it.

Fifteen minutes later, Crimmil came out of the building accompanied by a bulky shadow with a manta over his head like a nun's habit, hobbling next to him.

He opened the backdoor and stuffed the bulky man in the backseat. Brandy swung his plastic hair away from his eyes. "Who's that?"

Crimmil flopped down on the driver's seat.

Brandy went mute when he recognized Patxi's bloody face. "Wait one moment," he said with his full masculine voice. "Look, Mister, I don't want problems with ETA. They will kill us."

Crimmil unlocked the glove compartment and said, "Take the money."

Uncertain but eager, Brandy pulled out the wad of cash. "All of it?" he said, gawking at it.

"It's yours."

"I don't know—"

"You want that money?" Crimmil handed him a piece of notepaper. "Do you know this place?"

Brandy squinted at it. "The Mondragón *parque industrial*, yes, but not this address."

"Ask him."

"I don't know ..."

"Ask him, goddamn it."

Brandy laid his arm on the backrest. "You are Patxi, true?"

Patxi nodded yes. "And you are with him?"

"No. I only met him tonight, just a client."

Crimmil cut in, "What did he say?"

"*El Americano*," Brandy said to Patxi. "He wants directions."

Brandy translated. "It's off the Vergara Highway."

"How do I get there?" The car's engine snapped on.

Brandy said he'd show him. He peered back at Patxi and then at Crimmil. "You are not going to kill him?" he said in English.

"Me, kill him? What do you take me for?" Crimmil answered, faking Al Pacino's accent in *Scarface*.

After he broke into Patxi's apartment, Crimmil thought he had again picked on the wrong *etarra* to interrogate when Patxi came charging at him like a suicidal gorilla, ignoring the Glock pointed at his face. It all turned in his favor after he caught Patxi's wife hiding in the kitchen. Once he stuck his gun in her mouth, the gorilla turned into a lamb. All he had to do after that was articulate Symphony Messina's name and he had the big ape eating out of his hand.

"You tell me where she is," Crimmil had told him, "and I no bang-bang you and your wife and your son when he gets home. *Comprende?*"

They zoomed past a road sign with the name Arrasate-Mondragón with two red lines across it.

"How far is this place?"

"Very close," Brandy said, his Adam's apple twitching with every dry swallow. "One kilometer more."

Crimmil grinned at himself in the rearview mirror, his eyes in the light of a passing car. He'd have to remember that look in his eyes for the movie, zoom right into it and fill the screen with it. The weary but burning eyes of a man on the verge of triumph.

Brandy would not dare look behind him anymore. Out of the corner of his shadowed eye, though, he noticed Patxi squirming under the blanket, untangling himself from his bindings. He glanced at Crimmil in terrified silence, unable to sit still, expecting something terrible to happen at any second.

Crimmil caught sight of the words *Parque Industrial* on the sign over the highway. Above it, the first light of daybreak appeared over the hills. A million-dollar, red carpet day was about to dawn.

"Tell him to go very slow now," Patxi said.

"What did he say?"

"He said to slow down, the turn is coming up."

"Tell him to slow down even more."

Brandy did as he was told.

Then, when Crimmil slowed the car almost to a stop as he searched for the turn, Patxi lunged forward with an animal growl and clasped his thick arms around Crimmil's neck in a crushing stranglehold.

Crimmil let out a choking groan and slammed on the brakes and both men shot forward against the steering wheel. Patxi landed piggyback on top of Crimmil. Brandy, too frightened to scream, grabbed hold of the wheel and pulled out the ignition key. The engine went silent but the car kept rolling on until it bounced over the divider curb and came to a dead stop across the opposite lane.

Like a bull wrestler, Patxi locked his forearms tighter around Crimmil's neck and tried to lift him out of the driver's seat and over the backrest. Crimmil clawed at the car roof, kicked the dashboard, choking and writhing like a fish. He tried to reach for his pistol, but Patxi's choke-hold was draining his head of blood, making him lose consciousness. Somehow, he felt the Glock in his fingertips and pulled it out of the breakfront holster in his belt. He fired one shot. The bullet tore through the backrest toward the rear.

Brandy shrieked and threw himself out the door and stumbled away from the car, his red hair wig in one hand, the wad of cash in the other.

Patxi knocked the gun out of the American's hand too late. Crimmil disentangled himself of the two hairy arms that had almost squeezed the life out of him, opened the door and pushed himself onto the pavement. Patxi fell back on the rear seat, his hands pressed over his gut, blood spilling over everything.

The sparse traffic on the highway came to a halt. No one risked coming near them.

"Where you going?" Crimmil yelled like a drunk at Brandy. "Get back here."

Scared of being shot, Brandy halted and started to walk backward away from him, as if something even more terrifying was looming behind the *americano*.

Crimmil wheeled and saw what Brandy had seen: a posse of four men in long raincoats, armed with hunting rifles and machetes, marching shoulder to shoulder toward him out of the morning mist. Beautiful photography had it been a movie.

Crimmil looked around but saw no place to hide. He aimed the Glock at Patxi, the light draining out of his eyes. "Come any closer and your friend's a dead man," he warned them.

Two more hunters in raincoats appeared from the other side of the road. Three others crossed the divider. "I'll fucking kill him."

They did not seem to hear or see him. They kept advancing toward him, resolute, like flesh-and-bone Terminator machines.

Crimmil squeezed the trigger and what never ever happened to the star of the movie at the end of the last reel happened to him then. His gun failed to fire.

With his face in a mask of horror, Gunther Crimmil dropped to his trembling knees, his eyes shocked awake by the here-and-now physical reality avalanching over him like the brightness of theater lights coming on when the show is over.

He begged, screamed for his life, his sweat-soaked nonfictional existence, until the machete-wielding ghosts, like butchers gone berserk, hacked him into silent lumps of blood-splattered skin.

TWENTY-SIX

New York City

FINISHED WITH THE day's billing, Tess tapped the enter button of her keyboard and looked at the time. Almost six o'clock, midnight in Madrid. She gave her cubbyhole a depressed look. Zeus should've called by now.

She grabbed a handful of files, research that had been piling up since the Messina case began consuming all her time. She dropped them on an adjacent worktable. There was still time to make it to the gym, if she left now. She needed to release some of the restless anxiety this case was causing her.

She opened her closet, brushed her hair in front of the mirror inside the door and grabbed her purse. She was about to exit when someone knocked on the door.

Spillman, shirtsleeves rolled to his elbows, opened the door before she had time to answer. "Going home?"

"Yes. Why?"

"Messina's coming at eight."

"I haven't heard from Aguirre yet."

"I need you anyway."

"OK. I'll be back before eight."

At ten to eight, Tess, fresh from her workout, stepped out of a cab. An ashy-blue light shone over Manhattan, reflecting off the glass-and-steel skin of the fifty-story skyscraper wherein Lance Cohen & Spillman Law Offices occupied floors sixteen, seventeen, and eighteen.

The hour-long session of aerobics and sauna had reawakened her spirit. It showed in the way she beat her heels across the lobby. "Hi ya, Walter."

"Back already?" The night guard smiled.

"Duty calls."

The LC & S receptionist was gone but the lobby lights were on, their white luminosity reflecting on the polished brass surnames on the long marble wall in the entryway. Tess moved past the empty offices and dark monitor screens. A voice, loud and harsh, held forth in the executive suite, too far away for her to understand the words. The sound followed her all the way to her office. She picked up the client's files and walked right out.

As she neared the executive wing, she recognized Joey Messina's unmistakable bark. Tess halted several steps before she reached the half-opened double doors into Spillman's office.

Messina was fuming. "I'm paying you a damn fortune to keep this kind of crap under control. What good are you if you can't keep track of the guy?"

"Aguirre has complete freedom of action," Spillman replied with his usual businesslike calm. "You approved it. Nothing we can do now."

"That's bullshit and you know it. What do you think I dished out ten Gs for an untraceable phone for, then?"

"It's only been a day since his last call. Have a little patience."

"Yeah, sure, but meantime my people lost him over there."

"Lost him? Wait a second—"

Tess backed away two steps when she heard Spillman push his chair and step around the desk.

"What do you mean lost him? Joseph, tell me you didn't have him followed. Tell me you didn't breach his main condition in the contract."

"Fuck the contract."

Spillman's voice sank an octave. "You better think about that. That man walks away because you breached; you still have to pay him the full amount. It's locked in."

"Do you honestly think I'm going to let those kidnappers walk away like nothing happened? After what they've done to my daughter?"

"Hold it there, Joseph." Spillman turned for the safety of his desk. "I don't want to hear any of that."

"Ah relax. I said I'll take care of the Cuban and I will. He'll get every penny coming to him. If he does his job. But the kidnappers—" Joey's mouth twisted with disgust. "Those pieces of shit are dead meat. No contract's ever going to change that. And if that Cuban thinks he's going to stop me once my daughter is back and he's been paid, the hell with him too. He's nothing."

"I can't sit here and listen to this." Spillman stood up, shaking his elegant baldpate. He opened the liqueur panel and fixed himself a scotch, no rocks.

This was not why he drove to the city each day. Suddenly no money seemed worth this kind of aggravation. He berated himself for getting involved with Thomas Pacelli's charade. All he had to do was keep coming up with maneuvers to keep Messina in town, nothing else. He had agreed to it because, between the two, Pacelli was the client to protect, the one to pamper. Thirty million dollars a year, of which a clean ten-percent went straight into his twin accounts in Israel, compelled him. But now this was getting out of hand. "Joseph, you must give Aguirre the time he needs. Think of your daughter."

"What the hell do you think I'm doing?"

Tess made an about-face and tiptoed back to her office. She slid down on her desk chair. This was not just a breach of contract as Spillman called it, or padding clients' accounts or bending tax laws, the kind of law practice she had learned to accept to keep her career. This was a boldface betrayal of all she held sacred.

She called Spillman's office. "Is Messina in yet?"

"Yes, get over here."

What angered her most as she marched back to the executive wing was Spillman's attitude. Was he going to allow Messina to violate the one condition that had made his agreement with Zeus possible? Was he going to let him backstab him like that?

The room was silent when Tess entered. Two standing lamps illuminated the area around the desk, casting shadows on their faces. New York was a chaotic pattern of light and darkness outside the window. Spillman waved a hand for her to come closer. "Has Mr. Aguirre called yet?"

Joey's armchair squeaked when he glanced over his shoulder at Tess.

"No," she said. "I haven't heard from him since before his flight."

"When did he say he'd call?" Joey asked without looking at her.

She shrugged. "Updates are at his discretion."

"No clue?" Spillman said.

"Why? Is there an urgency?"

"Damn right, there's an urgency," Joey snapped. "And there's going to be one every time I don't know where the Cuban is and what he's doing."

Spillman cast his eyes down at his desk. Tess averted hers toward the window. "If you recall, Mr. Aguirre is not subject to a schedule—"

"Woh, don't give me that crap," Joey cut her off. "This isn't about him. This is about bringing my daughter back home safe and sound. This is about me knowing if the guy's doing what I'm paying him to do, every minute of the day."

"Joseph," Spillman said, afraid of what he might say next in front of Tess. "I think Tess is aware of that."

"Oh yeah? I'll tell you what." Joey leaped off the chair, his finger aiming at Spillman. "The Cuban says he doesn't want interference. Fine. He only wants to talk to Tess here. Let'm. But if by tomorrow I still don't know where he is and what's he doing with my money, we're done here. You got that? Done."

Joey started for the door, then stopped. "This guy was your freaking brilliant idea," he reminded Spillman. "So I'm only going to tell you this once. Don't screw me on this, counselor. This isn't business. It's my daughter we're dealing with here. You find this guy and you find him quick. 'Cause, God forbid you don't. I won't be coming back here as a client." Joey glanced at Tess, stared her down, and walked away.

Tess waited until she and Spillman were in the elevator to ask the question that had been burning inside her. She glanced at the red digital numbers on the elevator panel. "Arthur, how long have you known the client has no intention of honoring the contract?"

"Of course he's going to honor it."

Tess glanced down at her hands, a sick feeling gripping her stomach. Her mentor, the man she admired, a man she had substituted for her father in her heart—why was he deceiving her? "It didn't sound like it to me."

"That's absurd. Don't you know Joey Messina by now? He was just venting, being his big-shot self. You were there when we closed the contract. Did it look to you then that he'd go back on his word?"

Tess's eyes glazed as she watched the elevator numbers light up like a countdown. Joey had not just been his threatening self. She had heard his mobster's rage in his voice. He was determined to kill the kidnappers, probably had been all along. The elevator eased to a halt on the main floor.

"Tell me something," she said, stepping in between the opened doors. "Are you going to let that man turn us into accessories to his revenge killings?"

"Oh please. What's wrong with you tonight?" Spillman stayed inside on his way to the basement garage. "We're not going to do anything of the kind. What makes you say that?"

She pressed her lips together, trying not to spill out what she had heard outside his office, aware of the implications. "You have to ask? You involved me in this case, Arthur. Practically threatened my position in the firm if I didn't succeed in bringing Aguirre around—"

"But you did," he said, without letting her finish. "And you did it because that is what we do. Look, I don't know what's on Messina's mind any more than you do. Whatever it is, it's out of our hands."

"Since when?"

"Since always. If the client refuses to follow our counsel there's nothing we can do. That's just the way it is. But whatever he does, he will remain our client and us his legal counselors. Because that is what we do."

"That doesn't mean we have to stand aside and let him breach his contract with impunity. Aguirre is also a client of this firm. It was your idea to represent both sides. I'm not going to look the other way on this."

Spillman tucked his chin and gave her a smile, his paternal version. "Tess, what's going on? Did something happen in Miami?"

"I did what you wanted me to do. That's what happened."

The lobby guard came up, drawn by their voices. "Everything OK?"

"Oh yes, thanks," she replied.

The guard scowled into the elevator. "Oh, good evening there, Mr. Spillman."

Spillman took Tess's arm and walked her to the glass doors. "Listen to me, Aguirre is going to need a cash transfer from us sometime soon. Am I right?"

"Yes."

"He'll probably call you tonight or tomorrow. When that happens, Messina will relax."

"When that happens he'll send his goons after Aguirre so he can get his revenge."

"No, he won't. He's just a control freak, and a desperate one at that. And with good reason. You'd be desperate too if you were going through what he's going through."

Tess bit her lower lip. They stepped out to the sidewalk. Manhattan's East Side was bumper to bumper with traffic in the evening glow.

"You know," Spillman said as if he had just seen the light. "I know what the problem is." He held her arms in his outstretched hands. "I've been overworking you with this case. I have."

She tried to argue.

"No, no," he insisted. "I saw the billing sheet. Thirty-two hours so far this week. And it's only Wednesday. You're a researcher, Tess. The best we have. This business with Messina, it's like you said, not in our job description. We've all been going out on the limb for this guy. Especially you. I think you deserve some time off. We'll look into it tomorrow. Promise. A couple of weeks, somewhere nice?"

"Arthur," she tried to protest.

"Do me a favor. Go home. Get some rest. It's what I'm going to do. Everything will look better in the morning. Trust me." Still grinning, he went back inside the building.

Tess watched him until he disappeared into the glass and marble surfaces. A dark breeze came cutting off the East River. Walking home, she could not help feeling like a traitor to her profession, to herself, and to Zeus. It was she who had sold him on the legitimacy of the case, assured him of Messina's sincerity. And it would be her who Zeus would accuse of betraying him if Messina had his way. Spillman's little speech when she started at the firm came back to her now, filled with new meaning. "In this profession of ours," he said, "emotions can and will interfere with our better judgment. That is a signal to go back to the beginning and ask yourself what made you choose the business of Law as a career. If you remember, you'll stay on course. If you don't, stay on course anyway."

It was precisely what Tess intended to do.

TWENTY-SEVEN

Madrid

THE TELEPHONE ON the night table rang with a foreign trill. Zeus rolled over and reached for it. It was nine-thirty p.m. and a slip of graying daylight was coming through the drapes. Summer in Madrid.

Pablo's mocking rasp came through the line. "*Soy yo, compañero.* Sorry to interrupt your *siesta*, but the work, it's ready."

"Already?" According to his wristwatch, he had been asleep for over two hours. He gave himself a weary look. He was fully dressed.

"I'll be there in an hour or so. You're still up by Ventas?"

"Same number, same portal." Then, "Want to have dinner?"

"Sure." He yawned.

"Then bring a couple of loaves of bread and we'll have some cold cuts and beer."

"OK."

"Don't forget the bread."

A half-hour later Zeus was on a taxi heading north on Alcala Street in Madrid's fluid summer traffic. He reached the Ventas area sooner than expected. The driver let him out in front of a convenience store near the Plaza de Toros. He bought two baguettes and walked the rest of the way.

A warm breeze accompanied him across the spacious grounds outside the bullring, its mysterious brown Moorish arches in the light and shadows of the streetlights.

On the Calero Bridge, over the multi-lane M-30, he noticed a white car slowing down to a stop for no apparent reason. It forced the other cars to veer into a single lane. Two blocks later, when he shuffled across the avenue, he saw the same car make a U-turn at the intersection and slow down to walking speed.

Zeus looked at the baguettes in his hand and back at the car and suddenly it hit him. The two-faced fat man ... He dunked the bread in a trash container and dashed across the avenue's six lanes and around the corner into a side street, climbed the stone stairway alongside the Comisaría de Policia building, and came back down on one of the dead-end streets behind the car parks. He was not sure if the white car had followed him as he made the corner, but now, looking over his shoulder, he was sure it hadn't.

He found the address. It was a building two blocks long and fourteen stories high, made up of tiny apartments. Zeus went inside and stood by the glass door for an instant. He did not see the white car.

Pablo answered the intercom and buzzed him in. "Fifth floor, the door across the hallway."

A sensor switched on the lobby lights as he entered. The elevators sliding doors opened and he pressed the seventh-floor button. When he reached it, he sent the elevator down one flight and took the stairs to the sixth floor.

From the corner of the stairwell, he peeked down the fifth-floor hallway and listened for a few moments. He noticed nothing suspicious, until he stood up and came face to face with an elderly woman in a print housecoat, glaring at him from one of the doors.

Zeus put his index finger on his lips. "Shhh. Got off on the wrong floor, that's all."

"Don't shush me," the woman snapped. "Are you also going to the fifth floor?"

"Why do you ask? Your downstairs neighbors are making too much noise?"

"Yes, much too much in-and-out. I am an old woman and I need to rest."

"Do not worry, *señora*," he told her as he stepped backward into the elevator. "Just go back inside, everything's all right."

Zeus rode all the way down to the main floor and rushed out of the building. At the corner bar, he asked for a public telephone and dialed Pablo's number.

"Where are you?" Pablo said. "Any problems?"

"Should there be?"

"I don't know. I'm hungry. Get over here. I'm waiting for you to eat."

"I don't think I'll be able to make it tonight."

"I thought you were in a hurry?"

"Not as much as you seem to be, old friend."

"That's a curious statement."

"Who's in your house?"

"Here? My wife and my cat."

"Are you sure? I've heard differently."

Pablo remained silent for a spell, and then let out a loud guffaw. "You are one cautious individual, *compañero*. I've always said it. But I'm sorry. You could not be more mistaken. There is no one here except us. Very disappointing, Aguirre. Very disappointing."

It was not what Zeus wanted to hear. "You're going to have to get your own bread tonight. I'll get back to you later."

He walked out of the bar, cut through the crowded sidewalks and hopped in a taxi in front of the fountain at the Donostiarra Avenue roundabout. He had anticipated some kind of interference. Except he had not expected it to come through Pablo, nor this soon. Now he had no choice but to prepare to go into deep cover, move as though he was on the run, work in the shadows. Now he was going to earn his money.

"To Callao Plaza," he said to the driver.

He didn't go back to the aparta-hotel on Fuencarral. Instead, he took a room at a hostel on San Bernardo Street. He called the hotel from his room, settled with the desk by phone, and had a taxi pick up his belongings and bring them to the hostel.

At around midnight, the night man brought his bags up to his room.

"Any problems?" Zeus said with a casual air.

"None," the young man replied as he set the suitcase and the briefcase on the bed. "I gave the *taxista* the gratuity as you said."

"Good. Here you are." Zeus handed the man two ten-euro notes.

He got a big grin in return. "*Muy agradecido. Buenas noches.*"

Zeus locked the door and called Cristina. She had nothing for him yet. He could not stop thinking about Pablo. Even back in the old days, you could count on the fat man for anything except his integrity.

The bathroom was out in the hallway. He grabbed a couple of towels and took a long shower. Afterward, he lay down on the stiff double bed in Spain's time zone and tried to put his thirty-two-hour day to rest. An edginess under his skin kept him awake. His back ached.

It was one in the morning, seven p.m. in New York. It was a good hour to telephone Tess. He knew she would be expecting an update. Except that was out for now. First, he would have to find out who had intercepted Pablo before he called anyone involved. The leak could be coming from anywhere, New York included.

TWENTY-EIGHT

Parque Industrial, Mondragón

THAT MORNING Baldo and brother Gorka arrived at the plant in the rented tuxedos they wore at their nephew's baptism ceremony and the subsequent dusk-to-dawn *fiesta*. They staggered out of the van in a nasty mood. They had missed the prisoners' last feeding and Baldo knew he too would be in mortal danger if Aitor were to find out the prisoners had gone unchecked for fourteen hours.

Squint-eyed in the early morning sun, Baldo removed his necktie and inserted the key in the metal door. When they entered, Carcelero was there waiting, tail-wagging, eager to welcome them after a day of fasting, his dusty paws all over their tuxedos. Baldo shoved the animal aside. The dog stuck his snout in the plastic bags with the food scraps he had brought from the banquet to save them from having to prepare the prisoners' meals from scratch. "Carcelero, fuck off."

Gorka laughed. "That poor dog is dying of hunger."

They hurried past the dust and grease-covered machines toward the kitchen area. Baldo removed his tuxedo jacket and glanced at the wine stain on his white dress shirt, also a rental. He opened the cupboard. No clean trays.

"Take off your jacket and wash two trays," he said to his brother.

"And what are you going to do?"

"I'll feed the dog and open the *zulo*."

A few minutes later, they piled the prisoners' food on the trays in the one-man elevator. Baldo was unworried of anyone catching his brother there, despite the grave violation it was. All the others were out of town on business and he was sick of having to feed the prisoners twice a day for days on end without anyone helping him, not even allowing him at least one day off for a family celebration. Besides, his brother Gorka was a Jarra youth and an aspiring ETA commando. More than enough credentials to give him the right to be there.

Gorka slid his chubby frame into the elevator capsule.

"Keep your fingers inside," Baldo warned him as he gripped the pulley chains.

The capsule-shaped elevator did its slow, creaking descent into the manhole. When it hit the *zulo* floor, Gorka felt for the light switch on the wall by the landing. He flipped it three times. "The light doesn't go on."

Baldo thought it odd. "Are you certain? I changed that bulb myself less than a week ago."

"Of course, I'm certain. What does it take to switch on a light?"

"You see any light under the cell doors?"

"Nothing."

"Wait then."

Baldo looked inside a metallic cabinet and came back with a new bulb and a flashlight, and dropped them into the manhole for Gorka to catch. After some trouble reaching the socket and changing the bulb, Gorka tried the light switch again. Nothing happened.

"It's still as dark as a wolf's mouth. What should I do?"

Baldo would have been happy to forget about it and go to sleep, but he thought he was already in plenty of trouble if he could not find what was wrong with the electrical connections. "Gorka," he hollered down the manhole. "I will raise the elevator and come down. In the meantime, feed the girl."

"What about the CD player? It does not go on either. There is no power in the entire *zulo*."

"We'll do without it." With cranky pulls of the noisy chain, Baldo raised the elevator one-arm swing at a time, a slow and clumsy operation.

Gorka picked up a tray from the floor and set it down by Symphony's cell door. Then he called up for the key. Baldo dropped it down one side of the manhole.

"Be careful when you open her door. Just leave the tray inside and get out."

After fumbling a few moments in the dark, feeling for the keys on the dirt floor while holding the flashlight, Gorka found it and unlocked the cell's door.

Symphony was ready for him in the darkness within.

TWENTY-NINE

Madrid

ZEUS FOUND A neighborhood bar near the hostel and had his first full meal since he landed.

He asked for Castilian soup and grilled hake and salad for his main course. A Metro map lay folded by his elbow as he ate. He studied it between bites, his gaze switching between the map and the loud TV set up on the wall.

The wave of violence against ETA dominated the national news.

"Investigations into the assassinations of alleged members of ETA continue in the Basque Country ... Another *etarra* was killed in a shootout early this morning in Guipuzcuoa ... a Gara newspaper article suggests industrialist Estrada-Uribe's possible involvement in the crimes ... attorneys for Estrada-Uribe reject it as shameful slander and demand a retraction ..."

Zeus was still trying to figure out who could have gotten to Pablo. Too many interested parties in this operation, starting with ETA itself. His business with Txomin was enough of a security concern for ETA to want to keep an eye on him. But his instincts told him they weren't the ones who'd gotten to Pablo. Judge Garzón's people had their motives too, for diametrically opposite reasons. The same as Spain's CNI, state security, and whatever other European agencies with interest in the case were good candidates. Then there was the FBI, of course. For all he knew they were onto everything like Spillman had said, hoping for a huge payoff in gangsters and terrorists and what-have-you. There was no end to it.

Zeus picked up a pen and circled several Metro train combinations on the map. He finished the last of his red wine and Casera and signaled the waiter to his table.

"Would you like your dessert now?"

"No, a solo coffee will do."

Zeus folded the map and slipped it in the pocket of the blue Real Madrid windbreaker he'd purchased that morning as a low-level disguise for his encounter with Pablo—if there was going to be one. He finished his coffee and walked to the public phone at the end of the counter.

"This is what you're going to do if you want the money," he said the instant Pablo answered.

"*Cojones*, Zeus. What's with you?"

"Do you want the rest of the money?"

"Of course I do."

"Then shut up and listen. You're going to bring me the work yourself. Go to the Metro station—"

"Are you *loco*? I'm not going down into the Metro. Have you any idea the stairs and walking I'd have to do? I'm too old for that kind of shit. Come to my house as we agreed …"

Zeus remained silent until Pablo ceased whining. Then, "You are wasting your energy complaining. You know me. This is going to be my way or no way. So pay attention."

"I know why you're doing this. Shame on you for thinking I'm setting you up."

"Don't personalize it, old friend. We all have outside pressures. Go to the Ventas Metro stop, go in the last door of the last car and take it until Diego de Leon, step off and call me from there."

"Wait, are you going to send me in one of those runarounds to see if I am being shadowed?"

"Do you want the money or not?"

Pablo was about to start up again but Zeus cut him off. "Get going and call me the instant you get there. If you call, I'll know you want the money. If not, it sucked seeing you again."

For the next thirty minutes Zeus had Pablo make several random Metro transfers, going from one underground station to another and calling him for instructions on where next to go. Zeus followed him at a distance until he was reasonably satisfied no one was tailing him. Then he called Pablo and told him to get off at a quiet station on the 9 Purple Line.

Zeus made his way toward the last Metro car. From the door between cars, he spotted Pablo's doughy bulk sprawled on the seat next to the last set of doors. There were a few passengers in the car now, most of them by the exits as the train approached the end of the line. "Get off and call me as you've been doing," he said into his mobile. "Stop whining and do what I say."

At the stop, Zeus zipped up his blue breaker to his neck and stepped onto the station's platform behind two women.

Pablo lifted his massive frame and dragged himself out of the car. He looked as though he had run a marathon. Perspiration had soaked through to the armpits of his suit jacket. He had his mobile phone in his hands, ready to call as instructed.

Before the train's doors closed, Zeus slipped behind him and hauled the fat Buddha toward the end of the platform as the train rolled off.

"Don't say a word," Zeus told him, pushing his forearm into Pablo's dewlaps and backing him against the tiled wall. "Just listen to me." Zeus glanced over his shoulder at the passengers leaving the station.

"Let go of me. You're going to give me a heart attack. I can't breathe." Pablo's face puffed up like a basketball.

A smell of chopped onions wafted into Zeus's nostrils. "Who had you set me up?"

"What?"

Zeus's forearm sunk deeper into the flabby skin between Pablo's chest and chin. "Don't make it worse. Who's setting me up?"

"*Está bien.*" Pablo stopped resisting. "Let go and I'll tell you. It makes no difference to me. It's your fault, anyway."

"My fault. That's a good one." Zeus got a grip of Pablo's tie and twisted it like a tourniquet. "Who are you screwing me for, old friend?"

"*Lo siento, de verdad.* Do you think this was my idea? You brought them to me." Pablo pulled out of his jacket the envelope with the counterfeit documents. "Here, you can have it. You don't have to pay me."

Zeus snarled, "You don't give up, do you?" He stuffed the envelope back in Pablo's jacket and gave the tie another turn. "You think I'm going to fall for that? A heart attack's going to be the least of your problems if you don't start talking."

"Please Zeus, you're choking me. I had no choice. What could I do? I'm at their mercy. They'll kick me out of Spain if I don't collaborate. I can't."

Zeus flashed over his shoulder at the station. A couple of people were looking his way from the opposite platform. He gave the tie another twist. "Stop wasting my time and tell me what I want to know. I'm not going to warn you again."

"What, you're going to kill me? You?"

"Oh not me, but the next train will when you accidentally slip in front of it."

"*Está bien.* It's Judge Garzón's agents. They just appeared in the house last night."

"Garzón?"

"That's right. That is who's after you. Garzón himself. That's what you get for fooling around with *etarras*. I told you."

Zeus looked disgusted.

"What do you expect me to do?" the fat man pleaded. "I'm in this country thanks to them."

"What does he want with me?"

"You know they don't tell me those things."

Zeus tightened the noose.

Pablo groaned, "They were going to arrest you on counterfeiting charges when I gave you the passport. But you've fooled them, Zeus. We lost them five stations ago."

Zeus stepped away from Pablo, a tiny sneer upturning his lips.

If Judge Garzón's agents needed him to make a mistake before they could pick him up, then things were not as bad as he'd thought. He could handle these kinds of limitations, almost preferred it, for motivation.

Fat Pablo would not look him in the eyes. "They really don't want to put you in jail or anything," he said as if to make amends. "They just want to know what you're doing in Spain. At least that's what they led me to believe."

Zeus scanned both ends of the platform. "I have a feeling they already know."

Another train was coming into the station. Pablo gave him a helpless look. "What are you going to do?"

Zeus shoved him away when the train's doors opened, then stepped in the car. "You take the next one."

Through the glass on the doors, Zeus watched Pablo button up his shirt and fixed his tie, a sheepish grin dribbling inside his greasy jowls. "No hard feelings?" he mouthed.

The whistle blew and Zeus took a seat.

~

At the next Metro station, Zeus dumped his windbreaker in a trash container and climbed the stairs to the street. He flagged the first taxi he saw. "To San Bernardo and Gran Vía."

He leaned back on the seat. It felt good inside the air-conditioned taxi. The driver asked which route he wanted him to take—a trick question some Madrid cabdrivers asked to see if it was safe to give the customer the runaround. "The longest one," he said with a weary laugh. "It's nice in here."

The taxi was inching up the M-30 in the three o'clock traffic when Zeus's mobile buzzed in his pocket. Cristina calling. "Good news," she said. "Your visit is on for tomorrow. We'll meet at dinnertime. I'll call back with a location."

Zeus gazed out the window at the municipal mortuary and at the billion-dollar white-marble Mosque over the highway, its minarets like missiles of faith aimed skyward. At least the day was not a complete waste. The meeting with Txomin was going to happen after all. The girl's liberation was one move closer.

On the corner of Gran Vía, the taxi nose-dived to a stop. The driver cursed apologetically and blamed it on the pedestrian traffic. Up San Bernardo Street, Zeus saw several patrol cars double-parked outside the hostel, holding up the traffic.

"Let me out here."

He paid the cab driver and walked up the block. He mingled with the people on the sidewalk, gawking at the police activity outside the hostel. Then he hurried off at double step, dodging bodies toward Gran Vía.

This was more serious than Pablo had made it seem. Much more. Now there was no going back to his room. Everything in it was lost. He slipped his hands in his pockets, feeling every item in them as he moved. It was all he could count on.

He rushed across the width of Gran Vía, sensing that old forsaken feeling of being out in the cold. Now he would have to dig himself underground for real. Deep enough where expert trackers couldn't find him.

Where could he go? Who had the most reliable system of evasion in this country? Who had the best network of safe houses and complete control of the underworld? The irony of it made him grin as he passed the tourists in T-shirts and bared knees enjoying the tempered air of Madrid in summer eves. He sat at a table at an outdoor café and pulled out his cell phone. Perhaps ETA was not his safest alternative, but it was the best he had. Besides, they had no choice but to give him shelter at least until he met with Txomin and for their own peace of mind.

Pablo was right about one thing, he thought as he waited for Cristina to answer. Somehow, he always ended up dealing with these Basques.

THIRTY

In the Zulo

BALDO KNEW THERE was an electrical short somewhere. He had checked the wiring and the circuit breaker box upstairs but didn't find it. That could only mean one thing: the problem was in the filth piled up in the *zulo*, the last place he wanted it to be.

With arms upflung, Baldo grabbed the chains and began to lower the elevator capsule into the underground. Gray patches of sweat formed on the underarms of his rented shirt, the bane of his existence. He had only given the pully one tug when a painful howl erupted out of the manhole.

"Gorka," he yelled down. "Are you all right?"

"She's out of her cell!" Gorka hollered from below. "She's got a knife or something ..."

For an instant, Baldo froze, terrified. "I'm coming down," he shouted, pulling the elevator's chains with furious yanks. "Be careful with her. Don't let her near you."

"Hurry, she's all over me ... I'm bleeding."

Baldo had sensed it coming for days. He knew it would happen sooner or later. Except he believed she had been saving it for him.

"She's going to kill me," Gorka hollered.

"Don't let that bitch dominate you. You hear me?" The cage descent was slow, a few squeaky centimeters at a time. "Hit her hard. Don't be afraid."

What happened between the moment Gorka opened Symphony's cell door and the flash of light he saw when the dehumidifier smashed against his head took but a second. But the preparations leading to it had been in the works for days. Ever since Symphony realized the persistent tapping she kept hearing during the dead of night was not a machine noise, or some burrowing animal, or her imagination, but coming through the raw dirt wall. A muffled pattering so faint at times she had to hold her breath to hear it. After a day or two she realized the tapping ceased whenever the kidnappers were around. There was a pattern to it, too. A rhythm pattern she recognized. Of course! It was the hand-clapping beat of a song Miguel Angel loved. Clap, clap, clap-clap-clap, Let's go! The realization sprung her to her feet. She picked up the bucket and started banging the same rhythm on the wooden-plank as loud as she could, crying out his name with all the force of her being.

Her cries echoed back to her with the muffled sound of her own name.

Two days of near euphoria followed, she and Miguel Angel shouting messages at each other, laughing, crying just to hear each other's voices, working themselves to sensory howls, past the low stink of their day-to-day confinement, until they went hoarse. "So close yet so far away."

To avoid suspicion, they played up their usual miserable appearance whenever the guards came with their meals. Hiding their secret joy was not easy at first, but they managed to do it. During the long unsupervised hours, they comforted and shouted their love for each other and made plans for their future, a future they were determined to have. They discussed escaping, decided on it.

Miguel Angel came up with the idea, simple as it was desperate. He based it on the off chance that a lone guard came to feed them, an improbable occurrence, but not without precedent. "They're getting careless," Miguel Angel told her. "It's become routine. They're bound to make a mistake. We must prepare ourselves for it."

Symphony was ready for anything.

That afternoon, thinking the new guard had come by himself, they went into action.

Using the exposed wiring in his cell, Miguel Angel short-circuited the *zulo* when he heard the elevator's chains rattling. It blacked out the area. Being the only one in direct physical contact with their captors, it was Symphony's job to initiate the attack when the time came.

Symphony had no problem drawing the violent energy and cold blood to do it. The instant the door opened, she slammed the metallic humidifier on top of the black ski mask, then pushed Gorka out of her cell. And now she had him trapped between the jagged stone wall and the sharpened end of her plastic knife pressed under his chin. "*Entra en la celda.*" She shouted at him in Spanish, pulling his mask off. "Get inside the cell, you fat ass."

Red-faced Gorka dropped his flashlight but would not budge. "Punch her in the face, goddamn it. *Dale una ostia, cojones.* You are twice her size!" Baldo kept yelling at him as he worked the elevator chains.

"I can't," Gorka shouted back, his chin on his chest, his stringy hair slicked with blood. "She's going to stab me in the neck."

Symphony kept screaming at him, too, being the *loca americana* Gorka had been warned about, pulling on his tuxedo shirt, kicking him, pushing her plastic knife deeper into his skin. "Get inside, you bastard. Get in the cell."

Miguel Angel's voice broke out now from inside his cell. "Symphony, are you all right? Do you have the keys? Do you have them yet?"

"I have the keys," she answered in English. "But I can't get him to go into the cell." She glanced at the elevator, only three feet off the ground. "Get in the cell, goddamn it. Move! I swear I'll hurt you ..." She poked him with the knife but could not go any further.

Gorka stayed one with the wall.

"Sym, what's going on?" Miguel Angel shouted. "Is the guard inside the cell yet? Unlock my door, hurry."

Symphony raised the flashlight menacingly and sank the plastic into Gorki's throat as deep as she could get it without drawing blood, but could not stab him. His boyish face was the first human face she'd seen since her abduction and she could not summon up that kind of cruelty. She glanced at the keys still hanging from the keyhole on her cell door. "Shit." All she had to do was shove him inside and race to Miguel Angel's door and set him free.

"Symphony, can you hear me?" Miguel Angel pounded the armored door with his fists. "Is he in the cell yet? Come on Sym. It's either us or them."

"He won't move," she yelled. "The guy in the elevator is almost here. OK, you son of a bitch," she said to Gorka. She smashed the flashlight on his head, hard. Gorka grabbed his head and nearly fell, screaming in pain. Symphony grabbed a wooden stool and kicked it under the descending elevator. The stool jammed the cage at a height where it blocked the door from opening. She turned her burning eyes toward Gorka. "You're going inside that cell now or I'm going to kill you."

She sank the plastic knife into the fatty bulge over his belt and Gorka let out an animal-like groan and backed into the cell, a patch of red on his tuxedo shirt. Symphony slammed the door shut, pulled out the keys, looked at them as if she could not believe they were in her hands.

Symphony went through the three keys in the ring, twice, but could not open Miguel Angel's door.

"Please, Sym, please." Miguel Angel begged her to hurry.

"I'm trying." None of the keys fit the lock. They were copies of the same key.

Meantime, Baldo kept stomping on the elevator floor like a caged ape gone berserk. He kicked down on it until the stool snapped apart and the cage tumbled to the ground with a loud metallic crunch.

Baldo did not rush out of the elevator cage. He stepped out slowly as if savoring the moment, the rubber hose in one hand. He stood at an arm's distance from Symphony and aimed the flashlight at her muddy face. "*Es esto lo que buscas, puta?*"

He held up a second key ring and jiggled it.

Symphony felt her soul drain out of her. "You fuck." She backed up to the wall, the plastic knife in her hand.

Baldo unlocked Symphony's cell. "Gorka come out, you fool," he yelled. When his brother stepped out, he showed Symphony the rubber hose. "You pay now," he said with his sneering, broken English. "For this and everything you have done to me."

THIRTY-ONE

Madrid

On Huertas Street, Zeus pressed the buzzer on a brass plate in the doorway of a centuries-old building. Across the cobbled strip stood an even more ancient house, number eighteen, with a plaque claiming writer Cervantes had once lived there. Zeus climbed up the five flights to the top floor, Cristina's and her brother's safe house.

Cristina was waiting by the opened door when Zeus reached the landing. "I would have preferred to keep away from you," she said as a greeting, a half-smile on her pale face. "To me, you are danger personified."

Zeus nodded in wary gratitude.

"But," she said, waving him into the apartment before double-locking the door. "High command's orders were very clear: 'Treat Txomin's Cuban compeer as one of our own.' So here you are. This is all we can offer you."

She swept her hand around at the place, crammed like a student's residence.

Zeus gave her an appreciative nod, then another to her brother, Natxo, who was sitting barefoot, in jeans and a T-shirt next to the computers. "Can't think of another place I'd rather be tonight."

"Maybe it's not what you're accustomed to," Natxo said. "But it's secured." He sounded like the born and bred *madrileño* that he was. "Welcome."

Despite Cristina's initial reluctance, a long productive night followed. Zeus was able to confirm Pablo's intel through their local sources. As it turned out, both his detention order and the raid on his hostel room had been issued by Judge Garzón's office, according to an unencrypted message they received from colleagues in Euskadi.

Natxo was not surprised. "There's little they don't know anymore." He sat with a keyboard on his lap, his bare feet on a work table loaded with computers, digital cameras, copiers, scanners, all the modern implements of forgery of the type Pablo had whined about. "The government has more access to intelligence now than they know what to do with. They've been on your case since you set foot in Spain."

Cristina nodded in agreement from an adjacent desk. "Tomorrow when you enter that prison," she said, working with the classic counterfeiting tools that Zeus was more acquainted with, scissors, razorblades, paste tubes, rubber stamps, "You must handle yourself correctly or you might not get out again."

Zeus tipped his head.

"I say it like this," she added, "because it's not just an in and out process. It will be risky. It could end up bad if it is not done correctly. Bad for you, bad for Txomin, and bad for us. You have to play the role we will assign to you with conviction. Do you understand?"

"I do," Zeus said.

"They do not care too much for ETA in that prison," Natxo said, grinning. The boy had a wicked sense of humor. "For you, it'll be the same as walking into the lion's mouth."

"This is why we are going through all the pains of making up these two new identities," Cristina added. "This is much work, too much to do in one night."

"Could I be of help?"

The inquiry put a tiny smile on Cristina's severe lip line. "You will be, but not yet. Go to the room and rest if you like, take a shower. Tomorrow will be a long day."

"You can help yourself to any of my clothes," Natxo said. "Just don't take my leather jacket."

In the rush to arrange Zeus's meeting with Txomin, they had to forge two different sets of identifications. One set to get him inside the prison grounds without alerting the press, and the official set, the papers he would use once inside the facility. The counterfeit Interior Ministry documents that identified him as the American attorney the Ministry had granted the visit.

"This way," Cristina explained, "the members of the press waiting for Txomin's mystery visitor will not be able to identify you."

"Smart, no?" Natxo said.

Something in Zeus's face made Cristina add, "We have done this trick before. It is the one flaw in their system. The only one we can exploit."

"If any problems arise," Natxo said, "you could always get rid of one set of documents."

"Your option," Cristina threw in with her half-smile.

Zeus gave a long look at the documents and identification cards, fanned out in his hands like playing cards. "Thanks. It's more than I expected."

THIRTY-TWO

North of Madrid

ON AN ISOLATED STRETCH of Old Castile, a modern, non-descriptive group of brick and metal-roofing structures appeared out of the brown sandy hues on the side of the road. At first sight, it reminded Zeus of a small airport because of the high concrete lookout tower.

"Is this it?"

"That is Soto del Real Prison," the driver replied.

The taxi stopped at the checkpoint. Zeus paid the fare and walked toward the security booth. He saw surveillance cameras hanging from eaves, atop metal stanchions, everywhere he looked, the extremes of maximum-security. Two parallel rows of high fencing topped with layers of coiled razor wire surrounded the perimeter like clenched jaws. It reminded Zeus of Natxo's description of Soto del Real Prison. It felt the same as walking into a lion's mouth.

"*Documentos*," the guard in the window said.

Zeus handed in a Spanish DNI card and the *solicitud* letter. After a brief wait the guard gave him a visitor's pass and an identification sticker made out to his cover name, the one intended to mislead the press. He put on a baseball cap and stepped through the turnstile next to the electronic barrier, then took his place in the queue, blending in with the other visitors heading in the same direction.

A guard with a submachine gun hanging from a shoulder strap swung his arm for them to proceed toward the administration building.

A loud buzzer sounded and two yellow metal doors opened. A knot of camera operators was waiting just inside the doors, no doubt hoping to pick out Txomin's American visitor from among the crowd bottlenecking past them. Zeus slipped on his sunglasses and lowered the cap over his face. Under his suit jacket, he wore a T-shirt that advertised a local business, courtesy of Natxo.

A couple of paparazzi types stood with video cameras in the ready beside the guards collecting visitors' passes. Zeus moved past them unnoticed. He followed the queue toward the main security check inside the visitors' hall, then on to the conveyor belt scanner and the long table for a rubber-gloved search. The inspectors made him open the package with the gifts he had brought for Txomin. Cigarettes, books, special foods for diabetics, all acceptable, nothing to confiscate.

"What's in here?" The officer pointed at his briefcase.

"My documentation and a change of clothing."

The officer gave the briefcase's contents a careful check then pushed them to one end of the table and signaled the people behind him to come. As Zeus gathered his belongings, he switched his documentation and replaced the identification sticker on his shirt.

A heavyset prison official stood leaning on an unused conveyor machine, eyeing the inmates' relatives as they entered, greeting the ones he recognized. Off to a side, a gaggle of reporters had gathered by the pressroom door. Zeus overheard them buzzing about Txomin's visitor as he walked past. He heard a reporter ask the heavyset officer if he knew who the mystery American visitor was.

The officer let out a scoffing laugh. "You do not know? I thought you people knew everything."

His colleague at the desk was still laughing when Zeus stood before him with his "official" pass in hand. The guard looked for his name on the monitor screen and frowned when he found it. "Come with me," he said, pushing himself off the chair.

"Is there a problem?"

"You have to go to the *capitanía.*"

The guard showed him to a room where two officers were holding an intense conversation. "*¿Que pasa?*" said the one with the mustache, upset by the interruption.

"This gentleman is the visitor with the special pass for five o'clock."

"Why didn't the gate call it in?"

The heavyset guard shrugged. "*No se.*"

The mustachioed officer waved for the guard to leave. He gave Zeus a scrutinizing up-and-down look. The glare of a tall glass brick window shone behind him. "You don't look like an American lawyer," he said, motioning for Zeus to have a seat.

Zeus chuckled. "You say it because of the informal clothing I'm wearing? Well, it's intentional. I didn't want the press to recognize me."

"You did a good job." Captain Hernández eyed Zeus's documents. "You are here to visit Txomin Arguelles?"

"I've come in answer to a petition he made, yes."

The captain glanced at the officer sitting behind Zeus's chair.

"What is the purpose of your visit, Señor Gómez?" the officer sitting on Zeus's blindside said.

Zeus replied without turning. "As the petition says, I'm a trusts-and-estates attorney from the State of Florida. I've come to settle a bequest for the Arguelles family."

Captain Hernández picked up the document with the Ministerio de Interior letterhead and seal—one of Cristina's forgeries. "Why is the actual amount of the bequest classified?"

"It's the family's wish."

The captain raised his dark eyebrows in fake surprise. "So, you have come all the way from the USA to give an undisclosed amount of money to the number one *etarra*. Interesting."

"My clients in Florida are within their rights to make this request."

The officer behind him stood up. "Condemned terrorists are not free to receive money or inheritances, much less from anonymous sources. Maybe in the United States, but not here."

"I'm aware of that, sir. However, Spanish law permits prisoners to assign these funds to a relative as beneficiary, if they so wish. It's the inheritor's right, and the reason I'm here."

A sudden tense silence held for an instant. "Do you know why this prisoner will be in prison for the rest of his natural life?"

"He was convicted of terrorism."

"Terrorism, yes. But that is only one word, Señor Gómez. It does not show the full picture of the kind of crimes this man has committed. Did you know that he masterminded the massacre of a busload of unsuspecting, innocent people? Not uniformed men, but innocent bystanders, men, women, children blown to pieces. Neighbors found body parts on the roof of a six-story building—"

"I am aware those were the charges against him."

"And this is the man you're bringing money to?"

"I bring money to no one. I am merely performing my professional duties, as you are."

The officer behind him spoke. "You have no misgiving in delivering money to terrorists and mass murderers?"

"No more than your own Minister of Interior had when he approved this visit. Or your own prison system that scheduled it," Zeus said without turning to face the officer. "I was informed that the visit will be recorded on videotape. Is this true?"

"Of course. We will be listening to the conversation with much care. You can be sure of that."

"Then, if you'd be so kind as to allow me to get on with it. You'll have the recording should you need further details."

The desk officer sprung to his feet. "You have ten minutes with the convict."

A prison guard escorted Zeus to a cubicle-sized room for a second body search. A half-hour later two guards accompanied him to the Locutorio, a soundproof cabin with a glass partition and an old telephone, heavy with the stale smell of cigarette smoke. They told him to sit down.

On the other side of the scratched plate glass, a lone green plastic chair sat empty. Zeus leaned back on his chair, eased by the notion that the only reason he had come this far was that Garzón's agents had no idea where he was this afternoon.

The muffled jingle of keys, footsteps, and murmuring of voices broke the silence. An elderly man, soft around the waist but not obese, wearing denim trousers and a white shirt sat down on the opposite side of the glass.

It was Txomin, looking one hundred years older. The hair left on his head, his craggy face and his thick beard were the same shade of gray as the walls. His eyes, once sharp like onyx billiard balls, peered at him through cloudy halos around their irises. He picked up the receiver, signaling to Zeus to do the same.

"*¡Coño, muchacho!*" he said in good humor, putting on a Cuban accent. "*Dichosos los ojos que te ven.*" Fortunate are the eyes that behold you.

"Señor Arguelles," Zeus answered with respectful affection. "A pleasure to meet you."

"You have no idea how very glad I am that you have come," Txomin said, his voice broken with age and emotion. "*Muy contento*. I have to admit, every time I lay eyes on a Cuban like you, I get the feeling something good is going to happen."

Zeus released a breath of modesty. "Can't say I've always been the bearer of glad tidings."

"But my first impression of you," he paused for emphasis. "That is something I will never forget."

Zeus grinned in silence. Some men were chased off by the idea of a debt of gratitude; then there were those who honor it from the heart. Txomin, the killer of innocent people, was of the latter kind. It didn't surprise him. He'd known that about him from long ago.

"This place." Txomin gave a tiny wave of his hand. "If this institution was made for anything, it was made for reflection. It is impossible to forget why one is locked up here. This gigantic complex of buildings of which I am only given ten narrow square meters of reinforced concrete to live in, cold in winter, hot in summer, fills you with a rocklike bitterness that one tries to fight off. But after a while ..." his brows raised with a sign of defeat. "People disappoint you. The ones that you least expect turn their backs on you. They are the ones who hurt you most."

"So how do you handle it?"

"One hour at a time. You can't let your guard down. They don't." He waved his hand again. "You must be the same as the prison guards with yourself. If you allow the bitterness to infect you, then you belong here. And I do not belong here."

Zeus tipped his head.

The old man said, "It is truly good to see you. Your mere presence returns me to a part of my life that now seems as if it happened to someone else. I am not saying it was all good—everyone knows it was not. But it was not all bad either."

"No, it wasn't all bad."

Txomin dipped his head and whispered, "Once you live through the horrors I have seen, including the one you saved me from, you become something else. You do not know it right away, but you do in time."

The old man laid his elbows on the counter and gave him an imperceptible nod to move closer. "Put the phone here," he said, placing the receiver over his mouth to block his facial expressions and lip movements out of the security camera angles.

Zeus leaned forward toward the glass partition, raised the receiver and held it over his lips, chin to chin with Txomin.

"I received word from the Family across the pond," Txomin said, referring to Judge Arsenio's coded message from Miami. "I understand you are here to arrange for the inheritance to be reassigned back to its people."

Zeus nodded. "Have you had the time to consider it?"

"Yes. I have already given instructions. But I wanted to see you and make it official. It was selfish of me, I suppose."

"I'm always glad to see my clients," Zeus said with a loaded grin.

Txomin chuckled and added with a tone of caution, "I hope the family over there appreciates what we are doing. This inheritance has aroused mighty appetites."

"They understand. But the question remains whether everyone on your side of the family will concord. The signals are confusing."

"Yes, well, unanimity has been rather elusive of late," Txomin said with a nod of regret. "There is only so much authority I can yield from here. I suppose you have heard that we are disbanding; or is it the other way around?" He laughed at his own irony. "The truth is we are a big family, full of discrepancies, but too big to disappear."

"I agree."

"Oh," Txomin said as if he had just remembered. "Our expenses, they will be taken care of. Correct?"

"Your beneficiary is willing to assume all expenses. If they're within reason. I would recommend avoiding a figure that he might misinterpret for something else."

"It will be a nominal fee," Txomin said. "We do not want any misunderstandings either."

Zeus nodded in approbation. He had Messina's approval to offer some accommodation fee if his daughter was returned in good health and without needless complications, but not a ransom. A ransom would free him to exact vengeance, which was what ETA's leadership wanted most to prevent.

Txomin said, "I've ordered for the inheritance to be handed over to you along with a note of regret to the beneficiary. We do expect the matter closed after the transaction is completed. Do you think we will have any problems afterward? We have suffered much loss over this already."

"That will depend on the condition of the inheritance."

"As I understand it, the inheritance is untouched," Txomin said. "Exactly as we received it."

"Then I foresee a happy conclusion."

"Do you have his word on it?"

"I have it."

"Is it good?"

Zeus gave him an uncertain smile.

Txomin waved his hand. "Never mind. You are not a fortuneteller. But do not forget, not everyone you will be dealing with here will have your best interests in mind. Expect some skepticism and you would be on the safe side."

"I understand."

"As I said, we have suffered much over this. Lost irreplaceable compeers and I want it to end." Txomin gazed at Zeus from behind his grayed eyebrows. "I have not asked what benefits you are drawing from this affair. Nor do I care to know. All I ask is for you to represent our interests with the firmness we deserve."

Zeus bowed his head. "Of course."

"*Bien.* Now, if that is settled—" Txomin leaned back, signaling the classified part of the conversation was finished. "Let us talk about the old days in Havana for the few minutes we have left. I have been looking forward to it for days."

Three minutes later the intercom line died. Txomin stood up and pressed the palm of his hand on the window plate, his beady old eyes glazed with emotion. Zeus placed his hand flushed with Txomin's on the glass. "*Cuidate, hermano,*" the old man mouthed. "Take care of yourself, brother."

Out of the booth, a guard escorted Zeus to the holding room. Captain Hernández was waiting for him, flanked by two armed guards. "Señor Gómez?" the captain said with a contemptuous little grin under his mustache. "You must accompany me."

"What is it now, captain? I have a flight-schedule to meet."

"You are being detained for questioning."

"Am I under arrest?"

"No. But we can arrange it if need be."

"What's the problem?"

"We will explain in due time. And please don't bother asking to call the US embassy."

"Why not?"

"Because they are already on the way, Señor Gómez. Or should I say Mister Aguirre?"

THIRTY-THREE

Parque Industrial, Mondragón

MINOT PARKED HIS Renault next to Baldo's bone-colored van outside the plant. He adjusted his beret and stepped out. No one was scheduled to be at the plant at that hour.

He circled the van, his nostrils in the breeze, sensing something in the air. He inspected the inside through the van's closed windows, the soiled T-shirts draped on the backrests, the dog-eared roadmaps inside the greasy side pockets, the ashtray brimming with cigarette butts.

When he reached the metal door into the plant, he took his keys out but found it unlocked.

The instant he set foot in the door, Carcelero let out a low growl. Minot shushed him and entered quietly. The dog followed him at a distance, sniffing menace in the gloomy air.

Minot came upon the tool-making machine left moved aside, the pulley chain hanging down, the one-man lift lowered into the *zulo*, and no one around. Careful not to soil his trousers, he knelt over the manhole opening. He tilted his head and listened. Faint but clear muttering grunts and scuffling noises rose out of the dark underground along with the stench. Then he heard Symphony scream.

His back stiffened upright.

Her second cry set him in wild motion.

The next instant he was climbing down into the underground *zulo* like a rock wall climber, holding onto the elevator grilled capsule just under the floor. He tumbled over the shattered stool in the landing and rushed toward the glow of flashlights inside Symphony's cell.

He came upon a rape scene—"*una violación*"—and he would stand by it until his last breath.

Baldo and Gorka had Symphony pinned to the ground, holding her legs and arms apart, their full weight on her, her torso bare except for her soiled brassiere, her girlish shoulders quivering on the ground, their sticky hands all over her.

"You miserable animals."

Baldo stood up and saw Minot's silhouette at the door. "She attacked us," he cried suddenly, aware of how it looked. "She was trying to escape with him and jumped us, the whore."

"You filthy pigs."

Gorka climbed off her. "She attacked us first," he yelled.

The instant they loosened their grip, Symphony shoved Baldo off her and clawed Gorka's eyes, making the boy squeal in pain. Baldo went for Symphony's arms. Gorka leaned back and swung his fist up to smash her face when a spitting noise, preceded by a muzzle spark that lit up the cell, stopped everything in mid-motion.

Gorka gripped his chest, made a wet gurgling noise, and tumbled over into the small walking space between the mattress and the wall.

Openmouthed, Baldo looked at the plume of smoke rising from the noise suppressor on Minot's pistol and leaped to his brother's side. "Gorka!" he yelled. "*Mi hermano—*"

Symphony squeezed herself into the corner of the cell, her arms folded over her chest, too frightened to make a sound.

"You son of a whore, *iparralde*. Why did you have to do that? " Baldo cried as he held his brother's shoulders. "Gorka, Gorka, talk to me."

A seizure rippled through Gorka's body. He coughed up a mouthful of blood, his eyes went white, and collapsed like in a make-believe death.

Symphony watched Minot emerge from the shadows, his downy facial hair, the single eyebrow over his slaughterhouse eyes under his ox-shaped skull.

Baldo released a long howl when he realized his brother was gone. "You'll pay for this, you deformed bastard."

"You brought this upon yourself," Minot replied as he unscrewed the silencer and sniffed it. "This girl is more important than you and your brother together. Only you are too much of a fool to see that. You're a disgrace to the organization."

Baldo stood up, his face twisting with fury and disgust, he let out a long, frenzied cry and leaped at Minot's throat.

Minot stepped back and fired and Baldo plummeted at his feet, dead by the time his bloody head hit the floor.

Miguel Angel screamed from inside his cell, "Symphony! Are you all right? Symphony! Answer me, please."

She wanted to tell him she was all right but would not dare speak. Minot made a gesture with his chin. "Answer your fiancé."

"Miguel, I'm OK," she yelled out without taking her eyes off Minot. "I'm all right."

His throat torn from shouting, Miguel Angel crumbled to the floor inside the darkness of his cell. "*Gracias a Dios.*"

"That in your hand," Minot whispered, pointing with his pistol at the plastic knife in Symphony's hand. "It is not necessary, please."

Symphony let it drop.

"Clever girl."

He lowered his pistol, picked up the battery lamp that had fallen during the scuffle, retrieved her shirt from the floor outside the cell and handed it to her. "Put it on."

Minot knelt next to the bodies of his compeers in their tuxedo shirts and trousers. He examined them for a moment, wiping the sweat off his forehead. They reminded him of two dead waiters caught in the cross-fire. "My apologies," he said to Symphony as he removed the content of Baldo's pockets. "This is much regrettable. Now we must depart."

"Go?" She shook her head. "I'm not going anywhere without Miguel Angel."

"Do not preoccupy, he will be OK. But you—" He gave a tragic nod.

"I'm not leaving without him. No way."

Minot removed Gorka's wallet and mobile phone and pointed at the cell's ceiling. "They will kill you when they see this."

"Why me? You killed them."

Minot stood up with a single motion and shone the lamplight on her face. "Did you want them to violate you? Rape you? Did you?" He swung an arm in a gesture of conclusion. "They killed themselves. Understand? Now you have to go. Come. Do as I say."

"I'm not leaving without Miguel Angel. Forget it—"

"Miss Messina," Minot said over her words. "You have no say in this.

You don't seem to understand. They will kill you. But they will not kill him."

"But Miguel Angel—"

"Stop this idiocy immediately." Minot's voice rose several decibels. "We depart now. Full stop."

"I can't. Miguel Angel," she cried. "He's going to take me away …"

Minot moved nose to nose with her. "Do you want to die? No. Of course not. Then you have to leave here, now."

Symphony felt her strength draining out of her. "Let me at least talk to him first, please. Let me see him and I'll go."

Minot lowered the flashlight. "I will permit you one minute to tell him goodbye," he said with his French inflection. "But only if you cooperate. Will you cooperate, yes, no?"

Miguel Angel, his ear pressed against the armored door, heard the *iparralde's* proposition. "Symphony, do what he says. Get out of here."

Symphony wiped her eyes with the back of her hand and zipped up her jogging shirt. "Where are you going to take me?"

"Somewhere safe."

She didn't know why she should believe him, but she did. "All right. Let me talk to him now."

Minot scrutinized her soiled face in the glow of the lamp. "Come."

Symphony tiptoed around the puddles of blood that had formed next to the bodies on the uneven raw wood floor and walked out of her cell.

Minot unlocked the hatch on the armored door in Miguel Angel's cell. "You have one minute."

When at last Symphony and Miguel Angel came face to face through the opening on the door, they choked, speechless, each imagining what the other was seeing. They stared into each other's tear-burned eyes and soiled faces as though seeing a vision. Miguel Angel inserted one hand through the opening. Symphony clasped it with both hands.

"You're trembling," she said.

"Sym, I'm so sorry. This is all my fault."

"Don't say that. I know whose fault it is. I love you, Miguel."

"And I love you so … But he's right, it's better if you go. He's not going to hurt you now. Once you're out of here—" He halted in mid-phrase and squinted at the flashlight. "It's better if you go."

"I'll know what to do."

"I know you will," he said, squeezing her fingers. "Your ring, where is it?"

"I don't know. Lost, maybe they took it."

"I'll get you another one. A better one. We'll start again. Clean."

For a couple of minutes Minot listened to their declarations of love, their whispering, aching voices, their undecipherable English in a mixture of amusement and impatience, then turned off the flashlight.

"Sufficient," he announced. "Now we go."

Symphony and Miguel Angel interlaced their teardrop-dampened fingers through the slot one last time. She held his fingers against her lips and said goodbye.

Minot kicked the trapdoor shut.

Inside his cell, Miguel Angel let himself crumble to the ground, buried in darkness, more alone than he could ever imagine.

~

Up in the greasy shadows of the plant, Minot didn't give Symphony a chance to weep. He showed her a syringe and a roll of masking tape. "I give you two choices. You can either be unconscious or comfortably bound for the next two hours. Which is your preference?"

She stared hard at his face for a moment.

"It is called synophrys," he said.

"What?"

"The overgrowth fusion of my eyebrows."

She winced, perplexed.

"Make your decision, please. Syringe or tape?"

She pointed at the roll of masking tape.

Minot told her it would have been his choice as well and proceeded to bind her hands and ankles.

He ripped one last strip and brought it to her face. "I will put this tape on your mouth only for the part we go through town. I take it off on the highway. OK?"

She did not bother to answer. He picked her up in his short, muscular Satyr's arms and carried her out of the plant and into the rear seat of his car.

Through the coarse fabric of a dusty hood, Symphony caught the first glimpse of sunlight since her abduction. She breathed the air, filled her lungs with what seemed like pure oxygen after weeks of inhaling her hell-hole's fumes. For a month, she had prevented her captors from seeing or hearing her weep and she was not about to quit now, but how she wanted to, she wanted to very much.

Minot set her across the backseat of his Renault as he tried to remember the English word for *se comporter*. "Ah yes," he said when it came to him. "You will behave, yes?"

She nodded yes under the hood.

"Clever girl."

THIRTY-FOUR

Soto del Real Prison

IT TOOK FORTY-FIVE minutes for prison security to forward the digital images of Zeus taken by the security cameras at the prison gate to AMEN-BASSY Madrid, where FBI experts ran it through the IdentaBase software, instantly pulling ninety-five match points in the name of Zeus Aguirre, and then transmit the results back to Soto del Real.

Captain Hernández signaled the two-guard detail escorting Zeus to halt in front of the *capitanía* door. Out of regard for Zeus's status as a former CIA "independent contractor," as noted in the report—a phrase the captain could not fully evaluate—he ordered a guard to remove his handcuffs.

"But," he told Zeus. "You and I are going to have a talk before my CNI colleagues come to take you to Madrid. You're going to tell me what you came here to discuss with Txomin."

"You're making a big mistake," Zeus tried to explain.

"It is you who have made a big mistake, Señor Aguirre," Captain Hernández said. "You've come here with forged documents, pretending to be a barrister. Mistake?" He forced a chuckle. "I recommend you think about that for the next few minutes until I get back." The captain opened his office door. "Better that you tell me about your business with ETA now than have my CNI colleagues interrogate you. Believe me, here in Soto, we are much nicer to *etarras*."

The captain swung one arm and the guards marched off with Zeus.

They walked past the *sala de espera*, where a large group of visitors, gypsy-looking types, waited to be called in to see their imprisoned relatives. The guards ushered him into a small holding-room next to the lavatories. The tall guard pointed at a metal chair. "*Sientese.*" The other guard slipped on a pair of surgical gloves and placed Zeus's briefcase on a metal shelf.

"What's in here?"

"Personal items," Zeus said. "Security already checked it. I have the voucher."

The guard ignored him and continued searching through the briefcase. "What is all this clothing for?"

Zeus was about to reply when a woman outside in the hallway let out a violent scream. The two guards glanced at each other and scrambled toward the door.

"A fight," the tall guard shouted to his partner and stormed out of the room. "*Jodío gítanos.*"

The guard with the surgical gloves stood by the door, yelling at someone outside. In an instant, the yelling and screaming multiplied tenfold. Zeus leaned his chair back to have a look. There was a huddle of people in the narrow hallway; two women were shrieking in the middle of it, ripping each other's clothes and pulling their hair. The guards yelled at them to stop; another two guards charged in with clubs swinging. The men accompanying the women jumped in their defense and the catfight turned into an all-out brawl.

The guard at the door shook his index finger at Zeus. "Do not move from here, you hear me?"

"Attend to your duties," Zeus replied. "I'm not going anywhere."

The guard flew out to rescue his colleague.

Zeus grabbed his briefcase and slipped out of the interrogation room. With his back to the wall, he jostled sideways, his briefcase over his face, past the blur of flying fists, nightsticks, and bloody noses all around him. He sneaked into the first door he found, the women's restroom, and rushed straight to the rear window. Up flush with the ceiling, the window had a metallic frame and heavy opaque glass panels. He dragged the wastepaper container by the washbasins to the wall, turned it upside down, climbed on top of it, and pushed the window opened and examined the vertical distance to the ground. Some ten, fifteen feet.

At that instant, several visitors burst in the restroom, screaming and toppling in a heap over an elderly woman. Zeus swung his briefcase out the window and climbed out. No one paid attention to him in the midst of the commotion, just a man jumping ship.

Holding onto the windowsill, he lowered himself, balancing with the tips of his rubber-sole shoes on the wall. Then, with his arms fully extended, he let go. A bolt of pain shot from his ankle to his knees when he landed on the pebbled strip. He dragged himself behind a wall, his back hurting so he could hardly breathe—another reminder of why men in the clandestine service retired by age fifty.

He sneaked a quick look each way and saw a cement passageway enclosed by a tall security fence with a single fixed security camera aiming in his general direction.

Frenzied shouts and scuffle noises poured out of the opened window above him.

Keeping to the camera's blind side, he half-limped, half-sprinted, around the corner and slipped behind a row of shrubbery fencing off two metal dumpsters. From here, he could see the roofed walkway and the front gate, a few meters' distance. He hurled the briefcase with Natxo's clothes behind the dumpsters, threw away the visitor's sticker on his chest, and slapped on the one he received at the gate.

He waited until he saw a large family coming out of the visitors' building on their way toward the prison's exit. With a slight limp in his step, he slipped out of the shrubbery and mingled in with the family, two women, a young boy, and the young man leading them. They scowled at him with their gypsy frowns but said nothing and moved on toward the gate together.

At the barricaded entrance, they handed in their visitors' passes to the guard at the booth as if they were all part of the family.

As a payoff for their silence, Zeus offered the young boy his sunglasses. "*¿Los quieres?*"

Too big for the boy, he accepted them happily nonetheless.

Zeus smiled at the family and limped away toward the parking lot, his ankles swelling with every step. Natxo spotted him from inside his Seat van and drove up to meet him with a smile on his face. "You did it."

Zeus groaned when he hit the seat. "Get me out of here. Go."

"With pleasure, my friend." Natxo gunned the engine and headed back to Madrid. "How did it go, tell me?" Natxo was still smiling.

"It went." Zeus said, grimacing and rubbing his ankles. "What are you so cheerful about?"

"I just won a fifty-euro bet, thanks to you. The chief said you'd never make it out of Soto del Real. I said you would. And you did." He laughed. "I owe you a drink."

"I rather you invite me to painkillers."

"Hope you are not serious. Tonight we go to Euskadi. To Mondragón. Apparently a local compeer has something important to give you."

Zeus gazed at the city lights in the early evening distance. For a moment, his ankle pain disappeared. "Did they tell you what it is?"

"No idea. The same as everything about you, man. It's top secret. I thought you would know."

Zeus leaned forward and massaged his swelling ankles. I guess I do know, he said to himself. This is where they give me the girl and I get to go home. Why the hell not? The pain and old age did not feel so bad anymore. "You know, maybe I'll have that drink with you, after all."

PART V

THIRTY-FIVE

In the Zulo

IN THE DARK OF HIS cell, all Miguel Angel could see was blackness whether he opened or closed his eyes. He crawled over the splintering floorboards, groping for the lidded tin can on the wooden box. Until then his hunger cramps had functioned like a timepiece in the perpetual night of his cell—hunger, his trusty reference of time's forward movement. But now his need for food had become a constant fatigue by which he could measure nothing except the early pangs, short breaths, and rapid heartbeats of starvation.

With extreme careful motions, he opened the can and extricated a small piece of the bread, the last of his food. He broke off a handful of crumbs and pushed it into his mouth. The bread soaked up all his saliva. He swallowed the dry lump in his throat and washed down the remains with a single sip of water. Blind, he capped the plastic bottle and shook it to hear how much water he had left. There was enough water and enough bread left for another survival meal. Then it would all be over.

Buried in darkness he had no idea how long it had been since Symphony had gone. A day? Two? Three? He thought they had left him there to die, abandoned to the crackling noises of crawling insects and the unremitting stench. It affected everything, his breathing, his senses. His mind dragged, too dull to tell whether he was asleep or awake, or whether the clanking noises he was hearing were real or imagined. Then he heard familiar squeaks, the metallic creaking of the lift frame in motion, followed by the crunch of slow, heavy shoe soles weighing down on the planked floor.

A yellow light beam cracked the pitch-black darkness under the door.

Miguel Angel crawled to the door, his heart pounding with anticipation, astonished that he had the energy to move. He listened to the slow-moving footsteps inside of what had been Symphony's cell. Had the killer come back to remove the shot-up bodies? To get rid of him, the only witness?

From the moment Symphony left, he had regretted telling her to go. But he had felt so sure her chances of escaping would be so much better outside he had not thought twice. Now it hurt him physically to think he might've made the wrong decision. Sweat drops rolled into the hollows under his eyes.

"*¡Dios!*" a voice cried out several times, each time angrier. It belonged to the man he knew as José—Aitor. Apparently, he had just discovered the dead bodies. He leaned the side of his face on the door and listened. Miguel Angel realized all that anger might divert toward him, so he removed one of the banquette's legs to use as a weapon.

Outside, in the dark of Symphony's cell, Aitor stood over Baldo and Gorka staring at their corpses in the beam of his flashlight. Twenty-four hours had not yet passed since he saw Patxi's dead body lying on a slab in the morgue and now this. "*Dios.*" He stepped around the brown dirt patches where blood had pooled and got down on one knee. Baldo's body was in rigid rigor mortis. His eyes wide open and dry. Aitor aimed the flashlight at Gorka and didn't recognize him at first in the brown-stained tuxedo shirt and the white mask of horror in his face. He couldn't understand what could have happened. The New York assassin was dead, his body dismembered and burned. Was this the work of another assassin from New York?

Where's the girl, then? And the boy? It hit him then. "Where's the boy?" Aitor rushed out of the cell, intolerable catastrophes flashing through his mind. In front of Miguel Angel's cell, he unlatched the trapdoor and yelled into the blackness. "Miguel Angel, are you in there? *¿Estás bien, estás ahí?*"

Stepping lightly toward the armored door's blindside, Miguel Angel stood in silence with the wooden banquette leg in his grip, ready to attack.

"Boy, are you in there? Show yourself." Aitor panned the flashlight into the dark of the cell, but would not go inside. "Show yourself. It's all right."

Miguel Angel could not hold his silence. "Go to hell, José. Where's Symphony? What did you do to her? Are you going to kill me too, you son of a whore—"

"Stop that," Aitor let out, confused but relieved. "I am not going to do anything to you. Move where I can see you."

"*No puedo.*"

"Why not?"

"Can't get on my feet." Miguel Angel was set to pounce on him.

Somehow, the intensity in his voice did not convince Aitor. "Come now," he said. "Let me look at you. I want to help you."

"You come in. I can't move."

Aitor now sensed the boy's hostility. "*Vamos.* Make an effort," he said, friendly-like, regretting having adhered to his own rule prohibiting weapons in the *zulo.*

"I'm dying of thirst." Miguel Angel squeezed the banquette leg ready to strike the instant José stepped inside. "Please bring me some water."

Aitor debated with himself whether to go back up to get his pistol or open the door and see what was wrong with the boy. Caution prevailed. "Wait," he said. "I will get you some water and food."

Miguel Angel leaned back on the wall, holding on to the banquette leg, drained of energy, feeling his moment had passed.

A few minutes later Aitor returned with the pistol in his hand, a lit kerosene lamp, and a shopping bag with a plastic bottle of water, a piece of chorizo, cheese, and bread. He pulled down the mask over his head, cocked his pistol and pushed the armored door open.

"I've brought you water and some things to eat," he said. "But you have to come out on your own to get it. Remember, I am armed. Come out in any manner you are able to."

Miguel Angel let out a long breath and dropped the banquette leg by the door.

Aitor watched the pitiful sight that emerged from within. A mélange of urine, musty sweat, and shame assaulted his senses. The weak lamplight made Miguel Angel cover his eyes with both hands. Aitor lowered the lamp but not the pistol and showed him the bag with the food. "Here, take it."

Miguel Angel looked him in the eyes. "Where's Symphony?"

"I was hoping you knew."

"Me?" Miguel Angel scowled at the eyes in the black mask. "How is that possible?"

"Go on, eat," Aitor said.

Miguel Angel, his face soiled with greasy dirt, uncapped the plastic water bottle and upended it over his mouth, then sat down on the boards. He bit into the chorizo sausage, into the fresh bread, took another swig of water, and bit off more of everything with the voracity of a shipwreck survivor.

Aitor watched him in silence. The boy's suffering shamed him. "Drink slowly. Don't eat so rapidly, you will get sick."

"I am sick already."

"Who took your girlfriend and shot my compeers?"

Miguel Angel wiped his lips and looked into Aitor's masked face. "You're playing with me, right?"

"Just tell me what you know."

"Why should I?"

"Don't you want to find out where your *novia* is?"

Miguel Angel stared into the mask's eyeholes as he chewed the ball of food in his mouth, sizing up the man, realizing he still could recognize an opportunity when it presented itself. "This is over," he said.

"What are you talking about? What's over?"

"This stupid, ill-conceived kidnapping, it's finished. I know who shot them and who took my *novia*. That's how I know."

"Then say who did it?"

"I will tell you. But first you have to swear you'd let me go."

"By God, you know I cannot do that."

Miguel Angel squinted at the sad gray eyes peering out the mask's eyeholes. "You have destroyed my life, tortured me, and maybe even provoked the death of the woman I want to marry—the hell with you, José. I can tell you all you want to know, but first you have to let me out of here."

"Don't be stupid. Do you think it's in my power to do that?"

"It is. It is you who are responsible for what happened here. It is you who are going to pay for everything. But I can change all that for you, if you let me go."

Aitor became silent.

"Think about it," Miguel Angel said, his face regaining the sheen of life. "I've given it plenty of thought. Only I can help you now, José. My testimony can save you. If I'm alive to give it."

Aitor nodded no. "It's useless. You'll be out soon. We are going to transfer you to another location, a comfortable one with a radio and—"

"This is my offer: Not only I will tell you who the killer is, but I swear to you here and now in God's sacred name, that I will never tell the police anything that would incriminate you. You have my word of honor. Truth is, I don't feel any animosity toward you, José." He looked up at his face. "Have you collected any ransom yet?"

"That is confidential."

"You have," Miguel said with a knowing grin. "I know it."

"How?"

"I know my father. Besides, you said I'd be out soon? I know you either collected the full amount or a good portion of it."

Aitor rubbed his masked face, exhausted.

"José, you and I know it's over. Why go on with it? Do it for your family, for my family, for the good of everyone involved in this tragedy. Let me go now and I swear I'll be a witness for your defense. My father will let you keep the money. Don't tell me this hasn't been done before. ETA has collected ransom monies after the hostage has been freed."

"It is not my decision to make."

"Please, José. It's too late for that. Believe me, what I know about the killer is something that you need to know immediately. You have no time to waste."

Aitor stepped back, motioning that he had heard enough. Miguel Angel insisted and Aitor let out a furious shout. "Shut up." He pushed the gun barrel into the boy's chest. "Stop your nonsense and tell me what happened here."

Miguel Angel froze in mid-motion. He glanced at the gun. "The murderer of your colleagues intends to collect a separate ransom from my *novia's* family. I heard him say it. Are you going to allow him to do that?"

"You are lying."

"With all my respect," Miguel Angel said, knowing he had scored. "In the month you have kept me and my fiancée in these inhuman conditions, have I ever misled you, tried to bribe anyone, been anything other than accepting? Don't you see, it's time to put an end to this madness. It no longer has anything to do with the Basque cause. No one will side with you after what's happened here—"

"Only one man did the killing?"

"Only one."

"Is he American?"

"American?" Miguel Angel looked at him as if he was deranged. "He's one of yours!"

Without at first understanding, that last phrase triggered the image of Minot in Aitor's mind. He lowered the pistol away from the boy. The *iparralde* had always been against freeing the girl, had his eyes on her from the start, and could not stomach Baldo. "The coldest man with a gun I've ever seen," Iñaki had once said of him. Aitor slipped the pistol under his belt.

"José," Miguel Angel said. "Tell me we have an accord and I promise I'll never press charges against you. I'll tell them nothing about you, nothing."

"You will not press charges against me?" Aitor grinned with sarcasm. "I will go free. Like nothing happened."

"Without my testimony I don't know how they can charge you. It'll be as if you were never part of this. You'll go free. And you already know how accommodating my father can be."

Aitor's limbs suddenly felt heavy as anchors. "You want to protect me."

"This has gone too far. Let's help each other. It's your decision and yours alone."

Aitor pulled off his hood, rubbed his brow and sat down on the boards next to the boy like a man gathering his own pieces. "*A la mierda …*" He looked the boy in the eye. "Now you've seen my face. You know what that means."

Miguel Angel nodded yes.

"Do you want to help me?"

"I said I would."

"Then start by helping me bring the cadavers of my compeers out of here."

Miguel Angel placed the plastic bag with the remnants of the food aside and stood up. "Does this mean we have an accord?"

Aitor stood up. The darkness solid around them. "*Vamos.* Let's take them out while you tell me what happened here."

THIRTY-SIX

The Spanish-French border

MINOT'S RENAULT BUCKED onto a hilly goat trail near the Bidassoa River, the dividing line between France and Spain. "*Bienvenue,*" he said from the driver's seat. "You are now in my country."

"Your country?" Symphony said from the backseat, bouncing with every bump and stone on the track. "We didn't cross any borders. Where are you taking me?"

"Clever girl," he said, without explaining there had not been border controls for years. "Are you rested?"

"How can I, tied up like this?"

Minot breathed a little laugh through his nostrils. But they had made an arrangement. He would not tape her mouth or drug her if she promised not to scream or try to cause problems. Despite the discomfort of having her wrists and ankles bound with tape, Symphony could not deny the restorative feeling of being outdoors, on the open road. The sunshine, the clean air, the distant horizons revived her in ways she had not expected. "I'm starved and I'm thirsty."

"You drank all the water," he said.

"So? I'm your hostage."

"I will cook when we arrive. No McDonald's in the Pyrenees."

Minot became very talkative as they neared the mountains. He used the full extent of his English and a lot of his energy to try to convince her of something that he had no idea how little she cared to hear. "We didn't want to take you prisoner … it was all your fault … you forced us … the truth is that you have been a big problem for us."

"Not as big a problem as you are to me," she said without thinking, the road wind on her face.

His flat, ruminant eyes shone in the rearview mirror. "For you is so simple. You don't know the complications you have cost us. We are at war against a state that dominates us. And you—how do you call it? You are collateral damage. Bad for you as it is for us."

Symphony kept staring into the wind.

"We want our country to be ours. Be the masters of our territories, the same as you Americans. Land of the free, one nation indivisible. We want this too. How do you like to be forced to have ah—a Canadian or a Mexican passport? No, you don't like that. The Basques want the same thing. Our own passports."

"So you kidnapped us because you want your own passport?"

"You don't understand. You don't see. Why should you? You are American. So egoistic, so mighty, like rich children with nuclear bombs. Don't care to know of other people's dreams. Only the big American dream. Don't want to know of other country's hopes, of other languages except your own. Everything's got to be in English, if not, you have no use for it."

The Pyrenees foothills trembled in the heat haze.

"Look in your dictionaries. See what it says about us Basques." He knew it by heart: "'People of unknown origin inhabiting the western Pyrenees and the Bay of Biscay, with a language of no known linguistic affiliation.' As if we were some abnormality that does not fit in the world. When in truth we are the only pure race on this continent. Thousands of years old. Older than Europe. A nation to be admired. Yet we are ignored, dishonored to live under someone else's boot, like a caged relative you're ashamed of, hoping we disappear. Like what happened to the American Indians. But believe me: that will not happen with us ..."

Symphony turned her attention back to the wind streaming in the window until the sound of his voice became another road noise. She did not want to understand his sermons or know anything about him. All she wanted was that fresh air to blow on her face, for the passing landscape to absorb her, tell her if anyone anywhere under those dizzying vast skies of dusk had any idea of where she was.

THIRTY-SEVEN

AT A REST AREA ON the northbound side of the highway, Joey Messina stood vigilant watching the oncoming traffic, his eyes squinting in the August sun. At first, he saw no point in meeting with Little Tommy. He already knew what he was going to say. The rumor had filtered out way in advance, no doubt meant to soften the blow. He knew the German was history, probably offed by some Basque. But he wanted the little prick to tell him to his face. Joey needed someone to bear the blame for his missing daughter, for his impotence, for his crumbling self-respect.

A flare of silver sunshine flashed on the windshield of Tommy's Jaguar when it veered into the parking area. It looked as though a child was at the wheel.

Joey watched him come out of the car, chin up, all confident in the safety of his authority, now recognized by the Five Families, an endorsement that rendered him untouchable. And the reason he hadn't bashed in his little hairless head with the butt of the pistol he kept in the glove compartment. Joey was capable of many things, but suicide was not one.

"How you doing?"

"Thanks for seeing me, Tommy."

The somber expression on the don's face clashed with the sporty cream-colored shirt and baggy plaid golfer's pants and thick-soled shoes with the double heels. They patted each other's backs.

Joey leaned back on the SUV and crossed his arms. "Things are not looking so good."

Little Tommy wrinkled his sunburned forehead. "We've lost him, Joey.

Haven't heard from the German for days now. Not a word. You'd think someone out there in Marseille could tell me something." He shrugged his bulky shoulders. "Nobody knows. It's a disaster."

"A disaster?" Joey looked away, his lower lip in his bite.

"Wish I could tell you different. This tragedy affects us all." Little Tommy shook his head as though it was too much. "What else can we do but keep trying? Right?"

"What'd you think happened?"

"I think they got his ass. But who knows? Hey, we all agreed he was the guy for the job. Right? We didn't pick him out of a hat. The man hunted down Talibans in Afghanistan, for Christ's sake. Maybe we shouldn't have been so impressed by a military record."

Joey kept a close watch on Little Tommy's hand gestures and facial expressions, reading them for inconsistencies, looking for what the words did not tell him.

"What burns me is we trusted the guy. Nobody thought a plan B was needed. But this isn't over." The little man pointed his crooked index finger at the sky. "This impacts everything. Things you can't imagine. It could become a new trend against us and we can't have it. Maybe it's time you go out there and take care of it yourself."

"Is that so?" Joey wasn't listening anymore. He knew where the lying dwarf was going with it.

"I might've erred on this before, Joey ... But now I'm sure is the right decision ... You'll have the backing of all the Families ... Guaranteed ..."

Joey sneered at the ground. It had been one of the things the old Brooklyn don had said to watch out for. "If Tommy tells you to go, you can rest assure he's ready to make his move. With you gone, he'd have the perfect excuse to reassign all your territories. It won't take him long. By the time you get back you'd be left with thirty-five percent of your earnings, if you're lucky. And don't make the mistake of thinking anybody is going to stand up for you, either. Not even your crew. They'll be the first ones he'll offer a piece of the spoils. And what choice will they have? To remain loyal to you or martyrdom? If you go out of the country, it'll be the same as giving Tommy your life's work in a silver platter ..."

Joey gazed away at the Hudson River through the trees. Its blue-gray liquid mass flowing out to the harbor in the misty distance, the resting place of so many familiar names and faces, friends and foes, good and bad. He stole a glance at the midget, at his despotic little chin, at his pit-bull eyes. How easily he could break the little bastard's neck, faster than he could scream.

"So is that it? Now you telling me it's OK to go to Spain, a month after I asked you to?"

Little Tommy swallowed something bitter. "It's not OK, Joey. Except I can't honestly go against it anymore. Like I said, this isn't business. Never was. The problem is some of our people are not sure your daughter's really been kidnapped, you know."

"What?"

"You got to understand. Sometimes girls meet other people. Fall in love. They have statistics on it."

"Is that what you think?"

"Not me, but, hey. They keep telling me there can be no kidnapping without a ransom. That's a hard point to argue."

Joey was starting to hyperventilate.

"Be that as it may," Little Tommy went on. "I just can't deny your right to rescue your daughter. And wanted to tell you, personally."

"I'm a captain, Tommy." Joey poked his own chest. "Been one for eight years. And a made man for thirty. Are you telling me now it's OK to talk to the Feds?"

"Didn't say that. I'm just saying you got to do what you got to do."

"With all due respect, Tommy, you and I know very well there are some friends of ours out there who want nothing more than to squeeze me out. Move into my livelihood, the work of a lifetime. They're just waiting for me to do exactly what you're saying I should do now."

Little Tommy nodded in sad approval. He knew who he was dealing with. He also knew it was better to let his captain vent a little for the time being than to take him on and deal with the trouble that would surely come. "Have you a better idea?"

Joey gazed away at the traffic, nodding in silence and wiggling his fingers to counter the burning urge to pound Tommy's face into gook. He thought he did have a better idea.

THIRTY-EIGHT

New York City

"COME ON, COME ON, answer the phone." Tess redialed Judge Arsenio's number again. The third time in the last hour. She strode across her living room with her iPhone to her ear. For two days she hadn't stepped out of her apartment, living on Chinese and pizza deliveries, eating in front of the TV while pecking at her computers' keyboards, and waiting for Zeus to call. But the hours kept ticking by like a time bomb only she could defuse.

Judge Arsenio was the man Zeus had told her to contact in case of emergency, but the judge didn't answer or return her calls. Tess had no idea what Zeus's reaction would be when she told him of Messina's plans of revenge, but she had to warn him, ASAP.

She went back to her sofa, her command center, surrounded by her laptop and desktop and keyboards set up, her monitors logged on the Spanish news websites, her flat-panel tuned to TVE International, her iPad, her two cells and landline telephones sitting beside her at arm's reach.

She redialed Judge Arsenio's number. A gravelly voice cut in the ringing tones this time. Tess tossed her hair off her face and muted the TV.

"Hello, judge?"

"Who's this?"

"My name is Tess Bernard from New York, maybe you've heard of me."

"Certainly." Of course, he had. "What a pleasant surprise. To what do I owe this pleasure so early in the morning?"

"My apologies, sir. But we're experiencing a minor communications problem with Zeus."

"Oh?"

"We haven't heard from him since he arrived in Spain and we're concerned about it. I'm hoping maybe you can help us."

"He's only been gone a couple of days."

"More like three."

"You think he's in trouble?"

"I've no idea. I'm just trying to keep a step ahead in case he needs our help. There's been a lot about ETA in the news lately. We just feel he must have something to report by now."

Judge Arsenio was well aware of the firm's role in Zeus's operation, an operation that he had made possible through his links with the ETA leadership. He was also aware of Tess's personal interest in Zeus, a detail the judge let slip when he said, "Zeus speaks very highly of you, Miss Bernard." It was all in his tone.

"So you can understand my concern."

"I suppose it's never too soon for things to go wrong, but it's rather premature." The judge had not heard from Zeus since his phone message on the day he arrived in Madrid, but according to information he had received from other sources, there seemed to be no cause for alarm. "You have to keep in mind, this work Zeus is doing sometimes requires temporary blackouts. I think you should be patient. No news is good news in this business too."

"It's not just me," she said. "The client's been asking about him. There are other pressing issues we have to discuss as well. Are you sure you have no way of getting in touch with anyone who's in contact with him? At least point me in the right direction. Zeus told me if anyone could, it is you, Judge Arsenio."

The judge liked the way she had said that last part, the modulation in her breathy voice, the way it merged from businesslike to soft femininity in an instant. It explained Zeus' response when the judge asked him why he had accepted this complicated assignment, the helpless shrug and the love-bitten reply Zeus gave him. "Tell me something, Tess."

"Sure, anything."

"Can you be trusted to keep this business between us and only between us?"

"Absolutely."

"Not a word to anyone, not even to your business associates, much less to your client?"

"Not a word."

"Any violation is a deal-breaker," he warned.

"You have my word, your honor," she said as if in court.

Judge Arsenio chuckled. "I'm not that kind of judge, but OK. I'll get back to you at this number."

"When should I expect your call?"

"Give me a day or so." Then he added, his gravelly voice deeper, "And let me tell you something about Zeus that I think you should know. He's the most reliable man I know. He is one of those rare creatures that never lets you down. It's both his virtue and his weakness. His word is gold, Ms. Bernard. Remember that."

"Thank you so much, judge." Tess closed her cell phone and braced herself for a long day.

Three hours out of Madrid on the N-1 Highway, Zeus looked over his shoulder at Cristina asleep in the rear seat, then at Natxo at the wheel. "I'll take over if you're tired of driving."

"Me tired? How are your ankles?" Natxo said.

"Better. The ice bags cut down on the swelling."

"Feel like some coffee?"

"Always."

"There's a tavern near Briviesca. I know the owners. They make a very good coffee."

Natxo steered the Seat out of the highway. It was past nine p.m. and a dying light tinged the western sky. He pulled into the paved lot in front of an old roadside tavern.

They walked inside and stood at one end of the counter. A blend of old dingy bar smell and cigarette smoke hung in the air. The high ceiling made the dozen or so people inside sound like a crowd. The tavern owner, a Basque from Vitoria, came over and shook hands with Natxo. He and Cristina asked for cold drinks. Zeus had an espresso.

On the TV over the bar, the soccer game broke at half-time. Everyone shushed when the news report from the Basque Country came on and the reporter announced, "Forty-nine-year-old Patxi Mitxelena, a native of Mondragón, was found dead of gunshot wounds fired by unknown assailants during a shooting on the Arrasate highway."

A wave of murmurs rolled over the smoky tavern. Cristina glanced at Zeus. She believed Messina was responsible. It had been her theory even before she learned that Zeus was working for the gangster's daughter. Zeus responded with a mournful nod.

"I'm with him," Natxo said in Zeus's defense. "It's inconceivable that man would risk his daughter's life like that."

"Then who is?"

The tavern keeper came back to the end of the counter and engaged Natxo and Cristina in conversation. Zeus excused himself and stepped out for some air.

A chilly breeze came cutting down from the heights to the east. Good strolling weather, even on his sore ankles. He walked slow on the side of the unlit highway toward a gas station about two hundred meters away. The traffic was light. He pulled his new untraceable mobile out of his pocket. He had lost the Stealthphone in the raid. This one was a GSMK Cryptophone, latest generation, five thousand euros worth of peace of mind according to Cristina. Better be, he thought, as he tapped on it. He was about to make his first call to Tess.

He focused in on the silences between ring tones, listened for clicks and noises that might alert him of bugging devices. As far as he knew, the security concerns that had kept him from calling Tess still stood. The chances that the FBI had every one of her telephone lines bugged remained too real. But necessity and other essentials overrode his standards of safety. Tess answered after the third ring tone.

"Hi. Don't say my name," he said. "Know who's speaking?"

"Of course," she said, trying to control her emotions. "Are you OK?"

"Yes." Zeus continued walking on the graveled shoulder of the road.

"Why didn't you call sooner?"

"Things got a bit more complicated than we anticipated."

"Is everything OK?"

"Yes. Some progress has been made. That much I can report. How is it at your end?"

"I've been given two weeks off. Forced vacations. I don't think they want me around."

"What does that mean?"

"The client," she said, pausing for emphasis. "I don't think he's going to keep his word. It looks like he intends to get his revenge, no matter how this ends."

"How do you know?"

"By accident. Overheard them talking. My boss swears he was just venting. Didn't sound that way to me. I had to tell you." She paused, then: "Does that change things?"

"Quite a bit."

"How?"

"In unimaginable ways."

"Can you be a little more precise?"

"Not really. I'll have to reevaluate."

"What do you mean? Are you giving up?"

"No." He sounded sore. "I thought you knew why I took this job."

"I thought I did."

"I'm too committed. Certain gestures have been made that need to be reciprocated. I have to go the distance whether he keeps his word or not."

"I don't know what to say. I'm so relieved you feel that way, for our girl's sake. I guess you'll have to warn your friends at some point."

Zeus exhaled. "To tell you the truth, the way things are going he might not find anybody to exact revenge from. His contractors have done a pretty good clean-up job so far."

"That's another thing I found out with the judge's help," Tess said. "The client didn't hire the clean-up contractor, as you say. It wasn't his doing."

"Who did then?"

"His boss. The client's boss, who is also our client."

"The client's Family boss?" Zeus said, sounding both surprised and confused.

"Yes. I think it's part of a conspiracy my boss and the client's boss are in together, to prevent Messina from leaving the country."

"No names, please. What's the purpose of that?"

"To prevent him from talking to the authorities—quote, unquote. Yet there has to be more to it. Feels that way."

Zeus was nearing the Repsol gas station. "Well, it won't make any difference to the people here who hired the contractors there. Tell me, how about the transfer? I need those funds."

"You'll get them. Actually, you already have them. I made sure of it before I left the office. All I need to know is how to get the safe-deposit box key out to you."

"A safe-deposit box?"

"In San Sebastián, as you asked."

"I'm impressed. How did you manage?"

"Don't ask. The judge helped me with it. He said you'd know how to handle it at your end."

"How about the money in escrow?"

"That's secured. No one except you or your daughter can touch it. I made sure of that too."

"You're really something, you know that?"

"All I need is an address to get the package out to you."

"I'm on the road. I'll need an able body to deliver it by hand." Zeus started back toward the café, the lights of the gas station behind him.

"Have you anyone in mind?"

"Talk to the judge. Go with his recommendations."

"I might be able to tell him face to face," she said. "I was thinking of flying down anyway."

"It's kind of hot there now."

"I don't mind that kind of heat."

Zeus paused. "Sorry I'm going to miss you."

"You don't know the half of it," she said with a smile in her voice. "Get back in one piece, OK? Don't forget you have a debt with me."

"Only one?" A police squad car cruised past him.

"This one is important. You promised to play Chopin for me."

"That's one promise you can count on. Got to hang up now. We'll talk later."

Another police car zoomed past him, then another one approaching from the opposite direction, together with a Guardia Civil van coming on the quiet, roof lights off. The police vehicles poured into the tavern's parking lot.

Zeus doubled-back to the Repsol station. He walked casually past the station's cashier and into the men's room. He locked the door from within and dialed Cristina's number. Voice mail answered.

He went out to the convenience store area, grabbed a magazine from the rack, and watched the police activity down the road through the glass plate. The station attendants were out by the pumps, looking and pointing at the tavern.

Moments later, a knot of Civil Guard agents burst out of the tavern with Cristina and Natxo in cuffs.

Zeus crossed the road toward a block of low one-story shops. All the shops were closed, only the outside lights were on. He slipped into the hard shadows between two stores until every police vehicle pulled out of the tavern's lot. One of them drove up into the gas station. He knew then someone must have seen him there and took off at double-step in the opposite direction, toward the town lights, about a kilometer's distance.

Keeping to the roadside shadows, Zeus tried to think of what he could do for Natxo and Cristina. Not much, he realized. No use in telephoning them now. Looking over his shoulder, he saw the police cruiser pulling out of the station. It headed speeding in his direction, its blue roof lights spinning.

He sprinted into an open field by the road, climbed a stone fence, and kept moving over the dark grass and sandy dirt, away from the twirling lights. His aching ankles slowed his pace to a trudging hobble. He needed to rest and sat behind a tree, watching the cruiser. It moved slowly with its side searchlight beaming deep into the field, looking for him.

Not far from where he was, Zeus spotted a structure deeper into the dark of the field. He half-crouched toward it, following the smell of manure. There were three short horses huddled by the corral's fence. He shushed and hushed them in Spanish to keep them calm, and dropped on a large stone to rest his ankle, out of the wind. He waited until the twirling blue lights were gone, then took a deep breath and made his way to town, one painful step at a time.

At the entrance of town, he came up to the brightly lit doorway of a small inn, the bed-and-breakfast family-run type. He watched the doorway for a few moments from the corner, drying his sweaty face with his sleeve. The street was deserted, except for the occasional passing car. He rang the bell and leaned on the doorframe until the door opened.

Zeus tried hard not to limp when he entered. The innkeepers were a young couple in their thirties, cordial. They stood together behind a short wooden counter with a silvery desk call bell. They smiled at him in unison. He forced a smile of his own and asked for a room. "Just for the night."

"Would you like to see the room?"

"No, thank you."

Half-dazed by the pain, he handed over his passport and signed the ledger ... A single room with breakfast included ... No, no luggage ... No, he did not care for coffee or tea ... One flight up, the first door on your right. "Thank you."

He climbed the stairs, feeling his legs about to give. A homey, chemical scent followed him into the room. He double-locked the door and sat on the bed and peeled off his socks. His ankles had swollen into two shiny yellowish blue baseballs, the left one the worst. He took his cellphone out of his jacket and called the judge in Florida. He told him what happened to Cristina and Natxo.

Judge Arsenio said he would pass the information on to the interested parties. It could be worse, the judge said. "At least you now know where you have to be tomorrow."

Zeus knew where. The town of Mondragón. Where he would meet the kidnappers and get the girl, mission accomplished.

T H I R T Y-N I N E

Jaizkibel Pass, the French Pyrenees

AFTER NIGHTFALL, Minot drove the whining Renault up a mountain dirt road. He steered the car with the same bored motions as he'd driven on the paved highway in daylight.

The twisting road narrowed and rose into stony heights. Ash-colored tree trunks and large egg-shaped boulders appeared in the beams of the headlights. Since before Roman times, generations of Basque shepherds and smugglers—*mugalaris*—had used the Jaizkibel Pass and other crossings like it for trafficking with all forms of contraband back and forth across the Pyrenees. Modern law-enforcement technology, the size and nature of modern contraband, the disappearance of Europe's borders, had rendered these trails useless, except for incidental adventurous hikers, and ETA's *mugas* who still used them for gunrunning and as an underground railroad for fugitive members.

The Renault came to a halt beside two large boulders where the trail narrowed into a path with barely enough room for a man and his mule.

Minot backed the car onto a flat area in the trees. He glanced at Symphony sprawled on the back seat, her face in the shadows of the car's dim inside light. "We walk now," he said and drew a switchblade out of his pocket. "Turn around, please."

Symphony raised herself up on her elbows. Her features hardened at his sight. "Where are we?"

"We are in the high Basque Land—or France, if you prefer."

"Yeah, right."

A dog barked in the distance. He cut the layers of duct tape girding her ankles. "The tape on your wrists stays," he said and helped her out of the car.

Symphony suffered a moment of vertigo when she stood upright and breathed the pure mountain air. She leaned on the car for support. "The height and the cold must have given your lungs a shock," he said.

She pushed herself off the car with a look of defiance and scowled at the dark surroundings with escape on her mind. "I've got to pee."

Minot came back from retrieving his backpack from the car trunk and shone the flashlight on her face.

"Hey, stop that," she snapped, shielding her eyes.

"Look?" He aimed the flashlight around at the flat-leave trees and the unleveled ground, at everything as far as the light could reach. "Do you see?"

"I don't see anything."

"That is my meaning. We are no place. The dog barking? He is not a family pet. He is an Awoo—" he let out, howling like a wolf. "Hungry like you." He laughed, hissed. "No people anywhere, only the Pyrenees. Your father's assassins, they will never find you here. Understand? Now, go pee. I'll keep the flashlight on you."

"I'm not surprised you ..." she said, mumbling the rest out of hearing range, thinking the cocky ox-head was just speculating on that about her father's "assassins." She squatted half-hidden behind a stone. Minot held the light on her head, his pistol on the other hand.

Symphony stumbled back. "I can't walk. It hurts."

"You cannot walk? Uh, oh." He chuckled at her saboteur's trick. "Something bad with your foot? Poor girl. Do not worry. I will carry you on my shoulder. Only I warn you." He made as if sniffing his underarms. "Not complimentary."

"Forget it. I'd rather fall down the mountain than have you put your hands on me again."

"OK with me. Because you don't smell so good either."

After a long climb, they came upon an old shack silhouetted against the night sky. The old raw-wood door had a chain through it and a padlock. Minot had the key. "Sit there, please," he said, pointing at a log by the door. "I will start the motor for the light."

Symphony was glad to oblige. The muscles of her legs hurt and trembled after zigzagging through the mountains for an hour.

Minot came back with a small gas drum and got the generator going, its noisy engine jolting the night. A ceiling light fixture lit up the inside of his mountain hideout, a one-room, stone and wood cabin built in the shelter of a ridge, twenty kilometers from the nearest village.

Minot gestured for her to enter. He followed her in and dropped his backpack on the tabletop. A mixture of musty firewood, gasoline, and fertilizer penetrated Symphony's nose. The fore section of the cabin was set up as living quarters with a table and chairs and a couple of cots next to a cluttered cooking area. The rest of it was a combination of a mountaineer's refuge and a bomb-making workshop, with each corner of the rear wall set up with equipment and supplies for each endeavor.

Minot nodded as he opened an inner door. "It has a tub and a toilet."

Symphony walked straight into the bathroom. When she came out, Minot was by the sink washing a cooking pot, a kerosene lamp on the counter beside him.

"I want to shower," she told him, raising her taped up wrists. "Take it off, please."

He dried his hands with a rag and pulled out his pocketknife. His taurine gaze fixed on her face as he sliced the tape. "Your shoes, please. Give."

She hesitated but then slipped off the cheap lace-less sneakers and dropped them by his feet. He handed her a folded towel from a cabinet drawer next to the twin cots. "*Tout à vous.*" Then, "Oh, no hot water."

She shrugged.

"I will wait here," he said, dragging a banquette over to the bathroom door. "Five minutes. Then I will go inside." He slid off his beret, exposing his low cropped, bull-shaped head and sat down to clean his Beretta with the rag, the shadow of a grin in his wooly cheeks.

Inside the bathroom, Symphony locked the door and went straight to the window. It was small, shoulder-high, with a square wooden frame. She could fit through it if she tried, except it had been a month since her last shower and the idea of washing off the dirt and filth that had accumulated on her body was overwhelming. She found a used bar of soap on the sink, took a whiff of it, and ran the water in the tub. The pipes banged out gallons of brown water before it cleared. She twirled her fingers in it. Ox-head wasn't kidding, the water was freezing.

She wiped the scummy settlings before she stepped inside the tub. She would have screamed had the icy water pouring over her not stifled her breath. Every opened cut and scrape from her struggle with Gorka flared up as if she had poured salt on it. She lathered up her hair as fast as she could and rubbed away the grime on her skin after weeks of catlike washes.

Outside, Minot followed her every move by the noises she made, the water she poured over her, the movement of her feet inside the wet tub, the scent the soap gave off. "Your five minutes are up," he announced. "Come out."

Symphony came out dressed in the same green two-piece sweatsuit, but she looked and felt like someone new. Minot scrutinized her with a sideways gaze. She reminded him of a schoolgirl with her wet hair combed back away from her face.

"Sit down," he said, pointing at a field cot by the wall. "I cook dinner. We will eat and rest. In two or three hours we must go."

Symphony glanced at the cot. It had a mattress, thin as a cold cut just like the one in her cell. "I'll sit here," she said, nodding at a beat-up chair. She pulled it over and sat at the table, at the end nearest to the front door. "I'm hungry."

Minot sensed a new resolve in her attitude. It set off his alarm system. She stood up and paced near the door while watching him pick out several jars and cans with unfamiliar labels out of the cupboard. "When are you going to tell me where we're going? You said you'd tell me tonight."

"What is the difference if I tell you? You do not know this place."

"Yeah, but where?" Symphony found a piece of cord on the floor. She snipped it in half and threaded it through the lace holes of her sneakers. "You're not thinking of putting me in another hole in the ground, because I won't—"

"Do not worry. This time you will be in a big house. A magical house," he said with his back to her while stirring what was cooking in the pot. "It's any kind of house you want it to be."

Symphony had her hands behind her, closing in on the door handle. Minot glanced over his humped shoulder and dropped the pot in the sink, his inexpressive face darkening with an unfathomable ferocity. "Stupid girl." He marched to the front door and kicked it open. "You want to run away? Go. Yes, go if you want."

Symphony looked hard at his face. Was he for real? "Is this a trick?"

"No. Go," he said with the false conviction of a crossed lover. "I don't care. Go, go."

"Are you really letting me go?" She glanced at his gun in his holster.

"Yes, get out." He swept his hand toward the outside. "Bye, bye. Go."

Trick or not, Symphony could not pass it up, not with the whole world only a few steps from her. Without taking her eyes off him, she sidled down the stoop, one suspicious step at a time with her back to the night. She moved away from the cabin, watching him by the door watching her. Furious? Heartbroken? She didn't care.

She trudged on, half-turned, looking back at him, tripping over the protruding roots in the uneven ground, his ox-headed silhouette against the cabin light becoming smaller, wondering what had made him do it but not caring. A few yards from the cabin Symphony wheeled and broke into a mad dash downhill like a frightened wild animal in flight.

Out of the trees, she came up to a place where the ground turned into a vast lake of black air. She searched for a way around it, any direction away from the cabin. She tried to find the trail they had taken. She glanced up at the moonless sky through the dark outline of the pines to get her bearings, but it told her nothing. Every direction she took brought her back to the edge of the black cliff, as if the night had swallowed the trail.

Symphony realized then why he had let her go. She could not escape. And he knew it.

A chilled breeze rustled through the dead vegetation. It flew into her burning eyes. She sat down at the edge of the precipice, an endless sea of nothingness that stretched out into the black horizon. She hugged her stomach, tired of praying, of being scared, of taking it. And a sudden surge of fury lifted her to her feet. "I'm getting out of here, even if it kills me."

She lay face down flat over the edge of the cliff and, hugging the ground with her whole body and clutching onto any plant or root that held her, Symphony lowered herself into the darkness below. Carefully, she worked her way down the steep hillside, going from ledge to ledge until she reached a lip-like brink where the ground jutted out into the void. The wind and the night noises swelled to a roar around her. She dangled her legs over the edge as she had done before, searching for footing below, but found none, only empty space. She tried again to gain a foothold and this time the dry-dirt edge started to crumble under her. Terrified, she tried to climb back up, holding tighter to the flimsy roots, but the roots began to give, tearing in her grip, pulling out of the ground with spasmodic rips of her falling weight.

"Oh Jesus."

The roots snapped and the ground beneath her vanished; she dropped in a free-fall onto the slope below, rolling over the stone and vegetation, leaving her skin on the hillside, until she plunged into a thorny net of intersecting vines and branches trapped like an insect caught in flight.

Symphony kicked and squirmed inside the vegetable barbwire until all strength hemorrhaged out of her, too weak even to cry for help. Too much in pain to hope for anything but for it to end.

FORTY

In the Basque Country

THE FLORAL wallpapered room and the slivers of sunshine sipping through the blinds roused Zeus out of bed. He stood up slowly, feeling his ankles' response. They felt stiff and painful, but bearable when he stepped into the bathroom, and then even better after he took a hot shower.

He went downstairs for breakfast. The innkeeper couple was as cordial as they were the previous night. The small dining room had three tables of different sizes. There was a young couple, newlywed type, sitting by the window. He greeted them and asked the innkeeper for *café con leche* and toast. Near the tables, they had a rack with three different dailies, each announcing in bold letters the same headline: "Miguel Angel Estrada *liberado* ..."

Zeus picked up one of the newspapers and read it as he ate.

"Kidnapped son of industrialist Estrada-Uribe freed ... After thirty-one days held in a *zulo* by an ETA commando, twenty-one-year-old Miguel Angel Estrada is home ... Officials of the old Batasuna Party commend the kidnappers for the young man's release and sound state of health ... Judge Baltazar Garzón announced several 'search and capture' orders were issued for individuals allegedly implicated in the abduction ... The Estrada family asks the media for restraint, claiming the ordeal is not over ... Miss Symphony Messina, a US citizen and Miguel Angel's fiancée, remains missing ... ETA denies responsibility ..."

At noon, Zeus's rented car arrived. He settled with the innkeepers and drove off, eastbound toward the city of Mondragón.

On the road, he pondered whether to keep driving to San Sebastián instead and speak eye-to-eye with the Estrada boy. He discarded the idea immediately. Direct intel would be helpful, sure, but the police was going to be all over him. Besides, he probably only knew what his kidnappers told him about Symphony, what they care for him to know. The emphasis now was on swiftness, to keep two steps ahead of the police because once the boy was debriefed, the police would be off like bloodhounds pursuing every lead. The headlines demanded it.

~

The verdant hills and pastures of the Arlabán heights gave Zeus a fleeting feeling that he had been there before. He drove past familiar-looking fields of hazelnuts and centenarian chestnuts in bloom. Giant ferns shaped like eyelashes grew alongside the road. He remembered their shape from a book his father kept in the brown breakfront in his childhood home in Havana. The Basque fauna. He tried to recall their names. Dog roses, horsetails?

Zeus followed the signs to the center of town, past a welcoming billboard. Arrasate-Mondragón, the little big city of prosperity.

The sky was hot and bright, the traffic slow. He parked in Arimazuri Plaza and looked around at the elegant shops and eateries surrounding the square. Every international retailer was represented. No surprise there, he thought, as he meandered past the well-dressed shop windows and citizenry. There was money in this town. A lot.

Mondragón's cooperatives were legendary. They were twice as profitable as the average Spanish corporation, a fact that made them a true phenomenon in the capitalist world. They employed some 66,000 people in thirty-seven countries and, according to *Forbes* magazine, ranked as one of Europe's best places to work. Employee productivity surpassed that of any other Spanish organization. These cooperatives had made the town a showplace of Basque ingenuity. Hallowed ground for nationalists.

Zeus walked to Café Donosti. Contact was scheduled to take place after the lunch hour. He was early. He stood in the shade of nearby San Francisco Church and surveilled the café's activity. He had to assume that Miguel Angel's release would have a major effect on his mission. He could only guess what to expect from ETA's Mondragón cadres, now. He wasn't even sure if their arrangement would still be in place. Variables abounded.

When the lunch rush was over and most customers had left, Zeus pushed the café's door and stepped inside. Several young men—the local Kale Borroka hotheads, ETA's college-age crew—stood leaning at the stand-up counter near the door. The TV was on as usual, loud. Zeus approached the heavyset man by the register. They greeted each other. "Is *el autor* here?" Zeus said.

"You are looking for *el autor*?" the man repeated loud enough for everyone to hear over the blasting TV.

It was a signal. As if choreographed, the group of young men at the counter rushed toward Zeus. In an instant they had him locked in a multiple body-hold.

"Don't move or we'll kill you right here," one of them muttered in Euskara. They carried him feet first out of the café.

They had it all prepared. Zeus could not get a word out, could barely breathe with his head inside a plastic shopping bag pressing on his face. They swung him into a van parked by the curb. He landed with a boom on the metallic floor buried under a pile of knees, hands and feet. The man at the wheel started the engine and backed up to get out of the parking space.

A loud blow on the side panel of the van and at once all movement stopped.

The side door rolled open with a harsh growl and the figure of a graying-whiskered man appeared. "What the hell are you doing?"

It was Aitor, puffing mad, glaring at the sight before him. "Have you idiots gone crazy? Let that man go. Get off him."

The young men tried to argue. "He's the one they told us to watch for … the American with the rented car … he asked for you."

"Let him out. Who gave you those orders?"

Zeus untangled himself, leaped out of the van, and leaned his back against the side panel to catch his breath. He gave the bearded man a nod. "Good to see you, whoever you are."

"You are Aguirre, no?"

"I am. And you?"

"I'm the man you came to see."

The young men hopped out of the van in silence while Aitor helped Zeus back in the café. Once gathered inside, the Kale Borrokas offered their reluctant apologies to Zeus at Aitor's exigency. Then the host and guest locked themselves in the café's private dining room at the rear.

"Some reception," Aitor said as they sat at the table. "Are you all right?"

Zeus nodded. "I guess I came too early."

"These days some rumors sound too good to be false," Aitor said with a weary shrug. "Word got out that a suspicious American without luggage had rented a car from a local agency and was heading in our direction. It prompted our young ones to mobilize. These days we're somewhat sensitive about solitary Americans wandering into town. Those boys have every right to be angry. But I do beg your pardon." Aitor picked up the cognac bottle and filled Zeus's glass. They clicked glasses. "You have come highly recommended."

Apparently not enough, Zeus thought as he licked his cognac-burned, swelling upper lip. He actually said, "No real damage done."

The two men eyed each other, not concentrating on the physical as much as what their presence represented. "It's a good thing we're going to finally settle this affair," Zeus said.

Aitor's brow contracted. "I'm not sure if that's going to be possible. She's no longer in our care."

Zeus writhed on his chair. "What did you say?"

"One of our men has abducted the girl. Took the lives of two of our compeers in the process."

"Do you know where she is?"

"We know. But we will not be the only ones who know for much longer." Aitor glanced at the wall clock. "As of now, we have forty hours to get the girl back before Miguel Angel Estrada tells the police all he knows. It is part of the accord we made with him, to give us time to give the girl to you." He added with a grave grin, "Clearly, this was before our compeer took her."

Zeus was too stunned to process all he was hearing.

"The complications now are many, as you can guess," Aitor said. "I am afraid the boy knows enough about us for the Guardia Civil to reach some real conclusions. So we must act quickly."

"How much can he tell them?"

"No way to know for certain. Perhaps enough to lead them to the girl before we can find her. Maybe to lead them to this very room." Aitor gave him another cheerless grin. "Even to your house there in Miami, if they work fast enough. The crimes that have been committed here will have far-reaching repercussions."

"I don't follow," Zeus said. "If you know where Miss Messina is, what's stopping you from getting her back?"

"Time. Our compeer ran off with her only hours ago. While we were busy setting the prisoner free."

"Have you received proof of life?"

"No. But we know enough of our compeer to know he would not harm her. In his twisted mind, he did it to protect her."

"So where is she?"

"We've traced them to France. We are reasonably certain of where he is hiding her. Our compeers on the French side know the house. We just need corroboration on the exact location."

Zeus remained silent a moment. "This man of yours, did he force the girl to go with him?"

Aitor chuckled at the question. "Who knows? I do not believe she would have left her *novio* behind. She might have gone willingly, thinking it was a way out for her. Personally, I believe our compeer forced her. This compeer of ours, he's not the normal type. He suffers from some sort of deformity. Behaves as strange as he looks."

"This happened yesterday?"

Aitor nodded. "Late afternoon."

Zeus's mind was running it all down now. "Why do you think Estrada will wait forty hours before he tells the police all he knows? The police interrogators are probably all over him, as we speak."

"We made an accord."

Zeus's eyes flashed with disbelief.

"The boy gave me his word that he would wait two days before he met with the police. That was about eight hours ago. I trust he will do as he swore to do. The boy is a Basque. Besides—" Aitor took a drag of his cigarette and released a long weary puff of smoke. "Our accord is more utilitarian than you think, trust me. The girl's life depends on it."

"What happens when the time period is finished?"

"The deal reverses. I will not go into further detail. There are aspects of it that do not concern you." Aitor paused. "But do not worry, Aguirre. We will find the girl and hand her to you before the time runs out." Aitor topped-off his cognac tumbler. "Are you aware of what the man you are working for has done to us?"

"I know what the papers say and what your compeers in Madrid have shared with me."

"Then you don't know the half of it." Aitor hunched over the table.

Zeus leaned back and made himself comfortable on the chair. He was going to hear his host's version whether he wanted to or not. He could see it coming in Aitor's face, the burning need to tell it, every gruesome detail of it.

"Eleven people killed," he began. "Eleven that we know of. In only two, three days. Did you know that?" That's what that girl's father has done here."

Zeus listened.

"Each one killed in the most horrific manner. Including an entire family of four. Innocent people, women and children. Five of them my compeers and closest friends. Patriots, every single one of them, killed for not wanting to kill." Aitor knocked back the cognac and let the spirit burn down his throat. When it was over, he recited the full names and the places of birth of each of his "fallen compeers," a rehearsed eulogy by the sound of it.

"A terrible tragedy," Zeus said.

"This I will tell you," Aitor went on, looking deep into Zeus's eyes, as his coherence floated away by degrees. "Had it been up to me? That girl you have come for, she would have been set free a long time ago. And that beast her father sent after us would still be where he belongs, in your country, and my friends would still be alive—" Aitor took another sip. "But it was not to be. And you, sir. I am amazed you are still alive. It is by a miracle that anything connected to that man, Messina, will ever survive in this town from now on." Aitor shook his index finger in the air. "I promise you this, Aguirre, and I say it from my soul. Our response to your gangster friend will be slow in coming. But it will come. That, you can tell him when you see him."

"I've never met the man," Zeus said.

Aitor chuckled, unbelieving.

Zeus's eyes narrowed. "I'm not sure you understand my position. I'm here solely to send a kidnapped girl back to her parents—whoever they are. That is my one and only goal."

"I know who you are, Aguirre. Military man. I read your report. I, too, know Txomin. I met him once. In better days. Trust me, I know about you." A single laugh escaped though his nose. "Why else would you be here? Alive."

Zeus gazed at the tabletop. Suddenly the possibility that he would be working side by side for the next forty hours with a drunk bound to become the Most Wanted Criminal in Spain became too real. "So we have less than two days left to rescue the girl. When do we leave for France?"

"There are accounts that must be settled before you and I walk out of here together."

Zeus grinned, wondering when that would come up. "The money is in San Sebastián," he told him. "Is that a problem?"

"No. Donosti is on the way to France. If the funds are in our possession by tomorrow, we will proceed together. If not, you would be on your own."

"The money will be there."

They walked out to the bar counter together. The Kale Borroka boys were gone. "Tell me," Zeus said. "Why do you think this guy will give up the girl?"

"Because Minot is a compeer, and his basic nature is to follow orders."

Zeus nodded. "What's he really looking to get out of this?"

"Money will not resolve this situation, if that is what you're thinking."

"That's refreshing."

"There will be a negotiation, of course. But it will not be about money. It will be about what is best for the organization."

"What makes you so sure?"

"Because compeer Minot is a Basque, first and last. A patriot at heart."

"Then forty hours will be more than we need."

Aitor was starting to like the *cubano-americano*.

F O R T Y-O N E

WHEN SYMPHONY CAME to, the first thing she saw was a naked fluorescent tube hanging from a low, uneven ceiling. Then she noticed the yellowed, white bedposts at the foot of the bed, the standing fan swiveling with a soft hum in the corner, a print of bearded Louis Pasteur hanging over the bed. The longer she gazed at the room the less real it seemed.

Her head ached so bad Symphony could barely keep her eyes from closing. Everything in the room looked makeshift, rickety, off kilter. The walls were painted to look white-tiled, the window was frescoed on the wall, the worn-out furniture seemed like museum pieces or part of a theater set. The dusty air, the tomblike silence pressed down on her, oppressive like a bad dream. Still, she knew it could not be a dream or a nightmare.

Minot opened the door. She watched him approach. She no longer just feared him, she pitied him, too. He was dressed all in white, slacks and T-shirt, like a sailor. His ox-skull concealed inside a black beret as always. "How do you feel?" he said, halting two steps before reaching her bedside.

A cough broke her first attempt at speaking. "Where am I?"

"You are in hospital," he gestured with his hand at the evidence.

Her gaze wandered. "Where's the doctor, the nurses?"

"A doctor and a nurse have seen you. You don't remember? Anyway, you don't need them anymore. All you must do now is rest."

He stepped toward the door.

"Don't go," she moaned.

He came back halfway.

"Please tell me, when are you going to let me go?"

The labored rasp of her voice appealed to him. "I told you it is not my decision. My duty is to care of you until you go. And I am afraid I have not done a good job. I am sorry. You cannot be set free if you're not healthy. You will face the press on your two feet. This is the rule."

"When?"

"It is up to you now."

He left the room and locked the door.

From afar, Maison Lavryn, Minot's home, marked a bizarre outline in the flat of the valley. Once a roadside attraction to pay for its upkeep, it looked like a pileup of several houses of divergent construction and designs attached to one another. Structural wings extended from every side of the building like outgrowths of the walls. Three, four, even five stories high depending on where one looked. The building was Madame Della Marie Minot's creation. A gigantic maze-like dollhouse she had conceived as an heirloom and a hideaway for her only son. The product of a two-decade frenzy of construction and remodeling that did not cease until a life-size faux community with fake shops, cafés, schoolrooms, libraries, populated with costumed mannequins was built within its walls, wiping out the family's riches.

Inside Maison Lavryn, Symphony was no less isolated than she was in the cabin hidden in the depths of the Pyrenees, or in the *zulo*. The countless number of rooms, staircases, and corridors, some leading to doors installed on the walls, and pathways leading nowhere, guaranteed security.

Andre Minot, heir to the mansion, rolled a wooden cart into the *maison de santé* room where Symphony reposed. He picked up a saucer from the cart and placed his hand on Symphony's damp, feverish brow. Her hair was humid with sweat. "The doctor said you must start drinking these."

Symphony opened her eyes and wetted her cracked lips. Minot helped her sit up and watched her drink the pills. "Soon you will feel better, you'll see."

"Am I going to die?"

Minot took a step back, stunned. "No." His deformed head rose. "Why do you say it? You only need rest. The doctor said so. You are young. You are strong. I will not let that happen. Are you hungry? I have soup and I made a hamburger for you, American style. If you like something else is OK too."

Symphony closed her eyes and let her head drop on the pillow.

He observed her face from afar. He could not help seeing her in a different light now. In the mysteries of his thoughts, Minot felt personally responsible for her accident the night at the cabin. It took four men, he and three of his compeers, several hours and hundreds of meters of mountaineer's cord to untangle Symphony from the tree that had trapped her. Later, in St-Jean-Pied-de-Port, an ETA cadre whose wife was a nurse and a local doctor, a sympathetic intern, worked on Symphony's multiple cuts and abrasions, the worst ones needing several stitches. The doctor advised hospitalization because of her head injury. But Minot brought her home instead, to the make-believe hospital room in Maison Lavryn.

Despite his twisted sense of possession, Minot knew he could not hide the girl indefinitely. Not after so many of his compeers knew she was in his custody. She belonged to the organization and he would have to set her free, eventually. High command's directive had been quite clear about one thing though: "The girl must not be liberated until she can walk to freedom on her own." When would she be ready for that? Time will tell. In the meantime, he would only be following orders.

Minot's bovine eyes smiled at Symphony's slumbering face. He picked up the dishes and rolled out the cart into the hallway. He entered an adjacent room and climbed into a large fine-wood armoire. It led to a hidden stairwell. He pushed out a swiveling wall panel and went down a narrow stairway. It led into the yellowish tiled kitchen. The only kitchen in use out of the several in the Maison. It had a real window and a view of the mountains in the hazed distance.

He covered the plates and placed them next to a bowl full of pork sausages on the countertop.

In the shadows of the dayroom, Madame Minot was watching television. She sat prodded up on pillows on a metal-frame bed in the middle of the room amid a mismatched collection of furniture of styles that went back to an *ancienne noblesse* the house never possessed. Sitting beside her on a worn corduroy divan sat Gerard, a gaunt white-haired man in his seventies. He was the Maison's caretaker and the Madame's companion.

A taint of decay hovered in the room.

Minot's arrival drew no reaction from the old couple. They seemed in a trance, their unblinking gazes fixed on the TV screen. "I saw the sausages," he announced, lowering the television's volume.

The old woman's eyes blinked with annoyance. "Eat them if you want."

"You've already forgotten what I told you? No deliveries. No strangers coming to the house. No one."

"It's Thursday," the old man said.

Minot walked up to him, cupped his hands over his cheeks and shouted: "No one can come to this house until I say so. Do you hear me now?"

"Stop your braying," Madame Minot snapped.

"Mother, this is part of an operation—"

She shushed him. "Don't talk to me about operations. Since before you were born I've been involved in operations."

"Then have him call off all deliveries. I want no one coming into this house. This is serious, Mother. It's your duty and mine."

"The village holiday," Gerard said. "That's why the sausages came today."

Minot glanced at the old man, at his worn-out slippers, his bony leathery fingers. The village feast. "What else now?"

~

An hour later Symphony was still deep in a drug-induced sleep in the stale air of the fake hospital room.

Minot came in with a pan of warm water. He set a bottle with oxygenated water and one of mercurochrome, gauze, pincers on a saucer on the night table. To change her dressings and clean her wounds Minot needed to unclothe her to her undergarments. This time, though, he continued until she was completely nude. He panicked when he saw her in full. Averting his eyes, he soaked and squeezed the sponge in the warm water and gently began patting her skin, softly around the cuts and scrapes, the wiry black stitches on her arms. His face grew hotter with fright when he rubbed the sponge below her dainty shoulders, the purple bruises on her ribs, over her pierced navel and taut underbelly. He felt himself entering an unknown room when he reached her solid hips, her thighs, down the length of her slender legs to the red rose tattoo on her ankle ... There had been other glimpses of nude women in his life, drunken prostitutes he had paid for to see, to fornicate, bad-skinned women with panties around their ankles, laughing, practical jokers who always said something to disgust him and make him walk away without consummation. But the gangster's daughter was the first nude female he had ever seen in such clean clear light, in such gentle silence ... He drew the sponge around her breasts, circling them several times, his mountaineer's goat legs weakening on feeling the passing rustle of her warm skin on his fingers. He experienced the terror of her reddish-pink nipples compacting with the drops of oxygenated water. His breathing grew heavier, louder, pitiful ... Nothing shamed him as much as his own dishonorable urges, his animal impulses.

His eyes burned as he put her clothes back on as if dressing a cadaver, focusing only on his wooly hands, going through the icy motions of his self-loathing, a force ever fiercer than his natural desires.

Minot walked out of the room with tears in his eyes, his hands trembling, burning with fury as he only could be with himself.

F O R T Y-T W O

San Sebastián

Zeus followed the slow-moving traffic along the boulevard bordering the half-moon strip of La Concha Beach. A group of barelegged pedestrians flapped across the street, towels hanging, sunglasses gleaming in the early sun. The beach was his only memory of the city, a postcard childhood recollection of him strolling on the sand with his father during a nostalgic trip to the Old Country. He glanced at the wooded isle across the mouth of the bay, a few yards out offshore. A natural breakwater, he recalled his father pointing it out. A perfect beach. Zeus thought it so Basque of him to say so. It was August then as it was now when summer seems eternal.

Zeus found the hotel. He parked a couple of blocks away. The contact would be a recognizable face, Judge Arsenio's email had said, no special confirmation required. He could not help but wonder who the person was. The judge himself? Maybe. It would be good to have the old boy with him.

The Maria Cristina Hotel was one of the best in the city, a symbol of San Sebastián's opulence for a century. Zeus buttoned up his shirt collar and sports jacket, afraid his casual clothing might attract undue attention in all the luxury. He slipped on his prescription tinted glasses and went in the side door. Guests were streaming into the restaurant for breakfast. Several people were sitting at the lavish waiting area in the lobby. Two couples, a group of four, and a solitary woman. Zeus stood by the elevator doors expecting Judge Arsenio's elegant figure to come out.

He took another look across the polished brass and marble and recognized the solitary woman sitting on the lobby sofa. He pulled out a ballpoint pen and wrote on his notepad. The elevator doors opened and he cut in front of the bellhop coming out. "Pardon me," he said. "Would you be so kind as to give this note to that lady sitting over there?"

The bellhop gave him a questioning look.

"Don't worry," Zeus told him. "She's a friend. I want it to be a surprise." He folded the notepaper. "Just hand it to her, don't make it too obvious. Her name is Señorita Bernard." He slipped the bellhop a twenty-euro note.

Zeus entered the elevator as the doors closed.

The blue-uniformed young man walked to the sitting area, vowed before Tess and handed her the note. She bolted upright, glanced around, put her iPhone in her purse and unfolded the paper. *Take the elevator to the third floor. Alone. Z.*

Tess straightened her tan business suit and marched toward the bank of elevators, purse strap in the crook of her arm, briefcase in one hand, scarf aloft behind her. Several pairs of eyes followed her stride, men and women—the reason why Zeus had not stayed around to see who was interested. People always looked at Tess.

The elevator doors opened on the third floor. "Zeus." She rushed to him.

He took the heavy-looking briefcase from her. "Come on. We have to go. Quickly, please."

"What's wrong?"

"I'll tell you when we're out of here."

They raced toward the end of the hallway and into the hotel employees' exit. "Where's your luggage?"

"The concierge has it. What's happening?"

They dashed down the stairs, their footsteps reverberating in the closed stairwell. "Have you been followed? Did anyone look suspicious to you? On the plane, at the airport, anywhere?"

Tess was moving too fast for her heels. "I don't think so. No."

"Are you sure?" Zeus pushed the main floor door and glanced in both directions. "Try to think."

"I'm not sure. I didn't notice anyone."

He took her arm and stepped out calmly. "Hope you're right."

They slipped out through the service entrance. "Keep walking. The car's around the corner."

Out in the street, Zeus held on to her arm, his head panning like a radar, looking for any sign of surveillance. Tess kept up the pace, impressed at how alive he looked. She noticed a slight limp in his step but said nothing.

They sat inside Zeus's rented car. Their chests pumped from the haste. Zeus turned the ignition key as he assessed her face, her ruffled hair, her eyes bluer than he remembered them. "I think we're OK for now."

It was good to see her.

"Bet you weren't expecting to see me."

"Can't say I was." He backed out of the parking space and drove off. "Why did the judge send you?"

"That is exactly what he said would be your first question."

Zeus shifted gears, his brow in a knot.

"He told me you'd understand why with a single word: Necessity." She paused and added, "I'm the only one who cares, Zeus. Don't you know that?"

"Messina knows that too. Could've had you tailed. They could be on us right now. It's not good for you to be here."

"Arsenio took precautions to avoid anyone following me. I've been on four planes to get here. I didn't give my real name in the hotel—"

"We're past that."

"Zeus, I asked to come," she said firmly. "There just wasn't anyone else we could trust. Arsenio agreed. Besides, this is as much your project as it is mine."

"That has nothing to do with it."

"I don't think you understand—"

He cut her off, "Listen to me, Tess—"

"I am listening—" she cut him off.

"Garzón's after me," Zeus said.

"What?" she paused, her lips parting in shock. "Why?"

"*Asociación con banda armada.*" His switch to Spanish threw her off for an instant. "For associating with ETA. That's a crime here."

"I know that, Zeus. But how did he—"

"A former colleague of mine gave me away. Now I'm being chased as if I was another terrorist. And you," he glanced at her. "You have to fly out of here as soon as we're done with this bank business. Today. This afternoon, if possible."

Tess let out a long, tired breath.

He could see it had not been part of her plans.

She tried to say something. "Sorry, Tess," he interrupted her. "You can't stay in Spain. And definitely not with me."

Zeus took the roundabout toward the Boulevard, wondering why the judge had allowed her to come. He blamed himself, though. Had he informed him about Garzón's agents being on his trail, had he told him his true status, he wouldn't have sent her. He had also miscalculated Tess's resolve, how much she had taken Symphony Messina's case to heart. He should've known. Too late now. "You have everything with you?"

"Yes. It's all in my case."

They drove over the bridge across the Urumea River. They glanced at each other as glum lovers do. She placed the briefcase on her lap and showed him the passports and the rest of the paperwork Judge Arsenio had given her to obtain access to the cash. He stopped at a light and looked them over quickly. "Good work." He put his hand on hers. "You're one tough girl, Tess."

"You seem surprised."

He grinned. "Sometimes I'm a little slow."

"Yeah, I've noticed."

Zeus stopped the car on a shady street in the outskirts of the city, in front of a Caja Viscaya branch office. They surveyed the street and the bank. "It's a little neighborhood bank," Tess said.

"It usually is."

They went inside and introduced themselves to a bank officer. After a brief exchange, the man asked for their passports and excused himself. He came back with his supervisor, a stocky man with a friendly smile and a gray suit, the bank director. "Mr. and Mrs. Corona, please come this way."

He showed them to his glass-walled office.

"Will this take long?" Zeus said.

"Not at all," Director Casado said as he studied his "special customers" with a curious grin. "We've been expecting you. Your safe-deposit box account is ready." He retrieved several forms from a file cabinet. "Everything was handled at our main branch. All we need is a sample of your signature and that of your wife's for our records."

Tess and Zeus—Mr. and Mrs. Corona—signed the documents and placed the signed forms on the desk. Tess had to stifle a smile, thinking this was how married couples went through life.

The director looked at the documents. "Fine. Now permit me to show you to the vault," he said with an elegant sweep of his arm.

Mr. and Mrs. Corona followed the director down the stairs to the basement where the vault was located. He introduced them to the vault clerk, a grave prim-faced man in a double-breasted suit. "Pablo will show you to your box."

The slow-paced clerk ushered Tess and Zeus into the cool hush of the fluorescent-lit inner vault. They halted midway along the morgue-like wall of polished metal squares. "Your key, please."

Tess handed him the small envelope with the key the director had given her. The vault attendant searched through a mass of keys on a ring and held one up. He inserted the keys in their corresponding locks, opened the box, pulled out a gray metal drawer and placed it on an office cart. "Come this way, please." He showed them to a booth outside the vault.

Zeus stepped inside. Tess followed in and drew the curtain for privacy. "One hundred thousand," Zeus said when he finished counting the stacks of euros. "How did you get this much out of Messina?"

"It's not Messina's money. It's the firm's. Technically."

"You're really something, you know that?"

In a series of quick exhilarated motions, they transferred the stacks of one hundred euros from the metallic drawer to her briefcase.

That accomplished, he closed the briefcase and she locked it, then they glanced at each other in the half-light of the booth. He pulled her to him and kissed her as she had been waiting for him to do. When he began to ease away, she tiptoed holding on to him, unwilling to end it. Then they heard the man outside the booth faking a cough, and then another one.

Tess and Zeus looked at each other holding back a laugh and stepped out of the booth, an air of nonchalance in their manner.

They shook hands with the bank director and walked out of the sliding glass doors.

Outside, Zeus slipped on his sunglasses and scanned the street as they strode back to the car. "That wasn't too painful," she said with a cautious smile.

He opened the car door for her. "You and Arsenio did a good job, Mrs. Corona."

Tess watched him walk around the car. She liked the way he moved, those swift precise motions of his, like a dancer. "You haven't told me anything about Symphony," she said.

He glanced at her from the driver's seat. "Things have gotten a bit more complicated since we last talked."

"How so?"

"Two nights ago, one of the kidnappers shot two of his colleagues and ran off with her."

"Are you serious?" she said big-eyed. "Kidnapped by one of the kidnappers?"

"Afraid so." He started the car.

"This is crazy. What's going to happen now?"

"We're going to rescue her."

"Rescue? Where is she?"

"In France."

"In France?"

"Yes. About fifty kilometers over the border, not too far. If everything goes as planned, you might meet her personally as early as tomorrow night."

Tess stared ahead at the street, her lips parted, processing the information. "What about the police?"

"If the police intervene, she'll be killed. That's why we have to act quickly, use the manpower and material that is available. Part of this money is going toward that."

"How much of a ransom does this new kidnapper is asking for?"

"He doesn't want money."

"What is it he wants?"

"No one really knows what this guy has in mind. It makes no difference. We have to make our move tonight."

"You keep saying we."

"My Basque friends and me."

"Your ETA friends? The same people who kidnapped her in the first place? Zeus, tell me you're not doing this with them."

"It can only be done with them. They are serious about setting her free and there's no one else."

She tossed her hair back. "This is one strange country. What kind of rescue is it going to be? Sounds like a military sort of thing?"

"We have every reason to believe it will be solved with a negotiation. The weapons are only in case we need them."

"And this is happening tonight?"

"It has to be completed by tomorrow. Before the Spanish police can take more direct action. The press's been stirring up public opinion since the boy was set free. If the police find her before we do—" Zeus shook his head. "This guy will not surrender to the police. We are all she has."

Zeus pulled up to the hotel's side door and glanced over at Tess. He was really glad to see her. "I'll be back by lunchtime."

They looked into each other's eyes. "I was hoping to have coffee together," she said.

"So did I."

"Duty calls, I guess."

"Afraid so."

Tess leaned forward and gave him a kiss.

"Hey," he said. "Be ready to move when I get back."

Unsure of all that could be construed from his statement, she said, "I'm ready now."

"Good."

"See you later."

FORTY-THREE

Maison Lavryn

IN A TRIANGULAR space in the bowels of Maison Lavryn, Minot sat on a solitary school desk chair in the brown light of an overhead bulb. It was a place no one knew existed, created by an error in calculation. A wedge of dead space between three rooms, accessible only through the make-believe Fruiterer shop with the hanging dusty wax fruits and plastic vegetables, and the mannequin shopkeeper dressed in a faded blue frock. A secret alcove where he sought enlightenment and hid from his hidden life.

He sat holding his furry head in his hands and staring at the cluttered space, thinking of how he could rearrange it in case a backup hiding place for the prisoner became necessary. He tried looking at it through her eyes, and what he saw depressed him.

Since childhood, the triangular walled space had been his domain within the wall-less immensity of his imagination, his inner sanctum. But now he could not see it except as it really was—rows of nail points protruding from unpainted wooden walls, plastered with yellowed newspaper clippings and articles on ETA, and pictures of the Lavryn house in its heyday. There were several photographs of his father and one of himself as a babe when his malformation was vaguely noticeable and his eyebrows had not yet fused.

Underneath an *ikurrina*, the Basque flag, sat his books and booklets on and by Sabino Arana Goiri, his spiritual guide, whose idea of the Basque people as a special race in possession of an extra coil in their brain, which the average human lacked, had captivated Minot since he was a boy. To

Arana Goiri, Basques were not just another nation or another race with an undeniable right to their land, but a different species: the original Europeans.

Minot had searched hard in those books for confirmation of Arana Goiri's theory on the Basque people's extra-coiled brain. He believed the facts were in there, somewhere, and it was only a matter of time before he would find them. He already had his own buckled skull to prove it.

On the wooden shelves beside it were his books on human deformities. The studies on the Proteus syndrome, on neurofibromatosis, and other rare forms of Polyostotic Fibrous Dysplasia, a nonhereditary genetic disease that caused bones to turn into jelly.

On the smaller bookshelf sat the books from Minot's infancy, the ones he now detested but could not bring himself to throw away. Stories of talking animals, enchanted lovers, the Hunchback of Notre Dame, The Beauty and the Beast. The tear-stained pages of John Merrick's biography.

On the opposite wall, under a picture of Michelangelo's Leda and the Swan tacked on the wall, was his pornography collection, books on zoophilia, illustrated bestiality, all stacked carefully, titled spines to the wall.

A Chinese-made AK-47 with a fifty-round pan and an antique shotgun, a .22 rifle with a scope, stood on a corner next to a rapier and an army saber.

In the wooden chest, he stored cases of ammunition, cleaning brushes and tools. Inside a milk crate nailed to the wall was a pile of mobile telephones; in his desk drawer, he kept a short-barrel Smith & Western, a shoebox with coins from the world, wallets, passports, foreign currency.

On the single corner of the obtuse triangle, Minot kept his poetry, a stack of notebooks of poems in French, in Euskara, a few in Spanish, dating back to his primary school days.

Maybe he could set up the field cot there. It might fit if he cleared out space.

On the wall behind him hung an old crayon painting of his image done by a traveling artist on his thirteenth birthday, a deliberately flattering rendering that minimized the deformed shape of his skull. The version of himself he believed the person who would answer the silent calls of his soul would see.

He picked the notebook on top of the stack. He wanted to compose a verse in English, for her, for the one he no longer thought of as the *americana* gangster's daughter, or the prisoner, not inside his secret world.

He sat with the English-French dictionary on his lap, the New Cassells. He shuffled the pages, looking for inspiration. He liked the act of chasing down words and learning new ones as he went, following them to their purest symbols, their true meaning.

Calliope, Muse of the epic poetry ... He wrote a stanza and scratched out the words, then restrung them again ... Calliope, goddess of eloquence, patroness of Poetry ... He became lost in his own mental maze, down blind alleys of semantics, emotions he could not name. Calliope, why can you not see me? He slapped the dictionary pages. There has to be an English word for her kind of indifference ... How many times must I save you from certain doom before you recognize the inevitable forces that have linked us for life? You are mine as I am yours, he wrote, before his pencil smashed against the wall. A higher power has decided it.

FORTY-FOUR

San Sebastián

FROM THE DRIVER'S seat of his rented VW, Zeus watched Tess coming out of the hotel's side door. She had changed into a lovely pair of snug jeans under a tan blazer and was carrying a shoulder bag big enough to check as luggage at the airport, a woman primed for adventure. With a little smile on his face, Zeus unlocked the car door and started the engine.

"Got everything you need?"

"Yes," Tess said as she settled beside him, her blonde hair swinging like in a shampoo commercial. "I told them someone's coming to pick up my suitcase later. There's only one."

"Good." Zeus looked again at the hotel's door. No one had followed her out. It was past high noon, *siesta* hour, and the San Sebastian traffic was sparse in the muggy Basque sun. "You're staying the night," he told her as they drove off.

She smiled to herself. "Couldn't ship me out of the country, huh?"

"No seats left on any international flights until tomorrow."

"Pity."

"I've arranged for a place for you to stay the night."

"Where?"

"A town nearby called Fuenterrabia, next to the French border. You'll like it."

"How about you?"

He glanced at her. "Well, if all plays out as planned, I expect us to be on our way to New York by tomorrow, with the girl."

"From your lips to God's ears, my grandma used to say."

They drove eastward in the direction of France, the deep green Basque Country in the overcast light. Zeus talked on his cell phones for most of the drive, in Basque and Spanish, while Tess dozed off. Half an hour later, the car lurched to a halt. Tess opened her jet-lagged eyes to a hazy Monet painting of a sunset dock lined with small fishing boats with furled sails.

Zeus turned off the engine and gestured with his chin at the view of the angler's port and the shimmering bay. "How do you like it?"

"It's beautiful," she said.

"Told you. Your luggage will be here later. It's been confirmed."

"Where are am I staying?"

"See that bakery?" He pointed across the street at a gabled-roof building with white balconies on the upper floors facing the sea. "It's one of their *casa francas*—safe houses."

"Bread, bed, and board. Sounds wonderful."

He reached over, opened the briefcase, and took out several hundred-euro notes. Tess arched her eyebrow. "That's a lot of cash."

"For the piper," he said with his mystery tight-lipped grin. "Wait for me here. I'll be back with the keys."

The safe house was a two-flight walkup attic apartment over the *panadería*. Inside, it was shadowy and dusty from lack of use. The oddly arranged dark oak furniture in the living room, the big black plastic box TV set, the heavy-hanging drapes in the severe gloom, remained just as the old widow had left it before she died.

"I feel like I'm in Anne Frank's hideout," Tess said.

"Is it so bad?" Zeus set the bags of groceries on the table and put her briefcase in a closet by the door.

"Can we open the windows?"

Zeus walked to the floor-to-ceiling balcony Persian shutters and flipped them open. The late afternoon sunrays flooded in, breathing life into the room. They stepped outside and leaned on the grillwork railing. The scents of doughy bread baking and salty sea floated together in the air. Out on the Spanish side of the port a small forest of masts vaguely rocked with the tide. Visible in the near distance was the French shoreline in the setting sun.

Tess glanced at Zeus with a heavy-lidded smile in her eyes. "I am glad I came."

"So am I. But this is a safe house, Tess. We're here to keep out of sight. Come." He took her by the arm and escorted her back into the living room and closed the shutter doors but left the shades open. "It's better if we stay indoors."

"Can't even take a walk on the pier?"

"You have to stay here until it's time to leave the country."

"Are you grounding me, Mr. Corona?" Tess said with one end of her lips pulled up in a little grin of defiance.

He enjoyed her playacting, her put-on girly sass, but he could not have her in that frame of mind. "It all might look very peaceful out there but it could change on a dime." He spoke as he searched the kitchen cabinets. "We have to be careful. State security has been on my heels for three days." He filled a glass with tap water. "They damn nearly bagged me twice, in Madrid and the night we talked. Can't give them the slightest edge. If they catch you with me, well, you're going to need all the lawyer friends you have and then some."

"You're scaring me, Zeus."

"You'll be safe as long as you stay here. They have eyes watching over you that not even I am aware of." He raised the glass. "Want some?"

"I brought my own."

He'd seen the plastic water bottle inside her suitcase-like purse. She took a couple of steps into the shadows of the room, the sway of her hips and shoulders on stiletto heels doing the talking for her. She looked into his amber eyes.

"Aren't you going to show me the rest of the apartment?"

"There isn't much more to it. There's the kitchen. The bedrooms are that way."

"Which way?"

Zeus gave her his mystery smile, the one he knew she liked. "This way."

He pulled her to him for the kiss they had had to cut short at the bank. Locked into each other, they peeled off their garments, one by one, rolling on the walls down the narrow hallway into a bedroom, where they fell clasped together onto the narrowest and noisiest bed, laughing like juveniles at their own voracity.

Then it all turned serious, muscular and serious, as each took command of the marvels of their bodies coming together while the bedsprings screamed in rhythm with her single-syllable mantra.

When reality set in again, Zeus propped his head against the wall. Tess put her lips on the curve of his neck and rested her inner thigh over the warmth of his midriff. He knew as she knew they could never become each other's pastime. The twenty years of life that separated them and the issues and baggage they each brought, the very stuff they were made of, would not allow it. This had to be serious or not at all. He caressed her hair and listened to her childlike respiration until she fell asleep. Then he slipped away in silence. He found his cell phone and read the single message that lit up. It was time to go.

PART VI

FORTY-FIVE

New Jersey Turnpike

JOEY'S PORSCHE SUV and the Bureau's unmarked Chevrolet stood side by side at an emergency stop area off the highway. They kept the engines and the AC running, their backs to the oncoming traffic. Special Agent Pensotti, in a blue Oxford shirt and striped tie, shook his head at Joey from the opened window.

"That's not enough," he said.

"The hell it ain't." Joey showed them a manila envelope that had been sitting next to him on the passenger seat. It contained the so-called intelligence on the Cuban, for which he had paid through the nose. "Here. Take it. It's everything you need on the guy." He held it out the window.

The traffic roared.

Agent Pensotti did not bother to look at it. "We're going to need more than that if you want us to get involved."

"More? The guy's a fucking terrorist. Tight with those European Basques. All a bunch of terrorists. What more you need?"

Pensotti's partner, Special Agent Lomax, leaned forward on the steering wheel. "Listen Messina, stop wasting our time. We're not interested in your Cuban. You know damn well why we're here."

"We want Tommy, Joey," Pensotti drove it in.

"And I want my daughter."

"Give us something we can show our section chief. Then, maybe."

"You guys—" Joey winced. "You're supposed to serve and protect American citizens. My daughter's an American, a college student for Christ's sake, a good kid."

"It's out of our hands," Pensotti said. "Missing person's cases are a local matter."

"That's bull and you know it. Missing persons, kidnappings, abductions of American citizens anywhere in the world is Bureau business. I checked."

An eighteen-wheeler stormed by.

Lomax leaned forward again. "What the fuck's wrong with you, Joey. We come here to talk about Tommy but you keep throwing all this business at us. Your daughter's case is so far from our jurisdiction, I can't begin to tell you. And now you're going off about some terrorist crap. You're wasting our time. Talk to us about Tommy or call it a day—"

"This has got to be a give-and-take thing, Joey," Pensotti said. "I told you on the phone and I'll say it again. First you give us something solid on Tommy Pacelli, then we'll see about what we can do about your kid in Spain."

Joey rubbed the grease off his brow. "Look, I can give you Little Tommy on a silver platter if you want. But I know how this works. It'll take you Feds a year just to get him into court. Maybe five years to take him down. You actually expect me to wait for that? Meanwhile, my daughter's missing for a month already."

Pensotti shrugged. "It's how it's got to be, Joey. Nobody's getting something for nothing."

"The hell with you two. Find my daughter and then I'll give you everything you need to bring that piece of shit down. That's my offer." Joey threw the car into drive. "It ain't like youse are the only Organized Crime Unit around."

Agent Lomax said, "People who live in glass houses shouldn't be throwing rocks."

"What's that you said?"

"You heard."

"Yeah? You wish you had something on me. But you and I know you don't. All my business has been legit for longer than you've been a Fed. Longer than the statutes of limitations for anything you can ever dream of pinning on me."

The agents chuckled. "You're sure about that?"

"Like the song says, pal. Dream on."

Pensotti tapped Lomax's leg and said, "Hey Joey, don't forget you asked us to meet you. Not the other way around. We need your commitment on this."

The constant roar of the fast-moving turnpike traffic swelled in the sudden silence.

"Listen, I know you want Little Tommy more than anything. Or else you wouldn't be here. I wouldn't be here either if I didn't think you're the only way I got left to find my daughter. There's got to be something we can work out."

"Most certainly. You give us something worth our while on Tommy, and we'll see what we can do about your daughter."

Lomax cut in, "And so that you know, we don't care who you talk to on our side. You're going to get the same answer no matter who you talk to in the Bureau. Nobody trusts you, Joey."

"You think it's easy for me to sit here with you? This little meet. This is a feather in your cap. But don't you know what this means to me?" Joey hurled the envelope into the Chevrolet's passenger window. It landed on agent Pensotti's lap. "Talk to your chiefs there in Manhattan or in Washington D.C. or wherever. And don't take too long, neither. My offer can and will expire at any time. That's all I got to say."

Joey's Porsche Cayenne took off burning rubber.

Commitment, he said to himself as his SUV merged into the traffic heading into Manhattan. They want commitment, those stupid fucks. What more commitment do they expect? He had just ruined his life.

FORTY-SIX

Pyrénées-Atlantiques, France

BY SATURDAY AT sundown, everything that could be done had been done. Aitor's last telephone call to Minot had ended the same as the others, with Aitor or Zurgin shouting threats to their subordinate who refused to accept their authority or negotiate with what Minot called "the fate of a prisoner they had left to die."

None of their high-minded patriotic appeals to his Basqueness, to the honor of ETA, to reasonableness, to threats against his life had done any good. The girl was no longer their prisoner but a voluntary guest in his care, Minot told them, and it was of no concern to him if anyone believed him.

Zero hour was then set for midnight.

The email communiqué Zurgin had been eager to receive from high command in Toulouse, granting him full powers to decide on the course of action, finally came in at eight p.m.

A copy of the message went out to Aitor. It came in a coded text on Pedro's Blackberry handset.

Aitor immediately requested a meeting with Zurgin to discuss last-minute details. He still believed the standoff could be settled without an all-out assault on the house, as Zurgin had planned. Aitor wanted the Cuban's input before any action began. He not only trusted Zeus's good judgment, he knew Zurgin also respected him enough to defer to him if Zeus were to come up with a sound alternative. Most of all, Aitor wanted to determine whether his trigger-happy commander was sincere in his intentions of "preserving the prisoner's life at all cost," as the message from the leadership had concluded. A possibility that was much in doubt if they carried out the attack plan his commander had in mind.

At nine p.m. Aitor stepped out of the van. Pedro and Karlo followed him out. They stood by the side of the road, a country lane that swirled up the hillside over the valley. The fresh air felt good after hours stuck in the heat of the van.

A picture of summer-green tranquility lay before them under the dusky sky. The birds of sundown perched on the wires, chirping in the approaching darkness. The traffic in the valley had but died out as supper-time neared.

"Bring out the *bocatas* and the Coca-Colas," Aitor ordered.

"I brought a bottle of wine," Pedro replied.

"Leave it where it is. No alcohol tonight."

Pedro shrugged at Karlo.

The three men sat behind the high brush by the side of the road, supped on their sandwiches and drank their warm cola.

Aitor's baggy-eyed gaze kept switching between his wristwatch and the vista before him. He studied the layout of the streets around the Maison and the Maison itself, the absurd mess of fake doorways, mish-mashed windows, and artificial brick and multi-level roofs that sprawled in every direction. The men closest to the house had heard banging and hammering earlier coming from within, but it had stopped. He wondered what kind of scheme the *iparralde* had in mind.

The men ate their sandwiches and gazed at the Maison. "To me, that house looks as if a giant came and squeezed an entire village into a single building," Pedro said as he chewed. "Is it true it used to be a museum of some sort?"

"A tourist attraction for tasteless vacationers," Aitor said.

"That monstrosity of a house looks as monstrous as the *iparralde* himself," Karlo said. "If it were up to me, I would burn the whole thing down."

Aitor glanced at his watch again, debating with himself whether to call Zurgin or to wait another half-hour for his answer on the meeting. His orders were to stay off their mobiles unless unavoidable.

Zurgin's call came in at nightfall.

One of the Bilbao men camped at public campground across an open field from the Maison arrived on a motorcycle to take Aitor to the meeting. He rode pillion to a café in the town of St-Jean-Pied-de-Port, the old capital of the Basque province of Lower Navarre some twenty kilometers distance.

The red-tiled roof café was nearly empty, except for a middle-aged couple at the counter, murmuring and smiling to each other. Four elderly men were starting a game of *mus* at a rear table. Their loud southern French accents echoed in the room.

Aitor huddled with the others in a corner table. An assortment of ancient ox yokes, sickles, and braided baskets hung on the walls. Zurgin, the Bilbao man and their local support, Arlette, a nervous-looking, bottle-blonde schoolteacher in her forties, nodded in greeting and shook hands. The counterman set the coffees around the table and walked away.

When Zeus walked in, the ETA men were in the process of interrogating Arlette. He took a chair and listened.

Aitor looked annoyed. "These details are not enough," he was saying. "You told us you know this place."

The woman shook her head with a rapid tic-like movement. "You don't seem to understand. No one knows the complete layout of that mad house except for Andre Minot. It was purposely designed to confuse the eye, like a labyrinth. Nothing is what it appears. I gave you the only copies of the floor plans I found in the town hall archives. What else can I do?"

"But they are incomplete," Aitor said. "Many of the blueprints are missing or they are smudged or impossible to read."

Zurgin agreed. "This is unacceptable, Arlette. We were counting on you. You told us you have been to the house many times."

"And I have. Dozens of times. When it was opened to the public years ago. I gave you a sketch of the parts I remember. What else can I do? Each time we went into that house we encountered rooms and stairs and passageways we had not seen before. It was as if they materialized out of thin air. Even Madame Minot herself never ventures too far out of the living quarters, afraid she might get lost, or so I've heard."

Zurgin stirred on his chair. "People, it is raining on wet ground. We have heard all this before."

Zeus leaned his elbows on the table. "Has this man, Minot, given any proof of life on the girl in the last few hours?"

"Proof of life?" Zurgin laughed as if it was a bad joke. "He's refused to talk to us since lunchtime."

"To carry out this kind of operation without proof of life is impractical," Zeus said. "What if the girl is dead?"

"She might be, for all we know," Zurgin answered. "But we have other priorities."

"I thought this was a rescue operation."

"Only in part." Zurgin thought over his own statement as he gazed at the Cuban. "Have you any ideas?"

"I think we must first determine if the target is in any condition to be rescued," Zeus said, ignoring for now the ulterior motives ETA might be harboring. He had to keep the operation moving.

"Do you think we have not tried? That man is a lunatic. He would rather die than let the girl go." Zurgin gazed around at the café and lowered his voice. "We told him very clearly, if the girl dies, he dies. But do you think it made an impression on him? He's deranged. We have no option but to rush the house and get her by force and hope for the best."

Aitor looked at Zeus as if expecting to see an alternative solution form in his face. They knew the chances of the girl surviving an attack on the house were no better than if they left it up to the police to rescue her. Except Zurgin was not a man easily persuaded when set on a course of action. They needed to offer him an alternative that would at least delay the assault. Midnight was less than two hours away.

"If Minot's willing to give up his life for the girl," Zeus said as though thinking aloud, "Then we must find something that he's not willing to give up. You know this man," he said. "What's there that we can offer him, or take away, to get him back on the phone?"

"That is what I would like to know," Zurgin said.

Arlette said, "Andre loves his Maison Lavryn. It was his whole world for the first thirteen years of his life. Maybe—"

"The hell with it," Zurgin said over her words. "This is not only about the prisoner. That deformed cretin is a traitor and a murderer and he has to pay. We have our priorities."

"Why not just torch that monstrous house then? You'll see how fast they'll fly out of there," the Bilbao man said.

"That is savagery," Aitor said. "There are innocent people in there."

"Burning the house down is a possible solution," Zeus said to every-one's surprise. "But that's a weapon of last resort. We're not there yet." He cocked his head leftward. His eyes narrowed in thought.

Aitor watched him, cheering him on with his gaze. As if saying, spin those wheels, you were a Cuban revolutionary, Masters of Survival, propose a solution.

Zeus leaned forward on the table. "OK, I have an idea that might work."

Maison Lavryn

Minot sat facing the front door in the dark in what was once his father's easy chair. Fifteen years dead and he still could smell his bodiless presence in it, the fumes of a self-adoring animal. The Kalashnikov rested across his lap. The heavy armoire his mother kept near the small foyer sat flushed against the front door. Every door leading into the living quarters was nailed with cross-braced boards. A candle burned on the side table. Now and then, in the creaking silence of the house, he could hear his mother's muffled whining coming from the cellar, followed by the caretaker's consoling hums.

His cousin Damon appeared out of the dimness. He was wearing an iridescent tracksuit and carrying a shotgun in his hands.

"Cousin, let me turn on some lights. I keep hitting my knees on every-thing."

"No. Keep walking your rounds."

Cousin Damon muttered, "*Le roi le veut*," and stomped away.

Minot was ready. No one was going to find the girl inside Maison Lavryn, with or without lights. The police could search all they wanted: it would never happen. How many times did the social services come looking for him as a child? Did they ever find him? Never. Not until his mother decided to expose the truth of his existence did anyone outside the deranged confines of the house ever lay eyes on him. And his night-mares commenced.

A metallic ping of a noise made him prick up. It came from outside the house. He peered through the shuttered bay window. The lamppost over the crossroads had gone off. Burned out, he thought. One of his mobile phones vibrated in his pocket. The caller's number was unknown to him. He dropped the handset back in his shirt pocket. The mobile buzzed again. It was the same number on the screen. This time he listened to the voice message. A man with an American accent. "Monsieur Minot, my name is Joseph Messina, Symphony's father. Call me back. It's urgent …"

Minot bolted up, the Kalashnikov in both hands. He hurried around to every window, looking through the shutters at the outside grounds. He went into the dayroom and found his cousin asleep on his mother's bed. "Wake up, you fool. Pick up your rifle, I think they're outside."

Damon, dirty blond hair covering his deep-set eyes, sat up. "The dark makes me sleepy."

Minot went back to the foyer to guard the front door. He looked at his phone again, his bullish features solid as a sculpture, his eyes wide and glazed. He glanced behind him at the narrow door into the secret stairway to the *maison de santé* room where Symphony lay in her ketamine-induced sleep. Damon came back and stood next to the grandfather clock where time stands still. "I've looked through every window but didn't see anything."

The mobile in his pocket vibrated again. Minot brought the mobile nearer to his face and read the unidentified digits in golden LED shapes. It was ten forty-four p.m. He pressed a key with his thumb and put the phone to his pricked ear.

"Hello," said the voice at the other end. Then after a pause, "Andre Minot, is that you?"

"*Allô. Qui es-tu?*"

"Talk in English. I know you can."

"Who are you and how did you get this number?"

"Easy," the voice said. "I got it from one of your terrorist friends. You know who you're talking to?"

His American bluntness startled Minot for a moment, but he quickly recovered. "Umm, let me see." He could only think of one person who spoke with such an accent. "Mr. Messina, I presume?"

"Don't waste my fucking time, Minot. Is my daughter alive? Just answer that. Is my daughter all right?"

"Why should she not be? She's fine and dandy, as you Americans say."

A sigh of relief hissed across the line. "Then let me speak to her, so I can be sure."

"Of course you can, only she's resting at the moment. She's been through a lot, as you might guess."

"What is it you want, Minot? What do I got to do to get my daughter back?"

"I want nothing," Minot said as he meandered from window to window, looking for the enemy. "I am not preventing her from leaving. You can tell this to those policemen who are all around you listening to us right now—"

"Look, Minot, if you can believe one thing about me, believe this: There's no police. That's not the way I operate. If you don't believe me, just ask yourself this: Do you really think the police would give me your address and phone number? This has nothing to do with the police. This is between you and me now."

Minot chuckled.

"Did I say something funny?"

"Pardon, it's just the way you speak."

"Fuck the way I talk and fuck you. I want my daughter back, you hear me? And I want her now."

"I do not doubt it, Mr. Messina. Only I don't think she wants to go back. She's happy here with me. You see, with me she knows she is safe. Isn't that what all women want? It is not the same when she's with you, or with that bon vivant from San Sebastián she was going to marry. Therefore, I cannot help you. I am sorry."

"You're so full of shit—"

"I do not care what you believe. It is the truth."

"If that's the truth, then let her tell me herself."

Minot said nothing.

"Just put her on the phone, if you're so damn concerned for her well-being. So I know she's OK. So I know she's alive."

"Pardon me—"

"Look, asshole, I'm willing to pay you whatever you ask. Anything. So why not take the money and end this game of yours."

"Stop insulting me—"

"How much money you want? Just answer the question."

"I don't want your gangster money. I know who you are, Mr. Messina. I am not afraid of you. But she simply cannot speak to you now. There is no mobile reception in the room where she's recuperating." That was true; the only truth Minot had uttered so far. The room where he kept

Symphony was buried so deep inside so many layers of brick, wood, sheetrock and padding that mobiles rarely worked.

"OK, OK," the voice said. "Let me see her. I got to see her. Please. Bring her to a window, anything."

Minot let out a laugh. "Mr. Messina, who's the stupid one now?"

"What's wrong with you? Goddamnit!" Now pleadingly: "Listen. How about this? I have Symphony's sister, Aria, here with me. Let her go inside and see her sister for a minute. They don't have to exchange a word. Just a quick look so we know she's all right. Then we can take it from there. You don't have to trust me, Minot. But you can trust her sister. Aria's a good girl, just like Symphony. She'll go by herself. No tricks. The god-honest truth."

"Negative."

"For god's sake, Minot. She's just a young girl. She loves her sister. What could be the harm in that? Just let her in for a moment and come right out. What are you scared of? Think of the risk I'm taking as a father. What guarantees do I have that you will not keep them both?"

"None."

"You got absolutely nothing to lose by letting my daughter see her sister. You're holding all the cards. What more control do you need? Are you such a loser you don't know when you have the upper hand?"

"Insults will not help you, Mr. Messina. Your daughter is well and safe."

"If that's true, then do us both a favor. Let my daughter Aria see her sister and everything will be OK."

"I will think about it."

"No. You tell me now. Or goddamn it, I'll have my people burn down that amusement park madhouse of yours to the ground with you and your entire family in it—"

"Threats will not get you anywhere, Mr. Messina."

"This ain't no threat, pal. I'm just telling you what's going to happen. If you deny me this chance to find out whether my daughter is OK as you say she is, I'll know it's because you've killed her."

"I will call you back."

"When?"

"When I'm good and ready."

"You got till midnight. Then all bets are off."

Minot squeezed the mobile in his hand almost to burst. His cousin approached him. "Don't say a word to me," he told him, fuming. "Don't. Go back to your post by the window and stay there."

A couple of hundred meters away at a nearby construction site, Zeus pocketed his cell phone and looked around at the expectant faces staring at him in tense anticipation.

"I think he's bought it," Zeus said, smiling.

"I am impressed, Aguirre," Zurgin said, laughing. "You sounded just like Joe Pesci in that gangster movie."

The entire group laughed again twenty minutes later when Minot phoned back to speak with Mr. Messina, and agreed to have Symphony's sister come in the Maison for proof of life. "If the following conditions are met," he said.

To Zeus and the ETA men, all conditions were acceptable.

FORTY-SEVEN

The Rescue

OUT IN THE NIGHT's stillness, Zeus and Aitor stood in front of the construction site Zurgin had picked for his command post. They stepped closer to the curb upon seeing Arlette's car approaching with its headlights off. It came to a gravelly halt by a stack of bricks next to the sidewalk. Zeus watched Tess say something to Arlette before stepping out of the passenger's door. Arlette's car rode off in the dust cloud it raised when it pulled in.

Zeus gave Tess a quick up-and-down scan. "I like you as a brunette."

Tess missed the smile on Zeus's face in the dark. "We had to wait for Arlette's sister to bring me another pair of jeans, baggy ones, you know, to fit those things. Hers didn't fit me."

"You look fine." Zeus took her hand. It was damp with sweat. Zeus and Aitor escorted her up the dark stairs to the second floor of the unfinished structure.

"Is the wig all right?" Tess said with a stressed whisper. "I mean, is it too bulky in the back?"

"It's fine," Zeus said. "You're still OK with this?"

"I think so."

"You can tell me if you're not."

"I'm OK, Zeus. Stop asking."

"We could find someone else to do it."

"I said I'd do it. Somebody's got to."

"It doesn't have to be you."

"I'm the only one who can," Tess said, nervous but determined. "You know it and I know it. So please."

"Just making sure."

Zurgin and his men stood waiting at the top of the raw cement stairway. They assessed her as she passed them in the dimness. The Cleopatra wig and the dark makeup did give her fair features an acceptable Mediterranean shade. Zurgin pointed at a single folding chair on a corner of the floor for her to sit. Cement droppings crunched underfoot as each man took a seat on several upright cinderblocks set up around her, out of sight to the street. One of the Bilbao men stood by the wall next to a concrete slab balcony without a railing, looking out into the night.

Their faces glowed for an instant as each smoker lit up.

Zurgin tapped Zeus's knee. "Tell her we are very grateful for her help."

Zeus reminded him that Tess spoke Spanish.

"*Perdón*—my mistake," Zurgin said. He addressed her in Spanish, "Tess, first of all I want to thank you again in everyone's name for your help. I know Zeus has explained everything to you. But if you have any other questions—"

She shook her head. "None anyone can answer."

"Yes." Zurgin grinned sadly. "There is so much that we cannot predict. Have you memorized the windows you're to use as an escape if necessary?"

"Zeus and I have gone over it various times."

"Good. Do not forget to give Minot the mobile the moment you enter the house. Don't wait for him to ask for it. He will frisk you, but he will not touch you where you have placed the other one with the line opened. We know him. He will not do that."

"I won't let him go that far."

"If he tries and reacts with hostility to your defense, you give us your signal and we'll move right in."

Tess and Zeus exchanged glances.

"Were you able to properly conceal the pepper spray?" Zurgin said with a scowl.

"I did," Tess said. "In the hands-off zone. *Donde no se toca.*"

Her reply made the men chuckle. They seemed to be enjoying her nervous self-confidence.

"My only question is," she said addressing Zeus. "What if she gives me away without meaning to? I look nothing like her sister."

"Minot doesn't know that," Aitor said.

"I know, but—"

Zeus said, "That's another problem you'd have to deal with on the fly. Just be careful of whatever doublespeak you might use to get Symphony to play along. Don't forget Minot speaks pretty good English."

Tess nodded OK.

"Play it just like we discussed it," Zeus went on. "When you see her, keep cool and take control of the situation. I hear she's pretty smart. She'll catch on quick. But," he added with his index finger to the sky, "if you as much as sense the littlest thing going wrong, you get that pepper spray out and empty it on his face and run for the nearest window. We'll be out there waiting."

Tess nodded, her tense features lost in the shadows.

Zurgin stood up. "So, are we ready?"

She hoped she was. So did everyone else.

Zeus and Tess hopped on the commando's van and drove out of the construction site.

As they rode, Zeus asked her to go over the instructions list again. Tess recited it from memory—Symphony's and Miguel Angel's, even Aria's birthdates as well as their addresses, the names of all their immediate relatives—all of the information Zeus imagined Minot might think of asking to verify who she claimed to be.

"OK," he said when she finished. "Do you remember what to do if he asks something you don't know?"

"I'll make it up."

Zeus smiled. "You're really something, you know that?"

He stopped the van where the white-lined main road intersected with the road parallel to Maison Lavryn's private entrance. Tess dialed Minot's number as agreed and kept the mobile to her ear while she listened to the instructions he imparted from inside the house. Zeus could hear his compressed voice.

"Get out of the car and walk to the brown door. You'll see it when you reach the fence gate. Remember, I'm watching your every move. So no funny business. I have more than my eyes on you."

Tess covered the cell phone with her hand and glanced at Zeus. "Here I go."

Zeus could not hold back the redundancy of saying, "Be very careful."

Tess got out of the van, holding the phone to her ear. She waved at Zeus. "He says to drive away."

Zeus nodded once and drove off.

Anxious eyes followed Tess walking toward the side gate. She walked up the stoop. The brown door was ajar. She stepped up and an arm came out of the dark inside and hulled her into the house in a single motion. She wheeled free and found herself in almost complete darkness, staring into the black bore of a shotgun. A man who reminded her of Quasimodo yanked the cell phone out of her hand and began patting her torso, her arms. The black beret he wore seemed to be covering not a human head but some kind of hornless bovid.

"Are you hiding anything?" He frisked her ankles, her knees.

"No," she said, pulling away when he reached her thighs. "You think I'm stupid."

Minot nodded and his cousin lowered the shotgun and stepped away. He gave Tess a long scrutinizing look. "What is your name?"

"Aria Messina." She tried not to look him in the eye. "And you are?"

"What do you care? Where's your father?"

"In town."

"In St-Jean?"

"Yes."

"Who drove you here, the police?"

Tess winced. "Are you crazy? Do you think we want you to hurt my sister, or me?"

Damon came back from inspecting the windows. "Everything is quiet as a graveyard out there," he said in French.

"Go back and stand guard by the bay window. I am going to take her upstairs." Then to Tess in English, "You are going to see your sister." He opened his windbreaker and let her see the butt of his Beretta. "I will shoot you if you don't do exactly as I tell you. Yes?"

Tess nodded once, afraid to displace her wig.

Minot gazed into her eyes. "What nationality is your mother?"

"What? My mother? American."

"I know this. I want to know her origin. What is it?"

Tess felt a cold stab of panic. Her mother's ancestry? Was it a trick question? She had no idea. It never came up in the briefing, or anywhere.

She tried to stall by repeating the question. "My mother's grandparents, is that what you mean?" Minot remained silent, waiting for her answer. She tried to remember what Terry looked like. Think, think. Blue eyes. That's it. Terry's blue eyes. "She's part Irish," she said, feeling as if she had jumped off a skyscraper.

"Where and when was your younger sister born?"

Another trick question. Aria was the youngest, she realized. But he assumed Symphony was the younger one because of Tess's older appearance.

"Can't remember your sister's birthday?"

"Sure I do." She blurted out Symphony's date of birth and added, "Born in Brooklyn, like me."

Minot held her in his stare for a tense instant, his expressionless furry face impenetrable to interpretation. He opened a drawer in the armoire and unfolded a clean pillowcase. "Put this over your head."

"Is it necessary?"

He slipped it over Tess's head, took her by the arm, and led her to the narrow stairway in the kitchen.

Tess climbed the crawlway-like stairwells with Minot pushing from behind her. Breathing the mothballed air inside the pillowcase, she could feel the oppressive massiveness of the building as they went deeper into the structure. She counted the steps of each set of stairs they climbed—fourteen on the first one, twelve on the second, and nine on the last one. She tried to focus but it was hard with Minot yanking her arm in so many different directions.

Minot halted abruptly, her arm still in his powerful grip. "Aria," he said, his voice softer, closer to her face. "Don't fear me, please. I might look like an animal, but I guarantee you I am not."

His unexpected statement startled her. She said nothing, didn't even nod, amazed at how quickly he had sensed her frame of mind and how easily a kind word could spark a little hope in the midst of absolute panic.

They climbed in and out of something, walked a few steps, turned left and kept moving, her lumbering blind steps going wherever he guided her.

"Stop, please," he told her.

Next, Tess heard the jingle of keys, the snap of a lock, and a door handle turn. He pulled her forward and halted, the drone of an axial fan close by. "Symphony, look what I've brought you," Minot announced.

He lifted the pillowcase off Tess's head as though raising a stage curtain. Tess thought it was all over. But no. She took a deep breath, her eyes blinking. All she could see before her was the pale face of an ailing young dark-haired woman under white sheet covers, unrecognizable from the photographs she had seen of her. "Symphony? Can I approach her?" Tess asked before taking another step.

He waved her onward.

Stepping closer to the bed, Tess finally recognized the girl that had been on her mind every waking hour of her day and in every other of her dreams for a month, lying prostrate in the brown light of a sickly light bulb. On the night table beside her was a pitcher with water, a container of milk, and some packaged medication. She leaned over the bedside for a better look. The girl didn't look well. Her eyes were moving in jerky motions behind closed lids, there was a wide adhesive bandage of the kind used by surgeons as a backup to dissolvable stitches, and a long, scabbed cut along her jaw. "Hi, sis, how are you?" Tess whispered softly. "It's me, Aria."

Under the sheets, Tess couldn't see Symphony's legs and arms strapped to the under-bed, but she could tell there was something that did not belong there. Symphony was either ill or heavily drugged, that much she could tell. Tess had no way to know that Symphony was traversing the last stages of a ketamine withdrawal, lapsing in and out of hallucinatory states.

"Sym, it's me, Aria, your sister. Can you hear me?" she asked again.

Symphony opened her unfocused eyes, her brow in a knot. Tess leaned closer yet, keeping her back to the bullheaded man. She caressed Symphony's mussed hair and kissed her brow while trying to catch her eye. "Are you OK, sis?"

Minot stood at the foot of the bed. "Miss Messina, don't you recognize your sister?" He sounded more concerned than suspicious. "I said she was coming to see you."

"Daddy's here too," Tess said, winking an eye. "We've all been so worried."

Symphony's pallid expression hardened as though overwhelmed by it all. "Who are—?" she started to say between short breaths.

Tess cut her off. "Oh Sym, we've missed you so," she said over her words, her facial muscles going through every expression of warning. "Are you ready to go home?"

Symphony blinked several times and wet her chapped lips. "You said Pa is here?"

"Yes, yes. He's here too," Tess said, glancing triumphantly over her shoulder at Quasimodo. "Yes. We've come to take you home, if it's OK with you." Tess turned to face Minot again. "What's wrong with her? You drugged her, didn't you—"

"She was in pain," he said. "She suffered an accident."

"Yeah, right."

A noise that only Minot heard made his back stiffen up. He rushed to the door and looked outside, his neck goosed up, sniffing the air, and snarled, "I have to step out a moment." He pointed at Tess. "You stay here with your sister. Tess nodded and he slammed the door and locked it from the outside.

The noise of the bolting lock sent a shiver through Tess's nervous system. Symphony gripped her arm. "Who are you?" she said with a halting rasp.

"I'm Tess, a friend of your family. Part of a team that came to take you home. Can you get up?"

Tess's New York accent snapped Symphony to attention. "Take me home?"

"Yes. There are others right outside. Come on. Let's get you out of bed. I'll help you."

"Don't know if I can."

"You have to. We haven't much time."

~

Aitor and his men were waiting for Zeus in the shadows behind the vacant summer home neighboring Maison Lavryn. As soon as Zeus got out of the van, they handed him the Uzi and the ammo he had chosen for the operation.

"How was she?" Aitor asked of Tess.

"A little nervous. She'll be all right. Is Zurgin's group in position?"

"They should be by now. It will not take them long to force open the rear doors. The men from Bilbao are working on the electric line."

Zeus screwed the silencer on the Uzi as he followed Aitor and his team into the field between the houses, toward the Maison's chain-link fence. They crawled under it one at a time, then jogged crouching across the overgrown weeds of what once was Madame Minot's parterre garden.

They halted upon reaching the opened space before the Maison, its silhouette blacker and more massive against the jagged night sky. Zeus raced across the clearing and pressed his back against the wall next to the bay window. With the Uzi hanging over his chest, he looked around him. It was quiet inside and outside. Quiet was good. He waved the clear sign at the others.

As they slipped out of the waist-high weeds, a veined flash of lightning streaked across the sky over the hills. Seconds later, they heard the rumble of distant thunder.

Minot ran into the kitchen and found Damon standing in the dark, shotgun in hand. "Did you hear that?" his cousin said. "And I don't mean the thunder."

"Yes, you fool. I've heard it." Minot padded to the bay window. "Where did it come from?"

"I'm not certain. From the back, I think."

The few lights on inside the house suddenly went out. Minot froze. "They've cut the electric power." A second later he heard his mother shrieking in the cellar. "*Putain*," he snarled when it hit him. The *americana's* sister was a trick after all. A damn trick. He had sensed it deep in his gnarled skull from the start but now it was too late. Furious, he pulled the bolt of his Kalashnikov. "Damon—"

More banging noises echoed through the building. "They're coming in through the schoolroom, go run and take a look."

"Me? I don't know how to get there."

Minot kicked down on the floor to keep from smashing his cousin's head in. "You're a waste of a human being. Here, take the keys. Run to the *maison de santé* and bring me that lying bitch."

"The sister?"

"Yes, her! You do know how to find your way there."

"I helped you paint the room."

"Go and bring her to me."

Up in the faux hospital room, Tess unbuckled the leather straps binding Symphony to the bed. "Come, let me help you up."

"I feel so weak," Symphony said almost sweetly in her frailty.

"Please try. He'll be back any minute."

"Where are we going to go?"

"Our guys will be here at any moment."

Tess moved Symphony's legs to the side of the bed and helped her sit up. The iron bed was old and tall. Her feet did not reach the floor.

"What are you going to do when he gets back?" Symphony said.

Tess unbuckled her belt and squeezed her hand in under the baggy jeans. "I have a can of pepper spray and a mini cellphone with me," she said as she pulled out the lighter-size container and the tiny phone. Relieved as if it had been killing her, she said aloud hoping someone was listening, "I've got her. We're coming out." But Maison Lavryn's walls and ceilings weakened the phone signal to nothing.

Tess slipped her forearms under Symphony's underarms and lifted her. "Come on Sym, Let's get you up now. Help me." The instant Symphony tried to get on her feet her knees buckled under her weight and Tess lost her hold and both tumbled together onto the bed.

"I just can't do it," Symphony moaned. "I want to but I can't."

Tess looked at her lying across the bed, the plain white hospital-like gown pulled up by her waist, the heartbreaking scabbed lacerations on her thighs, the fresh scars, the black-and-blues on her legs, the sloppy stitches, and it broke her heart. Tess glanced over at the locked door, her mind bustling for a solution and finding none. Even if she could find her way out, she wouldn't be able to carry Symphony down the narrow sets of stairs. "We're going to get you out of here, I promise," she said half murmuring to herself, fighting back her tears. "Our friends will be here soon. Everything is going to be all right. You'll see ..."

Outside Maison Lavryn's walls Zeus, Aitor, and his men stole around the corner to Zurgin's position by the double doors the Maison construction workers used. A misty drizzle was coming down. When Zeus reached them, he found them in the middle of an argument. "What's wrong?" he said.

"The Bilbao team is on the way to the front door now, but we still can't pry these doors open. They are armored, soldered together. We're going to have to blow them up."

"We have to go in now," Zeus said. "We have no telephone signal with Tess."

"The Semtex is ready," Zurgin told him. "I have Pedro setting up the charge now. I will give the order whenever you say. You tell us when. With Tess and the girl still inside, it is only fair that it should be your call."

Zeus nodded. "Thanks. But it's going to get noisy."

"Maybe the neighbors will think it is part of the fireworks from the town feast," Zurgin said.

"Firework displays in this weather?" Zeus knew better than that. "Don't count on it."

The explosion was going to wake up the vicinity and bare everything out in the open, and cut down on the operation's timeframe along with it. But it had to be done. There was no getting around it. "Blow the doors as soon as the charge is ready," Zeus said.

~

Tess unclipped the cheap Cleopatra wig off her head and shook her mass of blonde hair loose. No point in carrying on with the ruse. She put the phone to her ear one last time. No signal.

"Don't worry," she said to Symphony who was watching her from the bed. "We'll be out of this madhouse before you know it. I'd bet they're on the way right now."

Tess rummaged around the room for something to pry the door open. The place was surprisingly orderly. "Did I tell you I met your mom?" she said, trying to comfort Symphony and calm her own nerves as she searched. "I did. She came with your dad to the office and we talked a great deal about you. She gave us a bunch of pictures so that we could recognize you. Zeus, the man in charge of your rescue, he has one. He thinks you're very pretty."

On one corner of the floor, Tess found a cardboard box with used cans of paints and hardened brushes. Among it was a can of Day-Glo spray paint and a screwdriver. She picked them up and walked to the door, stuck the screwdriver into the lock and tried to jimmy it open. Symphony watched her in a half daze.

Downstairs, Minot ran through a maze of doors, past the tiny library with the fake book spines, the fake post office, the beauty parlor with the female mannequin sitting under a chrome-domed hair drier. Years of dust lifted with his every footfall. He pushed a creaky door, worked his way past several school chairs, knocking over the plaster and mesh figures of two children in short pants. He shone the light on a set of double doors painted to depict a window with a view of an outdoor playground in the sun. He put his ear to the door, listened to the murmur of the drizzling rain outside until he heard what he had suspected. Footsteps.

A shotgun blast went off in the muffled distance. Although the shot was half-absorbed by the layers of walls inside the house, Minot knew where it came from. He let out a fierce grunt and raced upstairs to the *maison de santé*.

The blast from Cousin Damon's shotgun had shattered the framed picture of the bearded man above Symphony's bed to pieces. But Damon could not see what he had done, slumped back in the doorway, with his eyes swelling, watering, reddening from the pepper spray acids on his face. "*Je voulais seulement te faire peur,*" he cried. "I only wanted to scare you."

"Yeah?" Tess lunged at him and grabbed hold of the shotgun by the barrel, wrestling it up and away from him, pulling it with all her force. Damon tugged hard not to let go but he needed his hands to wipe off the burning liquids dripping out of his melting eyes and his nose. Tess gave the shotgun a potent reverse jerk and yanked it out of his hands.

Damon kept coughing and choking, waving one hand at her. Tess could only guess what the Frenchman was trying to tell her. She stepped back and with trembling hands aimed the gun at his chest.

Defeated, Damon slid down the wall to the floor, his throat swollen, unable to speak. Tess realized she needed him to take them out of there. So she picked up the pitcher with water and was about to pour it on his face when Damon cried out, "No, no! *Pas l'eau.*" He pointed at the tray. "*Le lait, me donnent le lait …*" he managed to groan between coughs.

"What?"

"He wants the milk, I think," Symphony said from her bed.

Tess handed him the milk carton and Damon splashed his burning face with the milk, rubbing it gently over his eyes. It blunted the irritation a little and he opened one eye through a bloodshot slit. The pepper chemicals were still at work and he was in no condition to wrestle her for the gun.

Tess shook the gun barrel at him. "Get up." She signaled with her head at the stairs. "Let's go."

Damon obeyed. Holding on to the wall, he got on his feet, his eyes swollen like that of a thrashed boxer, liquid and mucus dripping over his inflamed face.

"Walk," Tess hollered, taking charge of the moment. "Move it." She picked up the Day-Glo paint can and glanced at Symphony as she started for the door. Symphony was sitting with her slim tortured legs dangling from the bed. "I'll be back to get you," Tess told her. "I swear I will."

She stuck the barrel of the shotgun into Damon's lower back. "Walk and don't turn around. Don't look at me or I'll pepper your face again."

Walking behind him, Tess spray-painted an orange cross outside Symphony's door and marked the entire trajectory back to the kitchen with quick squirts of paint.

Downstairs, Minot ran to the bay window and saw two uniformed policemen—the Bilbao team—about to ram the front door with a sledgehammer. The heavy armoire he had propped against the door jolted inward with the first blow. He took the safety off his Kalashnikov, aimed it at the door, and fired four shots, then waited for their reaction. That was when the Semtex went off with a loud boom. The air-sucking blast wave tore its way through the stale spaces of the house and hit his ears with a solid thud, rattling every object around him.

Madame Minot went into a shrieking fit in the cellar. Minot, his nostrils throbbing, aimed his flashlight at the figure of his cousin bumping out of the stairwell, trailed by the "sister," who was holding Damon's shotgun in her hands. They halted at the doorway.

"You imbecile," Minot let out, huffing behind the glow of his flashlight.

"She shot me with pepper spray. You are to blame. You didn't frisk her properly—" Now the front door broke open with a crashing noise. The armoire beside it bucked into the room, screeching like a wounded animal. Minot wheeled and bump-fired his Kalashnikov at the door. Splinters and pieces of wood and spark flew in every direction. He turned and fired another wild burst intended to take out the "sister" but his cousin got in the way.

Damon plummeted to the tile floor. Tess screamed and squeezed the trigger involuntarily before she dove behind the table. The wild shot tore a hole on the panel wall next to Minot. A couple of pellets caught his right arm. He felt the burning sting and his blood dripping down his arm, piss-hot. Firing into the kitchen, he bolted into the dayroom.

Tess balled herself up in a corner of the kitchen while shrapnel-like pieces of tile, glass and wood shot over her head.

Outside, Zeus heard Tess screams and the AK-47's distinct sound print. This was not what he had expected. "That's not one of ours," he said to Aitor and ran toward the door, yelling into his cell phone, "Tess, Tess, talk to me."

Aitor's team scrambled to cover positions behind him. The Bilbao men in police uniforms tried to storm the house again, ahead of Zeus. Tess heard them outside and made a dash toward the door.

Minot leaped out of the dayroom and tried to catch her before she slipped out. He needed a hostage that he could kill without remorse and she was the perfect one. He found himself facing a police-uniformed man instead.

They fired at each other on sight. The ETA commando in police clothes fumbled with his rifle and two hits thudded on his chest; the man grunted and fell back out the door in a big crash. Out of ammunition, Minot dropped the AK-47 and bounded up the secret stairs, holding his bloody arm.

Tess ran out of the front door directly into Zeus's arms. "I saw her, Zeus." She couldn't stop panting. "I was with her. She's OK."

"OK," Zeus said. "Now take it easy. Breathe."

Tess took a few seconds to catch her breath and with a single verbal barrage, she told Zeus everything he wanted to know. "She's waiting for you. I promised her you'd come."

By this time, Aitor and his team had burst into the living quarters and found Damon lying on the debris on the kitchen floor sucking in his last breaths. Zurgin had two of his men rush the wounded Bilbao man to the clinic in St-Jean.

"Don't forget to get him out of that police uniform before he gets there," Zurgin told them as they lifted him into a van.

He then called Aitor aside. "This *iparralde* is willing to kill his own kin to get his way. God help me, he will not hurt another person again. Tell your man to get ready to set fire to the house."

"The girl still inside," Aitor told him.

Zurgin looked at him with his thick brows in a scowl. "We will do what we can to rescue her before the police put an end to this, which will be soon. In the meantime, have Karlo prepare to start the fires where we agreed. We are not leaving this place until I see this monstrosity of a house in flames. Are we in accord?"

"How about the old woman and the caretaker?"

"We'll ask them to come out of the cellar where they are hiding. If they refuse, well. That old woman created that monster. If she wants to die with him, so be it. Get all the gasoline canisters you can find. There is much building to burn."

Aitor came out to the roofed doorway where Tess and Zeus stood arm in arm. "This is a disaster," he said to Zeus. "The girl and the madman Minot are somewhere inside and Zurgin wants the house torched before the police get here. We will never reach the *americana* in time."

"I know how we can do it." Zeus glanced at Tess. "Let's talk to Zurgin."

After a short negotiation, Zurgin gave Zeus and Aitor ten minutes to go inside and get the girl. "When the time is up," he told them, "I will order to start torching the rear of the building. From there on, you will have whatever time the flames will give you. Or until the police get here. Whichever comes first. Ten minutes," he repeated. "Minot dies here tonight one way or another."

Before they moved on, Zurgin whispered to Zeus, "I'll take Tess back with me, if you don't come out on time."

"Thanks, but that won't be necessary."

They synchronized their watches in the rain. Zeus and Aitor gathered their equipment and dashed inside the Maison.

With their night-vision goggles on their faces, Aitor and Zeus scurried into the depths of Maison Lavryn. Following the Day-Glo aerosol paint trail Tess had marked out, they moved like two shadows in black jumpsuits through tangles of secret stairways and corridors in the blacked-out madhouse. Mannequins in make-believe shops appeared out of the black and green world of their NVDs, their disconcerting human forms startling them into firing position at every turn.

Tess's spray marks led them to a parlor-like room with a massive wooden wardrobe and dead-ended there. They looked at each other, confused. "What does this mean?" Aitor said.

They walked back to the last turn and retraced their steps to prove to themselves they had not strayed. They had not. Tess's markings cutoff at the foot of the wardrobe.

Zeus opened the wardrobe with one gloved hand, his Uzi ready to fire in the other. The wardrobe was empty.

He climbed inside, it was that big, and gave a firm push at the backboard and found it slid open into another room, a room arranged like a doctor's office. "There's more paint sprayed on this side."

They followed the shiny paint blotches on the floor into a long corridor, deeper into the building. The darkness became so complete that even with the night vision goggles visibility was almost zero.

They tracked the markings to another hallway where they saw an X spray-painted in front of one of the doors. A bright glow, made artificially brighter by the goggles, radiated from the room. A wooden plaque hung over the door with the words *Maison de Santé*.

Zeus did not expect to find Symphony in that room. He had to assume Minot had also seen the paint markings and taken her elsewhere. But it was a start. They had almost six minutes left.

With their backs to the wall, they began their approach, walking sideways toward the door, their weapons up by their goggles. Zeus could hear Aitor's heavy smoker breaths behind him. The light became even brighter as they reached the door. They removed their clumsy goggles. Zeus glanced at Aitor, nodded three times and they burst into the candlelit room.

Zeus and Aitor halted midway into their charge, taken aback by the strange sight they found.

Symphony remained in the same position that Tess had left her, sitting at the edge of the bed in her white cotton gown, her chin on her chest, her feet suspended over the floor. Like a peaceful pet by her feet sat Minot, cradling his bloody arm, his back to the wall, his wooly face wet with tears. He raised his malformed head and gazed at them without moving.

Symphony barely acknowledged their presence.

Zeus searched around for a weapon but found none. Aitor aimed his

Uzi at Minot's head, grabbed him by his shirt collar and dragged him out of the room. Zeus swung his weapon behind him, removed his gloves, and stepped closer to the girl. He smiled when their eyes met. "Hi, Symphony. My name is Zeus and I am here because your parents asked me to bring you home. Are you OK to go?"

"What happened to the lady that was here before?"

"Tess? Oh, she's fine, waiting for you outside. Come on, let's go see her."

"Are you really going to take me home?"

"You better believe it." He pulled out a plastic envelope from the inside of his jumpsuit and showed her a group photograph of the Messina family from the previous Christmas. When Symphony looked at it, her face twisted like a child about to break out sobbing. "I can't walk. My legs won't hold me."

"That's no problem. I'll carry you."

All the tears that Symphony had been holding back came pouring out in a silent flow. Zeus looked at his wristwatch. Three minutes left. He picked up a towel and wiped her face, then wrapped her in a bedsheet. He picked up her chin with his fingers. "Now we go home. Ready?"

He was about to lift her up when he heard the rumbling of knuckles and feet pounding on skin outside the door. Aitor burst in the room with his fists in the air. "I have to ask her one question before we go, and I need you to translate it."

"Ask her later. We haven't the time."

"I don't care. It has to be done now."

Zeus looked into Aitor's burning squint and nodded for him to proceed. "Go on then."

"Ask her if Baldo tried to rape her in the *zulo*."

Zeus hesitated.

"Just ask her. I have to know."

Zeus stepped closer to the bed. Symphony looked him in the eyes. "There's one thing we need to know before we go. OK? I hate to bring this up, but it's important. While you were being held hostage," he said with an awkward nod, "Did anyone try to molest you—sexually? Did anyone took advantage of you?"

A wrinkle of sadness formed on her scarred brow. She glanced at her hands then back at Zeus and shook her head.

Her answer needed no translation.

"Is she certain?" Aitor said.

"She said no."

Aitor's bearded face twisted, the red veins in his eyes flushed. Baldo and Gorka had not tried to rape her. "The lying pig," he said of Minot, who was prostrate on the hallway floor, listening to the exchange. Aitor unsheathed his commando knife and stomped out to kill the *iparralde*.

Zeus hollered, "Wait." Then he heard a scuffle, which he wasn't keen on interfering but was about to when Aitor suddenly reappeared in the doorway, his horror-stricken eyes and his mouth wide open in shock, and plummeted face forward to the floor with the knife stuck to the hilt in his lower back.

Behind him stood Minot, his hornless bullhead in the glow of the candles. He had Aitor's Uzi in his hands but hesitated to fire at Zeus, afraid to hit Symphony.

Zeus did not falter. He fired a burst but Minot vanished down the corridor, apparently no more hurt than he already was. Zeus charged after him with the goggles back on his face, firing at Minot's moving shadow.

Without halting to aim, Minot swiveled and fired back several times. Bullets drilled and cracked the mockup walls, objects shattered in a muted firefight, the Uzis spitting out their load through noise suppressors.

Zeus realized he had scored when he found the trail of fresh blood Minot was leaving behind. He tracked the brown drippings into a room set up to look like a fruit shop. It was not a big room but he was nowhere to be seen. Zeus searched for hiding places, felt the walls for hidden doors, kicked and pushed aside all movable objects, pulled the place apart trying to find him.

Minot could hear it all from behind the inch-thick sliding panel. Wedged inside his secret sanctuary, he tried to load his Beretta but the box of cartridges slipped out of his blood-soaked fingers.

Zeus was looking at his watch when he heard the noise it made. He looked at the faded fresco of trays of stacked fruits on it, went behind the mock counter, kicked the shopkeeper's mannequin out of the way, and slid the plywood board as far as it opened, then stepped back, the hot Uzi up by his aiming eye.

For an instant, Zeus thought he was looking down at a half-dead animal in the dark. Its blood, a black-looking substance through the night vision goggles. He kicked the Beretta away.

The animal wasn't alive enough to do anything but bleed to death.

Zeus glanced at his watch then back at the kidnapper. He felt neither pity nor satisfaction.

Minot observed the goggled-faced vision above him, his life energy like his blood, hemorrhaging out of him over the loose pages of his poetry spread out on the floor, soaking in his blood. "I smell smoke," he uttered in French.

Zeus remained silent, deciding how to go about the few seconds he had left.

"Am I in hell?" Minot said in Spanish.

"Not yet."

"I've never hurt her, you know. I couldn't."

"Sure, that's why you kidnapped her and drugged her, and who knows what else."

"I didn't do anything they hadn't done before."

"Why did you kill your compeer?"

"He didn't believe me."

"Friend, nobody believes you."

Minot's respiration was down to a few jerky chest spasms. He switched to Euskara. "All I ever did I did for the Basque Land. Hey, you," he said with a final breath of defiance. "Have I been a good ETA terrorist?"

The smoke thickened the dusty air. Zeus chuckled once. "Now you are." He slipped his finger off the trigger and took two steps backward and rushed back to Symphony.

Through the gunfire fumes and rising smoke along the interminable network of shadowed doorways and passageways, Zeus made it back to the fake hospital room. He picked Symphony up in his arms. "Let's go."

"How about him?" Symphony said as they exited the room.

Zeus glanced at Aitor's body. "Someone will get him later."

"No, I mean Andre."

"Someone will come for him too."

Zeus followed the orange Day-Glo down the stairs, chased by the invisible smoke.

Outside, Zeus found Zurgin and his commandos were gone. A couple of them had gotten rid of their weapons and mingled with the people coming out to see the fire.

He rushed past Madame Minot and the caretaker. They were standing in the rain under a black umbrella that looked like a hovering vulture over their heads.

"Where's my son?" she cried out him. "Is he coming out? Is anybody going to get him?"

Zeus kept moving with Symphony in arms toward the waiting van. Karlo was at the wheel gunning the engine. "Where is Aitor?"

"He's not coming. Go."

Karlo looked over his shoulder at Zeus. "I'm not leaving without him."

Zeus shook his head. "We can't do anything for him. Let's go. Where's Tess?"

"Zurgin took her. How about Minot?" Karlo said. "Did you get him? Tell me you did." It was the only reason Karlo had joined the operation, to avenge the killing of his brothers, Baldo and Gorka. "Is he dead?"

"Aitor got him before he fell. I saw him do it."

Karlo let out a quiet sob, peered into the rearview at the smoke clouds puffing out of Maison Lavryn's windows, the real ones, and kicked down on the accelerator.

As the van zoomed away, they heard the distant sirens of the rescue services and the police approaching from the far end of the valley.

Zeus covered Symphony with a manta and looked into her big Picasso eyes, already perceiving a certain glow about her. A radiance behind her pallor, which Zeus could not interpret in the urgency of the moment but would come to understand nine months later. He pulled a handful of Kit Kat candy bars out of his jacket pocket. "I heard you like these."

A ghost of a smile formed on the corners of her lips.

He put the weapons away in the knapsacks and sat next to the driver. "How long to Donosti?"

"We will be there in a few hours."

All along their path, they saw the area's neighbors turning on their lights and coming out in the timid rain to see the great conflagration at Maison Lavryn. It lit up the night as if the town was on fire. An event that many probably had wished for through the years of its absurd grandeur but now gazed upon with a pang of nostalgia, a landmark in the communal psyche, a historic gauge of before and after.

For more than a day, the fire built up into a volcanic inferno visible for miles, taking with it all the mad delusions that had conceived it and kept it alive. It took the entire region's fire units two days to put out the tons of compacted timber and building material that went up in flames. A tragedy foretold, the local news declared in its outreach for significance, for it to have happened on the Day of the Transfiguration.

FORTY-EIGHT

Pamplona, eleven months later

ALL HIS LIFE Orlando Estrada-Uribe had been a man of set ideas, of strict thought, a believer in that all things had their appointed places and no other. He functioned in a world of precision, formality, and moderation. Untidiness of any sort more than irritated him, drained his spirit. That morning as he flew over the Basque skies, his attention was engaged as usual, although not by the particulars of the business waiting at journey's end, but by the important details of his grandson's baptism.

At three thousand meters altitude, he did not brood over the profundity of the blue vistas of space or the physical nearness to God he felt sometimes when gazing out of the cabin window. Another perspective opened his thoughts along the scattered summer clouds and the jagged hilly ground below, the random patches of brown and green, the red roofs sprinkled over the landscape. It made him wonder about the many views that had passed him unnoticed in the course of his life. The experiences he had missed. Not that he regretted any of his major decisions: he would not go as far. He reflected on the decision process itself. How each conclusion arrived at is never the last. How every decision made irremediably leaves others unmade. What seemed so important at one moment could become so inconsequential the next.

At the airport, he stood curbside in his immaculate blue business suit and briefcase in hand in the early morning sunshine. He observed with a sense of isolation the holiday rampage of frenzied travelers exiting the terminal. The crass parade of disheveled heads under American caps, the gush of effusion, the merriment of intoxication. His limousine chauffeur arrived eighteen minutes late.

"Sorry for the delay, but the traffic today is infernal," the driver said with his tie loose below the opened collar and his face greased by heat and haste. "It gets worse every year with the *sanfermines*."

The twenty-minute drive nearly tripled in time in the stop-and-go traffic.

Señor Estrada-Uribe unfolded the newspaper and made an unprecedented departure from personal norm. He raised his clean-shaven chin and addressed the man at the wheel. "Your name is Salvador, correct?" he said with a curious grin.

"Yes sir."

"Tell me something, Salvador. Do you think this new ETA truce I've been reading about is sincere?"

The driver's onyx eyes flashed on the rearview mirror. "I hope so, sir. But there have been so many."

"Yes, but this time it looks like they mean it."

"They always sound like they mean it at first. Then, well, you know."

"Continue, please."

"Sir, we all know what they really want. No? They haven't been able to gain independence by force or by peaceful means. So, what is left?"

"So you think it is business as usual?"

"Who knows?"

Several blocks from the Ayuntamiento Plaza, the car came to a stop. The driver gave the rearview mirror another anguished peek. The barricades blocking the motorized traffic had gone up and a police officer kept waving an arm at him to turn to a side street. "Sir, we're not permitted past this point. I'll have to look for a parking garage and accompany you to Mercaderes Street on foot."

"It's all right, Salvador. I'll walk the rest of the way. You go home."

"Are you sure, sir? It's chaotic out there."

"It is only for a few blocks."

The driver insisted on walking with him, but the *señor* was determined. "I will call you when it's time to pick me up. Enjoy your holiday."

"At your service, sir."

Up in the oriel balcony, Aunt Virginia beheld a sight she would have never believed had she not seen it with her own eyes. "Miguelín," she called out. "Run. Is that who I think it is coming up the street?"

Miguel Angel came out to the balcony.

"Is that your father walking in the crowd or do I need new glasses?"

Miguel Angel laughed when he spotted the suit-and-tie figure of his father cutting through the thick of the red and white crowd. "It is he."

"Maybe you should go see if he is all right. When was the last time he even walked on the street, much less in this craziness?"

"I'll go, but don't tell Mother. She'll probably have a heart attack."

Miguel Angel flew down the stairs.

"Papa!" he yelled as he approached him, trudging alongside the security barriers crammed full of people. Estrada-Uribe scrutinized his son for a moment. He had expected to see him dressed in the colors of the mozo bull runners, but withheld from comment.

Miguel Angel took the briefcase from his hand. "*Padre*, what are you doing out here with the plebian? Couldn't get the police to remove the barricades for you?"

"I felt like walking," he said, fingering the perspiration off his receding hairline. "I have not been in Pamplona for San Fermín since I was your age."

"How do you like it?"

"It has changed. There are ten times as many people. I have heard more people speaking English than I did when I was in Miami."

"The *fiesta* is not just ours anymore. Haven't you heard? We're living in a global village."

Up in the apartment, the women gathered at the top of the stairs for Estrada-Uribe's entrance. It was his first visit to their home in several years and his elderly aunts were reeling with excitement.

Estrada-Uribe stepped into the sunlit living room and the effusive welcome. He gave his wife a kiss on the lips, double-kissed each of his aunts, and glanced around him with an inquisitive frown. "Where's my grandson?"

The women replied in unison, "He is having his breakfast ... his mother is feeding him ... she will bring him out in a minute."

Estrada-Uribe turned to his son, demanding an explanation.

Miguel Angel grinned. "She went into the bedroom for privacy—you know."

"Ah," Estrada-Uribe exclaimed. "To breastfeed him. Yes, of course."

Moments later, Symphony walked out of the cool shadows of the apartment with her babe in arms. She wore a white embroidered sundress and a pair of flat leather sandals, her dark brown hair loose over her shoulders, her slim figure seemingly unaffected by the rigors of childbirth. She gave her father-in-law the customary kiss on each cheek.

The grandfather studied the child's little face under the blue knitted cap. The parents called him Teseus, a name Estrada-Uribe had acknowledged but had yet to accept. He wanted his grandson to be named Orlando to correct what he felt had been a mistake when he failed to give his name to his only son. He still hoped to make the parents reconsider in time for the child's baptism. He removed his suit jacket and offered to hold the child.

Symphony handed him the baby.

Estrada-Uribe loosened his tie and sat on the living room sofa with the child in his cradled arms and an expression of analytical contentment. It had only been three days since he'd last seen his grandson, but newborns change from day to day and he intended not to miss any part of the process.

A circle of smiling faces surrounded grandfather and babe. The miracle child, this was how they thought of Teseus after everything his mother had endured. A tragedy no one spoke of anymore and only alluded to it with an admonitory rise of the eyebrows when absolutely necessary.

After her rescue, Symphony never returned to the States. Her abduction had by then wiped out every sign of her former life. Her home, every material and spiritual element that composed it, no longer existed, not even her family name.

Her parents now lived in a Southwestern state in the US, in the shadows of a government witness protection plan, deprived of passports, forbidden to see anyone from their past—supervised by the same people who denied her the protection they had sworn to provide to all Americans. With Tess's and Zeus's help, Symphony was able to track down her brother and her sister. They now resided in different states, also under different names. They communicated by email, though not too often anymore. Mama, her grandmother, was interned in a nursing home in Staten Island, her memory gone, they said, victim of a voracious strain of Alzheimer's disease.

Despite all the comforts of luxury, the servants, the free time, life in

Spain required some effort on her part. She was learning to enjoy the little triumphs that came with it. Every passing day she became more fluid in their language—the spoken one as well as the unspoken one. She drove herself to the supermarket, to the stores, to La Concha Beach. Motherhood was a hectic pleasure. The tricky part was getting everyone to stop their suffocating pampering and let her take care of the baby by herself. She enjoyed changing the child, didn't mind waking up in the middle of the night to breastfeed him, didn't mind any of it. She was lucky, luckier than she had the right to be. But to be loved by strangers took some getting used to.

She was sure that one day the strangeness would fade as it had the instant she saw Teseus wrapped in the blue hospital blanket, the little toy-faced stranger who could not live without her. The one who put an end to her night terrors. She was certain that when that day came all that would remain would be their love.

She also felt she now understood Miguel Angel's idea of being "a citizen of the world." Although it remained a concept her heart could not yet totally embrace. She missed her life, her family, her world. She could not help it. She didn't want it to be gone. Miguel Angel insisted that all she had to do was give "*Tiempo al tiempo*." Give time its time. "You're not even twenty-one yet. One day you will also look back at today with the same longing. And you'd have so much more to remember."

The rocket blast came then, a white puffy jet cloud across the clear blue Pamplona sky. It sent a rolling thunder through the multitude on the street.

Up in the apartment, it produced the opposite effect. A fleeting hush took over the family, an unplanned commemorative moment of silence. It lasted until Miguel Angel took the baby in his arms and led the family to the narrow balcony over Mercaderes Street.

The rising Iberian sun warmed the early morning air.

On every building façade as far as they could see, balconies bedecked with red and yellow flags were crammed spectators waving their arms at passing TV cameramen. People packed behind the street barricades chanted and cheered. On the hilltop, under the wall niche with the image of Saint Fermín, the bull runners in white and red hopped in place, holding their rolled-up newspapers high, working themselves up for the run.

Estrada-Uribe came to his son's side. "So that you know," he said as if he had just remembered and loud for everyone to hear. "The airline tickets you requested went out yesterday morning. One set to New York, the other one to Miami."

"First class, I hope."

"Of course," his father said. "We wouldn't want Teseus's godparents to travel any other way."

Miguel Angel glanced at Symphony, a satisfied smile on his face. Then he sat baby Teseus on the flat of his hand and lifted him up so the child would not miss a second of what was about to transpire. The July sun lit up Teseus's tiny three-month-old features.

A second skyrocket went off high over the city's red-tiled roofs.

"Here they come, son."

Surrounded by the roar of the multitude, the bulls of Pamplona burst out of the corral and charged down the hill again as it happened every year and probably will forever, people and animals racing together, driven by the indomitable desire to feel free and alive.

ACKNOWLEDGEMENTS

Writing a book is a most solitary struggle, but it takes a village to publish it. I'd like to thank everyone on the Vine Leaves Press team for believing in this work. Special thanks go to Jessica Bell for her vast artistic vision, and the legendary Peter Snell, to Melanie Faith for making developmental editing fun, and to Amie McCracken for her patience. A note of gratitude goes out to Tom Badyna, William Williamson, and Nancy Sartor, for their direct and indirect inspirational contributions. And, ultimately, a heartfelt show of appreciation to the Basque people whose singularity so energized this work.

VINE LEAVES PRESS

Enjoyed this book?
Go to *vineleavespress.com* to find more.